Vegan Vampire Vaginas

By Wol-vriey

Other Books By Wol-vriey:

The Bizarro Story of I

Meat Suitcase

Chainsaw Cop Corpse

Vegan Zombie Apocalypse

Boston Posh

Novellas and Short Stories By Wol-vriey:

Big Trouble in Little Ass
A novella featured in
Westward Hoes

Forever Ago Sunshine
A short story featured in
The Big Book of Bizarro

Vegan Vampire Vaginas

By Wol-vriey

Burning Bulb
PUBLISHING

Vegan Vampire Vaginas
by **Wol-vriey**

Burning Bulb Publishing
P.O. Box 4721
Bridgeport, WV 26330-4721
United States of America
www.BurningBulbPublishing.com

Cover designed by Gary Lee Vincent with the following licensed elements from Fotolia:
  - handprint © suslo
  - vector halftone lips illustration © hubis3d

First printing.

Paperback Edition ISBN: 978-0-69220-397-2

Printed in the United States of America

Library of Congress Control Number: 2014938527

Part 1: Boston to Boston

Chapter 1

Tom sat at a shadowed table in Sugar Ray's bar.

He nursed his brandy, cradling it in his palm like a baby. He rolled the glass side to side, watching the motion of the brown liquid with a languid eye.

The liquor felt good in his belly. Its spreading warmth nicely counteracted the cold night. In addition, it blurred the edges of Tom's emotions, so his appraisal of the day's lack of success didn't collapse into depression and self-pity.

***

Tom Palmer was tall and thin, with dark hair and calm blue eyes. He was thirty-two and ruggedly handsome.

Tom was a salesman. He worked for Grid-OMNI, the super-company that (under the supervision of the Boston City Council) now monopolized Boston trade.

Tom's job description was 'General Dispersal Employee,' meaning he went door-to-door flogging whatever the company handed over to him.

His previous commission had been selling portable repulsors—walking-stick-shaped stun guns with amped-up power charge to deter dinosaurs. The product demonstrations were impressive—a raptor hit by the portable's 'ground tip' had toppled over and lain twitching. The massive lizard hadn't died, but the time it was helpless was more than sufficient for any potential victim to flee. The portable wasn't a 'one-time' weapon either—each battery was good for ten zaps and easily replaced.

Yeah, Tom thought in alcohol-moderated anger, *it's a great invention; the clear solution to everyone frying up the city with blasters even more than it already is. A sure-fire seller too; the sort of device that could make my name in the company. Huge money as well.*

Tom had been delighted to be assigned the portables. His first few samples were snapped up on the spot. People were clamoring for more of the units.

Then . . . this morning, he'd been called into his supervisor's office.

"Sorry, Tom," Marge Brown had said, "you're off the portable team."

Marge was a short perky brunette. Pale-eyed, plump and with a kind face. Once-upon-a-time, she'd dated Tom.

"Off?" Tom looked at Marge like she'd just said she was his mother.

Marge sighed. She walked around her desk. Through the windows of her skyscraper office, Tom saw the grid splayed like a glass floor between the lower levels of Central Boston's buildings.

She reached Tom and placed a soft plump hand on his shoulder. "Not my call. I'd never do that—I know how much it means to you. The order came from above."

From above. The words rolled through Tom's mind like a new sort of language. He wondered if Marge was doing this to get back at him. *She's right—she knows how much this commission means to me. Is she still pissed at me for breaking up with her? No, she broke up with me, not the other way around. It can't be that; she seems genuinely sorry I've been kicked to the curb. This has to be some executive wanting their boyfriend or girlfriend getting the credit for marketing the breakthrough product. Nepotism strikes again.*

Tom forced a smile. "So what am I being reassigned to?"

Marge looked almost embarrassed as she told him. "There's this new novelty model of vacuum cleaner . . ."

***

Tom emptied his glass. He signaled Mei Ling, a pretty Chinese waitress, over. *Vacuum cleaners. I've been reassigned to sell miniature hoover machines for collecting rat droppings. Rat-shit.*

"Another double brandy," he told Mei Ling.

She left. Tom watched her sway back over to the bar and tell Sugar Ray what he wanted. The bar owner, a tall muscular negro with a shaven head, looked over at Tom and smiled. Tom smiled back.

Suddenly Tom felt foolish feeling so down. *Damn,* he thought. *So now I've got to sell rat-shit hoovers to rich housewives in North End. So what? Just knuckle down to it, man. Something better will turn up for sure.*

He looked over at Sugar Ray, who was now handing Mei Ling his order. *It isn't like I had the only thing I ever wanted taken from me, and I can't ever get it back. If Ray can smile, definitely I can too.*

Tom suddenly felt sad again. Only now it wasn't for himself, but for Sugar Ray. He knew Sugar Ray's story—everyone did.

The black bartender had been a heavyweight boxer—number one contender for the unified world heavyweight belts.

Sugar Ray had finally fought and beaten the unbeatable world champ Vlad 'The Punch Impaler' Utkin. Unfortunately for Sugar Ray, the fight had occurred on the same night as the dragons had destroyed civilization and he'd never been crowned as the new champ—the dragons had burnt their way into Madison Square Garden and eaten almost everyone.

Sometimes, Tom saw Sugar Ray smile sadly, and knew the man was remembering that night, six years ago, when he was almost crowned champion of the world.

Mei Ling brought Tom's drink. He paid. She gave him the eye then left, swinging her hips for his benefit.

Tom watched her depart. He sipped his drink, wondered what to do. This almost-thing with Mei Ling had been going on for a while now. The Chinese girl had given Tom so many green-light signals he'd need to be blind not to see them.

My excuse used to be that I was dating Marge, but then Marge . . .

Marge was now dating Bill Spector, who headed Grid-OMNI's finance department, and Tom was . . . available. So it was clearly time to chat—

"Hi, can I sit here?"

Tom jerked out of watching Mei Ling's hypnotic hips, turned his attention to the woman addressing him.

She was a tall blonde with short hair. Light green eyes, and a sharp nose in a chiseled face. Full lips like a red flower. Attractive like sex.

Heavy breasts strained against her blue halter top. Cut off denim shorts sheathed her hips. Black purse and shoes completed her outfit.

In her left hand she clasped a beer. Smiling, she offered Tom her other hand. "Hi, I'm Lynn . . . Lynn Jones. I hate drinking alone, can I join you?

Tom nodded quickly. He shook her hand. "Tom."

Lynn sat opposite him. Behind her, Mei Ling glared at him in utter disgust.

Oops, Tom thought, seeing the fire in the waitress's eyes. *But I honestly haven't done anything yet.*

Ignoring Mei Ling's anger, he gave Lynn his full attention. "Haven't seen you in here before," he said.

She smiled. "I'm new in this area. Used to live up north, on Endicott Street, but then a beetle laid its skyscraper almost directly on my apartment block. That freaked me out big time, and I began looking for a less bug-affected area." She licked her lips, her green stare suddenly intense. "Now I live just around the corner."

Tom laughed. Her reason for moving was a common complaint. He also noted the emphasis she'd put on her last statement—the evening could lead to something pleasant for both of them.

He smiled. Tray in hand, Mei Ling stalked past, pointedly ignoring him. She hissed loud enough for Lynn to hear.

Lynn caught the flash of Tom's eyes after Mei Ling.

She smiled at him. "Girlfriend trouble?" She made to get up. "I thought you were alone. Look, I'm really sorry to cause you—"

He stopped her with a hand on hers. "Please stay," he said. "There's nothing there. She's just pissed over a misunderstanding."

It was true, Tom knew, there wasn't anything between himself and Mei Ling, but still, he felt guilty saying it, like he was somehow still betraying her.

This is so dumb, he thought, *how the hell can I betray a woman I'm not in a relationship with?*

He relaxed as Lynn settled back into her seat. She leant across to him and whispered. "Well, not to disappoint her, we can ask your waitress back to my place for a threesome. Personally I love Chinese takeaways."

She laughed as Tom's face purpled in embarrassment. "I'm just kidding."

He sighed in relief. "I'm glad; she knows kung fu."

Lynn laughed louder. Tom smiled and finished his drink. Sex was definitely on the cards now.

He had no idea how he'd gotten so lucky tonight. And with a gorgeous blonde bombshell. It was a fantastic ending to what had so far been a horrid day. He remembered the little rat-dropping vacuum cleaner boxes in his car and grimaced. A really horrid day.

A note of caution flittered through his mind. *She could be working for an organ-harvesting syndicate. Before you know it your kidneys'll be down in Texas, your lungs in Los Angeles.*

Lynn laid a hand over his. His penis swelled, his worries deflated.

Then all of a sudden Lynn looked downcast, her face falling like autumn leaves. Tom's heart went out to her.

"What's wrong?" he asked.

"Nothing and everything," she replied, her face taut with strain, "I get like this occasionally." She waved expansively at the bar's street window. "Living in Boston really gets me down sometimes." She pointed up and out at The Grid, the transparent shield magnifying the night stars. "The thought that, except for The Grid, we'd all be dragon food now—"

"Except for we Chinese," Mei Ling said.

Tom and Lynn looked at her startled. Neither had heard the waitress approach.

Mei Ling smiled sweetly at them both. She pointed at the empty glass and bottle between them. "Can I get you both fresh drinks?"

"Another beer," Lynn said. She appraised Mei Ling with cold eyes. The other woman didn't flinch under her gaze.

"Beer for me too," Tom added. "I need something to dilute the brandy."

The waitress nodded coldly. She cleared the table and departed.

Lynn looked hard at Tom. "She really wants you," she said. "I can practically hear that Chinese cunt craving your Caucasian cock— screaming for penetration. You *sure* you don't want me to invite her back to my place with us?"

"Only if you've got a good dentist," Tom said.

Lynn was taken aback. She saw Tom wasn't joking. "You serious?"

He nodded. "She'll put out your lights with one punch. I've seen her do it before when a drunk got too frisky." He frowned. "Mei's a great girl. How do I put this . . .? I'm just not sure I'll be great for her . . ." He ran his fingers over Lynn's wrist. "Let's forget Mei, okay? Just for tonight?"

She frowned. "What if you and me turns into more than a one night stand? What if I want more after tonight?"

Tom mentally rolled his eyes. Exactly how did a one night stand threaten to become a relationship even before they'd had sex?

He searched wildly for an answer to soothe Lynn. It would be ruinous having two beautiful women mad at him.

"We'll worry about tomorrow, tomorrow, darling," he said calmly. "I'm loving your company so far, why let someone else spoil this beautiful thing between us?"

She visibly relaxed. Tom was now uncertain if she'd really been angry to start with. She'd seemed serious about asking Mei for a threesome.

Nah, he decided, *she just isn't holding down her beer very well.*

It flashed through Tom's mind that Lynn's mood swings weren't being caused by booze. *Maybe she's crazy.*

He studied her eyes for hints of insanity. She smiled back, pointed down at her chest. "You're looking at the wrong set, hon."

Tom realized Lynn wasn't mad. Just superlatively horny.

Mei Ling returned with their beers. She'd gotten over her anger. She smiled politely at Tom when he paid her, gracefully accepted the tip he gave her and left.

Lynn drank some beer. "Her pussy's still screaming your name," she said afterwards, "But that's one classy lady." She grinned at Tom. "Maybe you're right—maybe she is wasted on you."

Tom had had enough. Lynn's double-talk was doing his head in. Mei Ling had now vanished into the back room. No better time to make his escape.

He got up, jerked Lynn up after him.

"I haven't finished my beer," she protested.

He pointed. "I haven't even begun mine." He pulled her close, whispered: "I thirst for what you've got in your pants, my darling. I want to plunge my tongue into your wet depths and drink deep of your sacred fountain . . ." He pulled back and roved his eyes appreciatively over her cleavage, then looked deep into her green eyes ". . . Even as my hands take firm grasp, and like goats, scale your succulent mountains."

Lynn gasped. "Damn, Tom, if you fuck as good as you talk, I'll never let you go."

He grinned tightly, glad she wasn't familiar with the work of Iranian erotic poet Soraya Vagina. *Never let me go? Lady, you're not a stalker, are you?*

He relaxed. *She's just getting drunk.* Besides, his penis was now painfully erect—*that's why it's called a hard-on, bro.* He was screwing Lynn, this paragon of perfection, even if it killed him.

Lynn took her time with leaving the bar, lingering over a final extended gulp of beer. Tom prayed Mei Ling wouldn't return.

Lynn swallowed, then abandoned the rest of her beer.

"Ready to love you, baby," she giggled.

Tom sighed his relief. Waving to Sugar Ray, he headed for the front door, pulling Lynn—now skipping like a schoolgirl—after him.

Chapter 2

The moonless night raged like a storm in Lynn's head. Seated beside Tom as he drove from Sugar Ray's, north up Arch Street to her place on Milk Street, she fought to still the voice.

The voice—the soft female whisper in her head that spoke/commanded/insisted/demanded one horrible thing of her.

"Do it!"

"No," Lynn thought back, with equally violent insistence. "I'm not going to! It's mine now. Leave me alone."

"You have to!"

Lynn shut off her mind, steered her thoughts away from the horrid words in her head.

She was worried. It was getting harder and harder, not giving the voice what it wanted.

The pressure increased daily. In daylight, she easily ignored its soft urging, her everyday worries swamped it; but each evening, once she stepped out of her cashier's cubicle at the Citizen's Bank on State Street, it was like someone had opened a fire hydrant in her head—the words gushed like water, flooding her mind:

"Do it, you little pussy! Stop being such a coward. Do it! You've a gun at home, haven't you?"

"Yes, I do have a gun, but I'm not going to . . ."

It was the reason she drank so much now. Heard through an alcoholic veil, the voice was more ignorable. She could deceive herself that it was a figment of her soused delusion.

(Lynn didn't even understand how she was in this mess. She'd gone to use the ladies' room at work one afternoon a month ago, and then, just about to wipe herself dry after peeing, the voice had been in her head.)

The bad part of Lynn's drinking was how it made her talk out of turn. She'd been unable to resist pointing out to Tom how the Chinese waitress was clearly (to a woman's practiced gaze) in love with him.

She'd even relished the feeling of power of winning their mating contest. Even now, she still felt a thrill at 'dispossessing' the other woman of what was 'rightfully' hers. It was all the booze though; for all her obvious allure, Lynn wouldn't normally flaunt a victory in another's face.

She got worse the drunker she got. It was why she stuck to beer. Tipsy on anything harder, she became unbearable.

Lynn was pleased; she'd gotten lucky tonight.

She glanced aside at Tom, busy steering his gunmetal-grey Ford Camaro round a pile of charred rubble in the middle of the road. *Now, he's real cute.* Sex dulled the voice as well. All Lynn wanted tonight, was to get pumped good and HARD and doze off. Tomorrow was another day to be spent surviving: surviving Boston, with its dinosaurs and dragons; surviving the city's sky-high crime rate; but most of all, surviving *herself.*

***

"Damn!" Tom said.

Lynn jerked her mind out of itself. They'd reached the Arch Street/Milk Street intersection.

She draped a casual hand over Tom's arm. "What, baby?"

He pointed.

She inhaled sharply on noticing the dragon up ahead. "Slow the car."

Tom did so. They watched the dragon.

Over the open expanse of the intersection the massive fiberglass reptile prowled, restively trampling The Grid, Central Boston's dragon-proof shield. Sixteen feet overhead, it paced, flickering like a living diamond walking on air.

The dragon huffed and puffed. It glared hungrily at them.

Lynn's alcoholic fuzz cleared a bit.

She shuddered despite knowing they were safe. She couldn't help her reaction—she practically felt the behemoth's frustration. *This creature is death personified,* she thought. *All it sees as it looks at us is dinner. Thank heavens someone invented wiven.*

The dragon scratched and stamped The Grid, scouring it with bursts of fire to no avail. The Grid did what it had been built to do.

"Let's get out of here," Tom said, "before a pack of raptors find us."

Lynn nodded. "I'd forgotten about them. Turn left. Number two hundred."

Tom swerved the car onto Milk Street.

"It's between two skyscrapers," Lynn said, "the number's painted in bright red."

While he drove, she peered over her seat, kept her eyes on the dragon. Wings at half-mast like it was about taking to the air, the transparent monster padded after them on The Grid.

Damn, Lynn thought watching it move legs larger than the adamant steel pillars holding the transparent shield up. *It's fucking huge.*

She stared into the dragon's eyes, crystal-ball-clear ovals predicting death. Her death? Not tonight in any wise, but total annihilation for someone somewhere. One death or a million, Lynn knew, made no difference to the dragons. *They've burnt down the USA, fried the whole world, and they can't even have a concept of the amount of destruction they've caused.* Sadness entered her. She blinked back tears. *It's horrible. This beast is top of the food chain, and doesn't even know it.*

Alcohol rebuffed her sadness. Beside her, Tom appeared to have forgotten the dragon. She turned her attention from it also, watched Tom squeeze his stiffened crotch, the unconscious way he did it.

Typical guy, she thought, *he's most likely thinking of how to get me to agree to anal.* She sniggered lustily. *Darling, I'm not that drunk.*

She returned her attention to the dragon behind them. It had turned away. Lynn watched it run back towards the intersection, then soar aloft, heading east. An opalescent streak of death.

The female voice in Lynn's head returned. Now, like it was afraid of being banished for good, it cooed to her. "Tonight's a good night," it said. "Nice romantic moon, handsome man. A perfect night to do it."

"Go away," Lynn thought back irritatedly. "Leave me in peace!"

"I can't," insisted the silken voice. "I'm *you*; you're me, and—"

"I think we're here," Tom inserted into the unheard conversation.

Lynn smirked at the voice in her head. "Go screw yourself . . . with a psychic vibrator." She slipped a hand under her waistband. "Unlike you, I'm about getting laid." Her fingers roved under her panties, quested through her pubic hair, found her clitoris. She tingled.

"We've arrived," Tom said.

Lynn looked sheepishly at him. She groaned. "Damn, baby. I feel like a bomb about to go off."

"Yes! Yes! That's the spirit!" the voice cooed. "Lose it! Explode! Get out your gun and—"

"Get lost!" Lynn thought savagely back.

Tom stroked her thigh. "Let's go inside and explode together."

She leaned over and kissed him. "I think I love you. You know just what to say to me."

She frowned. "Unlike some douchebags," she thought pointedly at the voice.

"Oh, we'll see about that!" the voice replied. Dropping its coy act, it rumbled in her head like thunder, so that it was all Lynn could do to see straight. "You'll do it, bitch, or I promise you—"

"Shut up!" Lynn screamed out loud.

Tom gaped at her. "Are you alright?"

Lynn gripped her head hard in her hands. "I'm fine," she lied, with an effort holding back the tears threatening to spurt from her eyes. Her brain hurt now like it would soon start bleeding.

"You'll do it!" the voice thundered again.

She ignored her screaming mind. She regarded Tom calmly with her jade eyes. "Don't worry about me," she said. "I get like this occasionally. A bad migraine. It's almost like a voice yelling in my head."

He nodded sympathetically.

She smiled, stroked his penis through his pants. "But we can't let a little thing like a headache mess up our sex life," she said seductively. "I've some aspirin in the house."

She fumbled her keys out of her purse, waved them in Tom's face. "Let's go. I gotta have that thing in your pants." She giggled. "Unless you'd rather do it out here in the street?"

"Inside, baby. I don't want the pterodactyls watching us."

They got out of the car. As they stumbled up her front steps, Lynn steeled herself against the almost overwhelming noise raging in her head, the irate harpy screech threatening to render her blind, deaf, and dumb with its insistence that she execute its horrible course of action.

Worst of all, the voice relentlessly screaming at her was unmistakably her own.

***

Lynn's willpower crumpled as she and Tom staggered through her bedroom door. Like an overloaded scale, like an overstretched cord, her resistance to the obsessive voice in her head broke. From that point on, she was practically a walking automaton.

She bumped into Tom, tripped, almost fell.

"You okay?"

She looked at him, uncertain whether or not he sensed her mental strain, the battle she'd just lost. *No, he just looks worried about me.*

"Act normal," the voice said, its tone softly triumphant. "Don't let him think you're crazy. You've got to do this right."

Lynn nodded, both in agreement with the voice, and in answer to Tom's question.

"I'm fine, baby." She squeezed his ass hard. "I'm just dying to feel your cock caressing my tonsils—I'm wetter than a swimming pool."

And it was true. Now that she'd given in, agreed to do the voice's bidding, delicious arousal trickled through Lynn's limbs like she was a river valley being irrigated.

It's sad, so fucking sad, she thought, *I know I could really be happy with this guy. He's not a douchebag. Shit.*

But she'd do it.

She pushed Tom down on the bed.

"Get comfortable. I won't be a minute." Turning her buttocks to him, she wiggled out of her cutoff jeans, letting them drop to her ankles,

Leaving her thong on, she turned round again.

Tom had his cock out and was stroking himself.

Lynn felt eerily empowered. She giggled throatily. "Don't pop your cork yet. I want your first load of cream in my mouth."

She blew him a kiss, "Okay, gotta pee—too much beer," waved and traipsed off.

***

Lynn's bladder *was* full, so she peed. Kidney-filtered beer jetted from her in a long hot stream of piss that threatened to never end.

That out of the way, she got down to business.

The gun was in the bathroom medicine cabinet, hidden behind an array of body sprays. Lynn checked that it was loaded, then stuck it in the back of her thong waistband. The cold metal molded itself to her flesh like a body to a mattress.

She examined her face in the mirror, straightened her hair back with fingers. "I look like shit."

"You look hot," the voice—her voice—said. "Like a porn star. He's drooling for your cunt out there."

"Too bad he isn't going to eat it," Lynn retorted. "I was looking forward to some cunt-ilingus tonight."

She stared herself in the eye. Her beautiful reflection held no comfort for her; it simply confirmed the inevitability of her intended course of action.

"Okay," the voice said. "Don't keep him waiting or he'll get suspicious. He might run away."

"Oh no," Lynn agreed grimly. "We can't have that happening."

Gun pressing hard and cold against her ass, she returned to the bedroom to join Tom.

14

Chapter 3

Lynn slid her mouth up and down over Tom's phallus. He groaned. Her stroking lips were static electricity on his cock. The feeling was transcending—sheer velvet.

He lay naked on his back, hands folded behind his head on the pillow. Her heavy breasts caressed his thighs like masseurs.

Okay, so she's clearly slightly unhinged—so what? Half of Boston's population are only marginally sane,—

Lynn swirled her tongue expertly around Tom's glans.

"Fucckkk!" he groaned. She tightened her grip just behind his corona, licking his pee-hole whilst rhythmically stroking up and down his shaft, her thumb and forefinger formed into an 'O.'

The pleasure burning up Tom's penis subsided slightly to manageable levels. He resumed his mental examination of why he was here—in Lynn's apartment—despite clear signs she might be dangerous.

—Damn, just seeing the fucking dragons overhead, knowing you're protected from them eating you only by a see-thru sheet of plastic is enough to drive anyone—

Lynn raised her head from Tom's erection. Her mouth slipped off the penis with a loud slurp. Saliva dripped down the tumescent organ. Her slickened mouth glittered.

She sat up. Her breasts hung heavy. Her thong waistline dipped deep into her crotch, revealing a shaven mons veneris tattooed with a rose.

"Let me know when you're gonna cum, baby," she whispered. "I've something extra-special for you."

Tom nodded. She grinned back.

He suddenly sensed something synthetic about Lynn's lust, like she was playacting. Though her breathing was as labored as his now and her nipples engorged,—large, pink, stiff—her expression was strained, her facial skin taut like it was being yanked by her ears. Her eyes gleamed like she was concentrating on an assigned task. Fear whispered in Tom's head: *Or fighting against losing it big-time.*

He sighed. *So what—I already know she's crazy. I'll just avoid Sugar Ray's for awhile after tonight—drink uptown instead. The thought however saddened him. But she's so beautiful—sucks cock so good, better than—*

Lynn dropped her mouth back down onto Tom's penis, truncating his thoughts.

He groaned as she slipped over him again. Like his groin was a burning forest, the sensation ravaged him. *Oh, holy shit!* The feeling grew stronger. Tom's resolve to not see Lynn again weakened. *A blowjob like this is worth the risk, for sure!*

His hips lifted off the bed. He began thrusting, fucking her mouth.

Lips tight around Tom's glans, her eyes questioned his. He remembered she'd said to tell him when he was gonna cum.

"Yeah!" he gasped. The semen bubbled up out of his testicles, up, up, and away, like Superman off to rescue Lois Lane.

Lynn sucked greedily on the engorged penis, pushing Tom over the point of no return.

Tom began spurting. "Oh Godddddd—!"

He fell silent on seeing the gun Lynn had pulled out the rear of her thong. *Oh . . . no . . . she is crazy!*

The incongruity of the weapon's appearance magnified its size to him. The muzzle hole seemed large as a grave. It wagged in the air towards his face while Lynn kept her lips locked on his glans and swallowed his cum.

Horror streamed into Tom to replace the semen relentlessly streaming out of him. Horror and disbelief.

I'm about to die.

Frozen by disbelief, paralyzed by his orgasm, Tom helplessly waited for his life to end.

Lynn rammed her mouth down to the throat on Tom's cock. Then she placed the gun against her right ear and pulled the trigger.

Her brains blew out of the left side of her head.

She remained like that—her head impaled on Tom's cock, blood pumping from her wounds—while he finished cumming, too traumatized by what had just happened to do more than gape in horror.

Chapter 4

Lynn was dead. A white trail of brains was strewn across the room like she'd ejaculated out of the side of her head.

When he'd stopped shivering from shock and orgasm, Tom sat up and pulled Lynn's head off his penis. He rolled her corpse to one side.

A bone splinter was stuck in his penis. He pulled it out with a curse. Blood from the puncture mingled with the body fluids already smeared on him.

Dazed, Tom sat on the bed. He had no idea how he felt, no idea how he *should* feel. He worried instead that someone might have heard the gunshot and could come to investigate. And that the person might be armed.

(For the first time, Tom appreciated the advantage of Boston having no police force. There weren't enough people to employ, nor enough money to pay and arm them. A substantial chunk of the city's revenue already went towards keeping The Grid repaired, and paying/arming the military to protect the repair crews.

At work, Tom had heard talk of the city council buying security robots from Grid-OMNI. So far nothing had come of the plans. As Marge Brown had explained it, there was some trouble with reprogramming the machines— warbots imported from New Korea—so they didn't shoot up suspects for minor misdemeanors.)

Some of Tom's composure returned. He looked at Lynn's corpse.

He winced. *My cum's in her head, for crying out loud.* His mind flooded with memory of his orgasm, of his semen spurting into Lynn's dying twitching mouth . . .

Everything was suddenly too much for Tom. He rushed into the bathroom and washed Lynn's blood off his groin. Then he rushed out again and dressed as fast as he could. He had to be out of here, already. Away and gone from this place of death.

He stared at Lynn while dressing. The hole in her head yawned like a cave descending into liquid limestone—the messy exit wound looked excavated by minute miners. Her green eyes were glass orbs now, expressionless as mineral water.

Why the hell did she do it? I know the world's all fucked-up now, but I'd have stayed with her . . .

Tom thought quickly.

He made certain not to touch the gun. He knew not to leave fingerprints in the wrong places.

Tom wasn't taking a murder rap. With the DNA they'd get from his cum, any investigation (however belated) would definitely place him here when Lynn died. *But . . . her fingerprints are the only ones on the gun . . . so I'll walk free . . .*

Tom relaxed a little. He'd be fine as long as he was gone before anyone came.

But . . . He looked at Lynn's corpse, folded as haphazardly as discarded clothing. Her legs were splayed now, her thong dipping into her vagina beneath its floral tattoo.

Tom winced at another consideration.

I can't just leave her like this—like she was nothing, not worth bothering about. Five minutes ago she was a living, breathing person. What if no one finds her?

He picked Lynn's phone out of the cradle and dialed 911.

"Hello, Boston EMS here; what's your emergency?"

"Dead woman," he said. "A suicide."

"Where are you?"

"Two hundred Milk Street," Tom said. "Small bungalow cramped between two skyscrapers. Hand-painted red sign.

"We'll dispatch an ambulance right away. Please wait for it. The medics will want to ask you . . ."

Tom dropped the phone on the bed.

"Hello . . . hello . . . are you still there?"

Tom left Lynn's apartment.

He got into his car and drove off.

***

Tom drove like a ghost. His feelings were divorced from him, like he'd left them back in the apartment with Lynn's corpse.

Hell, when she'd pulled out the gun, I really thought I was a goner. Why the hell did she do it? I have to pick a messed-up chick on the day

18

she's tired of life. And the way she'd killed herself? I'll never have another erection.

He considered going back to Sugar Ray's for a drink to fill the void Lynn's death had excavated in his emotions. *Uh, uh, no fucking way—Mei Li's mad at me. Seeing her will just make this shit worse.*

Tom instead drove back to his apartment on Winter Street.

Once home, he got into bed. Encased in a mental fog of depression, he stared unseeing at the ceiling till sleep claimed him in blessed oblivion.

Chapter 5

Next Morning

Tom awoke feeling strange. An indefinable strange.

His nightmares had been comprised of phantasms refusing to solidify into coherent shapes. The only clear image? A familiar-looking blonde without a vagina ordering him to 'cum, baby.'

He sat up groggily. Memories of last night instantly flooded his mind: His glans stuck deep in Lynn's throat; his spurting like a fire hydrant; then . . . then . . . Lynn sticking the gun into her ear and . . . brains and blood spraying everywhere . . . her body splayed indifferently as discarded panties across her bed.

A car revved outside. Then loud shouting voices.

He was instantly awake and scared.

The voices clarified into a couple arguing over directions to the Boston Opera House.

The voices grew louder, till Tom couldn't stand it anymore.

He leapt out of bed, rushed to the window, yanked the drapes apart and yelled: "Keep going and turn right! It's two hundred meters down fucking Washington!"

The couple, a middle-aged pair, gaped at him in shock.

Tom dropped the curtains.

The car drove off. The fear remained. Fear of the nonexistent police force; fear—prodded by his weird dreams—of the dead woman's ghost.

He calmed himself. *It's out of my hands—*

My hand.

His left hand felt odd, like there was water *inside* it.

That didn't make sense. Tom raised his hand to see what the matter was.

He blinked, then gaped at his hand. What the . . . ?

There was a vagina in his palm.

The moist sex organ lay in his palm like an exploded life line. The urethral opening under its pale clitoral acorn was a purple puncture. Below this, between shaven labia, the vaginal opening was a tiny pink grotto.

It was a beautiful, fastidiously groomed pussy.

An impulse made Tom turn his hand over.

A red rose tattoo decorated the skin behind his knuckles.

He immediately recognized the flower as the same one tattooed on Lynn's mound of Venus.

He stared in confusion, then turned his hand back over and gaped at his palm. *Lynn's pussy? In my body?* The rose tattoo left him in no doubt it was the dead woman's vagina he was looking at.

Cold dread insinuated itself into his psyche. It gripped him by the throat and squeezed.

Oh no. This isn't happening.

Logic reasserted itself. This is America. People don't wake up with cunts in their hands. He forced a laugh. *Someone's playing a practical joke on me.* But his tree of reassurance bore worry-seeds. *But who? Who knows? Who could possibly know?*

Fear attacked his forced composure. *Did someone follow me from Lynn's place last night? Is this about blackmail?*

Calm hacked a resolute route through Tom's turmoil.

Joke, blackmail, or whatever; this vagina is nothing but glued-on latex—I'll pull it off.

Tom gripped the left labia and yanked hard. Sharp pain ripped across his hand. He yelped and let go.

With horror, he realized the vagina was part of him.

Bu . . . but . . . how?

Tom stared at his palm—at the incongruous sexual lake amidst a pasture of flesh. A smearing of white secretion now coated its rim.

He probed the hand-cunt with his right index finger. The entire digit slid into the aperture.

Tom slumped like a dropped handbag. He could no longer hide behind logic. This shit was real. He could feel his fingertip between his wrist bones.

He fought against freaking out. It was one thing waking up with a cunt on one's body, totally another thing knowing it was a *dead woman's* cunt.

Oh no, no, no, he thought.

***

Moving like a ghost, Tom got out of bed and shambled into his bathroom.

While brushing his teeth and showering, he pondered what to do.

He realized that if Lynn's vagina was on *his* hand, it was no longer on *her* body.

He regarded his palm. The vagina was all soapy. Like a male masturbation sleeve, it looked sex-ready. Tom, however, didn't have even the ghost of an erection.

How on Earth did her pussy leapfrog to me? His dream of the vaginaless woman returned. *Now I recall it, she looked like Lynn.*

He toweled dry. *The only place I'll conceivably find an answer is at Lynn's apartment. So I'm heading back over there.*

Tom dressed quickly and left, zooming his Camaro toward Milk Street.

Driving over, he realized he was being rash: *I called emergency services last night—Lynn's body would have been removed by now. But I can't just walk into Boston EMS and ask for her corpse, can I?*

Chapter 6

Milk Street was obscured by thick green fog. Tom had never seen the like of it before. Gushing as if from a reversed chimney, green billows poured from above, obliterating vision beyond a few feet.

Damn, Tom thought. *Something's cracked a hole in The Grid. This smoke might be poisonous.*

He considered returning later. Then his palm-vagina twitched, reminding him of why he'd come.

Wincing, he decided to brave the green smoke. He rolled up his windows, then, headlights on, drove into it.

Tom was out the other side of the fog almost before he was fully in it.

He heaved a sigh of relief, then realized the world had changed around him.

Milk Street had disappeared. Tom now drove on a highway flanked on both sides by grassland and trees.

He looked in his rearview mirror. The all-consuming green cloud he'd driven through was no longer evident. Instead, there was a city behind him.

The surrounding grassland was odd, but that *was* Boston in the rearview. With massive storm clouds overhead.

He stopped the car. *What just happened?*

Tom realized that, vision hampered by the green smoke, he'd accidentally driven through an OD—an Otherworld Door. The trans-dimensional space-time gates were notorious for appearing/disappearing at random in Boston. They were capable of hopping one anywhere from across the city to Alpha Centauri and beyond.

I'm lucky. The OD only transported me out of town. I could have wound up on Mars, or worse still,—

Then he noticed the giantess up ahead.

She was twenty feet tall. Her skin was mottled green and brown, like army camo.

She was walking across the plain, parallel to the road. Her gaze was turned inward, away from Tom.

He blinked in disbelief. *She's like a palm tree come to life.*

Despite the distance—about fifty feet—he made out the details of her body as she walked past. Rough but feminine curves and limbs, hands like a spray of tree branches. Palm fronds for hair. A white face under that. She turned toward him briefly, studying something in the sky. Her face was disturbingly familiar.

The giant woman passed Tom by. He watched her shrink in the rearview.

***

Tom tried rationalizing the giantess. It didn't wash. No theory he came up with covered the facts.

Finally, he turned the Camaro around.

Facing the city for the first time, Tom immediately realized he'd been mistaken. That wasn't a mass of storm clouds topping the city like a kindergartener's crayon smear. But what the hell was it? The thick green/brown mass extending across the Boston skyline looked SOLID. Like the world's largest cowpat.

Tom calculated that the mass extended out east across Boston's inner harbor. He had no idea how far west it went—its bulk thickened into the distance till it blended with the sky.

Like thread from frayed cuffs, black tendrils dangled from its underside, swirling in the wind.

Bemused, Tom drove towards the city. There at least, he expected some answers.

He considered the vagina in his hand. Hopefully, he'd find a fix for it too, maybe just surgery to remove the damn thing.

Chapter 7

Tom soon began passing houses. Shortly afterward, a sign confirmed his route as Washington Street.

He nodded, pleased to find something familiar. Washington Street ran all the way up to City Hall. It passed Winter Street, his old residence, and also Milk Street, Lynn's . . . Tom winced on remembering Lynn.

All the houses he passed were empty, seemingly abandoned. However, none of the buildings were burnt.

Which meant no dragons here.

That fact confirmed his spatial translocation.

Tom suddenly realized he'd also been shifted through time. It was now early evening. The sun hung low in the western sky, an orange circle falling into the distant horizon.

***

A car was approaching from behind, growing fast in the rearview mirror like the driver was hurrying to catch up with him.

Ah, yes, someone to answer some questions.

The car, a red Ford convertible with the sunroof down, drew level with Tom.

Tom goggled.

The car driver was a naked man. Fat and hairy, with short dark hair and a thick mustache. He had a hard-on which he was holding like a gear shift.

He grinned at Tom.

Tom waved. "Hey!" he yelled.

The naked driver preempted Tom's questions by calling back to his passenger:

"Hey, Pam, honey, come suck my dick!"

Pam was the equally naked voluptuous blonde draped across the Ford's rear seat. Her massive globose breasts wobbled atop her chest like cream topping on cake. Her nipples sat like cherries atop the cream.

She raised herself on one elbow. "*Now*, Joe?" She pointed at Tom. "He can see us."

"So what? He watches porn, don't he?"

"Joe, you're Chief of Police!"

The fat man laughed. "So we won't get arrested for indecent exposure."

"That's the lamest excuse ever to give someone a blowjob. "

"Pam, you're the one who wanted to fuck out in the open."

"We already did."

"Still hard. Need one more for the road."

"Lay off on the Viagra, okay?" The blonde scowled, then gave Tom a smile like strawberry ice cream. Her eyes were a light brown.

He glanced ahead, ensuring he was still driving straight, then returned his attention to the Ford's occupants.

"Hey!" he called. "I need directions!"

Joe ignored Tom. He flipped his erection with a finger. "C'mon, honey! Be a good dog! I got a bone in my pants."

"Darling, you ain't wearing any pants!"

Tom was about explaining further when Pam's neck began lengthening.

Mouth agape, Tom watched Pam's neck extend upward till it was as long as a giraffe's.

The blood drained from Tom's face.

Pam winked at Tom. She smiled evilly at his confusion and licked her lips. Then she bent her giraffe-neck down over Joe in an inverted 'U'. She ducked her head down into the man's lap and took his penis into her mouth.

Joe pushed her neck aside so she wasn't obstructing his vision. He turned and grinned at Tom. "Shit, man, this woman can sure suck dick."

Tom nodded.

"Hey!" Joe added, stroking his mustache. "Better watch where you're driving."

Tom turned and straightened out the Camaro. He returned to staring at the oddity beside him.

Pam's head was bobbing up and down in Joe's lap like a woodpecker drilling a tree. In the back seat her legs were spread wide, one foot up on the front passenger headrest, the other on the rear. Her vagina yawned at Tom.

While her head on its McDonald's-arch neck sucked Joe off, Pam caressed herself. Her left hand roved over her perfects breasts, squeezing and teasing. Her right hand dipped into her crotch, stroked and poked.

Tom was in a place beyond confusion now. After another quick glance at the road, he again returned his attention to Joe and Pam.

Pam took all of Joe's penis into her mouth. So deep—his pubic hair looked like it was her mustache. His fat thighs trembled around her chin.

One hand on the wheel, Joe shuddered with pleasure. He gave Tom a thumbs up, then tapped Pam's giraffe-neck. "Wow, man. Now this is what *I* call a deep throat—Linda Lovelace eat your heart out!"

Tom nodded back. The red convertible accelerated past. Tom watched it zoom off into a distant blur like a blood smear, Pam's neck a white hoop above it.

No way is that the chief of police.

***

When the convertible was out of sight, Tom parked.

He looked long and hard at the city ahead. Much closer now, the odd green-brown floating overgrowth looked like a massive clump of soil and grass.

Tom rested his head on his steering wheel. He breathed deep and slow to calm himself.

I gotta pull myself together, he thought, *before my mind ruptures from sheer disbelief. If I don't, I'll die here. I can't simply resign myself to the tides of fate, either. Apathy will prove as fatal as non-acceptance of the new status-quo.*

Maybe, he reasoned, *maybe I've always lived in this place and that other Boston was a dream I've just woken from.*

Chapter 8

Tom was roused from his meditation by a loud tapping by his ear.

Startled, he jerked upright.

A policewoman was rapping the door window-frame with her nightstick.

She stopped on seeing she had Tom's attention.

Tom looked her over.

She was *beautiful*. Lovely long-lashed gray eyes, full lips, high cheekbones, a perfect nose. Long raven-black hair.

Despite her severe black uniform, sexuality poured from the lady cop like heat from a fireplace.

'Sgt. Brooke Hayes,' her nametag read. Above it, the legend 'Boston Police' was embroidered on a patch beneath her left shoulder.

Tom felt instantly better. Coming from a city without a police force, the very *idea* of law enforcement was incredibly comforting.

"License and registration please," she said. Her voice was coldish, but not hostile.

He fumbled in his glove compartment for the documents. He handed them over. While she perused them, he looked around. Her patrol car was parked behind him.

He also noted that Sgt. Brooke Hayes had a large ass. Her hips spread before Tom like an unavoidable fact of life.

Sgt. Hayes looked up from studying Tom's papers. "Thomas William Palmer?"

He nodded.

She handed back his papers. "I should book you, Mr. Palmer sir, for self-endangerment, but I won't this time. But please remember—you don't stop out here for *any* reason. There's been a mass of sightings of vampire vaginas hereabouts. Several drained corpses too."

Tom raised an eyebrow. *Vampire vaginas? Nah, I misheard that.*

"You're free to go, sir. But if I find you parked out here again, I'll arrest you for being suicidal. Please always remember the ever-present danger of eaters."

He nodded. "Thanks, officer." *Eaters? What the hell are eaters?*

He decided to question the cop, try to glean some useful info.

"I had an odd experience a short while ago," he said. "A woman with a lengthening—"

He shut up. Sgt. Brooke Hayes was now pointing a very large gun at him. He gaped at her in surprise. "What's the problem, officer?"

She pointed to his left hand, draped on the window rim. "That rose tattoo looks familiar. Let me see your palm."

Tom gulped. *Damn.* He'd been so caught up in the weird shit going on, he'd totally forgotten about his hand.

"My *palm?* Why in the world—?"

Her lips curled in a scowl, her gray eyes thinned. "Just show me your palm, sir." A note of resolute menace had now entered her voice.

Tom turned over his hand. He watched her eyes widen on sighting the vagina. *Oh, shit.* "I can explain . . ."

Brooke Hayes nodded. "I'm sure you can, Pussypalm. I'd like to hear what you have to say." She smiled coldly. "Your fake ID almost fooled me, calling yourself Palmer. And your plastic surgeon's damn good—I suspect he even fixed your fingerprints too." She stepped back two paces. "Get out of the car, Tom. Keep your hands where I can see them."

Tom considered bluffing her and putting the car in gear. The unwavering aim of her gun at his head cautioned him not to. He doubted she'd hesitate to shoot him. Or that she'd miss.

He got out of the car.

"Turn around, hands on the roof, and spread your legs."

Tom did so. Sgt. Hayes kicked his feet farther apart.

"Look, officer," Tom said reasonably as she patted him down. "You're mistaken, I'm not this Pussypalm person you're looking for. My name really—"

Brooke Hayes tapped Tom's left hand. "What's that in your palm?"

"A vagina, but—"

"A *pussy.* Are pussies normally located in palms?"

Tom had no answer.

Brooke Hayes smiled coolly. "How much difference is there between the names Thomas Palmer and Tom Pussypalm?"

Tom had no answer for that either.

"You're under arrest," Brooke whispered into Tom's ear. "You can say nothing, or you can run your mouth. Whatever you say—"

"But I haven't done anything!"

She spun him round to face her. Her beautiful face was set like a carving in smooth white stone. "Oh you've done a lot, Tom Pussypalm, stop acting innocent. We've a pile of corpses back in Boston dying to testify against your ass."

Tom could only gape. *Murder?* This got worse by the moment.

Brooke Hayes scowled. "I'm a reasonable woman, Tom: I'll lay your options out for you nice and simple. You either come back to Boston with me quietly, or you can kick up a fuss, and I'll kick your ass. Which will it be?"

"I'll come quietly," Tom said.

She produced a pair of handcuffs. "Okay, turn around again. Hands behind your back."

He turned. She cuffed him then pushed him toward her squad car. She opened the rear door, pushed his head down, shoved him in. Once he'd righted himself to a sitting position, she slammed the door shut and climbed in the driver's seat.

She nodded back to Tom. "Behave yourself and we'll get along."

Chapter 9

Brooke drove fast. Tom looked out the window.

The landscape altered little for the first part of their journey. The scenery was just more and more abandoned houses.

They sped up Washington Street.

Now, the approaching overhead mass was undeniably solid. It floated over a hundred meters above the ground, well above most buildings.

The mass looked like matted seaweed and beach sand with swirling tendrils underneath, like an impossibly monstrous jellyfish made of humus and fungus.

Sun somehow shone through it. The world below the mass was undimmed.

It was much vaster than Tom had thought. It seemed to go on forever. East, west, and into the far-off northern distance where it had no end in sight.

They reached the Massachusetts Avenue intersection, where the overhead mass began.

"Hey!" Tom said.

"What?"

"Pull over for a moment, I need to talk to you."

Her first response was to point her gun back over her shoulder. "I've warned you not to be a prick, Tom."

Tom regarded her cold eyes in the rearview mirror. "Stop being so butch," he said. "You're too pretty to bitch effectively, anyway." He smiled. "I'm not making a nuisance of myself. Just park the damn car for a moment."

Brooke shrugged, mollified somewhat by his flattery. "Okay."

She parked at the intersection then turned to face him. Her eyes were no-nonsense adverts. "What's your problem?"

Tom gestured up with his head at the floating static mass. *"That is.* What is it?"

Brooke looked at him in surprise. "Bizarro?" She made a pissed-off face. "Don't tell me you're suddenly scared of the sky falling on your head?"

Tom rolled his eyes. "Just answer me: *What the hell is it?"*

Brooke's eyes smoldered. "For God's sake, stop acting like you're seeing the Boston Overhead for the first time."

But I am, Tom thought desperately. *I am, lady. That shit overhead looks as solid as the ground we're riding over, and it goes on for—*

Brooke cut into his thoughts. "Is this bullshit *all* you stopped me for?"

Tom decided that, maybe, like the beautiful cop was pointing out, 'Bizarro' a.k.a. the 'Boston Overhead' really wasn't a big deal.

Best pump her for other info.

"Forget it," he said. "How long have you been looking for me?"

"Don't screw with me," Brooke replied. "You can't talk your way out of this. King Eric wants you."

King? "I'm *not* screwing with you. Just tell me how long you've been looking for me. Please."

She shrugged. "One year. Since you pulled that bank raid. Eighty officers got killed in that, about fifty bank staff also. King Eric's been pissed off ever since." She looked hard at Tom. "What's this about, Pussypalm?"

"You'll find this hard to believe," Tom said. "But I don't remember who I am. Amnesia—I've totally lost my memory."

This perfect excuse/defense/lie had come to Tom at just that moment.

Brooke studied his eyes for hints of a lie. She found none. "You're serious?"

He nodded. "I don't remember any further back than a week ago. I woke up in a motel room with a bad headache and the ID you found on me. My name was Tom Palmer. I was a vacuum cleaner salesman."

Brooke's face was expressionless. "Vacuum cleaners?"

Tom nodded. He winced at the memory. "For collecting *rat* droppings. There were some in the trunk of my car."

"You didn't find the vagina in your palm strange?"

He smiled innocently. "Who wouldn't? Worst thing is—it looks fuckable."

Brooke smirked. "Oh, you can fuck Rose alright. We've heard stories about that at the precinct." She regarded Tom with cool eyes. "It does other shit as well."

Tom didn't ask what. 'Rose' was clearly his palm-vagina's name.

Brooke studied Tom's face. "You can't remember ANYTHING? The King's gonna love this."

"That's another thing: who's this 'King' you keep talking about?"

"The King of Boston of course—His Majesty King Eric the Young." She shook her head. "But you obviously don't remember that either."

Her steely gaze softened a tad. "Look, Tom, I'm getting convinced that you really don't recall who you are. That headache you mentioned? You got hit in the head or something—shit happens, okay? But we've had an APB out for your arrest since you pulled that bank heist—"

"Yeeeessss . . . that's the primary thing I *need* to know before I get into the city: who the hell am I?"

Brooke regarded him, her eyes cool as ocean depths.

"You're Tom Pussypalm of course—gangster, murderer, occasional hired gun." She laughed without mirth. "The FBI wants you for violent crimes in sixteen states. You were in Boston because her majesty Queen Shirley was an ex-girlfriend, and King Eric offered you amnesty and a job as his security consultant. You however had a pay dispute with the King and left his employ.

"Fast forward to a year ago. You and your gang of eaters hit the Federal Reserve Bank, kill everyone, and make off with three truckloads of gold. Six billion dollars worth. King Eric was pissed as shit. You dropped out of sight . . . till today."

Tom nodded. "I get it." He didn't.

"Time to get you back to town," Brooke said. "I can't keep his majesty waiting."

She turned and started up the car again. Across Massachusetts Avenue, they dipped under the suspended mass.

"Is there anything else I should know?" Tom asked as they accelerated.

Brooke thought a moment then laughed, "Just remember: Bizarro isn't going to fall on you."

Chapter 10

They sped up Washington Street towards the city center. Up through Shawmut, into Chinatown.

Everywhere was desolate, empty of people.

It was ridiculous how deserted the city was. The houses weren't damaged, just abandoned, like there'd been a mass exodus. Some buildings had broken windows, several walls were pocked with bullet holes. But that was all. There were no skeletons, no evidence of bombing.

Just like he'd noticed out in the suburbs, there was also *no burning*. Meaning, no fucking dragons. Hopefully no dinosaurs either.

So where the hell is everyone?

Brooke reduced the patrol car's speed.

Tom considered this 'new' Boston.

The biggest difference was the lack of a Grid. Here, no dragon shield protected Central Boston. Here there was Bizarro instead, a ceiling to the entire city, not just its lower levels. The floating mass reminded Tom that things here weren't by any means normal. Skyscrapers penetrated Bizarro, their uppermost tips disappearing into its substance like the buildings were its support pillars.

Once again his attention was drawn to the desolate buildings. Odd, if this version of home was safer.

"Where's everyone?" he asked Brooke.

She grimaced. Over in West End. Some in Beacon Hill. This part of town's too dangerous. There's eaters everywhere?"

"Eaters?"

"Cannibals. You don't want to meet them."

She drove on.

"Fuck," Brooke said suddenly. "It's an eater trap." Tom heard fear beneath her sexy toughness.

"What?"

"Up ahead in the road."

He looked. Across the road lay several nail-studded two-by-fours.

"We drive over those and we've no tires left." She scanned the roadside buildings, then pointed. "They're hiding in that house."

"How can you tell?"

"It's the only one with an open window, so they can shoot through it." She grinned. "Bastards just outsmarted themselves."

Tom was impressed with her deductive ability. "We reverse out of here?"

Brooke shook her head. "I'll take care of the shitheads. Just pretend you haven't noticed them."

She parked by the open window, then got out and walked over to move the nail-studded planks out of the road.

Immediately Brooke's back was turned, a figure peeped out of the window.

A completely bald woman with bright yellow skin.

Tom shivered at the sight of her. She was yellow as lemon peel. Good-looking, but with eyes as transparent as water.

The woman stifled a yawn whilst spying on Brooke. Her hand was normal, but her teeth were jagged, doglike. Like her eyes, they were transparent. Like glass.

She wore a tattered dress splotched with red.

She turned toward the police car. Tom quickly looked away like he'd not seen her. He sensed the yellow woman's pleasure on realizing he was handcuffed. She hissed back into the room: "Hey, Brian, wake up and bring the damn gun. Food's arrived!"

A chill went through Tom at her words. *Food?* Brooke meanwhile pretended she'd noticed nothing. She dropped one two-by-four loudly on the sidewalk and bent to shift another.

A short pause later, a fat yellow-skinned man with a shotgun joined the woman at the window. He too was bald, with transparent eyes and teeth. His clothes were as red-splattered as hers.

Tom suddenly realized that the red stains on both their clothes was blood.

"Where's the damn food, Lucy?" he whispered.

The yellow woman jerked a quick finger to her right, where Brooke was dropping another plank on the sidewalk. "Get the one in the car first!" she whispered back.

Brian fired at Tom. Tom flung himself down between the front and rear seats, cursing Brooke for handcuffing him. The rear window exploded. Glass and buckshot sprayed over him.

"Got that one," Brian said. "Now for the bitch over—"

Brooke was faster, popping the yellow man between his eyes. Brian's brains blew out the back of his bald head. His dying expression as he fell backwards was one of intense betrayal.

Lucy screamed. She disappeared from sight for a moment, then reappeared at the window with the shotgun in hand. "You goddamn cop sow bitch! I'm gonna eat your tits for that! I'm gonna—!"

Brooke shot her in the face also. She disappeared from sight for good.

Brooke walked around to the rear of the squad car. "Hey, you can come up for air now."

Tom was stuck between the seats. She opened the door and helped him up.

He gaped at her. "Who the hell were those psychos?" The blasé way the yellow-skinned pair had described he and Brooke as food horrified him.

Brooke's face twisted in disgust. "Not psychos—they're the eaters I was telling you about. Transformed Bostonians—those not immune to the Bizarro virus. Now they eat human flesh. The fresher the better. Forget the vavs—"

"The who?"

"Vampire Vaginas—plants evolved into women. Forget 'em; the eaters are the main reason you never slow down outside a safe zone."

She said no more. Tom asked no further questions.

His impression of this Boston being safer that home was clearly wrong.

***

Farther ahead, there were police patrols and roadblocks in the street.

All were heavily armed. The cops' faces were shrouds of menace haunting the darkness behind the grills of their helmets.

Brooke was waved past each successive roadblock.

Popular chick, Tom thought.

"Where are we headed?" he asked.

"City Hall—the royal palace. Where else?"

Chapter 11

City Hall

Bounded by a high perimeter wall that became a metal fence with guard posts, Boston City Hall wasn't the same as Tom remembered. This version was a smaller (six-story), more utilitarian construct, not the brutalist concrete monument of his home dimension.

Here too, it was built on a hillside that raised it above its surroundings. Instead of possessing a concrete plaza, however, this version was set amidst lawns dotted with impressive elms, cypresses, and beeches. More trees ringed the palace walls.

Peering in through the fence pickets, Tom imagined that most of the buildings in the rough triangle bounded by Congress, Court, Cambridge and New Sudsbury streets had been demolished to make space for the grounds.

He reconsidered; maybe they'd never existed. A large number of other buildings—including landmark skyscrapers—remembered from home were missing here. Several of those that did exist looked different. Both the Exchange Place and One Beacon Street skyscrapers, for instance, were half their normal height.

Travelling up here had been motoring along a familiar road in an unknown town. A familiar difference.

***

The City Hall guards waved Brooke through. She drove toward a group of policepersons standing by the building's north side stairs.

As she parked, Tom heard loud quacking to his right. He looked. A bevy of speckled ducks frolicked on an extensive pond that curved to City Hall's rear. Beyond them, the next door John F. Kennedy building was visible through the treetops.

***

"Who's this?" A tall, muscular man name-tagged Lt. Ryan Harding asked Brooke once she'd gotten Tom out of the squad car. Lt. Harding was dashingly handsome with deep blue eyes and dark hair. "Another suicide attempt?"

"You wouldn't believe me if I just told you, sir." She uncuffed Tom. "Show the lieutenant your left hand. Front and back."

Tom did so.

For a moment Lt. Harding gaped at Tom in disbelief, his mouth working like he was having a stroke. "Pussypalm!?"

Brooke nodded.

Seemingly a million police officers immediately surrounded Tom. Women and men with cold suspicious eyes pointing guns at him like they'd dreamt of making a sieve of him last night.

Oh, no, Tom thought.

"It's okay, sir," Brooke told Lt. Harding. "Tom Pussypalm has agreed to cooperate with the law now. He's here to meet with the King."

"Cooperate? Meet with the King?" Harding mouthed the words in seeming disbelief. Then his expression turned enraged. "Pussypalm! You son-of-a-syphilitic-bitch!"

Tom didn't see the punch coming. Harding hit him low in the gut, then twice in the face. Tom felt his lip split, blood flood into his mouth. Pain spun around his head like a roulette wheel.

Then the lieutenant began choking him.

Through the pain in his head, Tom saw that Harding no longer looked handsome. Rage had transformed the man into a demon—his face was drained of blood, his eyes were red with hatred.

What the . . . ?

Harding forced Tom to the ground, then straddled him, his hands still firm around Tom's throat. Tom saw the lieutenant's clear intent to murder him in his eyes.

Tom was vaguely aware of the cops around pulling Harding off him.

Brooke yanked Tom to his feet. Whilst struggling to breathe, he looked over at Harding.

The lieutenant, his hands fists, the cords in his neck bulging, was straining with all his strength against those restraining him.

"Let go of me!" Harding yelled. "I'm going to fucking kill that son-of-a-bitch!"

"Calm down, sir!"

"Fuck calm down! Let me go, you retards!"

More policemen joined the eight already holding him back.

"Only when you calm down, sir!"

A ginger-haired female sergeant ran across to Tom and Brooke. She gave Tom a disgusted look, then yelled at Brooke, "What did you think you were doing, bringing this garbage here!? You knew the lieutenant will fucking murder him!"

"Anne, I thought he'd be pleased we'd caught him."

The redhead gaped at Brooke. "Pleased? Brooke, are you fucking drunk!?" She gestured to Tom. "Get him inside before Harding breaks free!"

"Yes!" Harding screamed. "Get that piece of shit inside before I empty my gun in his guts!"

Brooke kicked Tom's ankle. "You heard him. Get your murdering ass in gear."

They ran up the stone stairs.

Once inside City Hall, guards immediately fell in step behind them.

Tom wiped blood from his mouth. "What the hell is going on?" he asked Brooke.

"Welcome to Boston," she replied. "Get used to the reaction, dude. You've utterly no idea just how unpopular you are here."

She led the way to the King's presence.

Yeah, I get that bit, Tom thought, matching his steps to hers. *But Lt. Harding out there isn't just upset over stolen gold or dead cops—the man clearly has personal issues with me.*

Chapter 12

King Eric the Young.

The throne room was on City Hall's second floor. A wide conference room with a wall of windows facing out to the harbor with Faneuil Hall Market on its right.

"That's King Eric," Brooke whispered to Tom as they entered, leaving their escort outside.

"Who?"

"The kid on the marble throne."

Tom goggled.

King Eric, ruler of Boston, was a little boy. A thin, bratty-looking, blonde-haired, blue-eyed child wearing a white suit and a gold crown.

King Eric's scepter was a large multicolored lollipop. He licked it continuously.

Tom stared at the child king in confusion.

"How old is . . . ?" he asked Brooke.

"His Majesty was six last month."

Tom gulped. His daylight nightmare showed no signs of improving to a routine bad dream.

There were two others in the throne room:

One was a voluptuous middle-aged brunette; large breasts, slim waist, nice ass. Tom placed her age at fifty. Extremely attractive, with nice cheekbones, a Roman nose and full lips. Her dark eyes were as jaded as a hooker's. Their crow's feet imparted her a quiet dignity.

She wore a dark blue suit and high-heeled boots.

"That's Megan Fox," Brooke whispered to Tom as they approached the throne. "She's head of palace security. Whatever else you forget, remember this: you *do not* fuck with her."

Megan regarded Tom with an amused expression.

The other person in the throne room was Joe, the fat dark-haired man who'd earlier overtaken Tom whilst driving buck naked on Washington Street. Joe was dressed now, in a grey suit, white shirt, and blue tie. He nodded to Tom.

"Captain Joe Bradley," Brooke whispered. "Chief of Boston Police. "He's okay, but can't keep his dick in his pants."

Tom nodded. *Yeah, we've met.* He wondered where giraffe-necked Pam was.

"Watch your back. Joe hates you as well."

"Thanks for the warning."

"The one person missing is Longneck."

"Longneck?"

"Pam Andersen. King Eric's secretary and Joe Bradley's squeeze."

They reached the throne.

Brooke saluted. "Tom Pussypalm, your Majesty."

King Eric smiled at Brooke. "Very funny, Sgt. Hayes, except that I don't feel funny today. This clearly *isn't* Pussypalm, officer, but, GOD, how I wish it was. That scoundrel impoverished us, and we need money for weapons if we're to defend our population against this plague of eaters."

"I'm not joking, sire," Brooke said. She nudged Tom, who duly presented his left hand for the King's inspection.

King Eric's eyes opened wide. Joe and Megan gaped equally.

"Pussypalm?" King Eric whispered.

Brooke nodded. "Modern plastic surgery is better than Photoshop, your Majesty."

The little boy regarded Tom angrily from his throne. Like a car accelerating from zero to sixty in four seconds, his eyes turned insane with rage.

"We meet again, asshole!" he shrieked. "I told you I'd get you in the end, didn't I!?"

His voice, a B-movie six-year-old's attempt to be badass, was made all the more disturbing by its utter conviction. "Now, where the hell is my fucking money? I mean, *Boston's* fucking money?"

"Er, you're not supposed to swear, your Majesty."

King Eric instantly looked embarrassed. "You're right, Meg; I keep forgetting I'm too young for profanity."

Tom wasn't listening to their exchange. He was watching Joe Bradley closely. The Chief of Police's fat face writhed with emotion, but he was keeping himself under control. It was quite a fight; Joe's hands were fists by his side, his mustache twitched. *Oh, yeah, he fucking hates me too.*

"Now, Tom," King Eric repeated. "Where's the gold hidden?"

Brooke saluted again. "There's a problem, sire: Tom Pussypalm has amnesia. It's how I caught him so easily, and why he's still not trying to escape."

The little-boy king raised an irate eyebrow. He took a lick of lollipop. "Seriously?"

Brooke nodded. "Yes, your Majesty. He doesn't remember you or anything else. He's been working as a vacuum cleaner salesman."

King Eric gaped in disbelief. He scanned Tom's face with cold eyes. "Is this true, Tom? You don't remember anything? You don't remember me?"

Tom bowed. He nodded. "It's true, your Majesty. I can't remember—"

"He's gotta be lying." Joe Bradley interrupted. "Pussypalm's a slippery prick."

"Yes," King Eric said. He speared Tom with a piercing look. "What if you're lying?"

"I'm not," Tom insisted.

"Check him out, Megan," the King said.

The fiftyish brunette walked across to Tom. Her eyes were pools of suspicion. "*Why should* a king believe a thief?" she asked.

Her voice was soft like a glove. A disturbingly erotic low growl.

She placed a scented hand on Tom's shoulder. "You seduced the Queen, deceived the King, robbed the city of six billion dollars. What better escape when caught than amnesia?"

"*I am* telling the truth."

She smiled. She raised Tom's left hand from his side and studied its vagina. She parted the sex's lips and pushed a green-nailed index finger into the opening. She worked the finger deep into Tom's palm-cunt, amused by his embarrassment.

Megan pulled her finger out of Tom's hand. It was creamed with white secretion. She licked her finger clean, then released his hand.

"Your second sex tastes like you."

Tom wondered how she knew. Was he supposed to have slept with her?

Megan walked around Tom. He neither saw her point meaningly to Brooke's nightstick, nor the policewoman hand it to her.

"You claim innocence," Megan said from behind Tom. She laid a soft hand on his shoulder. The smell of cunt wafted from her finger to his nostrils. "But as a crook, it's more natural for you to lie than be truthful. You're back to raid the King again."

Joe Bradley was scratching his mustache, unsure what to make of Tom. Brooke also watched Tom, a subordinate amidst superiors.

Tom stared at King Eric. Punctuated by lollipop licks, the little boy was thinking furiously, his brow deeply crinkled.

Tom knew adult concepts were difficult for a six-year-old brain to understand. *How on Earth, did this kid become king? I mean—King? In the democratic US of fucking A? And with all these adults bowing to his will? And does the brat have to keep slurping that damn lollipop?*

"You're lying, Tom," Megan insisted.

"You think so, Meg?" the King asked, his voice soft and dangerous.

"He's here to rescue the Queen, your Majesty. Sexual attraction is the primary motivation to gallantry." She smirked. "I recall that, before you wedded her, her majesty reputedly performed great fellatio." She ran fingers through Tom's hair. "The memory of a superlative orgasm regularly transcends common sense in determining male action."

Tom couldn't think up a retort. He was apprehensive—Megan was still behind him. He could hear her slapping something against her palm. The sound set his nerves on edge.

"If he wanted to infiltrate us," Brooke said. "Why would I find him parked by the highway?"

Joe Bradley raised an eyebrow. "Parked? Pam and I passed him on the way here." The police chief scowled so deep, the lines looked chiseled into his face. "So he stopped afterward?"

Brooke nodded.

Megan smiled like a cruel ghost. Her lovely lips curled down in a smirk.

Joe frowned at Brooke. "*Parked,* Sgt. Hayes? What does that tell you?"

"I don't understand, sir."

"Officer, Boston road law clearly states that *no one* stops in the unsafe zones for fear of the vavs and eaters."

Brooke nodded. "That's true, sir. But—"

"Think with me," Joe interrupted. "Pussypalm is here now because you arrested him. But you only *found* him because he *stopped* in a No Stopping zone, right? Considering we've been searching for him for a year, I find that too much of a coincidence."

He raised an enquiring eyebrow; smiled coldly at Brooke's bemused look. "Oh, you'd not considered that possibility? What better way to infiltrate us again?" He glared at Brooke. "Leave the thinking to me, Sergeant. Keep your opinions to yourself."

Brooke nodded respectfully. She stared at Tom in confusion, wondering if he'd really deceived her.

Tom stared back in equal confusion.

"You know, Tom," King Eric said. "I find Megan's explanation for your presence here convincing. Or maybe you can think of a good counter-explanation."

Tom stared at the boy in the white suit waving the lollipop scepter. "I've told you, your Majesty: I don't remem—"

Megan knocked him out cold with a violent smack of Brooke's nightstick to the back of the head. "This should bring back pleasant memories."

Brooke rushed to ease Tom's unconscious descent to the floor.

Megan handed Brooke back her nightstick. She turned to King Eric. "I believe he's telling the truth, your Majesty. He's not behaving like himself at all."

The little boy adjusted his crown on his head. "I think so too."

Joe Bradley nodded, his fat face creased with thought. "Why'd you knock him out, Meg?"

She smiled. "The most common cause of amnesia is a sharp blow to the head. In the same way, lost memories are often restored by a similar violent impact."

She turned to Brooke. "Leave us, Sgt. Hayes. Remain in the building. Expect to be summoned again shortly.

Brooke nodded and left.

"You know," Joe said, pointing to Tom. "We should hand him over to Dr. Oppenheimer. He's sure to jog his memory."

Megan snorted. "Oppenheimer's a dangerous quack and you know it. Science for science's sake is bad business. He'll fuck Pussypalm's mind up so bad he'll *never* remember where the city's money is."

"And we definitely cannot risk that happening," King Eric said, his expression very worried. "If the city doesn't get some money soon, we'll be overrun with eaters."

Chapter 13

Tom woke up. His head was ringing like a bell. His eyes slowly focused.

He was still in the throne room; now seated in a chair by the windows. He looked outside. Seeing Bizarro overhead instantly reminded him he was a long way from home.

He returned his attention back inside. Megan and Joe were still in attendance, seated by King Eric's throne.

"He's awake," the little monarch said. He peered sternly at Tom. "Do you remember yourself now?"

Tom remembered he had amnesia. He faked an effort of mental strain. With his headache, it was easy. He grimaced awhile, then shook his head. "No, your Majesty."

Megan rolled her eyes. "Violence was worth a try."

The King nodded. "We'll have to proceed as unplanned." He turned to Joe. "Have Shirley brought in."

Joe activated an intercom switch set into the wall. "Hey, Pam, his majesty wants her majesty."

Joe broke contact. "She's on her way, boss."

King Eric turned back to Tom. His voice was sad when he spoke, "You put me in a bad situation, Tom. I really want to punish you, but it's pointless when you don't remember committing the crime. And then there's the money to consider."

The little boy began weeping tears of rage. "Oh, the injustice of it all. The utter injus—"

The door opened then. Pam—in a short pink dress and pink high heels—entered, followed by two policemen rolling a gurney bearing a naked woman. The cops parked the gurney in front of the throne, saluted, and exited.

Tom looked at the Bostonian queen. She was bound to the wheeled bed, her wrists and ankles secured to its sides by leather straps.

Her pale eyes were open and staring. A honey-blonde, she'd have been beautiful, but fright and pain made her ugly. Her forehead dribbled fear-sweat.

She was gagged with a red gagball.

Her bare breasts lay on her chest like inflated pancakes.

The incongruity of her appearance/existence raged in Tom's head. *A six-year-old kid with an adult wife?*

Tom's eyes roved downward to her shaven crotch.

He felt sick. There was a long thin needle stuck into Queen Shirley's clitoris.

He looked away. Pam and Joe chortled.

The Queen hadn't noticed Tom. Her pleading eyes were fixed on her husband.

"Time for a reunion," the King said. "Shirley, darling, I've someone I'd like you to meet . . . again."

Shirley turned her head and saw Tom. At first there was no recognition in her eyes. Then Megan lifted Tom's hand so she saw the vagina in it.

Shirley's eyes instantly widened to circles. She began squirming against her bonds. "Hmmmmff, Hmmmfff!"

"Sorry, your Majesty," Megan said, placing a hand on Shirley's forehead, "but lover man here doesn't remember you anymore."

Shirley stopped fighting her restraints. Her eyes searched Tom's face for proof that Megan was lying. She saw nothing but bewilderment in his eyes. Hope visibly left her. She slumped back down on the table, breathing heavily.

Megan flicked the needle stuck in Shirley's clitoris. The Queen's eyes instantly gaped wide again. She began squirming violently in agony.

"Well, Tom," King Eric said. "This is my wife, whom you were servicing without stamped consent from me."

Tom shrugged in disgust. Disgust at himself for causing this outrage, disgust at King Eric and his insane officials for perpetuating it.

"What I don't understand," King Eric continued, "is why you had to *steal* her, creep behind my back. I'm six years old, duh, nowhere near puberty—*I can't have sex yet—I can't get it up.* Besides, Boston has very clear zero-tolerance laws against child-adult relationships. All you had to do was *ask* for my royal consent to romance the Queen."

Tom heard the boy-king's words in a daze. He looked at the Queen, unable to fathom the depths of her suffering. The blood on her pierced clitoris was a thick black clot, meaning the needle had been stuck in her body for a long time. He hoped it wasn't since he'd gone missing.

He wondered if he had sufficient leverage to save the Queen. *King Eric clearly won't rough me up till he gets back his money—six billion dollars? SIX BILLION? Fucking wow!—so maybe I can get her off too.*

It was worth a try.

"Let her go," he told the King. "So I fucking slept with her. So what?"

King Eric gaped at Tom in disbelief. His face reddened and reddened like he was holding his breath amidst a tantrum.

"No!" he finally thundered, smashing his candy scepter against the white throne. "Who do you think you are!? You're lucky you're still alive! Don't push your luck, Thomas Pussypalm!"

Responsive anger flooded Tom. Trembling with rage, he stood up. He considered rushing at the King, grabbing his stupid lollipop, and breaking it over his juvenile head.

Megan read Tom's frustration. She smiled at him. "Don't even think about it, darling." She opened her suit jacket. Its interior was tailored racks full of long steel needles. "If you dare attack his majesty . . ."

"Hey, Tom!"

Tom looked over at Joe and Pam. The police chief and royal secretary were both pointing guns at him.

"Don't be an asshole like you were when you hadn't forgotten who you were," Pam said.

"Please ignore what the lady just said," Joe said softly. "Please do something stupid. Pleeeeaase."

Tom was shocked by the desire to kill in the fat man's eyes. He raised his hands. "Okay, I won't start anything."

King Eric glared at Tom. Then the child suddenly brightened up. He grinned. "Tell you what, Tom. Watch very closely now—you'll learn it doesn't pay to anger me."

He nodded to Megan.

"With pleasure, sire." She pulled a needle from her jacket. It was a foot long and glittered like a ray of silver light.

On seeing the needle, the Queen began violently thrashing against her bonds.

Megan leaned over Queen Shirley. She positioned the needle teasingly over her left breast, then, slowly pushed the needle down into her nipple.

Shirley stiffened with the pain. Her body trembled like a dying fish's. A trickle of blood bubbled from the needle's entry point.

48

"Megan here is an expert in dishing out pain," the little king said. "She knows *three hundred* different types of torture."

Megan's face was taut with concentration. She pushed the needle through the fatty breast, wiggled it between Shirley's ribs, then forced into her chest.

Into her heart.

Shirley's back arched off the gurney so high she looked like she'd break in half.

Her eyes gaped wide as saucers. They rolled in their sockets then fixed on Tom, pleading with him to save her.

Megan pushed the needle all the way through Shirley's heart and out the back of her chest. Blood dribbled down the needle onto the gurney, ran over its edges to splash on the floor.

Pam extended her neck across the room. She hovered her head over the bound Queen, studying her face as though its rictus held some long-sought truth.

Shirley remained arched off the gurney. She jerked like an epileptic having a seizure.

"Now note, Tom," Joe Bradley said with a cold smirk. "Her heart's skewered like a kebab, but she's not dead. And she won't die. Megan is expert at this. She can keep her alive indefinitely in this suffering if the King commands her to. She can even insert more needles into her heart to amp up her agony."

Shirley's pain-seizure had intensified. Her limbs twitched like those of a dying bug. The expression in her eyes transcended pain. Spittle and incoherent noise dribbled around her gagball.

Up close to Tom now, Pam winked at him. Her giraffe-neck twined sinuously—a snake in slow motion. She turned back to regard Shirley's pain-racked body while licking her lips.

"Anguish must not be rushed," Megan said to no one in particular. "When the intention is to deal punishment, the desired effect is only achieved if the created agony is deservingly prolonged."

Shirley collapsed back down, giving off a long horrible moan.

"Fucking stop it, you bitch!" Tom yelled at Megan.

"Watch your tongue!" Joe snapped.

Tom stared Joe down. He turned to fix the King of Boston with a steely gaze. "Let her die, goddammit!" He asked for this because he didn't envisage Shirley surviving with a punctured heart.

The boy smiled coldly. "She'll only die when I get your word that you understand I'm not someone you fuck with. You piss me off once more and you'll get the same as she's getting. Understand, dickhead?"

"Please stop swearing, your Majesty."

King Eric leapt up in a rage. "Shut the fuck up, Pam! I'll fucking swear all I want. I won't have this asshole jerking me around!" He glared at Tom. "DO YOU FUCKING UNDERSTAND ME, DICKHEAD!!!?"

Tom's anger drained out of him like piss. He sat back down, nodded. "Okay, just let her die."

King Eric nodded at Megan. "Finish her off."

Megan nodded. She pulled another foot-long needle from inside her jacket. She placed its point inside Shirley's right ear, scowled pointedly at Tom—

"This is regrettable," she said. "When punishment is shortened, the desired lesson is never learned."

—then hit the base of the needle with her palm, driving it into Shirley's head.

There was a sharp crack as the needle broke through the Queen's skull. Shirley froze as if she'd been iced. Megan gripped the outer half of the needle and jiggled it so it sliced Shirley's brain to shreds.

Shirley instantly went limper than a rag doll.

Megan straightened the needle out again and hit it hard. In a spurt of blood, its tip punctured out through Shirley's opposite ear. Blood spurted freely, pooled around her head.

Megan curtsied to the King. "Her death is imminent, your Majesty. Three minutes maximum. I've shut down her respiration. Without oxygen, woman is simply an illusion of her own mind."

King Eric the Young looked at Tom, an enquiring eyebrow raised. For emphasis, he licked his lollipop. 'Get the point?' his eyes asked.

Tom looked from kid king to dying queen and shuddered.

Chapter 14

The dead Queen was removed by the policemen who'd brought her to the throne room. A maid was summoned to mop Shirley's blood off the floor.

The maid finished and left.

King Eric, Megan, Joe, and Pam all looked at Tom menacingly.

"Now, Tom," the King said, "listen while I lay down the law for you." His voice was hard as teeth. "Listen good."

Tom listened.

"Tom, you owe the city of Boston six billion dollars. A hundred and fifty-one tonnes of gold bullion. Until you remember where you hid it, you stay around. This is the ONLY warning you'll EVER get. You cross me and I'll have Megan give you the same treatment Shirley just got. Only, in your case, asshole, she'll keep you alive for years."

"And feed you chunk by chunk to the eaters," Joe said.

"And you definitely don't want that," Pam added.

Megan stared Tom dead in the eye. "Imagine being in Hell—a delicious human steak roasting in Satan's fire," she said. "The ecstasy of pain I'll introduce you to will be much more exquisite than that."

Tom believed her.

Joe walked over and draped a fat arm over Tom's shoulder. He smelt of sweat. "Now listen, dude. The King here, he don't mess about. He rules *all* of East Massachusetts. Remember that. You've no escape anywhere. We're watching you. Sooner or later, something will occur to jog your memory back to normal, and when it does, you return our gold and we let you go your merry way."

Tom doubted he'd be going anywhere other than six feet under once they had their gold back.

Thank heavens I've no idea where the gold is, he thought. *I can't ever remember what I don't know.*

The four kept looking at him. Tom became wary, sure there was something more he was about to learn. *But now? After everything that's already happened to me today, what the hell is so important that it can't wait?*

He was tired of learning. All he wanted was a warm hole; somewhere to hide himself till this storm of information overload blew over.

He was still deeply shocked by how callously King Eric had ordered the Queen killed. He was more shocked by the blithe efficiency with which Megan had done so.

Brooke was right; Megan wasn't someone he'd ever intentionally cross. If she said jump, the only question was; how high?)

King Eric's eyes bored into Tom's. "While you're here, I need you to make yourself useful."

"What . . . what do you mean?"

King Eric sighed. "We've a few security issues you're going to help us resolve." He nodded to Joe. "Fill him in, Chief."

Joe nodded back, then turned to Tom. "We're having trouble locating the eaters' main hideout in Chinatown. For the past three months bands of cannibals have been popping up everywhere, kidnapping people and disappearing again. Each time we track 'em down to Kneeland Street, then lose 'em."

Tom remembered the eaters—the horrible yellow-skinned couple who'd attacked he and Brooke.

The police chief was still speaking: "At the moment, our troops generally don't go lower than Essex Street 'cos of the vavs. The veggie vampire girls are worse than the eaters."

He smoothed his mustache. "We've cleaned the eaters out from west and north Boston. Everyone lives out there now—North and West Ends, Beacon Hill, some across the Charles River in Cambridge—but population pressure's building, so we need to reclaim downtown too. This sudden resurgence of the eaters is a setback we can do without. And they keep vanishing like magic."

He looked pointedly at Tom. "We need to know *where* in Chinatown the cannibals are hiding so we can take them out with a single decisive strike."

Tom was bewildered. He looked out the windows, where evening had segued into night, seeking illumination in the seaweed-like platform floating overhead. "How do you expect *me* to help?"

"You *really* don't recall anything," Megan said. "Rose can locate the eaters' hideout for us. It knows things."

Rose? Tom dubiously studied the vagina in his hand. 'Rose' looked like a flower sculpted from meat. Disgustingly pretty in pink.

He looked back at the others. "It *knows* things?"

"Yes," King Eric said. "It's how you successfully robbed my bank, and also how you hid the money where I can't find it."

"Unfortunately for us," Pam added, "Rose won't betray you. Even at point of death it won't tell us where you hid Boston's gold."

"Annoying," King Eric said. He smiled coldly. "But we'll take what it will do."

Tom was intrigued. "How does this work?"

"Someone screws your hand till it cums," King Eric replied. "Then it tells us what we want to know."

Tom looked at him in amazement. "Oh hell no you don't!"

King Eric laughed. "You've no say in the matter." He turned to Joe. "Get your dick out and fuck Tom's hand."

Joe raised his hands apologetically. "Sorry, boss. Me and Pam have already done it thrice today. I can't get it up right away."

King Eric made a face. "Why the hell do I keep you around?" He looked at Pam. "He telling the truth?"

She nodded. "We've been banging since 6 a.m. No lie, Pussypalm saw us."

The King licked his lollipop. He turned to Megan. "You do it then."

She nodded. "With pleasure, sire."

Tom heaved a sigh of relief. Her performing cunnilingus on his hand wouldn't be too bad.

Then Megan undid her fly. *Shit,* Tom thought, *She's not going to use a strap-on, is she?*

Megan dropped her trousers and panties and stepped out of them.

Tom winced. She had a penis.

Megan laughed at Tom's surprise. She fondled her penis at him. "You'd forgotten this too? Be relieved that it won't be stirring up your shit."

She caressed her cock till it was hard, then grabbed Tom's left hand. She spat on Rose, then after similarly lubricating herself, penetrated the palm-cunt.

"Oooooo, hell yeah," she moaned, her penis sliding deep into Tom's hand, up into his arm. "Shit, Tom, you've no idea how I've missed this."

"We've done this before?"

Megan didn't reply. She gripped his thumb and fingers tight and pumped hard into his vagina.

Tom was aware of the others watching him with amusement. Even little King Eric. He decided to tough it out. *Oh, no. I'm not getting embarrassed for their entertainment.*

It felt extremely odd. His wrist swelled and deflated as Megan's penis slid in and out of the passage between its bones. At full penetration, Tom clearly made out the bulge of her glans between the bones of his forearm.

Thankfully, it didn't hurt.

But then Rose began moaning. The vagina's words escaped the prison of the penis rhythmically slurping in and out of it.

"Ooh yes," it moaned. "Fuck me deep, honey!"

Tom froze. Its voice was dead Lynn's. And something else was happening too. Pleasure was now boiling in his hand. It felt like a penis having sex.

"Fuck me!" Rose moaned. "Pleeeassse!"

Megan obliged. The transsexual pumped Tom's hand hard and fast. Her dark eyes were glazed with lust, her brown curls whipped around her head like storm winds.

She stopped fucking a moment, reached down and yanked Tom to his feet. "The angle of your arm's wrong."

She resumed fucking it.

Tom fought to keep a straight face. The pleasure had now spilt over as sexual excitation into his body. He had a raging erection.

He faked composure. King Eric, Joe, and Pam watched him with interest.

Tom wondered how the law permitted a six-year-old to watch an explicit sex act. *Oh, I get it: This isn't 'normal' sexual intercourse— Boston has no legislation banning vaginas in hands.*

"Isn't there a law against kids watching porn?" he asked.

"I ain't gonna arrest ya, if that's what you mean," Joe retorted.

"Besides," Pam added, her eyes aglow with lust. "The King needs his sex-education classes."

Tom's hand came.

"Oh yeesssssss!" it gasped.

Its orgasm hit Tom like a truck. Shook him like a lightning strike. Pleasure streamed from Rose. It rushed up Tom's hand like a river and flooded him.

Tom twitched and ejaculated in his underpants. He stood there, drained and trembling. Megan came also, ejaculating deep into Tom's arm. Her buttocks clenched so tight during her outpouring of semen, Tom could count their muscle striations.

"Oh, goodness gracious fuck," she groaned.

The pair stood like that, then both collapsed into Tom's chair, Megan on Tom.

Megan said nothing. Her face was aglow with pleasure. Her lips were slightly parted. Her bust rose and fell rapidly. Tom could feel the needles through her jacket.

Tom's hand rested on the chair arm. Rose's labia moved like fish-lips. "Damn!" it gasped. Megan's cum dribbled from it over Tom's fingers.

Tom stared dully at the moaning vagina. He felt weaker than a newborn. The violence of his combined orgasms had wiped him out. Pleasure from Rose still coursed through him. He felt how it felt.

King Eric laughed. "Ha ha ha! You should see the stupid look on your face. Almost makes me feel as good as finding the lost gold will." His good humor reduced. "Okay, now to business." He fixed Tom with a stare. "Ask it where the eaters are hiding out."

"Can't *you* ask it?"

Joe waved his gun at Tom. "Ask it, jerk. It's *your* hand."

Pam giggled. She extended her neck over to look at Rose. "Better ask it quick, unless you want Megan to fuck it again. The effect only lasts about two minutes."

Oh no, Tom wasn't being fucked in the hand again. The sight of the semen dripping from his hand-vagina made him want to puke. Megan still sat on him, relaxed as if they were lovers. Her white ass was a soft pad. Her cock trickled cum down her thigh onto his.

"Where's the eaters' Chinatown hideout?" he asked Rose.

"Ninety-five Kneeland Street. A door in the back basement leads to their secret place." The answer was a sleep-languid, afterglow-sensual drawl.

Tom looked at King Eric. The little boy grimaced. "No wonder we missed it. The cannibals were tunneling under us?"

"One more question," Joe told Tom. "Ask it about Gail. What happened to her?"

Pam scowled. She ran angry fingers through her blonde hair. Her eyes simmered. "What sort of ridiculous question is that? We all know she's dead. The eaters ate her; we buried what was left."

"Fucking ask it!" Joe growled.

Tom had no idea what this was about. He repeated the question to his hand.

"The eaters," Rose drawled. "The eat—" Its voice faded.

Joe's face fell. Pam smiled.

King Eric frowned reflectively. "So now you have vaginal confirmation of Gail's death. Like you needed it. Sorry, Joe."

Joe looked horribly saddened. Pam was visibly hiding her glee over something.

Megan got off Tom. She picked up her clothes, began dressing.

Tom looked at Rose's labia, now folded together like petals at sundown. Pam's threat of his hand being screwed again rose horribly in his mind. "Is there anything else you want to know?" he asked King Eric, dreading a positive reply.

"No. Not for the moment."

Megan zipped up her fly. She smiled coolly at Tom, handed him a Kleenex to wipe his hand.

"Don't be ashamed that you soiled your pants," she said, bending to kiss him lightly on the cheek. "The pleasure of an orgasm must never be measured against public opinion as to its propriety."

Tom was surprised by how serious she sounded. There was no mockery in either her eyes or her voice.

Chapter 15

Brooke was assigned to guard Tom.

"Who's Gail?" Tom asked as she led him up a flight of stairs to his prison quarters. "Joe looked like he'd start weeping if the King hadn't broken up the meeting."

"Oh, Gail was the chief's ex-fiancée. She was manager of the Federal Reserve Bank of Boston."

"The Boston Fed? That's where I'm supposed to have robbed, right?"

A nod. "Gail and Chief Bradley were about to be married; then you pulled your heist, during which the eaters killed Gail."

Tom digested that. "They didn't find the body?"

"We did, but the eaters had done a number on her. It was her alright. Joe's just never accepted the facts."

"And Pam? She seemed pleased."

"Longneck? She's jealous and insecure. If Gail's still alive, Joe would leave her in an instant."

Brooke suddenly regarded Tom coolly. "I'd best tell you this, so you watch your step real good—Gail's full name was Gail Harding."

"Harding?" Tom drew in a sharp intake of breath. "Shit, you mean Lt. Harding?" The man's incensed reaction on seeing Tom now made sense.

Brooke nodded. "Gail was his younger sister. The pair of them were closer than two peas in a pod." She made a face. "You're living on borrowed time. Harding's gonna kill you first chance he gets."

Tom suddenly didn't doubt that at all.

***

The stairway led outside at one point. The night was silent and hot. Just like with the daylight, the night didn't seem any darker with Bizarro overhead.

Tom pointed to the massive overhead extension, its swirling earth-tentacles. "That's the oddest thing I've ever seen."

Brooke looked up, her face like sculpture in the night light. "For a man with a vagina in his hand, that's saying a lot." She shrugged. "Bizarro? You get used to it."

"And it floats? It must extend for miles and miles."

"Farther than you'd ever imagine. It rolls out over the harbor well beyond Logan Airport and South Boston. How it floats? No one's yet figured that out. It's a total mystery. Even Dr. Oppenheimer—Boston's top egghead—is clueless. I've seen satellite pictures of its upper surface, though. It's a totally fucked-up world up there. Animals; plants—things odder than imagination."

She ran a hand through her hair. "It's odd having another world a hundred yards overhead."

Tom pondered her words. *Yeah, it is weird.* "And the eaters, where'd they come from?"

"Some kind of virus."

"How'd it get here? From Bizarro?"

She nodded. "So the eggheads say." She regarded his shadowed form with tired eyes. "It's been a long day. How 'bout I just tuck you into bed?"

***

Tom's room/cell was on City Hall's fourth floor. It had a window and bed and an en suite bathroom and didn't look too prisony.

"You're not really a prisoner," Brooke said as Tom looked around.

"Really?" He walked over to the window and looked out. He had a great view of the Financial District.

Brooke walked over to stand beside him.

"Yes, really. You can go where you like. Thing is, you've no idea where to go. Try to run away? The eaters will catch and eat you."

Tom conceded her point. He left the window and sat on the bed.

"I saw the Queen get murdered," he said.

"I know. I escorted the cops who removed her body."

"You sound very blasé about it."

Brooke shrugged. "It wasn't murder, it was an execution. Queen Shirley was sentenced to death a month after you went missing."

"But the *way* she was killed . . . You're a cop. Don't you care about being humane?"

"Nope. A horrible death sets a good example to others who intend stepping out of line." She shrugged. "Besides, there's nothing I can do—

King Eric is ruler of Boston. He's the law." She peered at Tom. "You really don't recall anus or excrement or the toilet, do you?"

Tom looked at her askance. "I wish everyone would stop saying that. Besides, what the hell else is there to remember?"

"The way the city's run."

Tom laughed mirthlessly. "Run? By a six-year-old? How in Bridgette Kerkove's superfucked anus did that lollipop-addicted-brat become king?"

Brooke frowned. Tom clearly wasn't about to give up on this. She sat on the end of his bed.

"How else? This is America—democracy. We *elected* him as king."

"Let me get this straight: the city of Boston elected a six-year-old as king?"

She shrugged. "Even toddlers can enter the elections."

"And he's got power of life and death?"

She nodded. "For four years, then he's up for reelection. Someone else gets power of life and death. What could be more democratic than that?

Tom was lost for words.

Brooke was amused by his confusion. "You'll get used to it . . . again."

"I hope not. It's insane."

Brooke laughed softly, her gray eyes sad. "Since Bizarro, everything *is* insane, Tom. The world isn't what imagine you remember anymore."

Tom was pokerfaced. *You've no idea what true insanity is, sister. I wish I could give you a glimpse of where I'm coming from.*

Brooke got up to leave.

"Wait a bit," Tom said.

She turned. "Um?"

"What's the deal with Megan? Why does she talk odd like that? Drugs."

Brooke sat down again. "Drugs? Nah, Megan doesn't even drink. She's into some sexual religion thing. She's a follower of Iranian mystic Soraya Vagina."

Tom hid a grin; here at least was something he was familiar with. "I've read some of Soraya's work; she doesn't proselytize sadism."

"Nah, that bit is Megan herself." Her expression turned musing. "I often wonder if she . . . he . . . was abused as a kid. Some pedophile victims

59

turn out that way. And she's transsexual—her gender identity issues likely amplify her emotional damage . . ."

"Something's extremely damaged with her for sure," Tom said, "I've known nasty people before, but Megan seemed divorced from what she did to the Queen."

Brooke nodded. "Like she wasn't enjoying it, but it was *necessary?*" She shivered. "That's what scares me about her. She's a nut, believes her sexual salvation gospel."

She got off the bed and walked over to the door. Tom watched the policewoman's heavy backside sway unselfconsciously, her trouser rear caught in her ass-crack. The flicker of desire in his groin didn't neutralize the questions in his mind.

At the door, Brooke turned and stared pointedly at Tom. "And stop being so self-righteous. Queen Shirley got killed because you slept with her. She's only dead now because you didn't keep your penis in your underpants."

The accusation burnt Tom. "Hey, hey, hold on. Why do you assume the affair was my fault? Makes more sense that she hit on me. The kid already admitted he wasn't sleeping with her."

Brooke rolled her eyes. "It's ungentlemanly to blame the woman, Pussypalm. You forget: We're *never* guilty."

She slammed the door and left.

Tom stood up and walked back to the window. He looked out over the dark city, then up at the Boston Overhead, Bizarro. He found no answers in the black night, just more questions.

Finally he returned to bed. He lay there thinking till he fell asleep.

Chapter 16

Clothed in beads of sweat, Pam Andersen rolled over in her sleep. As she turned, face wrapped in her blonde hair, her right hand unconsciously quested for Joe.

The feeling of him beside her was so familiar that its lack woke her up.

"Joe, Joe?" Groggy, Pam looked around.

She was alone on the damp, sweaty sheets.

He's gone to the toilet, she thought. She was about falling asleep again when it occurred to her, that, maybe Joe wasn't innocently relieving himself.

Prompted by jealousy, the sleep drained from Pam's eyes in jerky stages. Even before she was fully awake, she was fully mad.

Pamela Andersen was an incredibly possessive woman. Dumped in an orphanage at the age of seven by her mother (after Pam's father left her for another man), Pam had never been able to lose the fear that everyone she loved would leave her also. Over time, through an unfortunate series of bad relationships, Pam's neuroses had only intensified.

Pam was a widow. Her husband Marv had been eaten by cannibals—the only reason Pam accepted that he'd not deserted her for another woman was that she'd seen it happen.

Nine Months Earlier

Pam Andersen sat on a kitchen stool, fixing herself a sandwich.

It was 1 a.m. Pam was butt naked. The night's sweltering heat caressed her body as she sliced a cucumber.

Pam was in a good mood as she arranged the cucumber slices over the layers of mayonnaise and chicken slices on rye bread. Next, she reached for an onion.

She and Marv had just made love. Marv had fallen asleep immediately after they'd broken apart. That was fine with Pam—he'd fucked her nicely tonight, long and gently, just how she liked it. Her pussy and nipples tingled pleasantly.

She wished Marv would be home more nights. Sex compensated for the heat—made it not half as bad.

***

Marv Andersen was a senior supervisor with Boston Cannibal Watch (BCW), which meant lots of nights spent watching heat radars for suspicious levels of eater activity.

Marv oversaw Beacon Hill district, the northeast of the city. Originally he'd worked down in Chinatown, but Pam had whispered in King Eric's ear, and he'd been reassigned. Even when Marv wasn't home, the knowledge that he was nearby made Pam feel better.

They also lived on Canal Street for the same reason. Their Avenir Building apartment was equidistant from City Hall and Hull Street by the Charlestown Bridge, Marv's observation post.

(Boston could never totally rid itself of eaters. "I believe the virus is still active," Dr. Oppenheimer had told King Eric in Pam's hearing, "transforming normal citizens into cannibals everyday.")

Marv and BCW monitored eater concentrations. This was easy, as most Bostonians now lived in the west of the city. Once the BCW detected high eater numbers anywhere, they forwarded the location to the police, who rushed in to decimate them again.)

***

Pam's pussy clenched deliciously in memory of the sex she and Marv had just shared. She forgot her sandwich for the moment. She giraffe-extended her neck down, till her head dangled upside-down in her crotch. Mingled love juices sheened her thighs, her anus a tiny pucker behind them like the entrance to a train tunnel seen through cloistering hills.

Like a loincloth, her blonde hair hung down to her knees.

Parting her labia with her hands so she was looking inside herself, Pam inhaled her vagina odor deeply.

She grinned at the pussy and cum stink. The delicious smell of past carnality triggered a desire for a repeat performance. *I don't care how tired Marv is. Once this sandwich is down my upper hatch, I'm waking him up for some more cock down here.*

Pam took another deep sniff of herself. The smell of semen gave her a sense of accomplishment. Neck curved like a swan's, she licked her clitoris, tightening her lips round the bud, teasing and sucking deep on

62

herself. Pleasure hit her like a hammer. She had to adjust her posture, spreading her pussy lips with one hand and gripping the kitchen table with the other—her legs felt like buckling. She sucked her pussy, relentlessly drawing out remnant trails of Marv's semen.

With supreme effort, her body trembling, Pam yanked her head away from her cunt and shortened her neck back to normal.

She licked her lips, her chicken and cucumber sandwich now totally forgotten. Her nipples stood up on her breasts like thimbles, tingly nubs. *Oh no,* she thought grimly, heading for the kitchen door with purposeful strides. *No self-cunnilingus tonight. Giving myself head simply isn't the same thing as having a hard man. Marv had better—*

The loud sound of breaking glass shattered her lust.

Pam froze. Her mind instantly linked the noise with possible scenarios. Had a peacock smashed into the window by mistake or a windblown . . .

Then Marv began screaming, his voice siren-loud from two rooms away.

That could mean only one thing. Eaters! They'd somehow broken into the house.

Panic instantly filled Pam. She rushed to the kitchen window and peered out, just in time to see a yellow leg lift off an improvised ladder into their bedroom window.

Pam was dismayed at the eaters' ease of access to them. *Just a ladder?* Urgency replaced her panic: *I need to fucking help Marv.*

She rushed to the knife rack and jerked out a huge cleaver. From down the corridor she heard a single gunshot.

Brandishing the cleaver, she ran out of the kitchen, heading for their bedroom, all her previous sexual arousal now converted to battle readiness.

Pam knew her only chance of saving Marv was to take the eaters by surprise.

There were two guns in the bedside cabinet, another in her bottom dresser drawer. This last was an experimental laser Dr. Oppenheimer had given Marv. It wasn't practical for military use—it quickly overheated—but Pam had once seen it reduce a live turkey to charcoal. She wished she could get her hands on that laser gun, but the dresser was on the room's far side, by the window. To reach it she'd need to pass through the eaters. The bedside cabinet however was right by the door once she opened it.

Marv screamed again as Pam reached the bedroom door. This time much weaker.

He's fading! she thought desperately, scared of being left alone again.

She tried the bedroom door. It was locked from the inside.

Damn! Pam thought.

"Please, no! Don't!" Marv screamed on the other side of the door. "Don't—!" It was horrible to hear Marv, so vital, so virile, crying like a baby. She realized then, that he wasn't yelling her name, calling for help. Her husband clearly didn't want the eaters knowing she was in the house. He was trying to protect her.

"Noooooooo!"

Pam didn't wait to hear any more. She darted into the next room and opened the window.

Like an alien invasion, the hot night wind blew in hot and heavy over her naked body.

Pam stuck her head out of the window. She extended her neck, slithering it along the exterior brickwork like a snake towards the bedroom window. She had just one chance of saving Marv, if it wasn't already too late.

(Not for the first time, Pam Andersen cursed her possessiveness. She and Marv lived on Canal Street because she didn't want Marv too near the other BCW wives. Pam firmly believed familiarity bred desire, not contempt.

Her insistence that they live apart from everyone else now meant they had no help.

But this sector of Boston has been totally clear of eaters for two years now, her mind screamed in disbelief. *They've never dared come this way before now.*)

Her head reached the bedroom window, its lower sash now devoid of glass.

She stared in and recoiled in horror.

Marv was dead. His killers had cut a deep rive in his torso from ribcage to crotch.

The eaters were grouped around Marv's corpse. There were six of them, two women, four men—yellow as lemons and bald as vultures. One man was pulling out Marv's viscera in handfuls and passing them around. The others—their eyes like empty pits in their skulls—ate the shared organs ravenously. Their transparent teeth ripped kidneys, intestines, and liver chunks apart as effectively as knives.

Marv's dying expression was of the most horrible pain imaginable.

Pam stared at the mutants eating her husband. All wore threadbare blue denim dyed red by faded layers of blood. Marv's blood was red and fresh on their bodies and jaundiced faces with those horrid transparent eyes.

One of the eaters had a chunk of arm missing from where Marv had shot him. A yellow hole in yellow meat. Pink blood dribbled down his arm. Marv's nerveless hand still gripped his gun, as bloodied as the rest of him.

An almost impossible rage filled Pam. *Oh no, you fucks have gone much too far.*

For a woman eternally scared of being dispossessed of her man, the eaters had unwitting pushed all of Pam Andersen's red buttons.

She calmed herself, however, enough to put her plan into effect.

It was a suicidal plan, but Pam's sense of outrage transcended such considerations.

With the eaters consumed with eating her husband, she slithered her head and neck in through the window and down to the floor.

Silently, she moved across to the dresser, now fortuitously placed to aid her. She raised her head to the lowest drawer. She swiveled once to check that the eaters were still engrossed in their feast, then, gripping the drawer knob between her teeth, she pulled it open by careful inches.

She stopped every few seconds and checked on the eaters. She needn't have bothered. The cannibals never noticed her. They ate loudly and noisily, smacking their lips as if Marv's guts were the tastiest thing ever.

"Give me some kidney, Jose."

"Don't be greedy, Maria, just eat the liver."

"You're the greedy one, jerk. Gimme some damn kidney!"

"I still think we should have cooked him first."

Pam wished she was deaf. Once she got the drawer open, she rooted through her undies for Dr. Oppenheimer's laser pistol. Like a pig snuffling for truffles, she nosed her intimate apparel aside.

Shit, this is taking forever, she thought angrily.

Her lips touched cold gunmetal. She clamped her teeth around the gun's barrel and pulled it out of the drawer.

That was when she noticed that the loud feeding sounds in the room had stopped.

She raised her neck and saw the cannibals staring at her in shock. All were red like they'd been spray-painted.

Pam was disgusted. A female eater was kneeling between Marv's legs. She had Marv's penis in her mouth, was sucking on it.

One of the male eaters got over his surprise. He leapt at Pam, grabbing her neck. Pam twisted her head right and left to no avail in her attempt to get free.

"We're gonna eat you, bitch," the yellow man growled. "Looks like there's plenty meat in that long neck of yours."

He opened his bloody mouth to bite Pam's throat. She winced at his bad breath, a stink of decayed meat.

She reared back and head-butted him. The eater let go of her neck. He staggered back, blood pouring from ripped lips. "Shit!"

Pam quickly reeled herself out of the room. Behind her, she heard the eaters talking.

Back in the next room, she heard their confusion as they stared out of the window after her. "She's disappeared!" a thin female voice yelped.

"She's just another freak, Maria," a male voice soothed. "Bizarro keeps making 'em."

Pam was incensed. *You mutants are calling me a freak?*

"Yeah, a freak. Some kind of woman-snake. Her neck probably was her body."

"What did she want the gun for then?"

"Don't sweat it, Julie. There's only one of her and six of us. We got guns too. Hey, Jethro?"

"Mo?"

"Watch the door."

"Why? It's locked."

"Because I fucking said so, meathead. I don't want that longneck bitch disturbing dinner again. It's bad enough we didn't cook it first."

Pam flicked the safety off the prototype laser. She tested it first on a chair in the corner of the room. The chair dehydrated instantly, crumbling to the floor.

The gun was hot in her hand, but she'd manage.

She smiled coldly. *Longneck freak bitch, huh? Disturbing dinner, huh? Well see about that, assholes.*

***

Pam fried the bedroom door. When it crumbled to ash, she saw the eater named Jethro waiting behind it, pistol poised.

Before he could get over his shock and fire, she fried him too. Jethro burnt up like a matchstick.

Longneck bitch huh?

She stepped into the room.

The remaining eaters instantly leapt up from around Marv's corpse.

"Hi, assholes. The bitch is back. And for your info: that's my husband you're eating."

Before any of the cannibals could grab their guns, she crisped them all, sweeping the laser from left to right and back again. All it took was a single touch of the laser beam to set each alight. The room filled with smoke as the eaters burnt.

The single eater she didn't fry was the woman who was still—to Pam's disbelief—sucking Marv's cock. The eater bitch's necro-fellatio pained Pam almost more than seeing Marv dead.

The cannibal woman was kneeling, seeming entranced as the laser beam flashed left and right over her head.

The four remaining eaters reduced to piles of ash.

Pam yanked on the cock-sucker's right ear, yanking her off Marv.

She spun her round so they were face-to-face. "Stop playing with my husband's prick, you stupid bitch! That's mine alone!"

The woman leapt at Pam, jaws bared, her teeth transparent knives from which strings of saliva dripped. "Gonna eat you!" she yelled.

"Eat this instead!" Pam stuck the laser pistol in the woman's mouth and pulled the trigger. Her head exploded into flames.

Pam played the laser beam over the woman's body. She caught fire, then coated over with white ash, her interior glowing like it contained red-hot coals.

Pam dropped the now scalding-hot gun, kicked the disintegrating woman aside, and leapt to Marv's side.

Her heart broke. The cannibals had made a total ruin of Marv. In addition to the gaping chasm that had housed his bowels, huge chunks of meat were missing from his chest and thighs.

Shit, shit, shit! her mind screamed as she knelt beside her dead husband on the blood-soaked bed, cradling his head. The corpse's blood smeared her, his head lolled in her embrace.

Pam's adrenalin/anger rush died. A flood of emotional horror, pain and loss kicked in to replace it. She wept loudly over Marv's corpse, crying like she'd never stop.

Around her, the six eater corpses—charred black mounds like anthills made of coal—smoked on.

Pam wrenched herself out of yesteryear. The horrid memories swirled stubbornly in her head for a moment, then dissolved into fetid emotional ghosts, a lingering sick feeling.

She lay in bed, sweaty body glistening in the dappling night light. With the moon blocked off, here beneath the Boston Overhead, Pam always had the illusion of moonlight being spread like butter on burnt toast. Night light bothered her for seemingly having no source.

"Imagine Bizarro as a massive solar panel," was how Dr. Karl Oppenheimer had explained it to King Eric, "with reflectors studding its underside." He'd adjusted his glasses, then continued, "But the reflectors are of course invisible. Try visualizing them as massive fiberglass cables running through the mass, leeching in light from topside and streaming it out downside, bypassing Bizarro like it's not even there. Now finally, also visualize the Overhead as having an automatic regulator that adjusts the amount of light projecting downward to a constant, determined value. One value for day, another for night."

Pam yawned. *Egghead shit, but then Oppenheimer's too smart for his own good anyway.* The explanation made sense to Pam, but it also smacked of Bizarro being somehow alive, which she found disturbing, like it was a vegetable Big Brother watching her.

Her mind returned to what had woken her up. *Where the hell is Joe? He ain't in the john, that's for certain.*

***

Standing by her bedroom window, hands on the ledge, Pam extended her neck along the outside wall towards Brooke's room. Brooke also lived on the third floor, six apartments away. *Damn you, Joe, you dog! You can't be trusted for a minute. Oh, yes. I did see you watching that policewoman's ass swing. I should have you neutered.*

Neutering Joe Bradley sounded nice to Pam as her neck elongated rapidly in a profusion of added vertebral links towards Brooke Haye's window. She'd heard that castrated dogs never strayed from their mistress's side.

Chapter 17

Brooke Hayes was alone. She lay on her side in her sweat-drenched bed, her hands between her legs, pleasuring herself. One hand tickled her clitoris, the other fucked her vagina with a mertopus tentacle. The mertopus was one of the myriad strange hybrids created by Bizarro—an ugly carnivorous black fish with red tentacles instead of fins.

As Brooke sexed herself with the red tentacle, it released hormones into her vagina, heightening her enjoyment.

Her pleasure rose. She rode it expertly, sliding the tentacle as deep as it would go inside her cunt, but it simply wasn't enough.

Not the physical sensation—that was superlative as always, but the emotional component. Masturbation by any other name—sisters doing it for themselves—was still jerking off, still just a relationship with your hand.

Brooke wanted a man.

Brooke Hayes knew she was beautiful and had full confidence in her sexuality. There were lots of men to be had; only none Brooke really wanted . . . till now.

Okay, she liked Joe Bradley too, but she wasn't trespassing on Pam Andersen's turf. *Damn, that bitch is jealous—crazier than Jeffrey Dahmer where boyfriends are concerned. She should be called Ms. Clingfilm. Worse still, she's got the King's ear.*

She gritted her teeth as orgasm washed over her like the waves of a sea. At her crest of pleasure, Tom Pussypalm's face exploded through her mind. His eyes behind her eyes bored into her disapprovingly as she came.

Screw this, Brooke thought when her orgasm subsided. *Something about that man gets to me. No, I don't trust him, I definitely don't love him, but—*

She pulled the mertopus tentacle out of her dripping vagina, tossed it aside, and leapt to her feet.

—but I most definitely want to fuck him.

She wrapped a robe around herself, tidied up her mussed hair and left her room.

Chapter 18

Pam watched Brooke masturbate without feeling the slightest glimmer of arousal. Her eyes widened, however, when she saw what the policewoman's sex toy was.

A mertopus tentacle? Pam cringed in revulsion. *Damn, girl, no wonder you ain't got time for guys. That thing will crisp your pussy—fry your G-spot so bad, you'll never cum again.*

Pam personally knew two women burned by mertopus tentacle usage. Both now complained of a continual 'buzzy' feeling in their vaginas. "It's like that ear ringing thing . . . tinnitus . . . ," one had explained miserably, "but much worse. My pussy feels permanently halfway between arousal and orgasm, no matter how much I jerk off or how many cold showers I take."

Oh, no seafood sex for me, Pam grimly reaffirmed.

She watched Brooke turn off the room lights and leave. *Where the hell you going now, girl? You off to fuck the fish itself?*

Pam forgot Brooke. She floated her head away from the window to peek into the next room. Her neck had begun aching now. She looked back at her body, almost thirty feet away, her hands still clutching the window ledge.

She turned back to the night-dark brick walls, checking which bedrooms had their lights on.

(City Hall's ground floor contained mostly clerical offices and guard quarters. Like his throne room, King Eric's quarters were on the second floor, situated on the building's west side so the six-year-old monarch could enjoy the gardens and watch ducks frolic in the pond.

The apartments and rooms on City Hall's third and fourth floors were reserved for palace staff. The fifth and sixth floors were mostly unoccupied.)

Growing more and more agitated by the moment, Pam peeked in window after window looking for Joe Bradley.

She finally found him. Up on the fourth floor. In the one place she'd never have expected.

Pam laid her chin on a shadowed corner of the windowsill and peered into Megan Fox's room in utter disbelief.

***

Joe lay naked on Megan's bed. The bed, a plush pink heart-shape, reeked of rose perfume that wafted to the window and offended Pam's nose and emotions.

Joe was spread-eagled, his wrists and ankles cuffed to special posts built into the bed. He shuddered, like he was in the grasp of deep emotion.

His penis was stiff, hard and upright like a soldier on parade.

Megan was walking around the bed. She was completely naked. Sweat dripped down her back, ran between her breasts—distended white sacs, sexy despite middle-aged sag. Her engorged nipples stuck out. Her stiff cock jutted out in front of her. A thin string of pre-cum swung from her corona, catching light like a liquid chandelier.

In her right hand, Megan clasped a black whip that writhed.

That whip is alive, Pam thought.

"Painsure is the true sex," Megan was saying. "A blend of pain and pleasure far greater than the sum of its halves. We must transcend the inferior sexual experience."

Megan lashed Joe with the living whip. His fat body squirmed, his fat face contorted with emotion that was neither hurt nor horror.

Pam saw Joe's cock dribbling precum.

He's fucking enjoying it, she realized.

"No," she gasped, anguished emotion exploding from her in a tortured whisper.

Fifty feet away, Pam's heart beat angrily, her hands violently pounding the window frame.

Chapter 19

"No," Joe gasped. "Enough, please."

"*Enough* is for *me* to decide," Megan said. "The slave exists for the master's pleasure." She frowned coldly. "You need more painsure."

The lash fell again. His body shuddered first with pain, and then from the shock the whip gave him.

Megan was flogging Joe with an electric eel. With each lash she let it lay on him just long enough to shock him, before jerking it away and flailing it again.

"Drink this, darling," she'd told Joe earlier, pouring a thick unpleasant liquid down his throat.

Joe swallowed, then sputtered. "What is that shit?"

Megan stroked her brown hair. "An elixir. It will keep you alive. Painsure can be dangerous."

Now, Joe felt transcendent, like part of the Boston Overhead. His head felt detached from his body, which in turn felt like a multitude of separate parts floating in a swimming pool filled with honey. Each time Megan slashed him with the eel, the electric current split him into more and more pieces of himself.

And the feeling? Joe was unsure if he was in heaven or hell. It was beyond anything he'd ever experienced.

His cock felt a million feet long. His balls felt like Jupiter and Mars. His glans felt like a volcano, like he'd ejaculate molten lava.

"I warned you—after me you'd never love another," Megan said.

Joe wondered if she could read his mind. He stared into her eyes. A sexual universe reflected back in those brown eyes, spectacular truths that somehow bore no roots in lust or romance. Yes it was true, at the moment, Megan was the universe, all its truths, all meaning. Her incredible body, her fantastic breasts, the chocolate-furred mons veneris, the short knotty cock like a meat howitzer, the Junoesque legs . . . all was too much for Joe's mind to focus on.

Megan lashed him again. She deliberately let the eel lie on Joe now. Her eyes flickered with excitement as he spasmed/trembled in the pain that wasn't pain, in the painsure.

"I'm gonna cum," Joe moaned.

"Yes you fucking are, lover," Megan said. She pulled the eel's jaws apart and rammed its mouth down on Joe's penis as he began spurting.

Holding the fish's head firm over Joe's cock, Megan dropped its tail into his crotch, shocking his balls as he ejaculated in its mouth.

In an orgasm that felt like it went on forever, Joe shuddered and shuddered like he was dying. He felt the fish's mouth and throat over his erection like he was being rubbed by the silkiest pillows imaginable, a million miles away.

***

Watching from the window, Pam felt like she was dying also. She felt worse than betrayed. *A fish? Joe is cumming in an eel's mouth? A fucking fish?*

Frozen in place by masochistic impulse, Pam Andersen remained watching. Her heart beat so violently she felt her chest would explode.

***

Megan removed the eel from Joe's cock and dropped it over the side of the bed. She stood over Joe, placing one foot on his blubbery chest, and masturbated.

While she pleasured herself, she spoke softly to him.

"Love is power; sex is dissolution into the feeling; when we fuck there is no right or wrong, just desire and gratification of that desire." She grunted as the pleasure built up in her testicles. Her breathing came hard and fast as she asked, "Do you understand all this now?"

Joe nodded. He didn't understand a word of what she meant. What he did understand was that he'd just had an incredible sexual experience, and it had consisted of a transsexual and a fish. *Holy Guacamole!*

"Oh fuck," Megan grunted, her fingers working hard over her penis. "Are you ready to savor my cum, lover?"

"No, no!" Joe gasped in sudden horror. "I'm not drinking your cum."

Megan gasped. "You just came in a fish's mouth. What's a little semen between friends?"

Joe shook his head resolutely. With memory of the incredible orgasm fading, he now began worrying that Megan might actually force him to give her a blowjob, or worse still . . . and here he was tied down and helpless.

She laughed at his fear.

"I'm not into rape, my fat darling. Sex must be freely given and received. The sexual treasure is only revealed when the love key slots into a willing lock. Even in inflicting pain, coercion reduces pleasure. Get it?"

Joe shook his head.

"You're filled with worries about sexuality that don't bother me," Megan said.

"You have breasts *and* a penis—society already assumes you're sexually odd. I'm still normal."

"Normalcy is relative. Even 'relatively' is relative to what is considered normal. Your girlfriend has a neck like a giraffe, is that normal?"

Stroking herself fast now, Megan knelt beside Joe's head. She removed a hand from squeezing her testicles to caress his cheek and stroke his mustache.

He flinched. "Please don't, Megan."

She giggled. "The police chief is scared of a little prick?"

"C'mon, Megan—"

"Shut up. Drink my offering. Ejaculation is obliteration—of oneself, and of the other's liberty from you. Once you leave a part of yourself in someone, you are always with them, they are always yours. A gift of semen is greater than a kiss. Are you so obtuse that you don't understand this?"

Joe kept his mouth shut. *I don't care what you say, baby. I ain't drinking your damn love juice. Next thing I know, you'll be asking to fuck my ass.*

"You still won't accept my offering of truth into your mouth?" Megan laughed. "I'll be your beauty cream then. Here is evidence of my enjoyment of you."

She ejaculated on Joe's face. Her semen—thick white like yoghurt—spurted in loops all over Joe's cheeks, lips, nose, and forehead. His mustache looked soaked in milk.

He shut his eyes as she ejaculated more and more. Hoping she'd finish cumming soon.

***

And Pam watched and waited and hated and hated.

Shit. I am so going to kill this fucking son-of-a-bitch! she raged, finally retracting her neck down to meet her body.

I'm going to . . . I'm going to . . .

74

Angrier than a fly deprived of a delicious meal of excrement, Pam Andersen began racking her brain for the perfect revenge.

Chapter 20

"I want my vagina back," the woman said. She was dressed in a clown's outfit, blue polka-dotted with white. It had the crotch cut out, so Tom could see she was pussy-less down there. She had a whitened face, green-dyed mop hair, a yellow sponge nose, and a huge red painted-on smile, with large red dots on her cheeks.

They two were alone in Tom's bedroom.

The clown frowned behind her smile. She snapped her fingers. "Hand my cunt over, Tom."

Tom frowned. He was naked and his left hand was several times larger than his body, so big that Rose could easily admit an elephant. "Can't you just let it go?"

"Let it go? *Forget my vagina?* Are you stoned? My sex-life's a mess. Oh, sorry, I forgot—I don't have one anymore! I'm so totally not into anal. Vaginas only grow on trees in Pussytopia, dickhead."

The clown-woman reached into her impressive cleavage and produced a large cardboard gun. She pointed it at Tom and pulled the trigger.

"BANG! YOU'RE FUCKING DEAD!" read the triangular flag that popped from the gun's muzzle in a spurt of confetti.

"Oops," she said. "Wrong gun."

She threw it away and rummaged again between her breasts, finally coming out with an even larger pistol. This one was metal, and had a muzzle hole large enough for Tom to fit his cock in.

"Jokes over," the she-clown said. "I pull this trigger and guess who goes to the circus in the sky early."

"Okay, okay," Tom said warily. "You can have your hole back." He stared at the woman. "How'd I get it off?"

She pushed aside her green hair, pulled a switchblade from her ear. She handed it to Tom. "How else? Surgery."

Tom grimaced at the knife and its implications. "That's gonna hurt."

She-clown grinned. White teeth glinted in red paint. She pushed her gun between Tom's legs. "Trust me; this will hurt a lot more."

Tom nodded. He flicked the knife open. The blade's click as it leapt out seemed oddly to come from across his bedroom.

"Cut it out and hand it over," the clown said, eyes flickering angrily. Tom looked at her. She'd placed one fluffy-booted foot on a chair, and

76

was tapping her sexless groin for emphasis. "Hurry up, I'm missing a lot of fucking."

Tom nodded. He walked over to his massive hand.

"No, Tom, don't!" Rose wept. "I love you!"

"I love you too, honey," Tom said. "But the clown—"

"She's evil!" Rose screamed. "She wants to fill me with penises!"

The clown laughed. "For a part of my body, you're quite the drama queen you know. Fill you with penises? What the fuck else are vaginas for?" She waved the massive gun at Tom. "Stop dallying; hurry up."

Tom winced. He kissed Rose's massive clitoris—

"I'm really sorry, honey."

—then stabbed the knife into his hand just outside its door-sized labia.

Blood instantly spurted from the wound. It gushed and flowed, quickly filling up the bedroom. Up over Tom's ankles, then his knees.

"Fooled you, asshole," the clown yelled.

She began laughing manically, increasing in size as she did so. She grew massive, taller than the huge woman Tom had seen on his arrival here. She picked up Tom's left hand and rubbed Rose over her bare groin.

A haze rolled through Tom's head. He dropped the knife. A sudden flash of light made him shut his eyes. When he looked again, Rose was now seamlessly implanted in the clown's crotch.

Tom felt saddened. His hand was bereft of its vagina. His wounded palm bled endlessly, a sticky crimson flow that rooted Tom to the spot while it embalmed him.

The blood rose up to Tom's chest, then to his throat.

"Don't leave me, Rose!" Tom screamed. "I'm dying!"

"Tom, Tom!" Rose shrieked back, its voice growing distant as the clown strode off, her massive ass frumpy in her outfit. "Darling, darling! Tom, Tom!"

Rose's pathetic pleading sounded inside and outside his head at once.

Then Tom felt hands on his face, hands he couldn't see. "Tom, Tom! Fucking wake up, will you!"

***

Tom jerked awake, expecting assassins. Brooke's warning about Lt. Harding resounded in his mind.

It was Brooke. He relaxed, breathing hard.

"You were having a nightmare," Brooke said. Her robe pressed tight over her breasts. He saw her nipples were hard.

He looked at his hand. The vagina was still there, deforming his palm. "I wish the nightmare was real."

With a hand under his chin, she raised his face to look at her. "I couldn't sleep."

"I won't be able to now. It's ridiculous how hot it is."

Brooke dropped her robe. It streamed to the floor like water falling off her.

She scowled. "Enough talk already. You can guess what I'm here for."

Tom nodded. Brooke's body was sweet. Not voluptuous like Megan's, but deliciously feminine. Small breasts, heavy buttocks. Fleshy arms and legs—her muscles padded over with just enough fat. Delicate hands and feet. In short, all woman.

"Make love to me," Brooke said, climbing into bed with him. "Do it well or I'll hate you forevermore. And remember, darlin', you currently need all the friends you can get."

Chapter 21

Tom fucked Brooke with hard, slow strokes.

On her belly beneath him, she squirmed like a pinned worm.

It seemed to her in this congress of bodies, this conversation between their surfaces, that her vagina sucked his penis like a mouth. Brooke felt like she was eating Tom, using him for sustenance, her kegels chewing the rod of cock splitting her sex, a metaphorical hen scarfing corn. The weight of his groin on her ass, the rough spreading, the depression/compression of her buttocks with each pumping descent, the slurping incomplete withdrawal, then the delicious sluice of re-entry . . .

Re-entry. She was a meteorite from Venus, burning up in their sexual atmosphere . . .

Brooke transcended herself into orgasm.

A fat ass has benefits, she thought as she dissolved into sexual buttermilk. *Guys rarely ever turn you down.*

Brooke's climax lacked the desperate layers of sensation using her mertopus tentacle afforded her, but the blissful satisfaction of communing with another body, skin to skin—so close she imagined nutrients and oxygen from his blood penetrating into hers by osmosis—was unparalleled compensation.

Brooke splattered like dropped jelly, expanded like the universe, lay limper than a dead squid under Tom.

Thanks, she thought dreamily to no one in particular as the sensation destroyed her completely.

Tom groaned. He made one final thrust into Brooke and froze as his cum spurted from him.

Hot, the ejaculate was. Tom imagined it as solid, thirty million cells twisted into a desperate cord of fecundity, streaking like cheetahs to deadly solace, to a homely grave deep in the womb that so passionately craved them.

Fuckkkkk! He thought in the point of no return.

He gripped Brooke's waist tight. Rose squelched open and shut in his hand like it was chewing Brooke's skin. It buzzed with frustration as he came, sharing and yet not sharing Tom's orgasm.

Beneath him, his lover simply breathed and was.

***

Damn, that was intense, Brooke thought. She turned over, sat knees clasped to her chest, gray eyes afterglowing at Tom.

"You have no idea how good that was for me," he said. "I need to get arrested more often."

"Don't get cocky," Brooke said. "You were good, but not *that* good."

Tom grinned knowingly. "Boyfriend?"

It took Brooke a moment to realize what he meant. She hid her delight that he'd asked. "Let's just say," she said in a tired voice, "that I haven't spent my whole life waiting for you to turn up." In her mind she was chortling loudly. *Yeah, darling, I'm totally attached—I've got my beloved mertopus tentacle waiting at home.* Then seeing the disappointment that flashed across Tom's face at the thought that this was a one night stand, she added, as noncommittally as she could: "But now your pleasure raft's docked in my sexual harbor, I'll post warning to all the other luxury emotional liners on my horizon to steer clear of my ass." *Sexual harbor? Luxury emotional liners? Steer clear? Did I just reel off all that? Shit! I've been hanging around Megan too long.*

Damn, she thought next, *he looks more pleased than if he'd just got elected king.*

The mood between them was hot and sticky, more humid than the heavy night. Brooke liked it, liked it despite the fact that she'd just bedded a cop killer and made a date for second and third sexual helpings.

Who doesn't remember who he is, she reminded herself. *He seems more innocent than King Eric.*

She reached for Tom's left hand. He let her pull it to her.

"What's it feel like having this on you?" she asked, bringing Rose close to her face and examining it.

"Odd is the best word. Most times I forget it just like my penis, but then . . ." Tom tried to find words to explain the strange sensation of being sexually aroused in his left hand. He failed to. "It's just fucking odd."

Brooke sniffed Rose. "You need to learn how to douche. I can still smell Megan in it."

Tom winced. "Don't remind me of that."

"I won't need to if you don't remember where you stashed Boston's gold. It'll become a fact of life. King Eric may make Megan fuck your hand three times a day."

"Please don't remind me of that either."

(Tom remembered his dream. He was certain the vagina-less clown woman had been dead Lynn. Which made sense—a subconscious manifestation of his guilt feelings over her death. But the dream . . . had seemed so real. Horribly real.)

Brooke stared out the bedroom window. A sickle moon hung just below Bizarro's far end, looking like a birthday party decoration. Warm air blew into the room, wrapping them both in its gusts like it was dressing them.

She raised Rose to her lips and licked it.

She giggled at Tom's askance gape.

"No, I'm not into girls," she said. "But I've always wondered what eating pussy was like." She licked it again, then looked at Tom. "How does that feel to you?"

He grimaced. "It's warm and tingly and I can actually feel the lips swelling."

Brooke nodded. "Normal girly arousal feeling then." She licked Rose again, this time dipping her tongue into it.

Tom winced as sensation shot up his hand. His cock stirred in his lap. He pulled his hand away from Brooke, but she held it tight.

"Let's experiment," she said, her eyes bright with evil intent. "We're both going to pretend we're lesbians, okay? I'll be butch, you bitch."

She licked Rose some more, then stopped and pointed to Tom's penis, which was now engorged again. "It's okay if you want to masturbate."

Tom looked unconvinced.

"Go on," Brooke said. "I like to watch too."

She resumed performing cunnilingus on Rose.

Tom did as she said. While stroking himself, he focused on Brooke's breasts. The delicately veined white hemispheres hung off her chest like ripe pears, jiggling deliciously with the up-down motion of her head.

Her eyes as she worked were intent on him, watching him jerk off for her pleasure.

Tom's masturbation added to the sensation trickling up his arm. He wondered what it would feel like to jerk off with Rose—to fuck his hand. He quickly killed the thought. *Oh no, this only goes as far as this.*

"Oh yes, darling," Rose muttered around Brooke's lips. "Lick me good. Give it to me deep, baby."

Brooke's eyes widened at the honeyed pussy-voice, then she shrugged and resumed licking teasing and sucking. It was hard going. She'd not eaten pussy before and disliked the taste of it. She was uncertain if that was because Megan had cum in it earlier, or if all other vaginas tasted like this—this sourness that upset her tongue.

It struck Brooke as strange that she didn't really know what another woman's cunt tasted like. *But then*, she reasoned, *why should I?*

I know what mine tastes like from wetting my fingers while jerking off. She realized that she'd assumed everyone's would taste the same.

Mentally sighing at how complicated sex could be sometimes, she kept working on Tom's hand-vagina.

Brooke tonguing Rose's clitoris felt to Tom like she was sucking his testicles. He jerked off faster and harder, matching the sensation.

Brooke licked deep inside Rose. Tom's rectum clenched violently like he'd shit.

"Oh yessssss!" Rose hissed. Tom felt its orgasm rush up his arm like a cascade of explosions. His hand shook in Brooke's grasp as she tongued its clit frenetically to max out his orgasm. She gripped it hard; licked, licked, licked.

"Ahhhhh!" Tom groaned as the feeling burst across his body. He came. The semen spurted in a single thick translucent jet that splattered across Brooke's breasts.

Tom went limp, his body trembling.

"Nah," Brooke said, letting go of his hand. "I'll stick to dick, fuck you very much. Sucking cock is way easier than this shit."

"Oh, that was finger-licking good," Rose said in a satiated voice, its labia wiggling like trapped snakes. "Hey, Tom darling, is there anything you want to know?"

Tom and Brooke both gawked at it in surprise. Then at each other.

"Ask it where the gold is," Brooke whispered.

Tom was too wiped out by his orgasm to consider the danger. "Where is Boston's gold?" he asked.

Rose's reply was languid with pleasure. "Should still be right where you left it, you sexy man—up on Bizarro."

Tom got over his surprise at Rose's reply long enough to ask, "Where exactly?"

Its liquid voice a fading drawl, the vagina replied, "By White Lake."

It fell silent. Tom and Brooke stared at each other. Simultaneously, both looked out the window, up at the Boston Overhead.

"Up *there* all this time?" Brooke mouthed in wonder.

She looked back at Tom. "If you want to remain alive, I suggest we edit that information. Just tell King Eric you vaguely remember something about Bizarro. Don't mention gold—let Megan and Joe connect the dots. Then I'll suggest an expedition. As your guard, I'll be the one escorting you to the throne room."

Tom nodded dully. He'd do what she advised. Down in the throne room earlier, the King's officials had mentioned that Rose wouldn't betray him; but now it had spoken freely with Brooke present, which meant he could trust her.

He leaned over and kissed her pouty lips. She kissed him back, but distractedly, then pushed him away.

Her eyes were serious. "We need to think this through very carefully. You mustn't slip up. One inkling that you know where the loot is, and Megan . . ."

"Don't worry, I won't screw up," Tom shivered. The image of Queen Shirley with a needle through her heart was vivid in his mind.

"Then," Brooke concluded, "once we're on Bizarro, you need to get lost . . ." She smiled sadly. "And that of course will be the last I see of you. But before then . . ." she grinned broadly, ". . . I just ate your pussy, how 'bout you eat mine in return?"

She lay back between his legs, placing both feet on his shoulders and spreading her lush thighs, so he was staring directly at her sex. She splayed her cunt's lips. "You know, before you do, let's try something new."

"What?"

Brooke giggled. "Rub Rose over my pussy, let's see how that feels."

Tom blanched. Brooke rolled her eyes. "Don't worry. We'll stop before it cums."

Tom did as she asked, slipping his left hand over her crotch and caressing one vagina with the other. It was a pleasant feeling, if odd.

Brooke got off on it big-time, grinding her crotch up against his hand, squeezing her breasts, pinching her nipples and groaning.

"Oooooo," she gasped after a while, "that's *real* nice." She crooked a finger at Tom. "Okay, darling. Main course time. Start eating."

Tom pushed her legs sideways off his chest and knelt between them. He dipped his tongue into the glistening crevice of her proffered vulva.

As he licked her, his cut lip hurt, his jaw ached from Harding's earlier assault.

Brooke dropped her hands from her breasts to grip his head. Her moans resumed.

He raised his head after a few licks.

"Why'd you stop?"

"You taste like chicken broth."

For a moment Brooke wondered what he was talking about. Then it hit her: *Shit, the mertopus tentacle! I didn't wash!*

She scowled at him. "Get back to work, darling; it's just chicken-flavored pussy wash."

***

Afterwards, they talked some more. Tom voiced something that had really been worrying him:

"I've only been in town half a day, and having that kid as ruler already bothers me silly. You're an intelligent woman, how come you can't see that?"

"King Eric? Don't worry. He smarter than he looks."

Tom nodded. "Like a parrot, you mean. But, oh yeah, the royal brat swears like an adult."

Brooke grinned, then nudged him with an elbow. "No, King Eric *is* smarter. Smarter than most of us adults he rules over. That's what his lollipop's for."

Tom propped himself up, an amused look on his face. "You don't say?"

She nodded vigorously. "It's drugged." She laughed. "We're not that dumb to allow a kid rule unaugmented. The royal lollipop contains a mix of compounds, most important of which is IQ-soprene, which temporarily boosts King Eric's intelligence by a factor of three. There's also something to cut down on normal kid hyperactivity. And then . . . there's a tiny amount of heroin in it. Not much, just enough to keep him permanently licking the lollipop."

Tom wrung the words through his mind. "Addicting a six-year-old to heroin is a bit extreme."

Brooke shrugged. "Not my decision. Dr. Oppenheimer formulated the lollipop. Even Megan thinks it a great idea, and she normally scoffs at his inventions."

"Who's Oppenheimer?"

"I mentioned him earlier. Boston's primary egghead."

Brooke silenced Tom's next question with a kiss. She held her mouth over his, dueling tongues with him till he got the idea to keep quiet.

When she pulled away, her face was flushed, her breathing fast. "Use your tongue for something productive," she growled. "Like eating my pussy."

She grabbed his hair behind his ears and pulled him down to her vagina again.

The smell of her filled his nostrils as he tongued her sex, till finally he forgot all the day's oddity.

Everything was Brooke.

Chapter 22

"Pam will kill me if she finds out," Joe said. He was unbound now, seated beside Megan on the heart-shaped bed, their backs propped on pillows.

Megan kissed him. "She's a true lover. Love is as strong as death. Rather than share you, she'd prefer you as a memory. That way you remain hers alone."

Joe rolled his eyes. "If I didn't know you better, Meg, I'd think you were stoned."

"Sex is opium." She fondled his limp penis then pointed to the electric eel, now swimming in a transparent bucket. "Did you not feel this?"

Oh, I felt it alright, Joe thought in embarrassment. *Cumming down that fish's throat—shit, it felt like . . . something I want to experience forever.*

Megan studied his face intently. "We can be *really* good for each other," she said. "There's so much I can teach you."

Yeah, like how to suck cock, and get fucked in the ass. Joe found Megan devilishly attractive. Her penis, however, was a total *NO* in his book. It was the only unattractive thing about the gorgeous brunette.

Megan caressed her breasts. Joe admired them, sculpted alabaster hillocks on a flesh-and-blood Venus de Milo. The middle-aged wrinkling of her face, the slight sag of her skin, was a promise of sexual expertise. Sluggish blood flowed to his groin. *She's just perfect, just . . .* His eyes dropped lower and . . .

Her cock jerked in her crotch, stiff as a frozen chicken sausage, her scrotum like a bag of eggs below it.

"Do you care for something else tonight?" Megan asked in a hopeful voice. "Another dish of erotica, perhaps?"

Shit! She really does want to fuck me! Joe thought in horror. *That piece of meat is practically begging for my anus!*

He shook his head. "You're too much woman, Megan. Any more and I'll be useless in the morning. And Pam loves cock at cockcrow. If I can't get it up for her, she'll suspect something's up between us."

He appealed to her sense of duty before she felt her femininity slighted: "You saw how pissed the King was with me yesterday 'cos I couldn't get a hard on." He laughed. "That worked out great though. No way do I want to have sex with another man's hand."

Megan stroked his cheek with soft fingers, scraping his stubble with green fingernails. "It was a pleasant experience—like deflowering a virgin." She resigned herself to Joe's being finished tonight. "Concerning Pussypalm; we *must* jog his memory. The city needs weapons; for that, we need money."

"I wish King Eric would let me have him for an hour," Joe said savagely. "Oh, I'd definitely make him talk. I'd have him singing like fucking Pavarotti. That scumbag's the reason Gail's dead."

"And now she's a memory. Totally yours. No one else will recall how her vagina looked last, how she trembled under your penetrations, how your seed flooded her field—a gift too precious to despise. In that way she's forever with you."

The way Megan put it, Joe couldn't keep being angry. It made no sense, but it made loads of sense. It was her unaffected presentation—he knew he'd feel different later.

"Pussypalm could have robbed another town," he said simply. "There are Federal Reserve Banks in both New York and Philly . . . the reserve extension in Chicago . . . Cleveland . . . so much gold he'd have a cashgasm. Why the Boston Fed? Gail meant—"

"Your bank manger is dead," Megan interrupted. "I'm here with you. *For* you. To teach you things . . . like the delicious testicle acupuncture."

"The *what*?"

She grinned. "I stick the needles in just perfectly right and you'll have an orgasm without ejaculating at all." She winked. "The orgasm can last for hours, days even—for as long as the needles stay in place."

She giggled. "Sometimes I do it to myself. It's a superlative indescribable experience."

Joe saw she was serious, but then, Megan was *always* serious.

"Not tonight, though," he said quickly. "There aren't enough hours left." *Needles in my balls? You must be crazy. No, honey bunny, not just friggin' crazy—you're more insane than you're beautiful*!!!

He leapt off the bed before she convinced him to try the testicle acupuncture and began gathering his clothes.

Megan admired Joe's fat buttocks and anus while he was bent over. She caressed her erection sadly. His hairy hole looked so lovely, so virgin tight, so DEEP. A purple flower she'd like to spread open like she was the sun at dawn. But it was closed to her.

She sighed when he straightened up, let go of her penis. "Tomorrow then?"

Joe looked around from pulling on his shirt, grinning. "Most definitely. So long as Pam doesn't find out and kill me first."

Chapter 23

The policeman walked closer. Tom, hidden in a shadowed recess further along the third floor corridor, watched him approach.

The cop was young, with a blonde crew cut and a big nose. His brown eyes were tired; he'd clearly rather be in bed than patrolling City Hall's corridors so eaters didn't eat King Eric.

He had a rifle slung over his shoulder. His arm rested loosely on the gun.

The guard walked past Tom. Tom leapt out of hiding and broke a large vase over his head. He grabbed the fallen cop under the armpits and dragged him into a storage room.

Tom checked the policeman's pulse. The man wasn't dead. He'd have a bad headache on waking though—there was a bloody patch over his left ear.

At least no new murder rap, Tom thought.

He quickly stripped off the policeman's uniform, then bound and gagged him. He dressed in the man's clothes and shouldered his gun.

Okay, time to get the hell out.

Tom made his stealthy way along the corridor.

***

Brooke had left Tom's room shortly after he'd eaten her pussy the second time. She'd kissed him long and passionately, retrieved her dropped robe, and departed like the ghost of sex to cum.

Once the door clicked shut behind her, Tom had leapt to his feet. He was gripped by a sudden pressing urgency to be somewhere else. To get very far away very fast.

***

Moving cautiously, Tom quickly descended to the lower floor. The night corridors were shadow tunnels lit by dim bulbs.

The nametag on Tom's filched uniform read 'Josh Morris.' Tom figured he'd be better off not replying greetings. He kept pressed into the darkness, walking in the shadows like a figment of the corridor's imagination.

89

Three cops stood sentry outside King Eric's royal suite—two female, one male. None paid him any attention as he crossed the landing and descended.

Past the offices on the ground floor, Tom froze at the sound of a door opening up ahead.

Lt. Ryan Harding, wearing a T-shirt and shorts, crossed the corridor, exiting one room into the one opposite.

Tom waited till the lieutenant had shut the door behind him before continuing on.

Almost at the corridor's end, he froze again. He winced. The back door was guarded. A tall, muscular cop paced there, smoking a cigarette.

Tom backed away again into the stairway shadows. He waited. He was conscious of daybreak's fast approach, that escape would be impossible then.

The sentry finished his cigarette. He ground it beneath his boot, then started up the corridor again, towards Tom.

To Tom's relief, the man entered the room Harding was in.

With the coast now clear, Tom padded fast to the rear door. Passing the room Harding and the sentry had entered, he heard both conversing.

Tom silently slid the door bolts. He cracked the door open and peeked out.

The horizon was already brightening with daylight. In stark contrast to its dim interior, the grounds around the palace were awash in halogen lighting. Night like day.

He stepped outside and shut the door behind him. Concealed by a pillar, he looked around.

The duck pond ended on his right. A thirty-meter strip of lawn extended from the back door to the trees ringing the perimeter fence.

There were no guards in sight. But the lights . . .

He heard a sound overhead.

He looked up. Four floors up, heavy naked breasts plumped on the sill, Megan was peering out of her window. Tom pressed himself back into the doorway.

She-eit!

But Megan wasn't looking at Tom. Her eyes were intent on something above and beyond him. He followed her gaze and his blood chilled in his veins.

Practically indistinguishable from the trees ringing the fence, a massive green-and-brown-skinned woman stared over the wall. 'Sister' to

90

the one Tom had seen yesterday, she was at least eighteen feet tall. The ten-feet-high wall barely reached her bared breasts.

A vav, Tom realized; *a vampire vagina.*

(Megan's presence at her window had totally balled up Tom's escape plans. Unable to sneak along the wall for fear of her noticing him, he remained where he was and studied the strange woman opposite.)

The woman was clearly a plant. Her breasts were watermelons, massive green and yellow oblongs that stood high and proud like moored military airships. The left breast had chipped skin under its nipple. Juicy red melon flesh gleamed in the wound.

Her arms were plaited creepers, vegetable tentacles woven together into limbs. Each arm split at its end into four identical foot-long 'fingers.'

Her hair was a massive expanse of palm leaves; her face pale white fruit below it.

Her face? Tom's mind boggled. *Why the hell does she look like a thirty-something Marlene Dietrich?*

The vav's resemblance to the long-dead actress was perfect and entire. Eternally beautiful, smoldering blue eyes, made-up crimson lips, Marlene's iconic profile sat atop its brown neck-mooring like a misplaced hood ornament.

The plant woman screamed silently at Megan. It was eerie watching her, mouth open, tongue out, yelling soundlessly.

"Get lost!" Megan whispered above Tom.

Instead, in a lightning-fast motion, the vav flung a cord at Megan. The cord fell short of hitting Megan. It smashed into the lawn six feet from Tom.

He got a good look at the thrown cord lying in the grass before the plant woman reeled it back to her. It was a wet glistening tentacle dripping saliva-like liquid. The tentacle was pinkish, fleshtoned like mouth or vagina interior.

Its tip struck Tom as odd. He studied it as the tentacle retreated back through the grass like a snake. The tentacle's tip was a shiny six-inch black hook, glossy with slime.

The vav picked up the tentacle and flung it at Megan again. Again it fell short. This time a plume of clear liquid squirted from the tip of the hook on its impact.

"Death and sex don't always mix," Megan opined softly at the vampire vagina. "I've had physical heaven tonight—the afterlife can wait." Her naked posture was serene as an angel's.

The vav reared up angrily. Melon breasts haughtily aloft, she reeled in the tentacle again.

When she was done, she looked away from Megan, down at Tom.

Their eyes met. Hers flashed at him with . . . hunger? Desire?

The vav broke the gaze as abruptly as she'd made it, then turned and loped off into the distance.

Tom remained in the door archway until Megan had left her window.

He grimaced. The horizon was much brighter now, like five a.m.

Like he was about crossing a road, Tom peered left, then right, then left again. No one in sight. The simplest escape route was clearly a dash across the lawn to the wall.

Then the door behind him swung open and a hand grabbed him from behind.

***

Tom swung around. It was Lt. Ryan Harding.

Harding let go of Tom's shirt. His other hand held a fat ugly pistol. He jerked it at Tom. "Drop the weapon, asshole."

Tom unslung his stolen rifle, let it fall to the ground.

Harding tucked his own gun into his belt. His handsome face creased into an ugly smile. "Where'd you think you were going, Pussypalm?" he asked in a soft cold voice.

"Nowhere. Just looking around. Hot night, you know."

Harding smirked. "Yeah, right. In Morris's uniform?"

"I've heard so much about the eaters since getting here, I felt I needed protec—"

Harding ended Tom's inane spiel with a punch to the solar plexus. Tom crumpled forward. All the air sucked from his lungs. It felt like his guts had just exploded. Harding immediately hit him again, catching him flush on the temple with a right uppercut. Bright lights like a city skyline exploded in Tom's head.

Tom straightened up. "I'll come peacefully," he wheezed through a migraine of pain.

Harding smirked. "Only place you're going, Pussypalm, is six feet under a cold tombstone. This one's for my sister, asshole." The words were ominous,—a corpse's psychic caress.

He swung at Tom again. Tom rolled with the punch, or it would have knocked him out. As it was, Harding's knuckles ripped his cheek open.

Tom wiped blood from his face, then stared at it in horror. Then he glared angrily at Harding.

Harding swung again. This time Tom sidestepped and flung a return punch. The punch connected to Harding's ear. Harding reeled back, then instantly regained his balance. He shook his head to clear it, then scowled at Tom.

"That the best you've got, punk?" His voice was all the more menacing for its quietness in the halogen-lit dawning.

"Try this for size." Tom swung again, this time catching Harding on the chin. Harding grunted and closed with Tom, hitting him with a flurry of punches that left Tom breathless. Tom gave almost as good as he got, flinging punches that made the other man wince and grunt.

Harding pushed Tom off him. "This is a waste of time!" he growled.

Panting, and with bruised faces, each regarded the other.

Tom prepared to rush at Harding again. Then he froze.

Harding had jerked his pistol from his belt. There was murder in his eyes.

Hell! Tom thought, *this son-of-a-bitch plans on killing me.*

"I'm gonna kill you, you sick cunt," Harding said. "You've made it easy for me, knocking out Morris and stealing his uniform. All I need say now is that I shot an intruder who was running away and didn't know who it was."

"That's . . . that's murder!" Tom gasped. "You're a cop!"

Harding sneered. "So fuckin' what? You should have thought of the consequences before robbing my sister's bank and leaving her as eater food."

Harding retrieved Tom's dropped rifle from the floor. He flicked the safety on, then handed it back to Tom, barrel-first. He smiled coldly, his eyes arctic ice.

"Now, here's what you're going to do, Cunthand. You're going to take this gun and you're going to run away towards the wall. Then I'm going to shoot you in the back like you deserve, like the animal you are."

Harding laughed softly. He was enjoying himself now.

"And if you dare yell out for help, I'll shoot your balls and cock off before I kill you. No one'll miss them, you rapist prick. You bastard, you even . . . Gail . . ." Harding's voice broke with emotion. He motioned with his gun. "Get going."

"But . . . but . . ."

Harding sniggered, relishing Tom's horror. "No, you're not man enough to take a sporting chance, are you, coward? He raised the gun,

93

aimed between Tom's eyes. "I'll just shoot you here then; it'll be obvious that you attacked me first."

"You're mad."

The reply amused Harding. "Mad? *You're* calling *me* mad?"

Then he shrugged. "Goodbye, asshole. This one's for Gail."

"Revenge for her tortured soul must wait," Megan said, stepping from behind Harding and sticking a needle deep into his wrist. "You know how important this man—asshole though he be—is to Boston."

Megan's needle had paralyzed Harding's hand. His trigger-finger froze mid-squeeze. Furious at being thwarted, he tried jerking it back, to no avail.

Tom lived again.

Megan plucked the pistol from Harding's nerveless fingers. She pulled the needle from Harding's wrist, then scowled at him. "Return immediately to your duties, Lieutenant. Though I commend you for foiling Pussypalm's escape, you've greatly overstepped your authority by attempting to execute him. When day fully breaks, Chief Bradley will properly reprimand you. For this act of yours, you may even suffer a demotion." She nodded at the door. "Now go."

Harding was totally cowed; his posture visibly slumped like he'd been whipped. "Yes, at once, Ms. Fox. I apologize."

He reentered the building, leaving Megan alone with Tom. For the first time Tom realized that Megan was naked, her curvy body smelly with the night's sweat. Her belly glistened like it had been oiled. Her limp penis swayed between her thighs.

"That was very foolish," Megan said. "He was about to kill you."

"I won't try to escape again," Tom said honestly. Now the danger was past, headache fallout from Harding's punches had his legs wobbling.

"Of course, you won't," Megan agreed. "It's dangerous to run away from justice." She reflected a moment, then added, "Besides, this is a democratic society; one bound by the rule of law and order. If you are to be executed, it must be entirely on King Eric's orders."

She took the rifle from Tom's hand and escorted him back to his room.

Chapter 24

Pam fiercely *tried* to sleep. It was pointless. Her heart throbbed, ached, bled a river of hurt. *Joe—how could you?* The memory of her boyfriend with Megan and that snake, no . . . fish; *her* Joe with tranny cum smeared over his face. *Shit!*

Revenge stewed in her; it boiled over like a pot of untended broth. She was going to teach Joe a lesson he'd never forget.

How to do so stumped her, however. She sat in bed, legs clasped to her breasts, rocking back and forth, staring out into the sweltering night, that external universe of thrumming and chirping sounds. Her eyes recorded nothing they saw; her attention was focused deep inside herself.

She was tempted to 'giraffe' her neck up once more to Megan's room and spy on them. She quashed the impulse. *How pathetic,* she thought, *like a glutton for punishment desperate for a feast of degradation.*

She jerked upright at the hand on her shoulder. She spun round, found Joe had returned.

He was smiling down at her. "You're awake?"

Pam smiled back, her heart a black coal of hate. "I woke up and couldn't find you."

He yawned affectedly, began removing his shirt and pants. "I couldn't sleep either; too bothered about Pussypalm. I went to talk to Megan."

Oh, I saw your discussion. Pam wanted to yell at him, to scream so loud it woke King Eric up. But that wouldn't do. *Yelling the house down will just make me look spineless, dependent on this bastard for my self-worth.*

"I understand," she said. "It's always frustrating, having the solution so nearby, yet being unable to reach it."

Joe got into bed beside her. She turned her face away from his kiss. "Don't. You know that always leads to sex. Right now I feel like I'm frying in oil, tonight's just so damn hot."

She was upset that he didn't look upset at her rejection. Did he seem relieved even? *Oh, so she's used you all up, eh? I bet she fucked your ass too, sissy man!*

Then she sagged. Her unrelenting anger had tired her out. She leant over and kissed Joe. She kissed him long, slow and deep, all the while imagining she was poisoning him with her tongue. She pulled back and regarded him with smoking eyes. "I do want you too, baby. But let's sleep now. You know how much I love you in my crack at the crack of dawn."

He grinned. "Okay. Once it's six a.m. your ass is mine."

Ass? Pam's anger—which she'd been about postponing till morning—flared up again. *Ass? The asshole's already turning gay on me!*

Joe dropped off to sleep beside her. Pam however remained awake, running a million scenarios through her mind. She needed to do something to Joe to ensure he never, never, *never*, went near Megan Fox again.

It was almost six a.m. when the solution occurred to her. The outside sky was a white palette striped with gray trails.

Pam was amazed by how simple the solution to her problem was. It required King Eric's cooperation of course, but the child generally did whatever she suggested was best. Her plan also involved Pussypalm, but Boston's Public Enemy No. 1 was under house arrest, so that wasn't a problem.

Pam was so pleased by the thought of the lesson she intended teaching Joe that she woke him up. Sort of like a condemned man's last meal.

"It's morning, baby," she cooed in his ear once he'd opened his eyes. "I want to fulfil my promise." She tapped her crotch. "My pussy's lonely."

Joe woke up fast. His penis leapt to erection even faster.

Seeing the hunger for her in his eyes as she straddled him, slipping down on his penis like a glove over fingers, Pam almost changed her mind. But then her resolve hardened.

I'm doing what's best for both of us, she thought, relaxing herself to enjoy the sex.

With her revenge resolved, Pam saw no point wasting the hard cock poking up inside her like a Washington Monument made of meat. *If that aging tranny slut can have an orgasm with my man, I, who actually own the piece-of-shit boyfriend deserve at least four this morning.*

Chapter 25

Mourning Morning

Brooke slapped Tom hard. The blow reactivated the pain of Harding's punches. Tom gripped his head and winced.

She raised her hand to slap him again. He grabbed her wrist. "Stop it!"

She spat on him. "You tried to run away? You selfish jerk. I should have known better."

Tom let go of Brooke; she rubbed her wrist. "Harding almost killed me this morning."

Brooke paced angrily across Tom's room. "If you weren't so valuable alive, you'd wish he'd succeeded when I'd gotten through with you."

Tom gaped at her. "What the hell is wrong with you? You're overreacting."

Brooke walked up to him, and poked him in the chest with a finger. "You *really* don't know? You're a dick. We had a deal and you broke it." She retreated to the chair facing Tom's bed and sat glaring at him. When next she spoke, however, her voice was tired. "You don't trust me, do you?" She looked down at the floor. "After last night, that *totally* sucks."

"It's not that . . ."

Brooke looked at him again. "What is it then? Educate me: do I have pussy odor?"

Tom winced. "I was concerned for my own survival. You're just a sergeant."

"That's pathetic. You prefer female *captains*?"

Tom rubbed his chin. Talking hurt, like Harding had broken his jaw; his mouth still tasted of blood. "Just let me explain."

Brooke simmered.

"I trust you, Brooke."

"You've a crap way of showing it."

Tom sighed. "I honestly do."

"But you prefer pussy higher up the chain of command."

"Harding, who you accurately predicted wants to murder me, is a lieutenant and your superior. Now, imagine *you're* me, with my reputation. Bad odds there, right? No, not bad—downright horrible."

He sat on the edge of the bed and stared her deep in the eyes. "Think about it, Brooke: All Harding needs to do is dispatch you on street patrol or something and do me in before you get back. He chooses the right time and place, no witnesses."

Brooke smirked. "Witnesses mean nothing if Harding wants you dead. He could shoot you in the back in broad daylight and all the guys will say you attacked him first. Remember those eighty dead policemen? I'm the only cop on the force rooting for you at the moment."

She nodded, her eyes less angry, her face more friendly. "You're right about Harding sending me on street patrol—that's how I found you in the first place. I was checking out a missing persons report on some deluded heiress who'd run off to join the eaters."

"Join the cannibals?"

Brooke smirked. "You've no idea. There's a whole religious movement about how cannibalism is the true path ordained for man. MEM the fools call it—Man-Eat-Man."

"That sounds like a gay porn movie."

She walked over to Tom, jerked him up by his collar and kissed him hard, whilst squeezing his crotch even harder with her other hand.

When their lips separated, Brooke said: "It hurt me, thinking you were leaving. I felt like you were dumping me . . ."

"I'll never leave you," Tom said. "You can count on that."

Brooke smiled. She kissed him again, this time a light peck on the cheek. Then she walked off to stare out the window at the Overhead. "You guys all say that and it's great, and then one day it's over."

She turned back to Tom. "Only thing we can both count on is King Eric being mad at you now."

"Kid has quite a temper," Tom said.

"Not really his fault. It's the royal lollipop—there's some cocaine in it too."

Tom looked scandalized for a moment. Then he shrugged. "Let's go see his majesty the speedballer."

Chapter 26

Megan, Joe Bradley, and Pam were with King Eric in the throne room when Brooke delivered Tom there.

Against their expectations, King Eric was strangely calm. The little boy, now dressed in a Boston Red Sox jacket and cap over jeans and hush puppies, sat on his white throne licking his lollipop. His eyes brooded like he had too much homework.

"I don't think Megan has informed everyone about your escape attempt yet," Brooke whispered to Tom.

"I hope not."

Joe scowled at Tom. "We warned you yesterday not to try to run away,"

"Thankfully, Lt. Harding beat some sense into him," Megan said. "He'll not attempt flight again."

"Harding was going to kill me," Tom said.

The police chief scowled, his eyes cold stones in his fat face. "So? I don't blame him. I also want to kill you—"

Tom winced at the public admission.

"—but I'm regrettably more coolheaded and mindful of my obligations to the city."

King Eric lowered his lollipop. "Maybe Megan should give him some classes in her School of Pain," he said, stroking his chin with his thumb. "Few of her pupils ever reoffend."

Brooke cursed under her breath.

Megan curtsied. "Normally I'd agree, sire. However, in this case, I daresay he'll not attempt it again." She spread open her jacket, revealing the array of evil-looking needles holstered in its lining, then looked at Tom meaningfully. "Or will you?"

He hastily shook his head.

The King looked narrowly at Megan. "Are you getting soft on him?"

She let her jacket fall shut; smiled demurely. "No, sire. But I see no need to damage him further . . . yet."

The little boy monarch licked his lollipop. "Remember, Tom. Megan's School of Pain is always in session. But since teacher thinks you've passed the semester exam—"

"Hey, King," Joe interrupted, "How 'bout if Megan temporarily paralyzes Tom's right hand? Those needles of hers can do it easy; then you'll be *certain* he won't shoot anyone or knock them out. The Meds say he fractured Josh Morris's skull."

Both Brooke and Tom froze whilst the King considered this. "I think it's time to tell them you've gotten some of your memory back," she whispered to him.

She stepped forward. "Your Majesty—"

The kid monarch silenced her with a gesture. He rolled his eyes. "Please, Brooke, don't tell me *you're* soft on Tom now. I notice you two keep whispering together like lovers."

"It's not that, sire. Pussypalm here—"

"Shut up, Sgt. Hayes!" Joe yelled at her. "When we want your opinion, we'll ask for it!"

Chastened, her cheeks red with embarrassment and impotent anger, Brooke retreated into anonymity again.

"For fuck's sake, Joe, calm down," Pam said angrily. Tom realized she'd been staring at him for awhile now. Her gaze said she wanted something. But what?

Joe calmed. "I'm sorry, your Majesty," he apologized. "Your opinion on crippling his hand?

The six-year-old king was still thinking, his brow creased like the middle of an accordion. "Hmmm." He tapped his lips with his lollipop then pointed it at Megan. "What do *you* say?"

"I can do it, sire." She looked at Tom, then pulled several short needles from inside her jacket. She held the glittering slivers up. "Four of these around the wrist will paralyze his hand till we need it otherwise. He'll require antibiotics to prevent—"

She stopped talking. Pam had moved beside the throne and was whispering fiercely into King Eric's ear. The boy's eyes first widened in surprise, then he smiled, then nodded, licking his lollipop furiously.

All present waited to see what he was so excited about.

Pam, with a satisfied smirk on her face, stepped back from the throne. She didn't return to Joe's side.

"All work and no play makes me a dull monarch," King Eric said. "Time for some entertainment."

Megan, Joe, Tom, and Brooke stared at him, perplexed.

King Eric laughed. "I love circuses," he said. "I love those spinning wheels with people strapped to them and someone throwing knives at them." He clapped his hands vigorously. "We're going to have some of that. Right, Pam?"

Pam nodded. Her smirk remained fixed on her face.

The little king looked at Joe. "You got your gun?"

Joe nodded.

"Hand it to Tom."

Joe looked narrowly at the King. King Eric nodded. Joe handed Tom the gun. "Don't even think about taking his majesty hostage, asshole. You'll never make it out of—"

"Calm down, Joe. Nothing bad's going to happen to me."

He turned to Tom, who, along with Brooke, was staring in bewilderment at the pistol Joe had handed him. "Now, Tom," King Eric said with a gleeful expression. "I want to see a demonstration of your legendary shooting skills."

Brooke grimaced. Tom rolled his eyes. "Shooting? I don't—"

"You're famous for shooting teeth out of people mouths, fingers off their hands . . ." Pam said, extremely amused.

Tom winced at the descriptions.

Now Joe was looking worried. "Yeah, that's true. But what's he going to shoot now?"

Pam smiled. She reached into her handbag and came out with a large red apple. "This . . . off your head."

Joe's eyes widened in horror. "Oh, no, he ain't."

"Oh yes he is," King Eric retorted. "Shooting an apple off your head's easy. Just stand against the wall over there."

Joe stared at Pam, his eyes pleading. Pam extended her neck across the room, so her head was close to his, her lips caressing his ears.

"This is payback for you cheating on me, asshole," she moaned like she was desperate for sex.

Joe turned to look at her. "But . . . . ."

"Shut up," she whispered harshly. "I saw you and that slut Megan last night." She grinned. "Just take your punishment, like you do Megan's cock up your rectum."

"Pam, I'm sorry. It won't happen—"

"I'm sorry too; that I ever loved you." She calmed. "Don't worry. Pussypalm's a crack shot, it's not like he'll blow your head off."

"Pam, he doesn't fucking remember who he is."

"No difference. His muscle memory is still okay. You saw Harding this morning. All roughed up. He said Tom was throwing punches like Muhammad Ali. So he still remembers how to shoot, too."

Joe visibly withered, his fat body became somehow thinner.

"Hey," the King called over. "What are you two whispering about over there like you're Tom and Brooke?"

"There are beds upstairs for body talk," Megan added.

Pam drew her neck back a smidgen, so she was staring Joe dead in the eye. "And this is the *only* warning I'm ever giving you, Joey boy. If you *ever* so much as look at that tranny's fat buttocks again . . ." she giggled with pleasure at his distraught torment, ". . . Next time I'll have Pussypalm shoot a strawberry or ant off your cockhead."

"I'm getting tired of waiting!" King Eric growled. "Get your head back over here, Pam."

Pam kissed Joe once on the nose, smiled,—

"I'm doing this for both of us. So we'll live a happy fulfilled life together, loving each other till we're old and grey. I'll be yours even when my pussy's withered and flaky and all the Viagra in the world won't give you a stiffy."

—and retracted her head. She stood smiling by King Eric, draping a familiar arm over his shoulders.

Megan collected the red apple from Pam's free hand and walked over to Joe.

"She saw us," Joe whispered to Megan. "Pam's been spying on us."

Megan smiled. "I told you—she's a true lover—her passion for you is deadly."

"She's *mad*."

"We've always known that. Her mental instability makes no difference to the sweetness of her vagina, does it? Insane or sane, pussy is still delicious."

She led the trembling chief of police to the near wall with a firm hand in the small of his back. "Don't worry, Pussypalm's a good shot. If he's unsure he'll hit the apple, he'll aim to miss."

Megan turned Joe around, then set the apple on his head. She balanced it to ensure it wouldn't roll off, then stepped away.

"Okay, Tom, we're ready," King Eric said. He jabbed his lollipop at Joe, who looked like a convict before a firing squad. "Shoot the apple off Joe's head."

***

"I can't do this," Tom whispered to Brooke.

"You can."

"I've never shot anyone before."

"You're the best shot in Massachusetts."

"What the hell are you fucking waiting for, Pussypalm?" Joe Bradley growled. "Shoot this damn fruit off my head. I got police business to attend to."

"Hurry up," King Eric said.

Megan was silent; her face showed no tension.

Pam smiled tightly. Now she'd set the demonstration up, she was tense and worried.

Joe's face was most tense of all. Though fighting to hide his fear, it seeped through his unbothered expression like piss through jeans. Sweat beaded on his plump forehead.

Tom raised the cop pistol and sighted down its barrel. His vision reduced to a pinpoint with just Joe Bradley's head at its focus, like Boston's chief of police was the light at the end of a tunnel.

He raised his aim higher. The apple zoomed in at him, filling his field of view so it was the largest thing in the room. The *only thing* in the room.

Then . . .

Tom's head was suddenly filled with a vision; someone else's life seen through his own eyes.

***

He was holding a gun. Aiming it. A big, heavy pistol. Acrid gun smoke stung his nostrils from its recent discharge. He was outside. He was unsure where, but the Overhead wasn't overhead.

Opposite Tom, twenty yards distant, a naked woman was tied to a tree. Her arms secured behind her with duct tape, her ankles bound together.

Through his vision eyes Tom peered close at the bound woman. She was Chinese, and middle-aged. She looked classy, pampered. So what the hell was she doing bound up?

The Chinese woman had a great body—slim, long legged; nice breasts with nipples stiffened by the cold.

Then he realized he was aiming his gun at her, sighting at her. And also that he was standing at an angle to her, looking at her almost from the side, aiming at . . .

Oh shit, Tom thought. *Fucking hell no . . .*

He was aiming at her left nipple.

"Do it," a female voice said over to his right. "I want to see how good you really are."

Tom turned in his vision body. The speaker was a thirty-something brunette. She was handsome rather than beautiful, but he found her devilishly attractive. His heart beat faster on seeing her.

"Go on," the woman urged. "Yes I know . . . we *promised* Mr. Wu we'd return his missus once he delivers the trucks, but we never said anything about her tits being included." The brunette's blue eyes twinkled. "Don't be deceived. She's way too old to breastfeed—long past menopause."

Tom cocked an eyebrow. "You'd have fooled me." Tom's vision voice wasn't his own. It was deeper, more virile.

She laughed. "*Men*. Once you see T and A, you're putty. Her breasts are implants. The old hag's bags sagged long ago."

Tom laughed, kissed the brunette. "I love your sense of punnery, babe."

"Please don't kill me, Mr. Tom," the Chinese woman pleaded. "My husband will supply the trucks." Her voice sounded like she'd been drugged or tortured.

"Shut up," Tom said without looking at her. "I ain't gonna kill you."

He winked at his brown-haired girlfriend. Then in a fluid motion spun round to face the bound woman.

He fired. The Chinese woman shrieked as the bullet sheared her left nipple off her chest.

Tom was horrified at what he was doing. And it was him—it was— even though it wasn't. He didn't understand how. And no matter what he did, he couldn't stop it. He was trapped in the vision, as much a victim as the Chinese lady.

Even before blood had begun spurting from the woman's breast, the vision Tom was in motion. He sprinted fifteen yards to his left. There, with an unobstructed view of her right nipple, he squeezed the trigger again.

Another loud report and Mrs. Wu's right nipple also disappeared.

Mrs. Wu began screaming loudly. She made so much noise that Tom wished she'd faint from the pain and shut up.

Blood spurted from Mrs. Wu's aureole like she was suckling a brood of vampires.

Tom laughed at the sight. The brunette streaked across the grass to him, leaping on him and kissing him. "Wow, honey—I've never seen shooting like that in my life."

Tom was disgusted. He fought the vision, fought to extricate himself . . .

***

104

The vision winked out.

Tom stood horrified. He stared at Joe Bradley standing against the wall. *That was not me,* he thought. *It wasn't me.* He looked around the room with worried eyes.

"What the hell are you waiting for?" Pam said.

"It won't go away," Megan said. "Fate can't be escaped."

"Stop dallying," King Eric ordered.

Tom dallied some more. Against the wall, Joe looked like he'd explode from annoyance. "What the hell is wrong with you!? Are you trying to give me a coronary from anticipation!?"

Then Tom felt another hand inside his. Like his fingers were a glove being worn. Like the dream reversed, he felt this inner hand controlling his fingers, shifting them into time-tested alignments. Tom suddenly understood the gun, understood how to aim it, how to position it just right to hit the apple dead center.

I got this, he thought. *Easy as eating pussy.*

He lifted the gun, sighted on the apple again. Like the madman in his vision, his aim now was unerring. Tom knew he could shoot the apple on Joe's head to a million bits if he wanted, without damaging a single strand of the cop's hair.

Then, just as he pulled the trigger, the control over his hand faded. It left as its ghost a trembling sensation that dipped Tom's aim off target.

There was a loud boom. Like magic, a little hole appeared in the middle of Joe's forehead and his brains splattered the wall behind him. The apple rolled sideways off Joe's head.

The silence that followed was deafening.

Chapter 27

Joe slid down to the floor, legs pushing out in front of him so he ended up sitting. His hair dragged a red smear down the wall. His eyes were open and staring, his mouth agape. A line of blood dribbled from the hole in his forehead down over his nose and mustache.

Pam gasped loudly. She shrieked and ran over to his side.

"He's lost a lot of brains," Megan said softly. "That's usually fatal."

King Eric sighed: "Damn. I was really looking forward to seeing that William Tell trick."

Pam was cradling Joe's corpse, shrieking, "I'm sorry, I'm so sorry, baby! I never meant to hurt you!"

"Tom, you ass," Brooke whispered, "you've just killed the Chief of Police."

Tom's tunnel vision zoomed out again. Horrified, he lowered the gun and looked around. "I didn't mean to—"

Pam turned around and stared at the others. Her face looked whitewashed now, leeched of all pink. Her eyes bugged in disbelief. "He's dead."

"That's obvious, you twit," Brooke whispered.

"I didn't mean to kill him," Tom said in a strangled voice.

"Shut up," King Eric said. "We all know that."

Pam glared at Tom. She extended her neck across the room so she was face to face with him. "You murdered him, you bastard."

King Eric looked at her sternly. "Thanks to you, Pam, Boston now needs a new Chief of Police." He licked his drugged lollipop, then added in a sad voice: "I'm really gonna miss Joe; he was a good cop."

Megan walked over to Joe's corpse. Pam immediately retracted her neck back from glaring at Tom to glare at Megan instead.

"What the hell do *you* want?"

Megan smiled sadly. "Fat men make big targets," she said. "Easier to hit than miss. I'll greatly miss—."

"Oh fucking shut the fucking fuck up!" Pam screamed, her massive breasts heaving with her anger. "This is all *your* fault. If you'd kept your eel to yourself—!"

"No," Megan retorted soothingly. "You love fully, Pam. The more complete your emotional involvement in another, the more the likelihood of an accidental tragedy occurring."

She nodded at the other woman's teary-eyed confusion at her words. "But he's all yours now. No other arms will ever hold him, nor lips kiss his. No one else will ever fellate him to orgasm. Always remember, Joe's last-ever cum was up your bum."

Pam had no reply to that. Sobbing, she stared into space, not even seeing Megan, her mascara six black lines down her cheeks.

"Cherish his memory," Megan added. "What is recalled is much more concrete than what really happened."

"What the hell is she gabbing about?" Brooke whispered to Tom.

He shrugged back. He looked out the window. Outside the Overhead, the morning sky was a dull grey. Below it, the harbor looked like a painting.

"I need a new Chief of Police," King Eric said nervously. "I already feel like the eaters are coming for me." He looked pointedly at Megan. "If the government feels insecure, how do you imagine the public feel?"

Her eyes met his evenly. "The clear choice to step into Joe's shoes is Lt. Harding, your Majesty. I've reprimanded him harshly for this morn—"

"Harding's too much of a hothead," King Eric interrupted. "If I promote him he'll blow up my city. I . . . Boston, Massachusetts . . . needs someone who can keep their emotions in check."

He licked his lollipop awhile, brow creased in deep thought. "But where do I find . . ."

Then he looked at Brooke and smiled.

"You've impressed me with your efficiency, Sgt. Hayes. I, King Eric the Young of Boston, hereby appoint you as the city's new police chief."

Megan and Pam and Tom all gaped at King Eric.

He nodded. "Yes, yes. She is. I'm king—my word is law."

They turned and gaped at Brooke instead.

"Come to the throne, Captain Hayes." the King said.

Captain? Brooke gasped. Heart beating furiously, emotion swirling in her head so violently she almost lost her balance, she stepped towards the grinning six-year-old monarch.

King Eric rose. Face solemn, he dabbed Brooke on each shoulder with his wet lollipop.

"That's done," King Eric said, resuming his seat. "Now it's time to attend to the day's business."

Brooke stepped back to Tom's side. She surreptitiously squeezed his hand. He squeezed back, hiding a grin.

The King nodded to Pam. "Joe's death is a regrettable loss for the entirety of East Massachusetts. We'll hold a state funeral for him this evening."

Pam's eyes filled with a fresh flood of tears.

"Pull yourself together, Pam," King Eric said gently. "Boston needs you." He turned to Brooke. "Have the body removed, Chief."

She nodded, then stepped over to the wall intercom and activated the switch. "This is Chief of Police Brooke Hayes speaking. Joe Bradley just died. Send a morgue crew and someone with a mop to the throne room now." She cut the connection and turned back to the King. "Done, your Majesty."

"Good, good." He languidly licked his lollipop.

Chapter 28

The morgue crew arrived speedily—two male officers carrying a stretcher. They were followed by a skinny blonde police sergeant hauling a mop bucket.

All three policepersons stared at Joe Bradley's corpse in confusion. Then they looked in puzzlement from the King to Tom, who was still holding Joe's gun.

"What the hell happened in here, Brooke?" the blonde policewoman finally asked, speaking for all three cops. "Target practice?"

"Just clean up, Kim," Brooke said tiredly.

Kim stared her down. She pointed her mop at Tom. "Pussypalm just shot Chief Bradley? That's murder."

Now that Kim had voiced their thoughts, the two male cops were watching the women. Neither had made any move to pick Joe up. Both men's hands lingered close to their guns. Both regarded Tom with black glances.

"No crime was committed, Kim." Brooke said.

"This don't look like suicide to me, Brooke."

"It's *Captain* Brooke now. It's going to be a long enough day without your sass. I called you three in here to clean up the mess. Clean up the damn mess."

Kim looked at Megan, who nodded. "The police chief is dead." She pointed at Brooke. "Long live the new police chief."

"Why are you three cops standing like skittles?" King Eric asked. "Brooke is my new Chief of Police; anyone who doesn't like her appointment can go suck a candy bar."

Kim rolled her eyes. She nodded to the other officers, then got to work wiping down the wall.

Her companions followed her lead. The men gently moved the still weeping Pam away from Joe's corpse. Pam, hand in mouth, gasped as they lifted the body onto the stretcher. And carried it away.

"Go with them, Pam," Megan said. "Your heart is too dark now for work."

Pam looked at King Eric, who nodded back. "Take the day off. See you at the funeral."

Pam shambled off after the stretcher bearing Joe away. She was now a total mess, makeup smeared across her face, tears still spurting.

"She looks like a ghost," King Eric said. "Like someone stole her lollipop." He pointed *his* at Kim. "Hurry it up, sergeant; I have city business to discuss with Chief Hayes."

"Yes, your Majesty." Kim hurriedly finished her cleanup and departed.

As she shut the door, Tom heard her mutter, "*Chief* Hayes. Oh, Harding is going to just *love* this."

Chapter 29

Tom, Brooke, and Megan, sat in chairs facing King Eric.

"What's the first order of business, Megan?" the King asked, his eyes intent and sleepy at the same time. "Bring my new chief up to speed on the state of the City."

"The thing most needful of immediate attention is flushing out the eaters hiding in Chinatown. Since Pussypalm's hand yesterday pinpointed their location as—"

"Permit me to interrupt you, Megan," Brooke said.

Megan was about to reprimand her for impertinence, then remembered she was now Chief of Police. "Yes, Brooke, what it is?"

"I was about to report earlier that Tom has regained part of his memory. He says he has an idea where the stolen gold might be."

At her words, King Eric leapt up. "Where is it!?"

"That's the bad news, your Majesty." She pointed outside. "It's up on the Overhead."

King Eric looked out the extensive window, then at Tom in horror. "Up *where?*" He furiously licked his lollipop

Brooke nodded. "Tom says he remembers being up on Bizarro, but not where."

The little monarch stared at Tom with intense loathing. "I really wish I could kill you," he said finally.

Megan said nothing. She reached her hand across to Tom and delicately stroked Rose.

Tom didn't pull his hand away. The only reason he was still alive was because Megan had stopped Harding from killing him. Tom suspected that now, with Brooke being promoted over him, the lieutenant would be even more pissed off at him. But the man clearly respected/feared Megan.

Tom was counting on Megan's help at staying alive.

Megan winked at Tom. "Strange that the money has been so nearby all this while. When you vanished, we believed you went east or south. His majesty even had spies check out your friend Pablo Rodriguez down in Techxas—"

"Who?"

"The pedophile arms dealer. He, however, had no idea where you were, or even that you'd hit the bank."

"Well, it's settled then," King Eric said. "We'll organize an expedition up to Bizarro to get the gold back." He looked coldly at Tom, his young eyes so steely that chills crawled like caterpillars down Tom's spine. "You'll take us to where the gold is, and for your own good, it had better be there."

"Or else," Brooke said. "You're fucked."

Megan smiled dreamily at that. "The Chief of Police means *that* metaphorically, of course," she said. "She has no sexual interest in you at all; it's important that you understand this, or end up with your testicles shot off."

"The gold's there," Tom told King Eric. "Just get me up there. I'll find it for you."

Chapter 30

Tom didn't attend Joe's funeral. He'd wanted to, to express his grief/remorse, but Brooke vetoed the idea.

"You show up there, it'll be like rubbing salt into a gaping wound," she said from the chair opposite Tom's bed. "Kim's spread the word that you shot Joe."

Tom remembered the gutsy blonde sergeant with the mop. "Why would she do that?"

Brooke frowned. "It's true, isn't it? You did shoot him."

"And got your sexy ass promoted."

Brooke got up and kissed Tom. "I don't know how to thank you for that." Her expression turned concerned. "You didn't kill Joe intentionally, did you?"

Tom sighed. "What do you expect to happen when you hand a pistol to a man who's previously only seen them on TV?"

Brooke nodded, ran her hand through her hair. "I keep forgetting you don't remember yourself."

Tom didn't want to remember. That vision of him shooting that woman's nipples off . . . What sort of asshole was that heartless?

Brooke looked Tom dead in the eye. "Now, 'bout Kim."

"Yeah, what about her?"

"Make sure you're never alone with her."

Tom was taken aback. "I'm not thinking of hitting on her."

Brooke rolled her eyes. "I didn't say you were. She prefers girls anyway." She gripped his hand, eyes intent, face fierce with emotion. "Listen: Kim Fields is a lot like Harding—another hothead. And she's a crack shot . . ."

She scowled. "Yeah, you need to watch out for Pam too. You never know what a grieving woman will do."

Tom winced. "How many people want to kill me now?"

Brooke grinned. Likely everyone in Boston, except for me and Megan. Megan and I want the same thing: to fuck you." She grinned broader. "Lucky for me, you're not into dick."

Tom nodded out at Bizarro. "I'll be much safer once we're up there."

"Not really," Brooke said. "Harding's certain to be coming along. Likely Kim too."

Before Tom could express his dismay, Brooke grabbed his left hand and licked its vagina. "Lot of stress already. More to come today. Let's screw to relax, okay? Damn, I'm sounding like Megan."

"Brooke, if someone comes in . . ."

She sat beside Tom on the bed and pulled her boots off. "No one'll dare. Remember, I'm head cop now."

"That's abuse of office."

As response, Brooke's trousers and panties floated down to the floor. "Hurry up," she said, spreading her legs so her cunt gaped at Tom, "I've a funeral to attend."

Tom knelt between her thighs and lapped the beautiful vagina, with its black rat-sleek bush.

Brooke gripped his head and moaned deliciously.

***

"Give me a gun," Tom said afterwards, as Brooke buckled her belt.

Brooke gave a fierce shake of her head. "Uh, uh, darling. You've made enough corpses for one day."

Tom freed a strand of pubic hair stuck in his teeth. "It's strictly for self-defense."

Combing her hair with her fingers, Brooke studied him for a moment, then nodded. "Okay." She handed her pistol to him. "I'll get another from my room."

She kissed him, then checked her watch. "Dang, I'm running late."

Chapter 31

Joe Bradley's funeral, held at the All Faith's Sanctuary funeral home on Hanover Street, was a subdued affair.

Outside, the evening air hung heavy in the sky. Bizarro seemed to brood like it too sensed Joe's passing.

Dressed in a grey suit, King Eric sat in the front row of attendees, between Megan and Pam. The building was packed with police officers, all with sorrowful faces.

Brooke, expression severe, sat across the entrance aisle, with the other senior city officials.

Joe's corpse—in full ceremonial uniform with a glitter of service medals pinned to his breast—lay in an open pine coffin. The police mortician had patched up Joe's forehead—there was no sign of the hole that had killed him.

Joe's thick lips were creased into the ghost of a frown.

"He looks like he's sleeping," Pam whispered to herself. "Oh, Joe."

Pam, dressed in an ankle-length black dress with black lace hat and veil, was quietly dignified while the Reverend Janet Jackson—a tall aging redhead whose cut off 'Hell's Angels' leather jacket revealed an artist's gallery of tattoos on her arms—performed the service. During the reverend's sermon/exhortation Pam dabbed her eyes with a violet handkerchief.

"Dearly beloved," Reverend Jackson intoned solemnly, "we now commit this one into the bosom of our lord . . ."

"I'm sorry, Joe," Pam moaned in a strangled whisper, her eyes wells of tears.

". . . And so one day, we shall all rise again perfect and entire; freed from our cells of flesh . . ."

Pam sniffed loudly.

Reverend Jackson waved a cautioning finger at Pam. Her lined face expressed sympathetic disapproval.

". . . Joseph Bradley is now in a much better place than Boston, Massachusetts . . ."

Pam sniffed louder; then broke into tears. Behind her veil, eye makeup streamed down her face. Black trails of sorrow.

Janet Jackson smiled benignly down at her.

Megan reached across King Eric, who stoically licked his lollipop. The boy's eyes were stony—he was resisting crying himself.

She stroked Pam's knee. "Don't weep; he's now forever the man you wished he'd be."

The minister continued: ". . . Sisters and brothers, we now commit Joseph Vincent Bradley into the fire. This physical fire symbolizes the expurgation of sin from the soul, the divorce of contaminating dross from gold. Physical fire . . . a memory of the divine judgment to come."

Megan yawned loudly. Janet Jackson looked sharply at her. Megan smiled apologetically. The minister resumed, black fingernails tapping her notes for added emphasis.

". . . Ashes to ashes; dust to dust. May we all here be counted worthy to attain the resurrection of the dead, Amen." Janet Jackson bowed to the assembled cops, then retrieved her papers and left the lectern, high-heeled biker boots clicking on the stone steps.

The funeral director looked at Brooke. She gave a nod. He in turn nodded to his assistants, who sealed Joe's corpse into its coffin. The coffin was rolled into the furnace, the door shut.

***

(With the advent of Bizarro, bodies were no longer buried—if they were, the eaters dug them up for food. Nowadays, everyone—Muslims, Christians (of every denomination), Atheists, Rastafarians, Buddhists, etc.—requested incineration once their last rites had been performed.)

***

Pam fainted when the furnace burst into flames, a raging inferno like an artificial Hell.

"Don't leave me, Joe!" she shrieked in a piteous voice. Then she slumped back senseless in the pew, her neck elongating down till her head hit the floor behind the wooden bench.

The royal security detail seated behind King Eric instantly rushed to Pam's assistance. Two men lifted her head off the floor. Then after rolling up her neck and placing it in a neat coil in her lap, they arranged her head on it facing the furnace.

One of them then arranged her hat and veil on her head again.

Megan nodded her approval to the men.

King Eric licked his lollipop through the tears streaming down his cheeks. His little shoulders heaved with his sobs.

He wasn't alone; three-quarters of the cops present had tears in their eyes.

Chapter 32

For a while, Tom stood by his window, staring at the Boston Overhead. Bizarro's hanging brown mass gave him a feeling of the sky pressing in on him. He imagined it dropping and splatting Boston like a bug.

The feeling, nauseous like vertigo, drove Tom from the window.

He sat on the bed, considering the gun Brooke had given him.

He'd lied to her. He didn't want the weapon for self-defense.

Tom picked it up. He sighted out of the window and up. He concentrated; pinpointing on a low-hanging mass of the chocolate mulch.

This time it happened much faster. He felt again the hand inside his hand stabilizing his aim. Concurrently, his vision tightened, concentrated till he could almost pick out unseen details of his target.

Tom lowered the gun. The feeling faded after a minute. He raised the gun again, the feeling returned, sharper, keener. And now with it came a feeling of viciousness; of bloodthirst.

No. He felt himself 'shifting' again. The vision had him in its clutches before he could drop the weapon.

***

Tom was pointing a shotgun into the face of a bespectacled man with scattered white hair. He was entering a door, backing the man into the room beyond.

"Pussypalm? What do you want here?"

Tom laughed. Behind the white-haired man an old woman sat in a wheelchair.

"We're visiting Ma," a woman's voice said from behind Tom.

The vision dissolved into another:

A hand was secured to a stairway bannister by a metal hoop around its wrist. Below the hand hung a blonde boy of about twelve. The kid looked terrified.

"Now we see how good you are, amigo," a greasy voice said. "Remember: one miss and you pay twice as much for the rocket launchers. I get four fingers in sequence, so you need all five."

Once again Tom was aiming.

"Please don't shoot me, sir!" the boy shrieked. He turned to the unseen speaker. "Please Mr. Pablo! I'll suck your penis better! I promise!"

Someone poured a beer over the kid. "Shut up, little gringo swine! Señor Pussyhand is shooting!"

Tom fired. The boy's thumb flew off his hand.

The kid looked surprised. Then the pain kicked in and he began screaming.

Quickly, without pausing, Tom fired four more times. Each shot unerringly clipped off another of the boy's fingers.

"How's that?" he asked, blowing smoke from the gun's muzzle.

"Hmmm, Señor, you win today. I will throw in the rockets for free as agreed. But still, I think I am better shot than you. I think up a new— Mario, you shut up that crying gringo bastard already, or I will fuck your daughter tonight!"

There was a flash of metal. A knife whizzed through the air and buried itself deep in the screaming boy's mouth. The kid instantly shut up. His head fell forward. Blood streamed from his lips.

A sexy, but very scared Mexican señorita handed Tom a cold beer. Absentmindedly, he stroked her hair with his left hand. She shuddered beneath his gentle touch.

Tom saw Rose in his left palm as he ran it through the girl's glossy black hair.

He lifted her scared face to his. "Don't worry, hon. I'm not gonna kill you—just gonna fuck you to let off stress." He stroked her mouth with the vagina. "You like eating pussy, girl?"

To resounding Latino-flavored laughter, the vision cut out.

***

Tom dropped the gun like it was a snake. He was nauseated. It took an almighty effort not to throw up.

Man, this Pussypalm was one sick character. He glared at his hand-cunt with intense hatred. *But I'm not him, Oh hell no, I'm not him.*

Chapter 33

A policewoman tapped Brooke on the shoulder.

"Lt. Harding said to get you, Chief. Eaters."

Brooke was instantly out of her seat.

***

Harding was pissed off. At Pussypalm; at himself; at the world.

How in Boy George's tight backside could I have been so stupid? Fifteen years of dedicated service thrown away over some asshole. Damn! Damn! Superdamn!! I should be Chief now, not that Kim-Kardashian-buttocked minx . . .

On cue, Brooke exited the funeral home. Harding forgot how pissed-off he was and rushed over to her.

"Trouble, Chief. We've found a nest of eaters over in the JFK Building."

Brooke winced. The JFK Federal building was beside City Hall. "Holy shit. His majesty's gonna love that."

"He's going to poop his pants, Chief. Remember the last time?"

Brooke remembered. King Eric feared eaters like other kids feared the dentist. His lollipop was supposed to compensate, but adding valium to its drug-cocktail fouled up the candy taste. So he had separate 'stress marshmallows.'

The last time an eater had been sighted near the palace, the young King had moved the government west to Beacon Hill for a month.

"Who's watching them?" Brooke asked, following Harding to his Police Interceptor SUV.

"Kim Fields is over there with three SWAT teams." He looked at Brooke as he opened the door, nodded back at the funeral home. "Chief, I'm just hoping we can flush them out before they finish in there. Or else . . ."

Despite her worries, Brooke was smiling as she got into the SUV.

She liked Harding's constantly calling her 'Chief.' Being kowtowed to was heady stuff. It also meant Harding wasn't going to be a pain in her ass.

"Let's go," she said coolly. "We'll flush the bastards out. No way am I moving crosstown again."

***

They took the long route back to the palace: right onto Cross Street, left across Haymarket Square, left again, back onto Congress Street.

Once they hit Congress, Harding slowed.

"What's with all the cloak and dagger shit?" Brooke asked. "You're turning the vehicle like you're navigating someone's colon. And why aren't we going to the front of the building?"

Harding rolled the Police Interceptor to a standstill beside the JFK building, parking behind one of three SWAT vans.

He cut the engine. "The eaters don't yet know we know they're here. Cannibal Watch guys up at Hull Street—Marv Anderson's old post—sent HQ a message an hour ago about abnormal heat readings here in the JFK, so we rushed a team of our own over with a heat scope. It's a positive, but I told Kim to keep the noise levels down."

We're keeping the noise levels down alright, Brooke thought. *The place looks fucking deserted.*

They got out. Seventy yards away, in clear view over the palace wall, stood City Hall.

This had to happen on the day I got promoted, Brooke thought grimly.

"Where the hell is everyone?" she asked the single SWAT guard watching the road.

The man saluted quickly. "Getting set up, ma'am. Sgt. Fields is coordinating. She's around the back."

They hurried to the building's rear. Harding pointed ahead. "That's her over there."

Brooke made out Kim Fields behind a clump of oaks by the palace wall.

They ran across to her.

The skinny blonde sergeant had recovered from her earlier sassiness. She saluted Brooke respectfully. "You're just in time, Chief. We're going in."

They stared at the complex of two towers and four-story low-rise.

All the police activity seemed concentrated on the low-rise. Despite the evening cool, the air over it visibly shimmered with heat. Brooke imagined movement behind its windows.

Pressed tight against its ground-floor walls, heavily armed women and men in Kevlar vests and grilled/slatted helmets moved soundlessly into position.

There was NO noise. The police officers moved like armored ghosts, sunlight glinting off their assault rifles and shotguns.

(Brooke was very glad now that she'd fucked Tom before attending the funeral. Her body felt strong, tuned to the max.)

"What's the situation?" she asked Kim. "Please tell me the eaters aren't in either of the towers."

Kim shook her head. "We're lucky; it's too high to climb and both elevators are fucked." She pointed. "Our heat sensors pin-point all the eaters as being on the third floor of the squat here, west wing. A conference room beside the Paul Revere Library. Seems to be ten of 'em."

Brooke scowled. "They were really thinking of becoming royal neighbors." She jerked a thumb at the officers by the wall. "How are the SWAT teams deployed?"

Kim pointed left. "Joe Collins' guys are already in the corridor linking this building to the towers. Eaters ain't getting out that way. Lisa Gomez's unit is also inside, advancing along the main corridor. They'll take up positions by the middle stairwell, then signal. There she is now."

(Brooke sensed Kim's disappointment at having to coordinate the action and not herself enter the building. Sgt. Kimberley Fields was Boston's PD's best shot—almost on a par with Tom Pussypalm.)

Brooke followed Kim's finger. A red flag attached to a rifle barrel had appeared in a window. It waved thrice then was withdrawn.

Kim looked from Harding to Brooke. "The bolt-hole's been blocked, Chief."

Brooke scowled. "Time to catch the cannibal rabbits." She nodded to Kim. "Keep watch out here, in case you've any jumpers. Lt. Harding and I will coordinate the attack from inside." She thought a moment. "And send some guys up on the roof—I don't want the fuckers hiding out and re-infesting the place afterward.

Harding called two officers over and quickly divested them of their vests, helmets and weapons.

He and Brooke suited up, then joined the SWAT unit entering the building.

Behind them, Kim Fields quickly organized a second team to send up to the roof.

Chapter 34

Shrouded in sorrow darker than her dress, Pam Andersen was alone in company.

Accompanied by Megan and King Eric, she'd come to the harborwalk between Long and Commercial Wharfs on the Boston Harbor to scatter Joe's ashes. The royal limousine and two carloads of cops were parked a distance behind them.

Pam left King Eric and Megan. She walked alone to the sea's edge, stared out over the rusty chain railing into the dirty water. The late evening breeze rippled her dress. Distant gulls screeched at each other, their atonal cries like spirit voices.

Pam scooped a handful of Joe's ashes from his urn.

"Goodbye, darling," she said.

She found herself unable to open her hand and scatter the ash on the water. She couldn't do it. *I can't ever let Joe go. Not now, not ever.*

Laughing in sudden understanding, she raised the handful of ash to her mouth, and took a bite of it.

It tasted bitter. Dry, elemental. Like life, like death.

She ate the ash in handfuls, taking care that none spilled.

Behind her, King Eric turned to Megan in shock. "She's eating him."

"Yes."

"Do something! Stop her!"

"She loves him," Megan said simply with an approving smile.

Pam raised the urn to her lips and slowly trickled the remaining of Joe's ash into her mouth. She chewed, swallowed, gulped, chewed, swallowed. She elongated her neck so the ash would slide down it slowly, enjoying its one way trip to her stomach.

Eyes round, King Eric watched in disbelief.

"That's true dedication for you, your Majesty," Megan said.

"*Dedication?*"

She nodded. "Pam there is the sort of woman every man needs—one who goes the extra mile."

The boy king ruminated on that. "Her behavior *is* better than the way Shirley treated me."

"Exactly my point."

"It's very gross though."

"In love and war there are no rules."

Finally, Pam was done eating Joe's remains. She flung the urn far out into the harbor water. She grinned at the splash of its landing.

She turned back to Megan and the King, eyes gleaming. "I'm fine now."

King Eric nodded. "Dedication," he mouthed. He turned and walked off.

"There's some ash on your lips," Megan told Pam.

"Thanks," Pam replied. With a dreamy smile she licked it off.

Then she linked arms with Megan and walked back to the royal limo.

Chapter 35

Two cops hit the door with a battering ram. Once, twice, thrice. The wood splintered, then crashed off its hinges.

"Go! Go! Go!" The SWAT team charged into the conference room.

Brooke, running in beside Harding, had just enough time to glimpse the bodies strung from the ceiling before the room exploded into pandemonium.

Like their attackers, the eaters were armed. Like Sgt. Kim Fields had informed them, they were ten in number. Six men, four women. Hairless yellow abominations stained with Bostonian blood.

Caught by surprise, the mutant cannibals lost two of their number before rallying their defense and retaliation.

The hanging corpses got in the cops' way. Their bullets slammed into the half-eaten bodies, spinning them into one another.

Brooke was smashed across the chest by a salvo of bullets that knocked her off her feet. Her backward journey was halted by a dangling corpse that crashed down on her after she'd hit the floor. She stared into a fat female face—eyes eaten out of their sockets. The body was fresh; it dripped fluid, had no smell of decay.

Brooke lay under the corpse with minimal motion, faking her death. *Thank God for Kevlar,* she thought, eyes scanning the room.

The eater who'd shot her was now firing at another cop. Though concealed behind a stack of metal cabinets the man's lemon skin made him easy to spot.

Across from her, Brooke saw a policeman crawling across the floor, both his knees shattered by gunfire. Then bullets thudded into his buttocks, lifting him off the floor with their violence. Some clearly got well under his jacket: the man landed like a lump of meat and remained still.

She grimaced, resumed scanning the room.

There were four improvised barricades in the room, each shielding one or two eaters. Semi-automatic gunfire sprayed from each gun post in short bursts, shredding the swinging human corpses like paper. Windows exploded outwards in sprays of glass.

The uninjured SWAT team members had now taken refuge behind overturned metal furniture. Some were ducked behind reinforced riot shields.

There were several casualties. Most had had their legs shot to bits. Brooke saw Harding dragging a wounded cop toward the door. She wondered how the woman had lost her helmet—*maybe she slipped on some gore*—the entire right side of her face was a mess of blood.

Harding got the wounded woman out of the door.

They were expecting us to attack them, Brooke thought.

Holding the fat female corpse tight on top of her, she inched her way along the floor towards the eater who'd shot her.

The eater—a middle-aged man in a tattered three-piece suit—worked his machine gun from behind his barricade of rearranged furniture with a scowl on his face. His teeth were a mouthful of glass daggers.

The man randomly spat a finger bone in Brooke's direction. It hit her nose. Angered/insulted by the gesture, she resumed crawling.

She finally got into position behind the eater. Oblivious to her presence, the yellow man was now firing at Harding, who'd just dashed back into the room. The slugs dotted the wall behind Harding like punctuation.

The eater stopped shooting for a moment to rip a chunk of liver from the gutted body swinging beside him and pop it in his mouth.

Brooke pushed the fat woman's corpse off herself. She unclipped a grenade from her belt, pulled its safety pin, then rolled it between the eater's legs.

Eat this, lemon-face.

The grenade bumped the man's foot. Surprised, he looked down. The next moment he disintegrated into a thousand chunks.

Before the eater's pieces had all settled, Harding and two other cops had rushed over to Brooke's side.

Harding's eyes were flinty behind his helmet grill. "I've sent word to Kim to rappel down the roof crew."

Brooke nodded then returned her attention to the fight.

The explosion had confused the other eaters. Grabbing a swinging corpse for cover, Brooke leapt up and lobbed grenades at two barricades.

One scored a direct hit, blowing an elderly eater couple to bits.

The other blew its occupants' shelter over. The metal cabinet levitated like a hovercraft, then crashed sideways. Two eaters stood exposed.

Before the cannibals could hide again; the cops who'd accompanied Harding had mown them down with bullets.

Fresh salvos of gunfire spurted from the two remaining eater stations. The policemen ducked. Like jet fighters, hot metal streaked over their heads. There was a loud curse from behind them as ricochets hit a policeman in the leg.

"Persistent shits," Brooke gasped. "Where the hell are my roof crew?"

Like her words were a signal, the windows behind the eaters shattered. Four black-clad cops swung in amidst the glass shower, firing as they came.

There was an interlude of chaos—gunfire, explosions, yells and screaming. A flare gun accidentally discharged, a fire started up. A lot more shooting.

Brooke leapt up and shot an eater running to jump out of a window. His bald head exploded like Joe's had that morning. For a moment she wondered how the funeral was going. Pam should be done dispersing the ashes now.

And then it was over. Peace settled over the room again.

The room looked like the battle zone it had been. Smoke rose from multiple fires in diverse nooks, hampering vision, making it hard to breathe.

Cops were opening windows to let the smoke billow out.

Teams of medics were entering with stretchers. Others were entering with body bags. Harding left Brooke and went to coordinate the cleanup.

Brooke called back one of the two officers following Harding. "Get some fire extinguishers."

She watched the cleanup crew cut down the remaining human corpses. *This is the deepest into the city that the eaters have ever come*, she thought. *It's scary that they'd dare set up house opposite the palace.*

Walking to the door, Brooke kicked something. She looked down, then picked it up. It was an eater's lower jaw. A transparent curve of razor-sharp teeth embedded in yellow flesh. A chill of fear stabbed through her like it always did when she saw what Bizarro had brought to the world.

Monsters she could deal with. Monsters who'd once been—and in most regards still were—everyday people were another ball game entirely.

"Chief?"

Brooke turned to the speaker. It was a woman, one of the body-baggers. She pointed at the eater jaw Brooke held.

Brooke shook her head. "Nah. I'll keep it for a paperweight—the teeth look like jewels. I'll just trim off all the meat."

The policewoman's eyes widened, then she nodded respectfully. She stepped away, turned to scoop up a pile of human intestines.

The policewoman's deference reminded Brooke that she was running the show here.

"Hey, get a move on!" she yelled at no one in particular. The activity level in the room immediately increased.

Carrying the eater jaw like a trophy, Brooke left the room, satisfied that her first test as Chief of Police had been successful.

***

Kim met Brooke downstairs. "Hey, Chief, there were two eaters up on the roof; we took 'em out easy. We've no more heat readings from the building but Lisa and her team are sweeping the floors now for any stragglers anyway."

Brooke was amused at how pissed Kim sounded at not having been in on the action.

She pointed up at the room where they'd just battled the eaters. Inside, fire burnt fiercely, like it housed dragons. "I told someone to get extinguishers and put that out. It looks like they poured gas on it instead."

Kim studied the burning windows. "They'll douse it soon enough; we're lucky it wasn't the old library. All that paper . . ."

Brooke grunted. "The blaze is visible from the palace, specifically from King Eric's bedroom. Looks like we're burning the city down. What do I tell his majesty is going on out here?"

Sgt. Kim Fields thought a moment. Then she paused, uncertain whether or not to help her new boss out. Finally, she grinned.

"That's easy, Chief. King Eric's a kid, right? Just tell him we were setting up . . ."

***

129

"Fireworks?"

Brooke nodded respectfully to King Eric. She gestured out the window over at the JFK building where flames still burnt in two windows. (The fire extinguishers they'd found had been useless—some Bizarro fungus had reacted with their contents.) "Yes, your Majesty. In honor of ex-Chief Bradley. Unfortunately, some went off early—"

"Never worry about that!" King Eric exclaimed, leaping off his throne and rushing to the window in childish excitement. "Accidents happen!" He turned to Brooke, face feverish with anticipation. "When does the display start?"

Brooke checked her watch. It was seven-thirty. "Right about now, sire. We were waiting for darkness to fall properly."

She walked over to switch off the lights.

On cue, the night exploded into a kaleidoscope of shimmering streamers and trails of sparks. Green, yellow, red, orange, blue . . . the pyrotechnic ballet was a sight to behold.

King Eric stood watching the fireworks, entranced. Each cascade of light lit up the young monarch's face in diverse shades of color.

Megan was impressed. "That's quite a show you're putting on for Joe," she told Brooke.

Brooke whispered back the real cause.

Megan raised an eyebrow. "This close to home?"

"They'd set up a food camp in there—corpses swinging from the ceiling, kitchenette, the whole shebang." She realized someone was missing. "Where's Pam?"

"Indigestion. Something she ate after the funeral."

"Bravo, Bravo!" King Eric yelped in glee, clapping his hands. "More! More!"

Chapter 36

He lay in a bed that extended forever, a pink silken landscape with piled pillow-mountains. The cushion beneath his head smelt of Jasmine. The perfume both enticed and worried him. It filled him with anticipation.

Tom wasn't alone in the endless bed. To his left and right a multitude of couples—gay, lesbian, straight, transgender—were involved in a multitude of sexual activities, from gentle cuddling and heavy petting to the most strenuous fucking imaginable. The only catch was, all the sex, whether gentle caress or hard sweaty pounding, was anal specific. Ass to mouth, fingers in anus, cock to ass . . . he even made out two men in a sixty-nine position with hands wrist-deep in each other's rectums.

The couple on Tom's right were a lesbian pair. They were going at it doggy-style, the one topping pounding her lover hard with a glowing neon-green strap-on that made the bottom woman's plump ass look a firefly's each time the phallus slid out of it.

"Oh, fuck, Sheila; give it to me! Harder!"

Sheila obliged. Grabbing the plump woman's auburn ponytail, she yanked her head back hard and pumped, slamming her hips so hard, her partner collapsed onto the bed giggling.

Sheila fell on top of her. "Oh, I love your ass, Penelope." She kept fucking her hard, stroking her hair and kissing her neck.

The sexual action was similarly explicit all around Tom. A man pulled out of his wife's/girlfriend's asshole. Semen streamed from the distended pucker, down her thighs.

Tom had a raging boner. He was worried however. He was the only single person in sight in the endless bed. And the implication of all the same sex couples present weren't lost on him.

But . . .

He remembered Rose; maybe he was meant to fuck his hand. He was almost relieved, but then remembered Rose was a vagina, not an anus.

Then . . .

Oh, shit, no!

. . . Tom saw the man walking towards him. Slim and blonde with a moustache and beard. He wore tight black leather trousers and a black leather jacket. Black shades and boots.

Hell, no! This guy looks like one of the Village People.

Tom tried getting to his feet. His body refused to obey his commands to flee.

The slim man reached him. Without any ado or exchange of pleasantries, he knelt and began fellating Tom, sucking his stiff penis hard.

"No," Tom screamed as his cock vanished up to beard and mustache in the mouth. "Stop it!"

The man's response was to suck Tom harder.

"Stop it!"

The man removed his head from Tom's erection. He took off his shades; Tom saw his eyes were green. "Why? What does a lady have to do to get screwed around here?" She laughed at his shock at her female voice. "You didn't think you'd be rid of me so easy, did you, Tommy baby?"

"Bu . . . but . . . but . . . "

Her voice turned sweeter than sugar. "Exactly, honey. *Butt.*" She pointed up.

A huge orange/blue/green neon sign glowed:

'Welcome to The Butt: Club Backside, Where the Greased-Up Wise Cock Slides Up. Be Cool, Don't Fuck Like a Fool. Here the Asshole Rules.'

Tom winced through his relief. At least she wasn't a *he*, like several of the couples lustily screwing around them. "What do you want with me?"

Her face turned ugly beneath her mustache and beard. "Do we really have to go through this each time, Tommy baby?" While talking, she pumped his penis, keeping him rock hard.

Tom gaped. "We've met before?"

She was about retorting, then grinned instead. She unzipped her black pants from mons to ass.

He gasped when he saw she had no vagina, her crotch bare beneath blonde pubic hair. He looked at his hand. Then back at her again.

"Lynn . . . ?"

She nodded. "Yes, Tommy, the cunt is mine, all mine, it's mine, mine, mine."

Lynn didn't have any head wounds; but it was her alright. *How the hell didn't I immediately recognize her voice?*

He pointed to Rose. "I don't want it either," he said. "You can have it back."

Lynn frowned. "It wants you though. Likes to be fucked by your hard penis. All day long it sings to me of the incredible pleasure you give it, how fantastic a lover you are. How it needs you like you need air."

"Surely it can do that as part of you. Just take it off me."

She laughed, grotesque in her drag getup. "You're really accommodating tonight, aren't you?" She gestured at the multitude of copulating couples surrounding them. "Okay, I'll take it off. But this is Club Backside, Tommy baby. These loving couples everywhere have all got me so horny that I gotta have some rear action also. You dig?"

He nodded slowly.

She bent down and sucked the head of his cock, violent wrenches of her lips that made Tom shiver.

He looked around. The lesbian couple to his right were now asleep, Sheila's green strap-on buried harness-deep in her plump lover's expansive buttocks.

He looked back. Lynn was on her back now, buttocks spread with her hands so he could see her anus. It was an ugly hole with jagged edges.

She scowled at his grimace, stuck a finger into the slack sphincter. "Not my fault it's been abused." She smiled. "You know, Tommy baby, you've created all sorts of sexual identity crises in me by stealing my vagina—"

"I didn't steal—"

She shifted her left boot; planted its sole firmly across his lips. "I'm not done talking." She gazed at him, her expression neither smile nor frown. "You've reduced me to less than I am." She laughed at his querying expression. "How? *What?* Who ever heard of a woman without a vagina before?"

She trod her boot on his mouth to ensure he didn't reply. "What difference does it make? Do I hear your little mind asking that question? Am I truly a woman if I don't have a cunt? How do you think I have my period?" Her voice rose dramatically, to a shrill crescendo. "You've made me a honorary man, Tommy! Now you must fuck the consequences!"

Sheila and Penelope, the lesbian couple, woke up. "C'mon guys, we're trying to catch some shuteye here."

Lynn waved her right boot at them. "Sorry."

Both women fell asleep again.

Tom had used the distraction to free his mouth from her other boot. He spat a black stain of sanded rubber onto the bed. He sat up.

She looked at him expectantly. "We fuck now, yes?"

"At least take off the moustache and beard."

A head shake. "Of course not, this way's much more kinky. More fun. Imagine I'm a guy."

Tom imagined instead that she was Scarlett Johansson. That beautiful face, those perfect shoulders, that tight ass. He rolled her over so her facial hair was out of his view and slid himself up her anus.

Oh, yes.

Tom fucked Lynn's leather-clad ass hard and deep. Despite its ragged appearance the anus was airtight, like a second skin. Being inside her felt like wearing a condom. Tom pumped her hurriedly, rushing to come quickly, to rid himself of the gay associations of screwing someone with bristly facial hair.

Then he realized he was higher up in the air than before.

He looked down, saw they were rising on her extending arms and legs. "Whoa, there. What's going on?"

She turned her head a half-circle to smile at him. "'Whoa' is right, Tommy boy." She giggled. "You're loving me so good, I'm tripping out, and I'm taking you up with me."

Lynn's buttocks had expanded around Tom, molding to the contours of his hips and ass to form a support. He now sat amidst them, cock plugged into her anus.

In his surprise, Tom ceased making love to her backside as they rose to meet the expanse of brightly glowing tubes forming Club Backside's marquee sign.

Lynn wasn't having it.

"C'mon, baby, don't stop loving me. Poopie will come out if you do, and you've nowhere to run to."

Tom got the hint. Bizarre memories of an excrement monster he'd not yet encountered tingled his memory. He resumed the anal sex, a languid in/out motion, rocking back and forth. It was still pleasant, the asshole tautly welcoming, but confusion prevented him fully enjoying it.

Lynn turned back around and resumed moaning. Then she began singing 'fuck my ass hard,' to the tune of 'YMCA.'

They reached the neon sign. There was a yellow door to its left.

"We go in through here," she said. "Hold on tight and keep your head low."

She lifted her legs up from the bed, now invisible an impossible distance below, and climbed through. Tom lay flat on her, holding her breasts, as they made the transition.

His head banged the lintel. Pain and shock forced his eyes closed.

When he opened them again, they were somewhere else.

But where?

The landscape through the club sign was made/carved/molded/built whatever (Tom couldn't tell—at one point, it seemed all five simultaneously) from large white cubes. The white cubes formed dunes, hills and valleys. Everywhere was an endlessness of ascending/descending/spiraling steps, like semen from a Pablo Picasso wet dream. Or the Cubist's vision of Heaven or Hell, or both.

Tom clamped between her extruded ass-cheeks like a life-giving turd and fucking her as they went, Lynn tramped across the expanse of blocks with arachnid ease. She reduced the length of her legs till they walked only ten feet above the landscape.

Lynn's clothes melted off her body. They dripped down her extensive legs onto the white expanse as a trail of black foot prints. To Tom's relief, her beard and mustache also blew off her face. The shorn facial hair swirled and multiplied in miniature storms.

"Where are we go—?"

"Keep screwing me! Yeesssss! I'm cumming."

On those words, she finally shrunk down to normal female proportions again. Tom fucked her doggy-style on one of the white cubes, which wasn't hard like he'd thought. Instead, it was the texture of a marshmallow, softly resistant, like a well-rounded buttock.

Lynn reached back with both hands, pulling Tom deeper into herself. She screamed like he was raping her while he squeezed her breasts hard.

Then she was done.

"Thanks, Tommy baby," she moaned. "I'd marry you if I didn't hate you so much."

And with those words Lynn dissolved completely into air just as Tom began ejaculating, so he spurted his semen into his memory of her. Without her sweet rectum around him, Tom finished off by hand. His splattered semen seeped into the white surface.

"Shit!" Tom cursed, getting to his feet.

This crazy woman just used me for her own pleasure. And I'm winded, like I just bedded a thousand mares. But first . . . where am I? Where is this place?

Then he made another realization: *Shee-it, Rose is gone.*

It was true. There was no longer any stinky slurpy vagina in his left palm.

He began dancing a joyous jig.

"Yesss!" he yelled. "I'm free from the cunt-hand of horror!"

His pleasure was short-lived.

"Save me, Tom!" the familiar voice yelled. "Save me, darling!!"

NO! He looked up. Rose was being carried away by four twenty-feet-tall women with palm frond hair. The vagina, now monster-sized itself, hung between the quartet conveying it. It was suspended on the ends of the weird meat tentacles all four gripped, secured by four black hooks through its labia majora.

Rose—swaying, vaginal channel dripping—looked like a beached shark carried by four fisherwomen.

Sorry, darling cunt, Tom thought, grinning, *ain't no way I'm tangling with the vavs. Those sistas look superbad.*

"Save me, Tommy darling! Please, honey rod! Help me!"

Over Rose's screaming, Tom could just make out a humming, almost subliminal, sound. He tuned his mind to it.

It was coming from the vavs. The vampire vaginas were climbing a mountain of the white cubes—

Tom squinted hard.

—to a golden temple.

He listened harder. The barely audible humming was a song:

"Sing praise to Almighty Vagina.
Worship the bottomless pit, the sensitive front slit that does not shit.
Worship vagina, essential as air, that men love and fear.
Greater eternal enslaver, most delicious betrayer.
Worship Almighty Vagina,
All bow and adore, for she is above law, and rules over all."

The low melody thrummed the air without voices.

"Save me, Tom, you selfish bastard!" Rose screeched over it. "I'll see you gang-raped in hell for this!"

Tom instead sat down on a white cube. He relaxed back on an elbow. Grinning, he watched Rose borne away, far, far off, up the white cube mountain.

He tuned Rose's voice out by listening to the vavs' odd hymn.

"Worship Vagina, dripping like rain,
Succor from pain, release from strain, humbles the vain.
Tastier than honey, buys more than money.
Tunnel of darkness enlightening the soul,
Surpassing pleasure that mocks self-control . . ."

Tom awoke. Brooke was shaking him.

"What are you grinning about?"

"Eh?" He remembered his dream and quickly checked his hand. "Aw fuck, it's still here."

Her gaze narrowed. "What?"

He sat up. Regurgitated daylight filled the room. "Oh, never mind." He grinned at Brooke. "You look cute, Captain Hayes. Sexy new uniform."

Vanity pumped up, she sniffed, shaking her head so her black hair swirled around. "I prefer tough. Cute is for sissies."

"How about a kiss anyway, Chief?"

She bent so her lips grazed his. He reached up to pull her close. She drew back. "Don't French me, silly. You'll get me aroused, and we don't have time."

He grinned.

Eyes twinkling, she nodded at him. "Wash and get dressed, lover man. We've just enough time for some breakfast before meeting King Eric." Her eyes held his. "Remember what we agreed: you remember Bizarro and the lake, but nothing more."

"Don't worry," he said. "I won't mess this up."

***

Walking to the bathroom, Tom was very bothered. This was his second dream (vision?) featuring dead Lynn berating him over her vagina. He couldn't dismiss it as coincidence. And once again, the dream had been shockingly realistic.

Also, why didn't this dream Lynn have any bullet holes in her head?

Chapter 37

Now, the morning after, Pam felt composed again.

Sitting at her bedroom mirror, brushing her hair, she was surprised at herself. Not that she'd eaten Joe's ashes,—it had been the right thing to do—but that she felt so good afterwards.

I'm a black widow, she thought with amusement, *I ate my mate.*

Oddest of all, Pam felt closure. By ingesting Joe—her lover, her past—she'd cleared the stairway to her future. She felt bright and perky, ready even for a new relationship. And felt no guilt at that realization. *Megan was right: Joe's part of me now—I no longer need to mourn him.*

She grinned slyly at her reflection. *I'm an upwardly mobile thirty-something with an elongating neck, and I need a new man for some hot sex.*

Her grin broadened. *And there'll be lots of hot cop bods in evidence when we go up prospecting the Overhead.*

Humming a love song, Pam dressed. It would be a long day; preparations had to be made for the expedition to Bizarro. She'd been as surprised as anyone when Megan had told her where Pussypalm had stashed the missing bullion.

Chapter 38

"Dedication is of the utmost importance," King Eric intoned solemnly. His eyes skipped around the council table, alighting on people in turn. "Dedication to duty, dedication to one's nation . . ." His eyes settled on Pam, ". . . Dedication to one's family."

He frowned, took a lick of lollipop. "Since Queen Shirley died, I've been sad. Miserable and alone, with no one cuddling me close at night, reading me my bedtime story, tucking me in . . ."

Tom glanced at Brooke. "What's the matter with King Tut *now*? I thought we're here to plan our expedition."

Brooke didn't reply, didn't hear. Her gaze was fixed on Harding, who sat opposite her beside Pam, his attention riveted on King Eric. Brooke's thoughts were cold, appraising. True, Harding hadn't shown any sign of resenting her leapfrogging him, but nothing could be taken for granted. He might still decide to act like an asshole.

Megan sat on Harding's right. The transsexual brunette was impeccable in a cream-colored suit, her hair pulled back in a severe bun, her red lipstick perfect. She winked at Tom.

He nodded back. A moment later he felt the soft touch of toes on his ankle, next the silky sensation of a nylon-clad foot sneaking up the inside of his right leg. His eyes widened at Megan. She smiled coolly back.

King Eric tapped the conference table with his lollipop. "Yesterday, my secretary Pam surprised me . . ."

Megan's foot rose farther up Tom's leg, past his knee, by teasing stages creeping closer to his crotch. He felt increasingly uncomfortable; his penis began filling with blood. He however kept his face non-committal, affected to studiously follow the King's speech. *Shit, if Brooke accidentally looks down.*

". . . In all my years I've never seen anything it . . ." King Eric said, sounding close to tears. ". . . Such total devotion . . ."

Pam was first embarrassed, then confused by King Eric's words. Negative apprehension built in her, the sense that something very bad was about to happen.

Megan's foot nudged Tom's balls. A thrill of sexual electricity jolted him. He looked at her; her tongue moved slowly over her lips. He had no idea if she was horny or just cock-teasing him.

". . . Pam really impressed me with her dedication . . ."

Megan was now freely trampling Tom's penis, kneading it with her foot like she wanted him to ejaculate in his trousers.

Keeping his face straight, Tom reached under the table with his left hand and slapped her foot away. Megan laughed quietly. The foot instantly returned to Tom's crotch. He grabbed it and wrestled it back down, but Megan slipped his grasp and penetrated Rose with her big toe. As the toe slid in, Tom shuddered with sensation that froze him. Taking quick advantage of his shock, Megan foot-maneuvered Tom's left hand so it was wedged vagina-outward in his crotch. She then toe-fucked Rose—pushing her toe in deep, withdrawing it, pushing it in again—with a penis-smooth stroking motion.

Tom gaped at Megan. His eyes pleaded with hers to release him. He dreaded that Rose would start moaning.

Megan smirked back, daring him to make a scene. She kept the in-out movement going for a while, simultaneously levering his hand back and forth over his cock. Tom tried to focus on what King Eric was saying. It was a waste of time. Sensation kept building in his hand and penis. Rose began lubricating.

"Please," he mouthed at Megan. She turned her face away from him.

Tom felt Rose twitch, like a mouth coughing.

I'm fucked, he thought. *Brooke will love this.*

He forced his mind off the unwanted pleasure Megan was giving him. He nudged Brooke. "What's with his majesty?"

She tore her gaze from contemplating Harding and shrugged. "I'm not really listening." She listened a bit. "Kid's a politician. He's using the opportunity of Pam's grief to impress on the rest of us to do a better job. Or maybe he wants more fireworks." She tapped Tom's arm. "Hold on, I think he's finished."

It seemed to Tom that Rose's yelling to be fucked was only a few toe-strokes away. To forestall this, he turned and concentrated hard on King Eric.

King Eric smiled at Pam. ". . . Because of this, I hereby appoint my secretary Pam as my wife and Boston's new queen."

All present froze in surprise.

In her shock, Megan's foot stopped probing Rose. Tom quickly freed his hand from the vise of foot and crotch. He pushed his chair back so Megan couldn't start again.

"What did you say, your Majesty?" Pam finally managed to get out.

King Eric smiled benevolently. "You're my new wife. The people of Boston need a queen like you."

Pam stared helplessly at the others seated around the table.

"It is a great honor," Megan said. "You've no choice but to accept."

"But there's no sex," Pam said in horror.

"Well I'm a little boy," King Eric said. "Can't have erections yet. However, I'm magnanimous—you can apply for an adultery license. Only that idiot there . . ." he cast a black look at Tom, ". . . is off limits." He smiled at Pam again. "Now come over, my darling. Join me on the throne and let's rule Boston together."

Confused or not, Pam was nothing if not politically astute. She quickly got up and made her way over to King Eric.

He dabbed her once on each shoulder with the spit-slick royal lollipop and that was it.

There wasn't sufficient space on his throne for two people, so Pam ended up carrying him on her lap, his head pillowed on her porn-star-sized breasts.

"Okay," King Eric said, clapping his hands. "Now down to business."

Chapter 39

The rest of the morning was taken up in discussion with Boston University's Dean of Biophysical Research: Dr. Karl Oppenheimer, a short plump elderly man with thick glasses and disorganized white hair like he'd been electrocuted.

Tom winced on seeing the doctor. No doubt about it—Dr. Oppenheimer was the man in his 'gun vision,' whom he'd been backing away from the door with a shotgun in his face, towards an old woman in the background.

The doctor regarded Tom with hostility, confirming their unpleasant association with each other. Try as he might, Tom could find no inkling in his mind of what linked them together.

***

Dr. Oppenheimer explained why they couldn't reach Bizarro by aircraft.

"The substance forming the Overhead cuts off electrical function. Simple as that. Any plane or helicopter flown up there will crash. We've tried every sort of shielding imaginable, all sorts of vessels, to no avail. None that we ever sent up to Bizarro came back."

"How about balloons?" Tom asked.

"We sent three up; none returned either." He shook his head. "The nature of the place again: too fairytale for science. The crosswinds over Bizarro are simply too fickle for a balloon landing. I suspect those we sent up splattered like bugs into the mountainsides. Now, I believe the unreliable winds result from random buildup of massive static electrical—"

"So we can't *fly* up," King Eric interrupted, fearing a lengthy scientific exposition. He looked at Tom in puzzlement. "How'd *you* transport the loot up there then?"

"Maybe he gave himself head," Megan said. "Then floated away on orgasmic clouds of bliss."

"I very much doubt that," the little monarch retorted testily. He licked his lollipop moodily, kept staring questioningly at Tom.

"He likely climbed," Dr. Oppenheimer said in Tom's stead. "Which is what the expedition will have to do. Now please pay attention, everyone."

He unfurled a map of Boston against the wall.

"First, some background. You must all be aware by now that Bizarro isn't just a northeastern phenomenon. The Overhead extends far and wide across America, extremely high concentrations have been reported in West Virginia and Portland, Ore—"

"How far?" Tom asked.

Dr. Oppenheimer looked piqued by the question. "From my last info, it's everywhere now."

"Didn't look like it on my arrival. Everywhere was open sky."

"Down in South End," Brooke explained. "Bottom of Washington Street."

The doctor nodded. "No one lives out there in the suburbs. Too dangerous. In such places, Bizarro thins out to little walkways across the sky, routes of say, five meters width. You'll see them floating overhead, running for hundreds of miles. Over population centers, however, Bizarro thickens, almost like it can sense humanity—"

"That's creepy," Pam said with a shudder, "Like it's watching us."

Oppenheimer polished his glasses. "It isn't Big Brother, if that's what you mean. Nor is it any kind of malignant intelligence. I suspect it's just the increased carbon dioxide emissions from humans that attract it to form clumps. Like a plant seeking food."

He looked pointedly at Tom, his hostility only known to them both. "Does this answer your question?"

Tom nodded.

"Okay then. Now back to the matter at hand. Here in Boston, Bizarro starts at one hundred and fifty meters overhead. We're lucky. In Montana and Wyoming, it's only two meters above the ground. In Arizona, New Mexico, and Techxas, *it is* the ground."

"Do they have eaters there?" King Eric asked.

"Unfortunately yes, your Majesty. An excess of them. Towns like Buffalo and San Antonio for instance, are wholly eater territory, with the cannibals waging bloody genocidal war on humans. It's horrible."

King Eric's young face turned pale. He gulped and shuddered, began licking his lollipop furiously. Pam held him tight, rocked him to comfort him. "Please go on, Doc," she said.

"Now, back to Boston. Here, Bizarro is varying thicknesses. Seventeen of our skyscrapers penetrate it, only four exit it. Ironically, our tallest skyscraper, the John Hancock building, doesn't exit Bizarro—its upper floors are stuck inside a mountain somewhere up there."

"Which building do we climb then?" Brooke asked.

Oppenheimer tapped a point on the map.

"This here is the One Boston Place. It's one of the four skyscrapers that go all the way through Bizarro."

"One Boston Place? That's just behind City Hall. Outside, round the corner," Brooke said.

Oppenheimer nodded. "One and the same."

He unfurled another map over the first, tacked it down and tapped a red circle on it. "From satellite photos, here's the One Boston Place's roof exiting Bizarro's topside. It exits into a depression. Keep that in mind— the ground under your feet won't be as solid as you think."

"I've been up there," Harding said. "We sealed it off because of eaters."

"We'll temporarily unseal it again to let you through," Dr. Oppenheimer said. "If you find the gold up there, we'll ferry it back down."

He glared at Tom. "A lot of nonsense you're putting everyone through."

"Accept my sincere apologies," Tom replied drily. "I want this over and done with more than you do."

Brooke studied the new map. Even flattened in two dimensions, the Overhead looked odd. A landmark caught her eye. "What's that large white circle down in the left corner, with the brown dot in the middle?"

"This?"

She nodded.

"We call it White Lake. A body of liquid, but it's not water."

Brooke tensed. Tom did too. *Rose said I left the gold at White Lake.*

He kept his face calm. "I vaguely remember the lake; but not relating to money."

Dr. Oppenheimer nodded. "Either way, it's a good landmark to look for."

Tom pointed. "Is this a recent picture?"

The doctor shook his head. "Regretfully not. They're nine months old—the last available from before all the US's satellites went offline." He polished his glasses again, then scratched his nose, looking around the throne room at one and all in turn. "Now, since you'll be searching Bizarro, on to something important you each need to bear in mind at all times."

King Eric nodded. "What's that, Doc?"

Dr. Oppenheimer didn't immediately reply. First, he unscrolled another map and tacked it over the first. That done, he bowed to King Eric,

144

then pointed outside at the floating mass, its earth tentacles writhing in the morning air like octopus legs. "It's important for them to understand, your Majesty, that Bizarro—the Overhead—is not a totally stable construct."

"How do you mean?" Pam asked.

Dr. Oppenheimer pointed to the new map. "Do you notice anything different from the previous one?"

They all stared at it. "The lake's moved," Brooke said finally. "It's more central now."

"And several of the landmarks are in different places," Lt. Harding added.

"When was this photograph taken?" Brooke asked.

Dr. Oppenheimer smiled. "Three weeks before the other." He folded the map up so they saw the one below it for a moment, then dropped it again. "There are several other differences . . ."

His audience were quiet while he explained how Bizarro was constantly changing, being redesigned seemingly on a whim. ". . . What I'm trying to impress on you all is this—we've no idea what's waiting up there now."

"Except lots of vavs," Megan said. "It's bad enough them slithering down Bizarro's tentacles to us, without us going to visit them."

The doctor nodded. "And a whole lot of creatures you've never dreamed could exist. And variations on those you already dislike—"

"In short, we're watching for danger at every turn," Harding said.

"On the Overhead, we'll need eyes in the back of our heads," Tom said.

Dr. Oppenheimer nodded, his frown grim. "I couldn't put it better myself. He pointed out the window again. "About the only thing you've no need to worry about up there are eaters."

"That's a relief," King Eric said. "In that case I'll be glad to go on this expedition myself." He licked his lollipop in delight. "Just kidding," he added after a while; seeing all eyes were staring reprovingly at him.

Chapter 40

"Tell me about Bizarro," Tom said.

"Little to tell," Brooke replied without looking back. She was staring out of Tom's window, naked, her heavy ass pointing at him. Statuesque in the night light like a Greek idol come to life.

Tom walked over and grabbed her buttocks. "Tell me anyway."

She leaned back and kissed him. "There's a lot to tell, I'll just sound blasé 'cos we're all used to it now."

He reached up and caressed her breasts, rubbed his penis in the crack of her buttocks.

She grinned as she felt him harden. "If you really want to know, you'll have to stop that now."

"Your ass is mugging me," he said. "I'm the victim here."

She giggled, folded her hands over his on her breasts. "Just don't put it inside . . . yet." She nodded up at Bizarro. "We originally thought it was climate change, caused by industrial pollution. One morning there were patches of muddy air overhead, like dirty clouds. By evening the brown clouds had begun forming a single mass, by next morning it was complete."

"That fast?"

She nodded. "It wasn't this thick, but it covered the entire city. And it had already shut down all communications. Despite what Oppenheimer says, I think Bizarro has some intelligence. It's always struck me that knocking down communications was the most effective way to stop any coordinated attempt to destroy it."

"I'm not sure what you could do."

"Burn it. Back then it seemed a feasible plan to get the phones working again. But then we discovered our aircraft wouldn't work. After several choppers dropped straight out of the sky, we gave up on that idea." She scowled. "And by then we discovered we had a bigger problem, anyway."

"You mean the eaters?"

She nodded.

Tom nodded in sympathy. Her description of events was similar to that in his own home dimension, where the dragons and dinosaurs had appeared overnight and life had subsequently altered irreversibly.

Brooke tensed against him. "You know how it happens in all those zombie movies? Where the infection just spreads and spreads? This was nothing like that. Everybody who caught the Bizarro virus infection transformed at the same time."

"The same time?"

"Uh huh. They all caught a fever and turned yellow. By the next day they were eaters. Emergency services first thought they had liver disease 'cos of how jaundiced they looked, but then they all lost their hair too, and their eyes went transparent like they'd been bleached. Their teeth . . ." She caught her voice in a sob. "Do I have to keep telling you this?"

He nuzzled her hair, pushed his penis deep down her ass-cleft, felt its topside slicked from her vagina. "You can stop if it's getting to you."

"It is getting to me. I saw friends and family get eaten by other friends and family. Even that wasn't like the movies . . ."

Tom turned her to face him. "I'm sorry I asked. You don't have to say any more."

She looked at him with tear-filled eyes. "Oh, but I want to, Tom. I need to." She laughed. "My father ate my mother and younger brother. I got home to find him making a stew of them while singing Jimmy Buffet's *Cheeseburger in Paradise*—I'll hate that song till the day I die now. But that wasn't the worst thing. You know what the worst thing was?"

Tom said nothing. Brooke's tears were flowing freely now.

She jabbed his chest with a finger while talking. "The worst fucking thing was, that when I shot him—shot my father who was cooking his family for dinner—he was confused. He didn't understand what he'd done wrong."

Tom remembered the eater couple who'd ambushed he and Brooke two days ago, how they'd sounded convinced about the rightness of their actions. That had been the most creepy part of the encounter.

Brooke wiped her eyes and laughed bitterly. "Get it? That's the biggest mindfuck with the Bizarro virus: in addition to transforming human bodies to that hideous hairless mustard yellow, it also alters the victim's minds. Now they don't see anything wrong with eating people. They think all immune, untransformed humans are food animals."

"That's absurd."

She nodded, composed again. "Yes it is, but you saw that couple who ambushed us, right?" She laughed out loud. "Oppenheimer's unsure if the eaters have evolved or devolved, top of the food chain or lower down."

"How can cannibalism be the peak of evolution?"

She shrugged. "Easy enough. If the cannibal is as smart as you, speaks English, and eats you without ethical compunctions . . . Oh fuck this

147

conversation." She turned her back to him, leaned out of the window. "Put your cock inside me. I really need it now."

Tom obliged. They did it like that, leaning out of the window, while the hot night winds caressed their straining forms.

Brooke winced and grunted as they screwed, like she was in intense pain. Tom understood that she was purging herself of her demons. He held her hips and pumped her hard, kneading her ass like it was dough. She ground back against him, rolling her heavy buttocks like she was a sea and they its waves.

The heat and tomorrow's threat of the unknown up on the Overhead intensified the experience. Both their orgasms were animal releases, silent except for explosive gasps of air announcing their conquest of each other.

Afterwards, with his semen dribbling down her legs, she leaned over her shoulder to kiss him. "Where the heck have you been all my life?"

He kissed her back, ran fingers through her hair, black liquid locks that seemed part of the night.

"Let's go to sleep," he said. "Long day tomorrow."

"Not till I finish my explanation about the eaters."

He screwed up his face. "Forget it; it upsets you."

She grinned. "It's okay. I'm fine now. Fuck me again if I start crying."

They sat on the bed. "I'm all ears."

"Coming down to race? With the eater virus, the end product's the same—a yellow person. Someone called the virus the 'melaneater' 'cos it doesn't matter how much melanin you've got, if you're white or black, you'll 'fade to yellow' either way."

"That's fucked up."

She nodded emphatically. "Extremely. Only way you can tell a previously black eater from a white one is by redundant facial characteristics . . . occasionally. Shape of nose . . . lips, and even that's unreliable. But the 'melaneater' name's wrong anyway."

"How so?"

"The color change occurs all through eaters—their flesh and organs are totally yellow." She scowled. "Yellow meat? It's sick biology. Their bones are cookie-soft, but reinforced with a web of thin aluminum threads, their blood's pink . . . totally crazy."

Tom nodded. He could hear both weariness and a return of her previous depression in her voice. "I think you've enlightened me enough for tonight," he said, patting her thigh. "Okay, Chief, run along to bed now."

She looked at him slyly. "You're getting rid of me?"

"Actually yes. If you don't leave this moment, I'll end up screwing you again, and then we'll both be useless in the morning."

She laughed. "What a sweet way to kick a woman out." She winked. "I actually could go one more time."

He shook his head.

She giggled with amusement. "C'mon. One for the road?"

He laughed and reached out his hands to her. "Oh, come on. You're so hot my dick's hard again anyway. I'd have to jerk off if you left now."

Brooke grinned at his erection. "On second thoughts, I think I'll be going now."

She stood up quickly and slipped her sandals on.

He stared at her. "You're actually leaving?"

She giggled. "You recently wanted me to."

Tom leapt up to grab her, but she'd already picked up her robe and fled the room.

He stood staring at his erection, hearing her laughter trail back down the corridor.

"Just go down," he told his penis. "I am not giving her the satisfaction of being right tonight."

Part 2: Bizarro

Chapter 41

They travelled to Bizarro by elevator.

Eight made the trip up. Tom, Brooke, Megan, and Harding. Then four officers handpicked by Harding for their toughness: Sergeants Lana Perkins and the redheaded Anne Smith, and two male cops, Detectives Tony Jones and Leo Lucas.

Conspicuous by her absence was Kim Fields. BPD's best shooter had been dispatched—in Harding's stead—to flush out the cell of eaters Rose had revealed were infiltrating the city via the basement of an apartment building on Kneeland Street in Chinatown.

Harding was along because he was the force's top survival expert.

Both he and Tony Jones were wearing metal-detector bracelets.

"Likely a waste of time since Bizarro messes up electrical signals," Dr. Oppenheimer had explained. "But they might work briefly at some point, and then you'll have an idea of the right direction to search."

***

Rose was currently covered in a black cop mitt Brooke had given Tom. Hidden like this, it was easy to forget he had a vagina in his hand.

"How did your hand feel last night?" Brooke whispered to Tom in the elevator. "Sweet like me?"

"You wish." Tom had had to masturbate in the end. Images of Brooke's massive rear endowment had kept floating before his eyes. Each time he'd tried to count sheep he'd wound up counting asses instead.

***

The One Boston Place's roof access door was comprised of three sheets of metal sandwiching two slabs of concrete. Similar reinforcement had been afforded the 'interior' walls of all seventeen skyscrapers that penetrated Bizarro.

The foot-thick door slid aside on rollers.

"This is one thick fucking door," Brooke said.

The black cop rolling back the door laughed. "L'il King Eric got enough trouble sleeping with eaters about, Chief. Kid don't want no additional beasties slipping down from Bizarro and turning up in his dreams."

The door opened fully. The party moved out. The door wheeled shut behind them, an impervious buttress against the infiltration of definite weirdness into almost-normalcy.

They looked around.

"You've got to be shitting me!" Anne Smith said.

Tom heartily agreed with her. His attention was riveted on the unlikely vision facing them.

They'd exited the skyscraper into a street. A paved aisle through red-brick houses with flowers growing out of their walls and roofs. Between the houses grew HUGE flowers—massive carnations, tulips, dandelions, and roses that draped over the street like street lamps.

Up ahead and farther off—visible over rooftops—were other even weirder architectural constructs. Animal-shaped buildings—massive glassy dogs and cats with levels of arched windows studded all over them. Behind those rose mountains, the size of which seemed impossible considering that they were on a floating mass of earth suspended over a city.

"Remember what Oppenheimer said," Brooke reminded everyone. "Nothing up here is what it seems. Behind any of these doors might be an ambush by something impossible."

Tom said nothing. *I can now see how this place—Bizarro—must have seemed the perfect location to hide all that gold.*

He considered the buildings facing them, the flowers growing out of the walls—monster luxuriant blooms filling the air with exotic perfumes.

Overhead the clouds were fluffy white, the sky blue.

"It doesn't even look like part of Boston," Detective Jones said. His face was confused. The other three escort cops looked even more troubled than he did.

"Bizarro isn't part of Boston," Brooke said sharply. "It's a solidified dream." She was uneasy. This place—the sights, the smells . . . everything—unsettled her cop calm.

Everyone looked left and right. Each direction flooded their minds with a collage of wondrous sights.

Brooke tugged Tom's arm. He turned to her.

"Look behind you. Look up."

He did. His breath froze in his throat. What should have been a simple concrete rooftop hut was here the lowest floor of a four-story building.

His eyes slowly rose up the building's red walls.

154

The others had also turned now. "What on earth are those things?" Megan asked.

They studied what she was pointing at. Six human-sized creatures sat on a ledge two floors up, peering down at them from between a profusion of huge orchids.

"They look like eight-legged lizards," Brooke said.

"With monkey faces," Tom added.

The lizard-monkeys had scaly brown skin, and blonde manes ringing their faces. One yawned, revealing pointy teeth.

Harding flipped off his pistol's safety. "Meet a potential foe." The other cops did the same.

The lizard-monkeys however showed no aversion/threat to the humans. One after the other, they lost interest in the party below and began wildly copulating with each other. The males had short red penises, the females, white squirty vaginas. Both sexes grunted like pigs.

Tom returned his attention to down around him.

He looked pointedly at Brooke. "Can I have a gun now? Just in case at some point we have to fight our way through this oddity."

Harding laughed mirthlessly. "A gun? You should be glad we aren't dragging you along in handcuffs."

Brooke shook her head at Tom, flinging her black hair around. "No gun for you. You're not murdering us in our sleep."

Megan laughed. "I agree with Brooke. You're such a horrid shot, Tom, you'd likely kill us without ever meaning to."

Tom winced at her reference to Joe Bradley's death.

He pointed up at the rutting lizard monkeys. "Their bites may be poisonous. We need to avoid getting bitten."

Megan nodded. "Obvious, but still true."

Brooke scowled. "Keep your fucking opinion to yourself, Pussypalm. This shit's all your fault to start with."

It was an act, to prevent any suspicion of their relationship. She adjusted her pack on her shoulders, looked coldly at the others. "Let's get out of here. I hate this Bizarro place already."

Not waiting, she set off down the flowered-bordered avenue ahead.

155

Chapter 42

They hurried after Brooke. Floral perfume assaulted them from all sides. The smell was thick, cloying, sucking oxygen from their lungs.

"Hey! Wait up!"

Brooke didn't hear. She was a block ahead of them and plodding grimly away, her form slightly distorted by the thickened air.

"This smell is choking me," Harding growled. "It's like I'm swimming in soup."

"Best we run then," Megan suggested, "before it asphyxiates us totally."

"No," Tom disagreed. "Running make you breathe faster, which makes things worse."

The others realized he was right. Tony and Leo, the male officers, spat simultaneously in disgust. Lana angrily stabbed a monster dandelion petal. The petal flinched back like a human would. Anne said nothing; her eyes flickered left-to-right as she walked.

"I can't shake the feeling we're walking into a trap," Harding said. He gestured to the red-brick bungalows on either side of them, to the flowers. "But where? There's no one here."

Except for the lizard-monkeys, Megan thought, sighting several having sex on a slatted yellow roof. *And they're more interested in fucking than attacking us. Still something isn't right—I feel it too.*

Tom was studying the huge blooms they were passing. Their stamens were transparent as if made of glass. Faint hints of color reminded him of LEDs.

"What's with the Chief?" Anne asked suddenly. "She looks spooked."

They all looked, saw what she meant. Up ahead, Brooke had stopped walking. She was looking around her, 'touching' the air in front of her, seemingly perplexed by something. As they neared her, she called something out to them. A question of some sort.

"We can't hear you," Megan said. "Speak louder."

"Why *can't* we hear her?" Tom asked worriedly. "She's shouting."

"Chief's gesturing us to go back," Leo said.

"I think he's right."

"Shut up, Pussypalm. Keep walking, I don't see any danger."

Next thing they walked into an 'absence of sound.'

156

Stepping out of the silence, they found themselves both face to face with Brooke and in the middle of a forest clearing.

They looked behind them. The street was totally disappeared—there were trees everywhere now. Tall thick gnarled trunks, strewn with dangling creepers beneath lush foliage from which came animal noises.

Oddest of all were the monster pale mushrooms obscuring the bases of the northward mountains. One of said mountains had a sheer eastern face, perfectly geometrical and with indents, as if that side of it was an artificial construct.

I think we just found out where the John Hancock Building ends, Tom thought.

Harding gawked. "What the . . . ?"

"This is what I was trying to warn you meatheads about," Brooke said. She tapped a solid patch of air. "It's one way—we can't get back through to the street."

Megan smiled. "Welcome to the jungle then." She took a deep breath. "At least the air's normal again. But *where are* we?"

"Will someone explain to me what the hell just happened?" Harding growled.

"We've just stepped through a matter transmission system," Tom said. "It's sent us across Bizarro." He pointed. "Look! The mountains are closer now; and check out back over those trees—there's the glass cat and dog houses."

The others checked out what Tom was saying. They made out their erstwhile point of entrance to the Overhead in the far distance.

"One more thing," Tom said. "This 'system' shifted us through time as well. It's now evening, hopefully of the same day."

"Huh?" But it was true, the sun, which had been east of them five minutes ago, was now far to the west.

Tom shrugged. "I think it calculates temporal differences; how long it would normally take us to walk over here, and—"

"Shut the fuck up, Pussypalm!" Brooke snapped. "This shit is confusing enough without you yapping away like Oppenheimer!"

Everyone looked at her. "What now, Chief?" Harding asked.

She scowled. "Rethink plan, of course. We've just lost seven fucking hours to a footstep. We need to find a vantage point and look around. I was heading for one of those cat houses—tallest things in sight—to see if we could locate White Lake. That's fucked now."

Tom pointed to the nearest mountain, a brown mass that looked disturbingly like a chocolate cake, the snow on its peaks like icing. "How about climbing that instead? The view should be unparalleled."

Harding looked coldly at Tom. "I thought the Chief just told you to keep your shithead opinions to yourself."

"I'm only trying to—"

"You know, Pussypalm," Brooke interrupted, her voice cold, "the sooner you regain your memory, the better. I hate the thought of tramping all over Bizarro without even a working metal detector, overturning every damn rock just 'cos an asshole like you . . ."

Brooke was proud of her irritated performance. "No way must they get to know we're lovers," she'd told Tom before they'd left. "With Harding and his goons along, that's suicidal for us both."

She'd packed her mertopus tentacle to keep her vagina happy.

Harding smirked. "Hey, Chief. How 'bout I have the guys and girls work Pussypalm over? Might jog his memory."

Brooke scrunched up her face in mock-thought. *Trust Harding to seize on an opportunity for violence. I'll be damned if I let his apes get their hands on Tom. Now, how the hell do I get out of this?* "Hmmm," she grunted after a 'see what I mean?' sideways glance at Tom. "That's not such a bad idea, Lieutenant. The—"

"Not right now," Megan interrupted, "Physical violence drains strength, both his and ours. Pain is always best utilized where it will be most productive."

The policepersons sniggered. Harding laughed. "I love the way you talk, Ms. Fox. Okay, we'll wait till you and the Chief think we can give the bastard a constructive beating."

"You and I have a lot to discuss, Lieutenant," Megan replied, her eyes appraising. "Maybe during a relaxation break."

"Sure thing, Ms. Fox."

Brooke scowled. "As much as I hate to agree with Tom, I think the asshole's right. Climbing the mountain seems our best option."

Harding nodded. "Okay, Chief." He turned to his unit and pointed toward the foot of the mountain. This was visible through an aisle bounded on the left by thirty-foot palms, on the right by an intermingling of oaks, birches, and equally massive mushrooms.

"Anne and Leo, you two take point. Lana, Tony, you guys bring up the rear. Keep your eyes peeled for—"

Harding's voice froze in his throat. A long thick tentacle had whipped out from the palms towards them. Its end wrapped twice around Leo's

158

neck. Next, its tip, a black hook, dug deep into Leo's throat, embedding itself so deep into his flesh it was invisible. Next moment, the cop was yanked off his feet and through the air, toward the palms.

The palms began moving.

"Vavs!" Harding yelled.

"Shit! Take cover!" Brooke yelled.

Everyone rushed for what shelter they could find.

Brooke's admonition hadn't come quickly enough though. Another meat tentacle snared Lana. The policewoman gargled and bled from the hole in her neck. Like Leo, she too was jerked up through the air towards the palms.

Chapter 43

Tom and Brooke hit the dirt behind a giant mushroom.

Pain jarred Rose. Tom was glad he was wearing a glove, else the hand-vagina would be packed with sand now.

He checked how concealed they were. Profuse foliage and brush hid them from side view.

He peeked out. "Vavs?"

"Over there."

Across from them, a large number of the palms now revealed themselves to be giant women like the one Tom had seen outside City Hall.

All were at least twenty feet tall, with trunk-legs half that length, woven-creeper arms and massive breasts. Brown and green mottled bodies. Fingers and toes that were part leafy-branch, part tentacle. Spread palm-frond hair curled like hairdos.

All had the faces of early 20th Century Hollywood superstar actresses—Marlene Dietrich, Lana Turner, Grace Kelly, Zsa Zsa Gabor, Jean Harlow, Fray Wray, Rita Hayworth, Ingrid Bergman, Elizabeth Taylor, and others. The faces were repeated. Tom made out four 'Dietrich' vavs, two 'Kellys,' and three 'Monroes.'

Tentacles wrapped tight around their necks, Leo and Lana hung penis-limp from the crotches of two of the foremost plant women. Both cops struggled weakly to free themselves. They jerked, clearly dying. The vavs that had them captive were both giggling soundlessly like they were stoned. The other plant women watched them jealously, then looked around, searching for Tom and his companions. Each vav gripped a slick pink/purple tentacle in her hand, the black tip hook dangling with menace. Occasionally they swung the tentacles, which seemed to come from between their legs.

It made no sense to Tom. He looked at Brooke. "What is going on?"

"Sssshhh," she replied. "We can't take them on."

"What are you talking about?" A few feet away, Tom saw Harding, Anne, and Tony crawling silently deeper into the underbrush beneath the oaks. Further on, Megan was also distancing herself from the giant women.

Brooke and Tom were the only ones stationary, but the giant mushroom shielded them so completely they might as well not have been there.

The other vavs were meanwhile peering into the maze of oaks and pines, looking for the dying cops' companions.

The searching giantesses made no conversation among themselves. Their mouths opened and shut in silence.

"Can't they talk?" Tom asked Brooke."

She shook her head. "They're telepaths."

"They can't hear our thoughts, can they?"

Another head shake. "They can however sense our minds."

"What's the difference?"

"Because they share faces, vavs identify each other by their different brain wave patterns. Same thing with humans—they read our minds rather than our faces to differentiate between us. But because humans aren't telepathic, we can't communicate across the species divide. And they don't understand any human language; not even sign language or symbols."

Tom quickly mused on that. "And now? Why the hell are they attacking us?"

"The vavs are vampires," Brooke explained. "They feed on human blood—through their vaginas. That's where those tentacles comes from—their cunts. They're rooted in their wombs like placentas, coiled up inside them like gestating infants, exiting their sex when needed. Those two who've snared Lana and Leo are now draining all the blood from their bodies—the tentacles are hollow tubes, and lots more efficient than a pump. The hooks at their tips—meat hooks—are barbed; once one's embedded in your neck, you're fucked six million ways—it ain't coming out without surgery."

Tom gulped. The vav draining Leo—a 'Joan Crawford'—suddenly jerked like she was cumming. She reached down and jerked her meat hook from the dangling man's neck, an action that practically ripped his head off. There was no blood,—

Brooke winced. "Like I said, they're demonically effective."

—Leo's neck was as blanched as meat taken from a fridge. The vav's cunt-tentacle unwrapped itself from around his neck. His body flopped useless to the ground. The vav stretched. Her tentacle slowly reeled up out of sight into her vagina, its meat hook tucking away neatly between her buttocks.

"Seen enough?" Brooke asked.

Tom nodded. "More than I want to." Lana's drained corpse joined Leo's on the ground. Like his, her neck was ripped open all the way back to the spine.

"Time we get the hell out of . . . yikes!"

Brooke ducked just in time.

The vavs had uncovered their hiding place. A vav's meat hook ripped a deep gash through the mushroom concealing them. Brooke rolled over and looked up. A 'Dietrich' vav stared intently at her. The vampire vagina woman's beautiful face was flushed like she was aroused. She jerked her meat hook back out of the mushroom, tearing the fungus' cap completely off.

No shit! Tom thought as the dripping tentacle flashed back over their heads, simultaneously reeling back into the vav's cunt.

Then another vav flung her meat hook at *him,* and he was rolling, dodging her murderous vaginal tentacle.

Unconsciously, he rolled out of the mushroom cover into the passage dividing the palms and mushrooms. He bumped to a halt against Leo's corpse.

He stared a moment into the man's throttled bloodless face. Then he grabbed Leo's pistol out of his belt.

Not now! he thought desperately, as a vision dropped like a curtain over his current reality . . .

***

A wasted-looking junkie woman by a street corner somewhere. Watching from inside himself, Tom understood that her name was Kiki, and that she'd stolen money from Pablo Rodriguez, the arms dealer. Then she'd fled from Techxas to Boston.

Tom and his brunette girlfriend stood in shadow, fifty meters from Kiki, watching her twitch on the comedown from her last fix.

"Well, there she is," Tom said with relief. "Time to kill her, get Pablo off my fucking back."

The brunette kissed Tom, then shook her head. "Pablo's a greasy slob, no class whatever. Disfigurement's better in a case like this. A walking notice to others to not fuck with him. Just shoot her nose off."

Tom considered. "You know you're a sociopath, right?"

She grinned back sweetly. "If you shoot her nose off, I'll let you piss up mine."

He was taken aback. "Piss up your nose? Why the hell would I want to do that?"

"Dunno. You ever done it before?"

"Hell no!"

"Me neither. It'll be a new experience for both of us then."

Tom mulled on that a moment. Then in a fluid motion, he fired twice at Kiki.

Kiki's nose seemed to leap off her face.

Tom turned to the brunette. "That okay?"

"Wow!" She was staring wide eyed at Kiki, who was trying to work out what had just happened, why air now seemed to be directly entering her head.

Then the noseless woman began shrieking like an air-raid siren.

* * *

The vision faded. Tom gasped with nausea. *This guy's a total nutcase, and his girlfriend's even worse!*

He remembered where he was. Ducking airborne meat hooks, he dived back to Brooke's side. She lay on her back in a hollow, panting hard, watching tentacles rip the mushroom to shreds.

They quickly retreated between a clump of mushrooms and trees. It wasn't perfect protection—there was space to their left and right, but the vavs would only be able to attack one at a time.

Brooke hissed angrily. "Vavs aim for the neck. They'll wait till they can see us clearly before attacking."

"We're lucky—they're not armed with swords."

"They don't need swords; those meat hooks are weapon enough. They weren't expecting us, are probably here for some fertility ritual."

"We'll take them out one at a time," Tom said confidently. He'd felt it immediately he picked up Leo's pistol—that other hand inside his, taking over control.

Brooke shook her head. Around them was the loud rustle of the frustrated plant women. "Trust me, darling, it's not that easy. We need to get our butts away from here so fast it'll feel like we're leaving them behind."

A meat hook slung into the narrow alley at them, its cunt-tether taut. It missed. Tom let off several shots at its vegetable owner.

His aim was perfect as US bombs hitting terrorist camps. The bullets, fired in a down-to-up sequence, severed the vav's right arm at the shoulder. The arm flopped off her body, crashed to the ground. Green sap seeped from the wound.

"That's a waste of ammo," Brooke said.

The green giantess scowled at Tom, monster irritation in movie-star perfection. Then she picked up her right arm—the fist of which still held her tentacle—in her left. She placed the wounded shoulder joint back together.

Tom's eyes widened as brown roots grew out from both arm and shoulder, linking them firmly together again. *The lady is self-sealing? Oops.*

In twenty seconds flat, the vav's wound was healed. Her shoulder looked repaired with surgical sutures. She reeled in her meat hook, its wet length slurping back up into her vagina. She peered intently at Tom, watching for a clear shot at his neck.

Brooke tapped him on the shoulder. "See what I mean? I reckon there's twenty of those plant bitches out there—only way to kill them is to burn them down like trees. Let's haul ass out of here before they surround us. Hopefully Harding and the others will be able to cover us."

Tom nodded.

Brooke leapt to her feet. "Go!" Firing at random, Tom hard on her heels, she charged out of concealment.

Taken aback by the suddenness of their charge, the vav who'd been watching Tom leapt out of their way. The other plant giantesses hadn't even seen them coming. Before they recovered enough to attack, Brooke and Tom had turned right, down an aisle between the mushrooms, and were running hell bent for leather.

Chapter 44

"This way," Brooke gasped, jerking Tom left at the first side-aisle they reached. Neither looked back to see if the vavs were giving chase. They ran toward the mountain, parallel to the route they'd been on, the huge fungus's caps hiding them totally from view. The mushrooms they passed grew gradually bigger and bigger to story-building sized.

They stopped, gasping, and looked back. The vavs were searching for them in the opposite direction. The loud noise of the giantess's ripping apart the mushroom field carried to the fugitives.

"Thank God," Tom wheezed.

"Yeah," Brooke agreed. She looked around frowning. "Now we need to link up with Harding and Megan. They'll have headed for the—"

At that moment, Harding and Megan stepped around the side of the mushroom. Then Tony and Anne. All held guns at the ready, their faces taut except for Megan, who was pokerfaced.

Harding's eyes widened in surprise. "Chief?"

"We were just coming back to look for you two," Megan said. "We first thought you were dead. but the vavs clearly don't think so—it had to be you they're searching for."

Brooke nodded. She pushed her hair back from her eyes and adjusted her pack. She jerked her thumb back at the angry vavs. "We'd better get lost before they realize they're beating around the wrong bush."

Harding saw the gun in Tom's hand. He swung his pistol to cover Tom. "Hand the weapon over, Pussypalm."

Brooke shook her head. "Let him hold on to it. The asshole's learnt his lesson. He knows we need to stick together to survive here."

Harding was conflicted. He stepped close, whispered, "Chief, we can't trust this guy, you know that."

"Unfortunately, we need to," she whispered back. "He's remembered how to shoot again, and you remember how good he was. Way better than Kim Fields. We need that in a tight scrape."

Harding winced. "Chief, that's what's worrying me. Pussypalm once shot the nose off a hooker at fifty yards. I handled the case. In addition to having no nose, the woman also had a 'PP' carved into her cheek. She said his girlfriend did it."

"Also, remember too when he stole the gold? We wondered why John Wu agreed to provide those military shipping trucks for him and never alerted us that his wife had been kidnapped. That was until Betty Wu showed us her breasts. Pussypalm had shot both her nipples off. Also from a distance."

"I never heard that," Brooke said.

"You were lower rank. Wu helped fund King Eric's election campaign. King asked us to keep it quiet, no need to embarrass the lady."

Broke stole a glance at Tom. *He shot her nipples off?* She quivered with revulsion at the horrid image. *Is this the man I have feelings for?*

She realized Harding was right. Outside of her personal bias, there was no reason to let Tom remain armed. She turned to him.

"Hand it over," she said.

Tony and Anne, who'd been looking ready to revolt, lowered their guns when Tom handed Leo's pistol over to Harding without protest. The pair nodded to each other, walked off in opposite directions through the mushroom field to watch for trouble.

Brooke pointed over at the vavs, now far in the distance. "Those girls don't look about to give up looking for us."

Megan followed her finger. "It's their nature. They're persistent as male dogs following a bitch in heat." She pointed up. "The sun will set soon. An unfamiliar mountain can prove very inhospitable at night."

They pondered this.

"We need to camp somewhere. These mushrooms stretch forever, and the longer we remain out here—"

"Hey, Chief! Come look at this!" It was Tony, rushing back from patrolling the mushrooms, his eyes wide with excitement. The cop wolf-whistled to summon Anne back, then led them to the next mushroom.

"It's a *house*, Chief," he said, pointing to the door in the fungus. "Just like down below."

Anne came running up, her face flushed. "They're houses," she gasped, making an all-encompassing gesture with her semiautomatic. "All the mushrooms are houses!"

Megan smiled. "Now we've somewhere to spend the night."

Brooke looked at Harding. "This is too good to be true."

Tom looked down the aisle, imagining how many fungi were planted here in this single field. Not to mention all over Bizarro. *But . . . fungi houses?*

Harding pushed the door open, peered inside. "Looks empty. Time to make ourselves at home."

166

The mushroom interior was like any normal house. Pleasantly decorated in pleasant shades of blue. It was furnished with tables and chairs, some plastic, some wood, some grown from its own structure.

"Hold on a moment," Harding said. "This house smells occupied."

The others looked sharply at him. He nodded. "It does." He looked at Tony. "You check upstairs yet?"

Tony shook his head. "Came to call you once I opened the door. I'll have a look now." He climbed a staircase to their right.

Harding gestured to Anne, then to the corridor leading off the living room. "Check out the downstairs rooms."

She hurried off also.

"What is it, Lieutenant?" Brooke asked. "You're expecting elves and fairies?" She was being facetious, of course: Where eaters were concerned, Harding was the expert. He knew as much about the cannibals as could be learnt without being digested by them.

Harding didn't reply. His mind was pondering the fungus house's lack of a musty smell of disuse.

Tony reappeared at the top of the stairs. "All clean up here, sir."

Harding nodded.

A moment later, Anne returned, her face strained. "Lieutenant, Chief, this way. We got a problem."

They rushed down the corridor after her.

The corridor led to the house's rear entrance. This rear door was ajar and bloodstained. Telltale red footprints led inside from it, branching off into the first two rooms on either side. Each door was marked with multiple red fingerprints.

"Yeah," Brooke whispered, "We *do* have a fucking problem."

Holding her gun ready, she nodded at the nearest door.

"Oppenheimer was wrong then about the cannibals not being up here," Megan said.

"We'll soon make them wish they weren't," Harding said.

Tony covering him, he pushed the nearest bloody door open with the muzzle of his gun. The door swung in silently on lubed hinges.

"Damn!" Tony gasped from the doorway, his face turning pale. "The shitheads have been having themselves a party."

The room was filled with bloodied human bones.

Harding quickly examined the bones. "These are about a month old."

"Safe to spend the night here then?"

"Not sure, Chief. The eaters should be long gone now, but you never know. His brow furrowed. "What I'd like to know, is both how they got up here in the first place, and, more important, where they found humans to eat."

Tom heard none of their discussion. Catalyzed by what he'd just seen, his breakfast was forcing its way back up his throat. Staggering, he knocked open the opposite door and puked on the floor. Bent over, intent on voiding his belly, he didn't look at the room.

"Fuck my ass!" Megan gasped behind him.

Tom looked up then. There were six half-eaten corpses strung from the ceiling. All were disemboweled. All looked disturbingly fresh.

He resumed puking.

The others didn't wait for Tom to finish upchucking. They rushed out of the house via the bloody door. Brooke yanked Tom along by his collar.

"This mushroom's residents will soon be back," she told him to his sick face while he puked along the way. It's almost sunset."

"No vavs in sight," Megan announced.

Outside, in the fading light, there was now no sign of the vampire vaginas. "Yeah, that's something to be grateful for," Harding said. "Now we just need a mushroom to room in for the night.

Chapter 46

Tom woke up. The room was hot; humid and uncomfortable. The window was open the merest crack, through which he could see the moon.

The room was illumined in a golden glow from the mushroom's walls.

("Natural solar energy panels," Megan had called the process when they'd moved in. "Stores energy by day, pumps it out by night."

"Like Bizarro itself," Brooke had duly noted. "Just wait till Oppenheimer hears about these.")

Tom's bladder was full. *I gotta go pee.*

Swinging out of the bed, a square mound of fungus, he realized Harding wasn't in the room. Tom was sharing rooms with Harding, Brooke with Megan.

He shrugged. *Less I see of that meathead the better anyway*. Harding was likely checking on Tony and Anne. Both officers were camped in the living room downstairs keeping watch.

Tom paused in the doorway. The toilet was on his left, at the far end of the corridor. He turned toward it, then back again. A beam of light sliced across the corridor from an ajar door at the corridor's right end.

Tom scratched his head. Brooke and Megan were sleeping in the room opposite his, and Tony and Anne were downstairs. So who? Eaters?

Cursing himself for handing back his gun, he edged his way toward the part-open door, ready to yell blue murder the moment his eyes confirmed his fears.

He reached the door, peeked in, and froze.

Harding and Megan were in the room. The pair were naked in bed, their clothes strewn everywhere like they'd undressed in haste.

Megan was kneeling behind Harding and fucking him hard in the ass. Harding, his face taut with intense emotion, gripped the edge of the bed to steady himself, his fingers penetrating the fungus. He pumped his buttocks back hard to cushion Megan's thrusts.

"Oh, yeah," the beefy lieutenant groaned in a hoarse whisper.

"Don't relax yet," Megan grunted. "Tighten your man-cunt till it hurts."

She was bracing herself with a hand in the small of Harding's back. Her other hand was under him, jerking off his penises in time to her strokes.

Penises.

He's got two cocks, Tom realized with shock. His amazement kept him glued to the spectacle, eyes agoggle.

Lieutenant Harding's two penises, side-by-side rods of turgid aroused flesh, throbbed in his crotch to Megan's ministrations.

Megan collapsed on Harding's back. She rolled him onto his side. Breasts squashed against his back, she began masturbating both his erections simultaneously while fucking him. Her grease-slicken penis slid smoothly in and out of Harding's anus.

"Now *relax*! Reach for the highest pleasure!"

Then her tone softened.

"You must *relax* your ass. It will help you come more enjoyably. Relax, imagine yourself as an immense anus, about to push out the world's largest turd. Imagine my penis is that turd. Give in to the feeling. Unwind, let your stress seep out of you like my semen soon will. Fuck without concern for this quest, for worries, for anything else, but this cock, this satiation of our shared desire; let—"

"I'm coming, Ms. Fox!" Harding groaned. He ejaculated; simultaneous streams of semen squirted from both his urethral openings, a duo of opaque loops that splattered the bed.

"Yes, baby, cum for me!" Megan kept fucking him like she'd never stop.

As Harding's erections detumesced, Tom recovered from his daze. He padded away, his mind full of the odd sight of the lieutenant's twin organs.

Chapter 47

Megan fellated Harding back to full erection, then got on her hands and knees, her buttocks facing him. Her anus pouted above her scrotum. "My turn now, sailor," she said over her shoulder. "Give me both torpedoes at once."

He scowled at her tight little sphincter. "They'll rip you up."

She laughed, caressing her hard nipples with cum-coated fingers. "I'm a woman of extraordinary capability. "I am because I am, not because I should be. Always ensure you give me what I want—not what you think I should want."

Harding rolled his eyes. Not her sex-magic now. "Okay."

"Hurry up, I need filling."

He did as she bid him. Her anus admitted him like an old friend. Harding was surprised. Most of his boyfriends only wanted one cock at a time. Harding often wished he was heterosexual—women had two apertures for penetration—but vaginas completely turned him off.

Just like breasts did.

Megan's pillow-soft mammary endowment did nothing for Harding. Nothing was better than a hard male body straining against his, sweaty muscled flesh and a hard penis up the ass. That filling/fulfilling deep penetration. Like just now. Yeah, despite all her mystic bullshit, Megan Fox could fuck. Her cock made up for her feminine defects. She acted/sounded oddly detached though . . .

"Deeper," she moaned, "Force yourself all the way into me, like you desire to be one with me." She moaned louder. "Yes like that—like a wolf ripping into meat."

The simile chilled Harding. He froze against her, unconsciously stopping the penetration.

Megan's cool voice floated over her shoulder. Calm and non-erotic, like she was inflicting torture on Harding, not enduring an almost anus-rending penetration.

"Pain is itself pleasure. I'm enjoying this because I want to, not because it feels good or excites me."

Whilst speaking, she jerked off hard and fast, her white fingers floating over her sex like angels.

"I choose therefore I am. This pain I feel is affirmation of my superiority over you—how I willingly take what you have to offer, and even more, if you have to spare." She grunted. "Now fuck me HARD, you wonderful, lovely, double-rodded fool. Do it super-hard or expect to be demoted once we return downstairs."

Harding fucked her as hard as she requested. For himself too, the pleasure, the sheer ecstasy of marauding Megan's rectal cavity was sublime. Pleasure trembled his legs.

"I'm dying!" Megan gushed, a solitary exclamation accompanied by a torrential squirting of semen. Masturbating furiously, she fell forward flat onto the bed, sweaty white body collapsing like the proverbial deck of cards into her jetting cum, her breasts squashing wet circles onto the fungus. She let go of her throbbing penis and lay splayed out like a corpse, letting Harding maintain her ecstasy by the slick friction of his two cocks on her prostate.

Harding shortly came again. And collapsed on her.

"Don't you dare move," Megan ordered. "Keep me corked. Leave your babies inside me."

They lay like that, him on her, Harding stroking her dark lustrous hair, while she thrilled to the sensation of being simultaneously filled and flooded.

***

Brooke jerked awake. Her pussy was wet. Despite the sleep, she was tense.

Too much excitement and responsibility makes me a horny girl. She drew a finger through the slit of her sex. *Watching Tom's ass all day doesn't hurt either.*

She remembered properly where she was. In bed, beside Megan.

She turned. *Where's Megan? Ah, gone to pee.* She grinned. *I'll just have a quick wank before she gets back.*

When Megan wasn't back from the toilet after five minutes, Brooke got the mertopus tentacle out from her pack and slipped it into her pussy. The tentacle's creamy sensations as she stroked herself with it soon eased away the day's stresses.

172

Tom's cock would be so much better, she thought, sighing into luscious orgasm. *But with Harding watching over him, empty pussies can't be choosy.*

***

"I can't stand that son-of-a-bitch," Harding said. "If he makes even the slightest sign of running off, I'll—"

Megan giggled loudly. "Only after we find the money, honey."

She stroked Harding's hair. He lay with his head in her lap, her large breasts shadowing his face. "Pussypalm might be gone already, we've been enjoying each other for two hours." She laughed at the instant change in Harding's expression. "Don't worry. He's still in your room. He'd never try fleeing, not after seeing the vavs in action today."

"He might still try. He's remembered how to shoot."

"Don't be silly. You've got his gun."

She reached across into Harding's crotch and grabbed his left penis. "Once we find the gold, it'll be expedient to dispose of Pussypalm before he recovers his memory."

Harding turned his face up to stare at her. "You're serious?"

"As a grave. He'll be dangerous then." She squeezed the cock that filled her hand like a fat sexy worm. Its twin reflexly filled with blood. "Think you can make it one more time?"

Harding liked Megan like this. He grinned. "I can try." He frowned. "I don't understand. Why'd you report me to Joe and King Eric then?"

"The beating you gave him was sure to be noticed. And Tom was sure to tell Brooke you'd tried to kill him."

He winced. "You handed Brooke my promotion."

"Are you angry over that?"

"Shouldn't I be?"

She bent, kissed him. "I did what was best at the time. No one knew Joe would have his 'accident.'" She laughed coolly. "There's still hope; Brooke's new at this. She's also naïve as a bunny. She'll likely get killed up here. Then I'll ask Queen Pam to have his majesty make you Chief instead."

He frowned. "Clutching at straws."

"No other options." She tapped his shoulder, her eyes glowing down into his. "Look, suck me hard and let me fuck you again. Your muscular body turns me on no end."

Harding made to get up. "I gotta pee first."

Megan held him back. "How fortunate. I'm thirsty, darling; do it in my mouth."

He goggled in disbelief.

She yawned. "Why not?" She laughed derisively at his surprise, "Where there is consent, Lieutenant, nothing is taboo."

He nodded, unable to resist her, unable to refuse the odd experience she offered.

"Lie on your side."

He did so, she positioned her head in his crotch, and took both his penises into her mouth. She looked up at him and nodded.

Harding urinated in Megan's mouth. She drank the piss down, gulping fast so he didn't spill out her lips. She luxuriated in the odd feeling of the twin squirting organs laving her throat with liquid jets. There was a lot of the pee. Her flooding belly felt warm, like she'd just drank good Scotch.

Harding finished. Megan removed her mouth from his cocks, sucking each penis empty in turn. Raising herself up on her elbow so she looked down at him, she gargled loudly with the last of his pee.

She swallowed. "Wonderful mouthwash," she said.

Harding said nothing. She bent to kiss him. He turned away from her lips.

Megan studied his face for a moment, her eyes unoffended. "You've much to learn about love, Lieutenant."

"This isn't love. It's depravity."

"What's the difference?" She stroked his face. "Every night is full of secrets. If bedroom walls could talk, what unbelievable stories they'd tell."

"Everyone should draw the line somewhere."

"I lost my pencils in grade school. Don't play the innocent with me. You enjoyed pissing down my throat, didn't you?"

Silence. Emotion wriggled across his face like worms.

She feigned incredulity. "You're *scared* to admit it?"

"Ummm . . . it was *different* . . ."

"And if I'd asked you to *shit* in my mouth instead of using the toilet?"

"You'd . . . you'd never do that."

Megan laughed. "And why not? In a loving relationship there are no limits, no taboos—only bodies enshrined, cocooned in mutual trust. Except you told, who'd ever know I ate your excrement? A little toothpaste and we're back to normal."

"*I'd* know. It's so . . . so . . ."

She stretched like a cat, licked her upper lip with her mouth open. "I just drank your urine, Lieutenant; tell me, in what way am I any different than I was ten minutes ago." Her eyes pierced his like she'd blind him. "Answer me; am I less desirable?"

"Do you really believe all this crap?"

"I love it when you talk dirty, baby. But don't evade the question. Answer me!"

"Perversion is perversion."

She laughed loud. "And a rose by any other name is sixteenth century English bullshit. You've nice pouty lips, you know. Maybe *I'll* shit in *your* mouth instead."

He blanched. "Oh, no you won't."

Megan stifled a yawn. "You're so boring, Lieutenant. But you've potential—I'll make a man of you yet. Now let me fuck you again. Your ass understands me better than your brain." She tapped her cock. "Chew my love bone a bit first."

Harding took her penis in his mouth. She grew on his tongue like a child becoming a teenager.

She giggled, pulled him off her by the ears. "You'd make a fantastic rent boy the way you suck."

She rolled him over. She lay flat on him, breasts on his back, hard slick rod in the crack of his buttocks, poking his testes. "Just relax and take it like a man."

Harding relaxed. Megan reached a hand between them and guided her cock into Harding's hole. She began moving, then stopped. She withdrew.

"What's the matter?"

"Too slippery. Too much cum still in you from last time. Hold on."

She moved down his body. She spread his buttocks and stuck her tongue into his anus, then pouted her lips around his sphincter and sucked hard.

A wet snake, the cum slithered out of him into her mouth in a salty stream.

"Yes," she said after a while, rising and wiping her lips. "You'll feel better now."

"You're odd, Ms. Fox."

"I'm just true, that's all. Everyone else is false." She slipped her penis back into Harding's ass. "Now hold still and let me love your body. No— *don't move.* Let my cock pilot you in the plane of pleasure."

Harding did as she'd instructed. Turning his body over to her, however, resulted in his mind wandering; his thoughts finally journeying back to that horrible day a year ago.

Part 3: Bank Corridors Pt. 1

Chapter 48

One Year Ago.

Kim Fields on his left, Marlon 'Trouble' Barrett on his right, gun steady at the ready, Lt. Ryan Harding stalked down a third floor Boston Fed corridor.

Harding's sister Gail's office was at the end of the corridor.

On either side of the trio framed faces of past bank presidents glinted like glass ghouls.

Kim spat in disgust. Beneath her helmet, her expression was pained. "I honestly can't believe this shit—eaters so hungry for human flesh they hit a bank? And the Boston Fed at that?"

"You'd expect the sheer firepower here to put the bastards off," Marlon added.

Harding grunted. "Bank's obviously less secure than we thought."

Kim concurred. "The cannibals keep seeing people coming in and out day after day. Soon they start wondering why they aren't helping their yellow mitts to lunch."

Harding and Kim had rushed over from City Hall immediately word came in of the eater attack. They'd met the front plaza, entrance hall, and entire two lower bank floors in scenes of blood-soaked carnage—guards, bank staff, and customer corpses lay everywhere with eaters feeding on them.

It was ironic. The reason the Federal Reserve Bank of Boston hadn't shifted location from the harbor since the eater plague started was because the city felt the cannibal threat would help keep the vaults safe from attack.

Harding winced. *Yeah, right. Like the eaters weren't a threat enough.*

Like she could read his mind, Kim added: "In retrospect, a real bad idea—over a hundred people working in one building. Food begging to be got."

Downstairs was a war zone now. Both SWAT teams Harding had brought over were now engaging the cannibal mutants in close-quarters combat with all sorts of heavy ammo being used by both sides. Harding had sent for every officer who could be spared from the South Terminal Precinct Station, down on Atlantic Avenue.

Every now and then the floor rumbled from explosive detonation.

Harding groaned. *It's going look like fucking Lebanon down there afterwards.* Harding had no idea if the eaters had penetrated the Bank's upper floors yet. He had a horrible vision of streams of blood flowing from offices to form a river draining down the steps.

But this floor first. He had to ensure Gail was okay, get her out safe if she was.

How in hell did so many of them get in here unnoticed anyhow?" Kim asked.

"Likely by boat, meaning Harbor Patrol must be counting corpses now."

"More food for the freaks."

The conversation was really worrying Harding. *Dammit, Gail, don't be dead. Please don't be dead.*

Harding had been expecting trouble for a month, just not this kind. There was currently five billion dollars in bullion—likely a lot more since the Charlestown reserves were also stored here—in the Boston Fed's basement vaults. And his sister Gail was Senior Acquisitions and Transfers Manager—Boston/East Massachusetts's de-facto treasurer.

Gail had suspected that Tom Pussypalm—that psycho bandit freak—was having her watched.

So Harding had been expecting a kidnapping attempt.

***

Harding had reported his suspicions to Police Chief Joe Bradley. (With Joe and Gail's wedding barely a month away, Harding could simply breeze into Joe's office. Having the boss in love with your younger sister had benefits.)

Joe walked around his office, throwing angry glances out the window at Bizarro. "It's too damn hot! Why the hell doesn't it rain? This city would be more tolerable if that airborne blob of absurdity up there wasn't drinking all our cloud water."

He controlled himself, returned his attention to Harding. "Don't bother your head, Ryan. Oppenheimer has so many security devices on the vaults, it'll be easier to blow Boston to bits than get the gold out."

He grinned. "The good doc assures me that the only safe way to open the vaults is to cut the electric power supply for the whole of Downtown, and the control switch for that is in the South Terminal Precinct Station basement half a mile from the bank. Come off it, man. No one's going to attack a district HQ."

"I know that, Joe, but . . . Pussypalm? That hand-cunt of his might . . ."

Joe nodded. "I know. I've thought about it too. I don't think it matters."

He raised a beefy hand to silence Harding's next statement, then moved away from the window and stood facing him with both palms on his desk. "It's one thing breaking into the bank, another thing altogether getting away with the gold. He'd need an army to move it out of Boston." He grinned. "I'm a firm believer in pussy power being able to accomplish stuff that we guys can't, but even a psychic vagina will have a problem doing that."

Harding nodded. "Yeah, I guess you're right. But I'm real worried about Gail. I hate the thought of Pussypalm stalking her. The problem is how slippery the bastard is. No one's seen him since he flipped King Eric the bird." His face began reddening in anger. "If that freak dares so much as—"

"Nothing will happen to her," Joe said quickly, mindful of Harding's temper. "I've assigned two officers to watch Gail. If Pussypalm dares show his face . . ."

Harding cooled down a bit. "Who've you got on it?"

"Marlon Barrett, Anne Smith."

"'Trouble' Barrett? Thought he retired after that Chinatown incident."

Joe shook his head. "Nah. Backup arrived before the eaters made it all the way through his leg. Marlon's a lucky guy—somehow none of the cannibals' teeth ripped his femoral artery. The medics grafted skin and plastic muscle to replace the rest. He's good as new now, but he's having nightmares—needs an assignment till the shrinks clear him."

Harding nodded. Detective Barrett was tough. "Good man to watch Gail."

Joe grinned. "I partnered him with Anne just in case there's fisticuffs. You know how she likes a fight."

There was a knock on the door. "Come in," Joe yelled.

Pam Andersen entered, carrying a sheaf of papers. King Eric's busty blonde secretary nodded to both men.

Harding smiled back. He knew Pam's husband Marv; they'd worked together last year flushing out a band of eaters from Copp's Hill Burying Ground. He smiled at Pam. *Utterly beautiful woman, more breathtaking than many movie actresses.* He found it creepy, however, how she could lengthen her neck. *Even now, it looks two or three inches longer than normal.*

He shrugged. *And I've got two penises. A freak's a freak.*

181

Pam dropped the files in front of Joe. "On his majesty's service, Chief."

She sat on the edge of Joe's table, waiting, while he leafed through. Harding thought he detected animosity in the air, like Pam was pissed-off about something.

Not my worry. He got out of his chair. "Gotta run, sir."

Joe looked up from the files. His face was suddenly weary. "Don't go too far, Ryan; looks like we're about to have another eater epidemic."

Harding winced. He looked at Pam.

Her lips creased into a wry grin. "Yes, Lieutenant. King Eric's accidentally found out about it. His majesty is thinking of moving the government to the west part of town—Beacon Hill."

What? He can't do that, Harding thought angrily. *Relocate the government? Someone needs to bend that little brat over their knee and give him a good—*

Joe interrupted his thoughts. "Ryan, 'that little brat,' is the elected King of Boston, Massachusetts; granted power of life and death in the last city elections by we, its devoted citizens. He can do whatever his shitty five-year-old ass wants."

With a start, Harding realized he'd been thinking aloud. He looked in horror at Pam. *Hell no. She heard me. There goes my future promotion to Captain out the window.*

Pam smiled sweetly back at Harding. "Don't worry, I'm not telling. Wow, Lieutenant, Marv's right—you *do* have quite a temper."

***

Four weeks ago, Joe's optimism had seemed sensible. Not now.

Now, Harding winced. This seemingly endless lime corridor wasn't doing his dour mood any favors. Its color was too similar to the eaters' body color.

And the occasional blood smear on the walls . . .

"Ssssshh." Harding pointed up ahead. Gail's office door was open.

Oh, shit! he thought next. A bright crimson splash stained the carpet outside it.

Harding broke into a run. Kim and Marlon thundered after him.

All three froze in the office doorway, staring in horror.

Chapter 49

Gail Harding lay across her desk. Two eaters were eating her. They'd ripped her belly all the way open and were stuffing handfuls of her guts into their mouths. Their guns were slung across their backs.

Gail herself was long dead. Half her face had been eaten off, revealing blood-streaked skull bone, her nose and lips gone. Her dark hair hung off her bloody head, dripping red like a paint brush. Her legs were splayed wide apart, bare feet dangling in midair. Her skirt, panties, and shoes lay discarded on the floor.

The eaters realized they had company. Both swung toward the doorway, scrabbling for their guns. "Shit!" one yelped. "It's the pigs! Shoot the porkers!"

Harding and his companions were faster. Feeling like a bomb had detonated inside him, like he'd died, Harding began firing, pumping hot leaded hatred at the eaters.

Beside him, Kim and Marlon did the same.

The merciless gunfire ripped the eaters apart, blowing yellow skin and flesh off their bones like fragmenting boiled-egg yolk. Pink blood splattered everywhere.

Harding stopped firing only when his clip clicked empty. He walked across to his sister's side and stood looking down at her in disbelief. One blue eye hung from its socket on a nerve, the other was a bloody puddle. Her breasts were slashed open like pillows an intruder had searched.

He dreaded looking down at her exposed vagina, then did so . . . Damn, she'd been raped; there was cum in her cunt. A trail of the semen had dripped to pool with blood from her torn anus.

Harding was confused. *Now this is odd for sure: eaters don't rape human women, they just eat you. And why the hell am I looking at my sister's vagina anyway?*

He popped out his weapon's empty clip, inserted another.

Kim and Marlon joined him. "I'm sorry this happened, sir," Marlon said. "I really am."

Harding turned to them, eyes full of pain. "Why? Tell me why it had to be her?" He was choking back tears now. "You know, we planned for everything but *this*."

He frowned at his sister's corpse. "We've work to do," he said coldly. "We're gonna clean out their nest, wherever it is." He turned to Marlon. "You were watching: where exactly did the eaters come up from?"

The black man looked troubled. "That's the odd thing, Lieutenant. They came out of the bank doors; like they were already inside the building."

Kim scowled. "That makes no sense. They clearly got in the back way, via the harbor."

Harding parted the window drapes, peered down into the bloody plaza out front. "South Terminal guys should be arriving now. The eaters won't get away."

"We're missing something here," Kim said.

Harding looked at her sharply. "What?"

"Two things strike me as odd. Why would eaters target a bank anyway? Not their style; too much security."

"Kim, who gives a shit about *why*? They just fucking did. Maybe they're just not as smart as everyone assumes."

Kim ignored the pissed-of crack. She gestured around. "And also— this really bothers me, sir: Why are all your sister's files scattered everywhere?"

Harding and Marlon saw what she meant. The evident mess was more than just a fight with the eaters.

"Someone ransacked her office before killing her," Kim pointed out. "Who and why?"

Harding considered the mess with puzzlement. Someone had clearly been searching for something. "This is begins to stink."

The lights went out then. The air-conditioning unit ground to a halt. The three of them stood in half-darkness, dappled with shadows.

"Damn," Kim said. The clear sound of her spit splatting the floor hit them both in the silence that followed. "This is just what we don't need with eaters everywhere. They see in the dark almost as good as cats."

The lights remained off. Artificial twilight. A switch however tripped 'on' in Harding's mind.

A month-old statement bounced around his skull like a concrete basketball.

Harding's grief instantly rolled off his shoulders. Instead he felt like he'd been punched in the stomach.

The lights came back on.

Harding glanced one last time at Gail's savaged, raped, corpse. "I swear on your grave, sis: I'll kill that HIV-infected-asshole if it's the last thing I do in my life."

"Thank heavens, someone's efficient," Kim said. "I can't imagine what the—"

"Come on," Harding interrupted, pushing past her out of doorway and breaking into a quick jog. "Hurry. We've got to get downstairs already."

They rushed after him. "You sure we shouldn't take Gail's body with us, Lieutenant?" Marlon asked. "In case any more eaters are up here."

"Later. This isn't just a random cannibal raid."

"Huh?"

They turned the corner, descended the stairs. "Nah. It's Pussypalm. This eater attack is a diversion to get everyone out of South Terminal Precinct Station."

"But what use is that?" Marlon asked.

Harding scowled. "Oppenheimer's fixed it so the only safe way to open the gold vaults is to cut all power to the Downtown district. The electromagnetic locks disengage then and the vault doors swing open. The master power control switch is down in the South Terminal basement."

He sighed. "Remember I sent instructions to bring everyone there over here to fend off the eaters. Next thing, the lights go off, and after a while come back on again."

Kim gasped. "Just long enough to open the vault doors and jam them. Damn! He's likely killed everyone left at the precinct!"

"Right. Marlon and Anne Smith have been watching Gail 'cos she suspected Pussypalm was having her tailed. Everything adds up—It's a robbery. That cunt-handed psychopath is in this building right now."

"Fuck!" Kim said. "We've got a war on our hands."

"Dude can't get away with that much gold," Marlon said. "Much too heavy. Greed done killed the fool."

"I'd love to agree with you," Kim said, "but where there's a will, there's always a fucking way."

By now they'd reached the second floor landing. The corridor was lit up with bright gun-muzzle flashes. Smoke was everywhere.

They paused to consider their next move.

"So what did he want with Gail? Why rape and kill her?"

Harding's eyes turned cold as ice. It was Marlon, however, who replied her: "He's just a perv, that's all. Fucked her to rub it in Chief Bradley's face. You know: I took your cash, tore up your chick's ass."

"Dude, that's so crude," Kim said.

"Quit the stupid rhyming games!" Harding snapped. "That's my sister you're slanging about!"

Both officers were instantly apologetic. "Sorry, sir."

"Yeah, okay, whatever. Pussypalm hasn't got our gold yet. And I intend to see he doesn't. Concerning my sister; the matter's simple: She's dead, and I'm going to kill Pussypalm to avenge her." He looked coldly at the pair of them. "Either of you two bleeding hearts got a problem with that?"

They shook their heads. "We're with you," Marlon said.

Kim nodded. "Justice is too good for an asshole like that."

The shooting and bombing in the corridor intensified. Clouds of smoke reduced visibility to mere feet. Fire flickered between dark moving shadows.

"I've no idea which are our guys," Marlon said.

Kim agreed with him. "No way we're getting through here without being blown to bits."

Harding gestured back around the landing. "This way. There's a balcony out back leading down to the rear parking lot."

They retraced their steps.

Chapter 50

"Down!" Harding yelped immediately they reached the balcony.

The others instantly hit the floor along with him. They peered out through the gap beneath the metal/glass parapet.

Kim gasped. "What the fuck?"

The rear parking lot thronged with vavs—green/brown-skinned giantesses each taller than the second-floor balcony.

The plant women milled restlessly, their beautiful movie-actress faces intent with almost sexual concentration. Most of the vavs had dying police officers dangling in their crotches, helmets missing, faces purpling from being throttled by the vagina tentacles wrapped around their necks, twitching helplessly between the mammoth thigh-trunks as each vampire vagina leeched them empty of blood.

Overhead, Bizarro floated like a massive squashed turd, its sheer expanse mother to a new form of claustrophobia.

Those vavs who didn't have captives were whirling their vaginal tentacles overhead lasso-style and flinging them. Around the vavs lay a multitude of uniformed bloodless corpses of the already drained.

A Vivian Leigh vav hungrily whirling her tentacle pouted prettily at the second floor balcony, but didn't notice the concealed cops.

Kim grimaced. "That's our South Terminal Precinct backup."

Between the vavs patrolled armed eaters, eyes alert for more police to kill. Some eaters were ripping apart the dead bodies and feeding on them.

Harding scowled at the carnage. He'd already lost count of how many dead officers he was responsible for. Today just got worse and worse.

"What the fuck do the vampire vaginas want here?" Marlon asked. His dusky face was strained, his eyes bugging out like he was seeing a vision of Hell.

"What does it look like they want, sergeant? They're draining the lifeblood out of the BPD. Pussypalm set us up."

"That's not what I mean, sir. They shouldn't be—"

"Forget it," Harding snapped. The sight of the dying officers dangling from pussy tentacles was unnerving him. He ripped his eyes from the sight, pointing. "Those trucks are how Pussypalm intends to convey the loot."

There were three trucks, white 18-wheelers, each with a fifty foot trailer. "Wu Dock Trucking' was painted on each tractor unit in bright red lettering over a green Chinese dragon. The lot walls had been demolished to permit the trucks entry to the premises. All three massive vehicles were backed up to the bank, parked side-by-side in the basement driveway, their rear ends well out of sight under the balcony.

Marlon whistled. "That way's direct access to the vaults."

"He loads those, there goes Boston's gold," Kim added.

Harding scowled. John Wu Trucking's office was around the corner, on Dorchester Avenue up by India Wharf. Harding knew the Chinese businessman. Wu was honest and hardworking, handling shipping for most of East Massachusetts. He was tight with the royal family too. Three Wu trucks rolling down to Summer Street would have attracted no suspicion whatever. But how the heck had he got involved with Pussypalm?

"He won't load them up," he said. "Take too much time. Gold weighs a fucking ton."

"He will," Kim said. "Those aren't normal trailers on those trucks. I've seen those before. Military uses them to ferry missile components and broken-up aircraft and tanks. They've got both a built-in forklift and a conveyor belt. Automatic. More efficient than a Ford assembly line. Once the gold's loaded on the conveyor . . ."

Harding looked at her, a pained expression on his face. "Stop being a smartass."

"Sorry, sir,"

"We don't need to make it to the vault itself. Pussypalm's likely right below us right now, directing operations—"

"Sorry to interrupt, sir. But what I was trying to say before about the vavs? It's odd them being out here. They and the eaters never get along."

Harding scowled. The black cop had a point. Vampire vaginas and eaters hated each other. Both species fed off a limited resource,—humans—were competitors in the food chain. "I don't fucking know why, okay? Listen, here's the plan: We crawl to the end of the balcony. Round the corner, the stairway leads directly down. We can't take that now—the vavs and eaters'll be waiting; but the corridor to the records rooms opens directly onto the landing."

He looked at Kim. "You're the sharpshooter; once we turn that corner, blow the friggin lock off . . . our lives depend on that door opening once we slam it."

She nodded. "Gotcha."

"Good. We charge in shooting. Watch out none of our guys are in the way. Marlon, you keep going to the front of the building—let Anne realize the shit's hit the fan out back. Tell her to send for reinforcements and flamethrowers. Kim, you come with me. Halfway along the corridor, on the left, is the stairwell to the executive underground car park. That's right under the building. The landing's a vantage point—we can see the rear vault doors from there—and we can hit and run." He looked at both sergeants quickly. "Got it?"

They nodded, then froze. On the other side of the barrier hiding them, the Vivian Leigh vav previously looking their way had now snared a policewoman.

They watched the hapless woman simultaneously choke and empty of blood, whilst swinging like a pendulum. Her eyes—almost popping from her head from the pressure of the tentacle triple-wrapped around her throat—clearly conveyed to them her horror at the pathetic nature of her death.

Her eyes met Harding's. They pleaded with him to kill her. A hand reached toward him, beckoning a bullet. A merciful shot to the head, not this draining away, exiting life like Coca-Cola sucked through a straw.

Kim lifted her gun. Harding pushed her hand down. "You'll give our position away."

She spat in disgust. "I feel like murdering these plant bitches. I fucking *hate* their only weakness being fire. The way this cunt is draining her, jerking like she's cumming, makes it even worse."

The dangling policewoman went limp in the vav's crotch. The vav shivered with pleasure.

Harding nudged Kim and Marlon, "Let's go."

They set off down the balcony, running crouched like apes.

They almost made it unnoticed. But as they neared the turnoff to the landing, a Brigitte Bardot vav turned and looked directly down into the balcony. Her crotch was occupied with a dangling, dying cop, but her smoky hazel eyes momentarily unglazed from their feeding sparkle.

She made no sound,—everyone found that creepy about the vavs, how they didn't talk—just pointed down at the trio scuttling toward her.

The three cops realized she was screaming telepathically at her sisters.

"Run for it!" Harding yelled.

They leapt up and ran. Their mad scramble for the landing, toward the Brigitte Bardot vav who'd blown their cover, was punctuated by their ducking a sudden rain of meat hooks as the vavs, lusting for their blood, now converged on the balcony.

"Look out!" Marlon yelled to Kim. He knocked her down, out of the path of one of the black bone sickles. The meat hook shattered the window over her head.

Harding, in the lead, heard the noise of breaking glass. He turned back to check that they were both okay.

Marlon quickly pulled Kim up. "Are you al—"

His question was literally cut off as a follow-up meat hook implanted itself deep into his throat. The next moment Marlon was jerked off his feet up into the air.

Kim leapt after him and grabbed his feet. Marlon gurgled blood and screamed wordlessly while the vav—a Joan Fontaine—yanked on her tentacle to get him over the balcony. Kim held on fiercely.

Harding beat at Kim's hands. "Let go of him!"

"Hell no!"

With an almighty yank, she pulled Marlon back down over the parapet.

The black policeman fell on her and Harding. He was minus his head; the meat hook had cleanly decapitated him.

Kim stared at Harding in horror.

He spat. "That's what I meant!"

Blood pumped in jets from Marlon's neck. It painted the walls and floor and splattered Kim's uniform.

Harding dragged Kim away from the dead man, off toward the landing. The meat hooks still came fast and furious, but they evaded them now by running close to the wall, preventing any encirclement.

The eaters down in the lot began shooting at the balcony, blowing glass shards everywhere.

"He saved me," Kim wept as they ran. "That would have been me."

No shit, Harding thought. "Door's coming up!" he yelled. "Get ready to hit it!"

Beside him, Kim transitioned out of grief and back into kickass mode. Her brain focused like an optical laser.

They turned the corner. Kim took one look at the position of the lock and hit it with five perfectly placed shots that fucked it up completely.

A human battering ram, Harding hit the door shoulder first. They crashed through. A stream of vav tentacles trailed after them.

In full view of the frustrated plant giantesses watching through the doorway, they stopped and caught their breaths.

The corridor stretched before them, beckoning like a throat desiring to swallow them.

Harding placed a hand on Kim's shoulder, his eyes soft. "I'm sorry about Marlon back there. Nothing we could do to save him."

She nodded. "I'm fine, sir," then scowled. "Sir, what the hell do we do? Body count's rising here like it's the Vietnam war all over again. Only thing missing are evacuation helicopters."

"We still got napalm. Time for Plan B. You go find Anne and get a message to HQ for flamethrowers. "

"And you, sir?"

Harding's face set in ruthless lines. He gestured to the stairwell bannister up ahead. "I'm going to find that psychopath Pussypalm and kill him." He shook his head at the question in her eyes. "This is beyond revenge; with that asshole dead, the robbery's over."

"Better to wait for backup, sir." She looked back out through the landing door. The vavs had now dispersed.

Harding scowled. "It'll take them forever to arrive. These are the times when I wish Bizarro didn't screw up radio reception."

"And chopper electronics?"

Harding grunted assent. "Only good thing about this mess is that Chief Bradley's up in Charlestown again, looking for King Eric's imaginary eaters. I can't imagine what he'd do now if he knew Gail was dead."

"Likely bomb this building to dust. "But, sir, *why does* the King keep sending the chief up there? We both know Charlestown's clean."

"Kid's five. Maybe he sees eaters there in his nightmares." He nodded Kim down the corridor. "We're wasting time. Go."

Gun at the ready, Kim loped off.

Harding paused at the top of the stairwell for a moment, listening. Then he descended fast to the underground car park.

Chapter 51

Kim Fields disliked Anne Smith intensely. The pretty orange-haired sergeant was a cunt-tease.

It was almost impossible for Kim to see Anne without feeling a wet warmth in her vagina. But the feeling wasn't mutual. Or maybe it was, but no, it wasn't, or maybe . . .

Fuck, Kim thought, reaching the stairs at the corridor end. Here with no smoke or corpses, progress was fast. *The little bitch has me on a high wire. She's totally messed up my head.*

Kim had a MASSIVE crush on Anne. Might even be love—Kim wasn't sure. She'd watched from the sideline through Anne's ceaseless string of relationships with totally unsuitable women—Anne had a thing for bull dykes who kept beating her up.

Two Months Ago in Dollhouse:

Up on the stage, the punk band SOS—Strap-On Sisters—were playing *Ballad of Screwy Yu.*

Lead singer Josie Kutchner, a tall muscular blonde with a crew cut and a voice like a kennel of pissed-off dogs, yelled out:

"Why why why did you run away?
You had enough of our bedtime play?
Now I'm brokenhearted all over again,
I'll never never never never love again.

You tight-assed little Asian whore,
I'm gonna permanently widen your back door,
Forget that fashion victim, I got more,
You've never been loved like this before.

So why'd you up and run away,
Back to that cunt of yesterday?
Come home, darling, it's time to play.
My itty-bitsy kitty's feeling lonely.
Yaaaaaaaaaaaaaaaaaaaaaaaaaaaaaaaaaaaaaaaa!"

The bloodcurdling scream lifted the small hairs on Kim's neck.

Goddam, I utterly hate Josie's voice. She made her way to a free table. *Stupid dyke endlessly moaning about her ex's infidelities. Grow a pair, willya? Stop whining, knock out her teeth next time!*

Kim became aware of a commotion on her left.

It was Anne Smith in a fight with her girlfriend.

Woman, you've asshole—total shit—taste in women.

Anne's current girlfriend was a short fat brunette with a beer belly—her gut hung over her belt like a sack. Kim couldn't remember her name—Anne changed women so frequently, she'd need to be a sprinter to keep up. She simply thought of the woman as Fat Woman.

Seeing Anne, a pang stabbed Kim. *Shit, girl. I LOVE you, can't you see that? I'd treat you so much better than that sack of guts. Better than anyone ever has.*

The fight between Anne and her girlfriend got louder.

SOS began their next song, *Ribs or Studs*; a Josie Kutchner exposition on why interchangeable penises were better than the natural kind.

"If you're flowing red at that time of the month,
I'll use my big horsie and plug you up.
And if you feel slutty, want a double fuck,
I got a little toy that does two at once."

"You slut!" Fat Woman shouted drunkenly over the band. "I saw you making eyes at Tonia!"

"And so what? You don't own me!"

"I gotta little dick, I gotta big dick,
I gotta lotta dicks, just takes your picks.
And if you hate dick, I really got no dick,
Real dicks make me sick, I prefer plastic."

Then the argument turned physical, with chest-poking, hair-pulling, and shoving. Fat Woman, despite her blubber, had the upper hand.

The other women drinkers watched their spat with little interest. Anne was *always* fighting with her girlfriends. No one would interfere, so long as things didn't get too out of hand.

Despite her deep longing for Anne, Kim couldn't help but be amused by the fight. It was hilarious, seeing Sgt. Annabelle Smith being womanhandled by her out of shape girlfriend.

Love sure does make you weak. Anne was extremely tough,—in cop threads Kim had seen her kick some serious ass—but this? It was almost karma.

Well deserved payback for rejecting someone who truly loves you.

Then the fight turned really violent. Fat Woman slapped Anne's face. Anne glared drunkenly back at her. "You hit me?"

"It's what you deserve."

"Oh, yeah?" She grabbed her beer bottle and shattered it against the edge of the table. "I'm cutting you a new cunt!" She stabbed at Fat Woman.

Fat Woman batted her hand aside. The bottle flew off towards the stage where Josie Kutchner was yelling the lyrics to *Vegan Vampire* over Mandy Morrison's jagged guitar riffs:

"I'm gonna suck your lemons dry,
Suck both your lemons dry.
Your melons are so full of juice,
Gonna drain it all out of you.
Your banana is so hard,
You wanna stick it in my backyard fruit salad,
But I'll suck it till it dies,
Drink it down to baby size,
Then you'll realize,
This ain't no veggie paradise!"

Fat Woman slapped Anne again. Anne's head cracked sideways. A stream of blood oozed down her chin from a cut lip.

The watching women got up. "Hey, cut that out!"

Kim leapt to her feet and rushed over.

Kim reached the battling couple before the other women.

In the interim before her arrival, Fat Woman had hit Anne twice more, another slap that worsened her cut lip, and a punch to the left breast.

"Fuck you," Anne lisped through bloody teeth, her eyes a golden glare. "My pussy's mine. No one tells me who to fuck."

Fat Woman's eyes widened in rage. She raised her hand again.

Kim grabbed her wrist. "Okay, that's enough. Hit her one more time, and I'll book you for assault."

Fat Woman turned to see who'd spoken. She recognized Kim as a cop, and also recognized the cold sober hatred in her eyes.

She dropped her hand. Sat down. "Fucking pigs."

Kim bent over her. "Did you say something?"

Fat Woman didn't reply.

Kim picked up the woman's beer and emptied it over her head. "You need to cool off."

Fat Woman sat motionless while the beer sloshed over her.

Kim turned away from her to Anne. Anne's ginger hair hung scattered over her face. "Damn, girl, I thought you could kick butt."

Anne spat blood. "Being in uniform helps."

SOS began the next song, *Ellen DeGenerate*:

"Ellen says,
I like fisting best,
And sucking Portia's breasts,
Ellen DeGenerate.

Ellen says,
I love chocolate,
Because it looks like shit,
Ellen DeGenerate."

Kim winced at the lyrics. *Get a life, Josie.*

Everyone knew the story. Josie Kutchner was still irate at talk-show host Ellen DeGeneres for kicking SOS off 'The Ellen Show' four years ago (when there was still TV) after studio security caught her masturbating with a HUGE carrot in Ellen's private toilet.

Ellen DeGenerate was her comeback.

"Come with me to the ladies' room," Kim told Anne, "I'll clean you up."

That night, it had almost looked like something might happen between them. Anne had wept and Kim had hugged her, been supportive, wanting to kiss her but not daring.

"I'm breaking up with that bitch," Anne insisted as Kim washed the blood from her mouth. "I'm moving out for good."

Good for you, girl, Kim thought with delight. *You deserve so much better.*

***

As they were leaving the ladies' room, Josie entered, roughly pushing between them.

"Hey, watch it!"

Josie turned to them. The blonde's face was screwed up in an expression of intense pain. She was gripping her belly hard. "Sorry, my period just started."

She left them gaping after her and rushed into the nearest cubicle.

"Was that a *carrot* in her hand?" Anne whispered to Kim. "She's not—"

Kim nodded back mutely. Both women stood by the door, rooted in place by expectancy.

Loud crunching sounds started coming from the toilet cubicle Josie had entered. Like someone eating ravenously. Then a deep sigh of relief, then more crunching.

Kim giggled. "She's just hungry."

Anne stared at her wide-eyed. "In the toilet?"

"It could be worse; at least she's not dildoing herself with it. She just finished singing *Ellen DeGenerate* after all."

Giggling, both women left the ladies' room.

***

Inside the cubicle, Josie Kutchner pushed the carrot deeper inside her vagina. She heaved a deep sigh of relief as her pussy teeth ground it up to paste, then swallowed it up into her womb.

Her pussy finished swallowing, began sucking again. She pushed the carrot in farther. The vegetable was half-gone now. Another round of voracious chewing and swallowing, another push.

Josie made herself comfortable on the seat. *Damn—it's hungry today. Has to be that cocaine I took. Bad decision, that—hyperactive vagina.*

Living with vagina dentata was the bane of Josie Kutchner's life. *At least it's vegan—content with cucumbers, carrots and apples. I can't imagine what my life would be like if it wanted meat all the time, like Alison's. What'd I do then?*

Her pussy finished eating the carrot. Josie pushed the green shoots out of sight inside it, waited till it had chewed those up. Then she unrolled a tissue from the dispenser and wiped the orange/green pussy spittle off her crotch and thighs.

She pulled up her jeans and returned to the club stage for the next song.

***

That night, Kim definitely felt things were looking up.

But, next morning,—Kim didn't know if Anne was simply too hungover to recognize the want in her eyes, or simply just a masochistic asshole—next morning Ann greeted Kim like nothing had happened the previous night.

***

Walking into *Dollhouse* that night, Kim couldn't believe her eyes.

Anne and Fat Woman were wrapped around each other on the dance floor, kissing passionately while Strap-On Sisters played the bluesy *I'm Sorry, Pussycat,* the only love song in their repertoire:

"I never meant to hurt you, baby,
But you make me so mad,
When you should make me glad,
And my clit and nipples hard.
I never meant to hit you, darling,
It made me so, so, sad . . . afterwards.

I'm sorry, so, so, so, so sorry,
All I've done all day is worry.
Please take me back, honey,
You can have all my money.
Just forgive and forget,
I'll kneel between your legs,
And get you oh soooooooooo wet."

Fat Woman was squeezing Anne's hot-panted ass so hard Kim could see white finger indentations in the pink skin. Tears were running down her plump cheeks.

"Feeeeeeel me—I'm so wet for you,
Both my mouths are wet for you.
Mouth-to-mouth in sixty-nine,
I'll kiss you till the end of time.

Ah ah ah ah ahhhhhhhhhhhhhhhhhhhhh!"

When Josie Kutchner grabbed her crotch and began faking an orgasm, Kim left in disgust.

After that, she'd found another bar to drink in.

***

And yet, each day at work, Anne kept giving Kim come-hither glances, only to freeze her out at the last instance. Like an ice wall between them.

"So that's it," Kim said aloud now. "I'm done; for good. Lot's of nice girls out there who'll appreciate me. I ain't a waste of space."

She just hoped she'd maintain her resolve once she saw Anne. She practically dreaded seeing her now. *There's just something about those slim hips and that ass that lights my cunt on fire. Anne doesn't have a big ass, but the way it slopes down into her pants . . . like a massive meat spoon, and when she's in shorts . . . I can just see my face between those buttocks, squashing my cheeks together . . . my nose dipping into her . . .*

Kim pulled her mind back to badass mode. *Okay, enough's enough. Six months of hard-to-get is more than the doctor prescribed for me. Bitch, get off and stay off my radar.*

Now additionally pissed-off, Kim descended the stairs. She wanted some ass to kick.

Chapter 52

Kim had arrived back in the entrance hall. The place was totally demolished, its support pillars so bombed they looked like monsters had bitten sections out of them. Kim felt only one of God's miracles was holding the building up. Amidst the rubble and wreckage, groups of eaters and cops were firing at each other from makeshift gun posts.

Damn! It looks like we're playing Middle East Peace Process down here!

The police were being pinned back behind doors, behind the pillars, behind bullet-riddled marble counters.

Now where the hell is Anne?

She spotted two officers reloading a machine gun behind a pillar so pockmarked it looked corroded—its metal skeleton was visible.

She leapt into the open, ran across the hall toward them.

An eater stepped out of cover on Kim's left. He swung his rocket launcher toward her and fired.

Kim flung herself to the floor. The rocket streamed over her and out the entrance to blow a crater in the front plaza.

Crawling like mad, Kim reached cover. The cops loading the machine gun looked up at her. "Where the hell is Lt. Harding? We need backup, we're getting plastered here."

"Out back doing a Jason Bourne impression. Where's Anne Smith?"

The man started to reply, but another rocket streaked past, trailing sparks like splinters. It blew out part of the wall. A backwash of dislodged plaster and smoke rained down on them.

"These damn cannibals are better armed than we are," the cop spat bitterly.

"Hold on a minute," Kim said.

She leapt out of cover, sighted and fired twice. The eater with the rocket launcher toppled over backwards, both his eyes blown out.

She ducked down again. "I was asking: Where's Anne? Harding sent me to her."

The man pointed left. "Through there. She took a unit to circle round the eaters."

Kim looked in the indicated direction. Anne was somewhere through a doorway blasted so devoid of stone it was now circular. Smoke poured from it like there was fire on its other side.

She turned back to the men. "Cover me."

The cops hauled their machine gun into the open and began shooting. Kim took off for the demolished doorway like Satan was after her for her soul.

***

Wading through smoke again. Tense like each step would be her last. Kim took the possibility of death in her stride. Fear didn't count here—it was too late now to renegotiate her karma. She'd live or die. Hopefully live.

Then noise up ahead. Oranges flashes through the acrid mist on her right.

Kim rushed forward, peered in through a glassless window.

She was just in time to see an explosion blow Anne—ginger hair streaming—backward through a doorway.

Kim's heart stopped. *Oh, no. Anne!* All her dislike of the other woman instantly evaporated. Her heart filled with a massive sense of loss.

The room itself was a mess of smashed computers and tables. Anne's unit had all been blown to bits. Human body parts and mangled steel were twisted into bloody sculptures. The trio of eaters who'd blown Anne through the door were laughing. They dropped their weapons, searched the tangled wreckage for people bits to eat.

Kim padded quickly to the doorway. "Hey, cannibals."

The eaters spun around, gaping blood-dripping transparent teeth.

Kim pumped them full of bullets, kicked their falling bodies out of the way, then leapt through the mess to the far door. She skidded once on someone's intestines, but righted herself.

Then she was through. She froze in the doorway, her heart in her mouth.

Annie!

Anne Smith lay untidily, her body totally limp. Her uniform was ripped and bloody. Worst of all, she wasn't breathing. There was no motion from her chest, no rise and fall of those little breasts that Kim had lusted for so long to chew and suck on.

Kim flung her gun down and rushed to her side. "Anne! Anne!"

She unstrapped Anne's helmet and slipped it off. Anne's eyes were shut, her head lolling amidst her cinnamon hair.

200

Hell, she's dead! In that moment Kim realized that she'd gladly endure a million years of the other woman's sexual torment if it meant having Anne back alive.

But . . . Anne didn't seem mortally wounded. *But she isn't breathing* . . . Kim decided to try CPR.

She quickly undid Anne's flak jacket.

Now how'd you do this? she thought desperately. *Hands on tits, lips on lips. No, no, no . . . don't kiss her, spread her mouth open, put mine over it and blow. Remove mouth, press down on her breasts . . . chest . . . don't squeeze . . . press . . . put mouth to mouth again, don't kiss, blow . . . What the fuck? It isn't working!!*

Desperate, she looked out the door, around the destroyed room. No medics, just pieces of people scattered all over. Dead eaters like giant smashed yellow crayons. Curtains of smoke. No point shouting for help, the sound of gunfire came loud from the adjacent rooms.

She looked back down at the limp redhead. *Don't you dare fucking die on me, you cunt-tease.*

Anne coughed. Her amber eyes opened. She looked at Kim in recognition, then scowled. "You're so desperate to eat my pussy that you can't even let me die?"

Kim was so happy. She grabbed the other woman to her and began kissing her face. "Oh, thank you, God, thank you, God. I always knew you existed."

Their lips met, slipped over each other into the wet spaces between them.

Oh what the hell, Kim thought, kissing Anne properly, *I've earned at least this one kiss from her.*

It took her a while to realize that Anne was kissing her back, with even more ardent passion than she was exhibiting. Then Anne wrapped her arms around Kim's neck and pulled her down onto her on the floor.

Their passion flowed like water. A warm, warm feeling flooded Kim. Her whole body felt like a dripping vagina.

After awhile, Kim freed herself. "There's a robbery on. They'll miss us."

"Screw the fighting," Anne said. "Just fuck me. I've been waiting for you to make a move on me forever."

"But I . . ." Kim was totally lost for words. *But I've been after you for six months. You really didn't notice? Oh hell, forget it.*

Kim quickly began unbuckling Anne's belt, before this all turned out to be a dream, a mirage of her unslaked lust, and she'd discover she was in fact holding a conversation with a corpse.

She removed her own helmet, flung it aside.

She now remembered she had a message to deliver to Anne, that they had to stop the ongoing bank heist. For a long moment she was conflicted. She'd always believed duty came first. But now the question: Duty to who? The city? Or oneself?

Then, whilst slipping Anne's pants down over those incredible hips, revealing the redhead's backside to her in all its scooped glory for the first time, Kim smiled. *Anne's right: Screw saving Boston's gold. Love is always more important than money.*

Her reasoning wasn't *all* lust-infused: *There's no fucking way Pussypalm can get the gold out of Boston anyway.*

She dug her mouth between Anne's thighs, began licking her gold-furred crevice. *Oh yes. I've found my own nugget right here.*

Chapter 53

With each step down, Harding's temper steadily worsened. Without Kim's wise-cracking, his grief was allowed full rein.

Visions of Gail, slit open like barbeque, guts spilled like roadkill. Her face ripped off, her vagina dripping rapist cum . . . Harding felt like holding his head and screaming.

A pot-bellied eater wearing a ratty striped suit was guarding the stairwell's ground-floor landing. When Harding reached him, the man was looking down over the railing at the car park.

Harding slipped behind the eater and broke his neck. Skin crawling at the contact with the cannibal, he dragged the dying man back into the shadows.

The eater was taking too long to gurgle his life away. He stared up at Harding, watery eyes like pools in his yellow face.

A rush of hatred flooded Harding. He stomped the eater's face. The man's skull shattered. Yellow brain matter and pink blood squirted from his ears and nostrils.

Harding winced. *They're like bugs, like roaches. Full of nauseating stuff.*

The dead eater's trousers were rotted clean away at the crotch. As was par for the fuck course, the man had a penis but no testicles. Eater men had sex, but never ejaculated.

Disgust flooded Harding. *No jism of their own, so they catch us normal men to knock up their women and make baby eaters.*

Harding lay flat on the landing and peered down into the lot.

Chapter 54

The vault access door had been expanded with explosives. Conveyor belts from all three trucks extended out of sight into it. Three trails of gold bricks streamed from the vault into the vehicle's rears. The flow of gold bricks seemed endless.

Harding winced. *That's three rivers of impoverishment if it gets away. I hope Kim and Anne get those reinforcements over here fast.*

Vavs stood between the trucks, the giantesses leaning on the vehicles like they were bar tops. The vavs' palm-fronded heads easily reached the lot ceiling. Male and female eaters patrolled below the vavs, watching the inner lot doors for break-in attempts. Occasionally an eater touched the gold stream and grinned.

Except for the clanking of the conveyor belt gears, the lot was quiet.

Harding scanned the enclosure. *Where the hell's Pussypalm? Show yourself you son-of-a-bitch.*

Then he saw the bandit, exiting the vault in company of a tall blonde. The blonde wore an open black robe beneath which she was naked.

The couple were laughing. The blonde lifted Pussypalm's left hand and licked its vagina. Both laughed louder. Pussypalm pulled the blonde's head close and whispered something.

Harding cursed. They were too far away for him to hear what they were saying.

Not too far away for a head shot however. Harding laughed. Everything was suddenly so simple. One shot was all it would take; just one bullet to the head and Boston would be free of the asshole for good.

He aimed his gun. The world shrunk to a lined focus along its barrel.

Harding got Pussypalm properly in his sights. The man's cold eyes and evil psychotic grin infuriated the police lieutenant. His finger tightened on the trigger.

The blonde was stroking the flowing gold like a lover, her face lit up with avarice.

Then, just as Harding fired, she shifted position, turning toward Pussypalm to say something.

The bullet hit the blonde in the head. She jerked upward once then flopped over. Pussypalm grabbed her before she hit the floor. He had his gun out, was scanning the lot, trying to pinpoint the shooter's location.

Shit, Harding thought.

Then he froze as the oddest thing happened. The woman he'd just shot withered to smoke in Pussypalm's grasp, then dissolved into thin air. Like she'd never been there at all.

The floor became a swarm of activity as eaters and vavs alike came alive.

Harding scooted back out of sight along the floor. He squatted facing the lot with the eater corpse on his right.

The instant after taking up this pose, there was a swirling of mist in front of him. The gas thickened into the blonde woman he'd just shot in the head.

She stood there before him, naked except for her open robe and high heels.

Harding looked up at her, his shocked eyes trailing her naked body. His gaze ascended her long legs, her crotch, her full breasts, to her beautiful face, with its lovely green eyes.

Blood gushed from the bullet hole in a shallow arc. Reddened brains hung down the right side of her head.

He blinked, speechless, then realized he'd just overlooked something. He looked down again.

The blonde had no vagina. Clearly visible (from Harding's crouched position), her crotch was a seamless stretch of white skin.

He looked back up at her face. She looked ill. He remembered the laws of reality. "You should be dead."

"I am, you bastard," she replied. "You just fucking killed me."

Harding winced. Blood was rushing down her cheek, over her collarbone, between her breasts, soaking her robe. Some was splattering the floor. "Then how . . . ?"

"This is a memory of myself. It'll expire in a short while."

Before Harding could say anything, the blonde lashed out with her foot. The tip of her shoe caught him in the chin; knocking him out cold.

Once he was unconscious, she dissolved again into gas. Harding disappeared along with her.

Chapter 55

Harding woke up. He was on the floor between two of the conveyor belts. A female eater was shaking him awake. He'd been disarmed and his helmet removed. His brain felt like a bomb site.

"Let him go, Gina."

The eater stepped back. She was short, curvy, and pretty, her bald head like the gold dome of an Oriental temple. Her eyes, liquid glass, regarded Harding with amusement.

Harding saw the speaker was Pussypalm. Anger boiled up in him. He leapt up, was forced down with the muzzle of the female eater's rifle in his face. A pleasant smell of flowers rolled off her, incongruously mingling with the smell of oil from the conveyors.

(Harding was facing the trucks. Seeing the neat shimmering rows of stacked gold—like bars of wrapped Belgian chocolate—disappearing into their depths, made him wince. *Where the heck have Kim and Anne gotten to? We're being impoverished here!*)

"Welcome to the gold rush, Lieutenant," Pussypalm said, his voice harsh. He pointed to Harding's left.

Harding looked. The blonde who'd abducted him downstairs sat cross-legged on the floor, gaping wound in her skull toward him. The wound no longer bled, looked like a dog had bitten into her brain. Her jade eyes were dull, like she was dead, but, seeing Harding looking at her, she fluttered graceful fingers in the barest of waves. Her lips parted: "Asshole." Naked thighs spread wide in her seated pose, her vacant crotch gripped Harding's attention.

"You killed Lynn," Pussypalm said. "Her memory of herself will shortly fade."

Harding spat. "And you, raped and killed my little sister, you piece of shit."

Pussypalm laughed. He ran a hand through his brown hair. "Gail? She was good in bed. Fantastic tight pussy. A screamer too."

Harding's hatred blew before his eyes like a sandstorm. Again he tried to get up. This time Gina, the female eater, stuck her gun deep in his crotch. "I'd *love* an excuse to castrate you."

Harding settled. He simmered with impotence. He glared at Pussypalm. The bandit stared back down at him in bored amusement. He held up his left hand, palm forward, the vagina dripping like it had just been fucked. "I'm not about killing you, Lieutenant. I should for killing Lynn—"

Stop saying that, Harding thought, glancing at Lynn. Her dead eyes creeped him out. *She's not dead. But she should be; that wound in her head . . .* Lynn winked slowly at him.

"—But I'm going to show my gratitude for Gail's supertight anus." His gaze hardened. "Now listen. Tell King Eric the Brat that I said thanks for the gold. Also, tell Joe Bradley I said thanks for the loan of Gail's superlative cunt. Extend also my apologies to him for summarily cancelling his wedding."

Harding's face reddened. "I'll get you for this, you bastard!"

"That's fine. Just don't try either it or my patience now." He smiled. "Now, I'll tell you *why.* Your sister was a snotty bitch, endlessly shaking her nonexistent ass at me in the palace and smirking." He touched his cheek in a gesture of remembrance, and laughed, "I called her a frigid tease; told her to put out or get lost. She was mad. She slapped me, told me she'd get me fired if I touched her; she'd have Joe lock me up, have you and your goons work me over."

Harding stared at him in disbelief. "That's all? And you weren't man enough to simply find a woman who wanted you?"

Pussypalm smiled. "What I want, I take. Today, I took what I wanted from Gail. Not bad, though I've had better. I might have let her live, but afterwards *she still kept bitching* . . . threatening to set Joe on me. so . . ." He shrugged. "There's only so much nagging a man can stomach . . . Besides, I was pissed off anyway—the stupid bitch was responsible for King Eric sacking me."

"Bullshit. You two had a pay dispute."

"I never complained to King Eric about money, Lieutenant. Your sister told the Queen I was discontent . . ." He laughed coldly. "She admitted to it after I'd ripped her ass up a bit."

"Screw you. Gail was nothing like that."

"And my dick is ten feet long. Believe what you like."

Pussypalm frowned. "I want you to live and hate me, Lieutenant, knowing I hurt you and got away with it, and there's nothing, absolutely nothing, you can do about it."

Harding glared, but said nothing.

Pussypalm nodded to the eater woman. "I'm done, Gee. Put him to sleep."

Harding looked up in anticipation. She grinned a mouthful of glass teeth back at him, "Sweet dreams, cocksucker," then slammed the butt of her gun against his head.

Harding went out like a busted light bulb. He collapsed between Lynn's knees.

The 'dead' woman absentmindedly stroked his hair.

Chapter 56

"Wake up, sir!"

Harding opened his eyes to a massive headache. It was Kim Fields shaking him. He felt his head. His left temple sported a bump proportionate to his headache. He winced as his fingers traced a shallow cut.

Harding was groggy till he looked around at the empty parking lot. Then he was instantly awake. No trucks, no eaters, no vavs, no Pussypalm, no brain-exploded blonde. Worst of all—

One peer through the vault opening confirmed this last.

—No gold.

He massaged his head in his hands, trying to force the headache somewhere he could retrieve it from later.

It didn't work. He looked helplessly at Kim Fields, noticing for the first time the other cops in the lot. "What happened to the reinforcements I ordered?"

Kim blushed. The reddening of her cheeks made no sense to Harding; he mistook it for battle excitement, like she was about to get a nosebleed. "It took her . . . I mean them . . . quite a while to come, sir."

Harding nodded. It didn't matter. He got to his feet. "Which way did Pussypalm go? Are our guys tracking the trucks across the city? He's a fool—no way he can get out of Boston."

Anne Smith answered. She'd joined them unnoticed. "Brooke Hayes and Unit Nine just got back from helicopter patrol across South End, Roxbury, and out west to Back Bay. Joe Lashley and Lisa Gomez's SWAT teams have already triple-checked Downtown, the Theater District, and Chinatown. They can't find Pussypalm anywhere."

Harding gaped at her. "What?"

"Yes, sir. He's gone missing. Harbor Patrol guys say no trucks went out over the bridge."

It was Kim who spoke. "Anne, Pussypalm has three 18-wheelers with him. Carrying six billion dollars in gold. They'll be moving slower than a snail with superglue for slime. How could we lose them?"

She shrugged helplessly. "I dunno. They're just nowhere to be found."

Harding's head hurt worse than it ever had in his life. "You're telling me they've vanished into thin air?"

For a moment, neither policewoman answered. Then Kim said: "They were gone by the time we got here, sir. No one's seen them since."

Harding walked to the vault door and peered in. Its emptiness assaulted him. "King Eric's going to be mad."

Anne stood beside him. "It's totally cleaned out." Harding looked sharply at her. Her voice was uncharacteristically mellow, her posture lax, relaxed. *Why the hell does she look like she's just had sex?*

Kim joined them. The three walked briskly away from the vault, out of the underground into the sunlight. They stood there watching the medics loading bloodless corpses into ambulances.

Brows furrowed in deep thought, Harding racked his brain, trying to understand how three huge trucks and a mob of vavs and eaters could vanish without trace.

Marlon Barrett's decapitated corpse was carried past, head arranged atop his neck.

Kim froze on seeing Marlon. *Damn, that would have been me!*

Tears sprang to her eyes. She quickly wiped them away.

Anne had noticed. She secretly, gently, squeezed Kim's hand. Kim glanced at her gratefully, her grief shared.

Their lovers' moment passed.

"I don't get it, sir," Anne said to Harding. "Pussypalm's a certifiable lunatic. Why'd he leave you alive?"

"To fucking rub it in my face."

Kim scowled. "Besides, it's nearing Christmas. Maybe he thinks he's Santa Claus."

***

The BPD combed the city like ants crawling over an anthill, to no avail. By evening it was obvious the city's money was long gone.

Chapter 57

Two days after the robbery, Harding visited the morgue. Judy Moran, the district coroner, led him across to Gail's body. Judy was tall and fat with sandy hair, buck teeth, and a large crooked nose.

"Don't be too upset," she told Harding, pulling back the sheet covering his sister's corpse.

Harding gasped. In a necrophile version of plastic surgery, Judy had both built Gail a new face and patched her eaten-up torso with bits from other people. Her skin was a mottled patchwork of color. It looked marginally like her.

Lost for words, Harding turned to the coroner.

"Chief Bradley insisted I do it," Judy said defensively. "He came down here yesterday, took one look at her body and began weeping." Her voice took on a tone of professional pride, "Fortunately, there were enough fragments of flesh lying about for me to borrow."

Judy covered the corpse again.

"You're absolutely *certain* it's her?" Harding asked as she drew the sheet over the corpse's head.

"Positive. DNA, fingerprints, dental records, everything checks out. She also had on her engagement ring."

"Damn."

"Chief Bradley was bawling like a baby."

Harding frowned. "One more thing."

"Yes?"

"The cum in her; was it Pussypalm's?"

She nodded. "Perfect DNA match. Signs of abrasion and bleeding in the vagina, bruising on her thighs, breasts, and buttocks also show that the sex wasn't consensual. He sodomized her too, ripped her anus up."

Oddly, on hearing this last, Harding began to feel much better. The simmering restlessness he'd felt since the robbery finally found a focus.

He was glad that Pussypalm had gotten away. Glad because it meant that he, Lt. Ryan Harding, would be able to find Pussypalm, wherever he was hiding, and kill him, butcher him like the animal he was, without justice interfering. And, yes, he'd really make the bastard suffer first.

Part 4: Morning

Chapter 58

Now Again

Downstairs in the mushroom house, nothing was happening. Sgt. Anne Smith sat in a chair watching the front door. Tony Jones dozed on a sofa opposite her.

She walked over and gently tapped the detective's shoulder.

He opened his eyes and yawned. "Is it four already? Feels like I've only slept ten minutes."

"You *have* only slept ten minutes. I need to go pee—don't want to leave the door unguarded."

Tony nodded and sat up. He lay his rifle across his thighs, yawned again. "Take your time. No way I'll fall asleep any time soon. We're really just watching to ensure Pussypalm doesn't escape anyway."

She nodded and walked off.

***

The toilet bowl was shaped like a set of human lips. It was green in color, clearly fungus, but so lifelike . . .

It was moist, but lacked water. It smelt like lemon.

Anne sat and peed, then froze in shock when something licked her vagina.

What the . . . ? Pants around her ankles, she leapt up, grabbed her rifle, and trained it into the toilet bowl.

She relaxed. It was just a tongue, a thick plant tendril licking the bowl dry.

She grinned. The tendril had given her an idea.

Anne sat back down. The tendril had begun retreating back into the toilet depths. She reached down between her legs and grabbed it. It felt rough, like a cow's tongue looked. She guided it back to her vagina. She moved it over her sexual opening a couple of times till it got the point, then relaxed, one hand on her knee, the other playing in her ginger-colored pubic hair, while it performed cunnilingus on her.

The feeling was exquisite, almost as good as Kim. Oh, damn, Kim—now *that* was a woman. Anne hadn't really known what it meant to be loved till they'd gotten together. She'd had great sex—mind-blowing sex even—with her other partners, but with Kim . . . the fact that the other

215

woman really cared for her made everything so special. Wonderfully special.

Yeah, honey, we're meant for each other.

She grabbed the toilet's tongue as it sought to drop back into the bowl again. "Not yet, honey." Her thighs felt like cream, the toilet lips like Kim's ass magnified a hundred times. She pulled the tongue up again, this time guiding it between her buttocks. She relaxed her ring, and pushed the tongue up inside her.

Her anus stung a little as it was penetrated. *Fuck, Kim. You almost destroyed me with that strap-on.* The pain brought pleasant memories however.

The tongue thrust up and down inside Anne. It was frustrated. The mushroom house sought excrement for nourishment. It could sense this food inside the hole in Kim's body, but had no understanding why the shit didn't drop into the mouth she sat on like it was supposed to. In its desperation to feed, it slid in and out with plant persistence.

Anne masturbated, her fingers fluttering over her clit in time with the tongue's strokes into her anus. She giggled as she came. *Oh God oh God oh God.*

Her orgasm over, Anne pulled the still-hungrily questing tentacle out of her ass. She leapt to her feet before it penetrated her again. Her legs were still weak as she pulled up her panties and trousers.

She was grinning while she buckled her belt. *I can just imagine the look on Kim's face when I tell what I just did. She'll be mad!*

Laughing, she bent to retrieve her gun. The sound froze in her throat as something hit her in the neck. She tried to straighten up, but found she just felt increasingly tired.

Groggy as shit, she managed to raise her head. She gaped at the grinning yellow girl in the toilet doorway. At the blowgun she held.

Oh, fuck, Anne thought, crashing to the floor unconscious.

Chapter 59

The room was first black, like night had been poured into it.

Slowly, in stages, it lightened, till at length he made out a huge gold temple at its farther end. A massive edifice that must've cost a king's ransom to build. Chaperoned by green clouds, the sun floated behind the temple, so brightly the lustrous metal seemed to flow like mercury.

The room's walls were still black. They rose forever like they were eternity.

Tom set off for the golden building.

He was filled with a compulsion to reach it, with the knowledge he'd find answers in it.

The temple's walls shimmered like glass. Likewise, the road to it was a strip of glass that duplicated him in reflection as he trod along it.

He realized he was naked. Thankfully, there was no one else around to see him. He reached the temple, pushed aside the silken curtains shrouding the door. Stepped inside.

"So you finally got here."

The speaker was Lynn—tall, blonde, beautiful. She sat on a golden throne in the middle of the gold temple, the walls of which now rose forever up to the sun somehow shining through the solid ceiling.

"What kept you?" Lynn's voice was smooth as dripping honey.

"You're expecting me?" he asked.

She frowned. "What a dumb question. Like I've anything else to do." Her eyes—green jade jewels, cold and pissed off—bored into his. "You've got my vagina. Give it back."

He looked at her. Then at himself. "What?"

"She means me," a squishy scared voice squealed from his left hand.

He looked down in horror. The vagina in his palm was trembling, dribbling secretion in its terror.

"The cunt's mine," Lynn said. "Sorry to pun here, but, *hand* it over." She laughed coldly. "Hand—get it?"

"I don't understand."

She rolled her eyes, then split her thighs, spreading them wide and high.

His eyes widened. "You don't have a—" he shut up on seeing her anus, a massive slack chasm like a child's yawning mouth. He wondered how she kept poop in.

"Butt plug," she said. "Huge one." She climbed down off the throne. She walked quickly towards him, gripping a gold axe that materialized from nowhere.

"Take it up the ass like I've been doing if you're so desperate to get fucked."

She reached him, swung the axe at his left arm. "Just a little separation."

"No!" Tom and Rose yelled simultaneously.

Tom twisted sideways, away from the axe, then flung a punch at Lynn. The blow knocked her flat on her back. She hit the floor hard, her gold axe spinning out of sight into the golden light.

She lay there, thighs splayed like a sexual invitation, breathing heavily. He stared hard at her crotch, then at his hand, then at her crotch again, willing the vagina to leap the distance between their bodies and implant itself in her pubic hair.

"No!" Rose shrieked, spitting fluid. "Don't ever leave me, Tom!"

"We're going to have to do this the hard way," Lynn said. She tapped her crotch. "Hey Poopie," she yelled. "Get your ass out here."

Rose began shrieking. "No! No!"

Tom tried to calm the vagina. "Shush! What's the matter?"

"Poopie's bad! We need to split before he arrives."

The blonde was still tapping her crotch. "Poopie! I said get your ass out here!"

A growly voice rumbled from her buttocks, "But it's nice and warm in here. I don't like the gold out there." Her extensive anal folds rippled like sails catching the breeze.

"Out here, already," Lynn snapped.

Her anus, already a massive chasm, expanded farther. At the far end of her rectum, Tom sighted something brown pushing outward, flowing like honey.

He froze. The rolling mass of shit had a face embedded in it. A corruption of a face, but recognizable as one.

"Ooh," Rose exclaimed. "Poopie's coming. Let's go!"

Tom was convinced—this was BAD. Only now, he was unable to flee, his legs felt welded to the floor. "Don't worry," he told Rose, soothingly, "We'll make it out of here alive."

He watched. The turd with the face seeped out of Lynn's ass. Behind its head it was like diarrhea, spreading under her buttocks. She smiled at Tom. "Poopie here will take care of you, tough guy."

The pool of shit completely exited her anus. It stank to high heavens. It began pulling itself into an upright shape, becoming a manlike monster a foot and a half taller than Tom. With those facial features that were holes and lumps sculpted in excrement.

More bothersome to Tom than the monster's size, however, was the size of its penis. Poopie's cock was a good two feet long. It was fully erect and curved upward, its fist-sized glans throbbing in front of Poopie's chest. The shit-penis was cracked like an old pavement. Grass-like fibers poked from it.

Poopie's stench rolled over Tom. He stared from the shit-creature to Lynn in horror. She still lay on the floor, leaning up on an elbow. She giggled, blew him a kiss.

"Oh, yeah, you're gonna get so fucked, Tom. I told you to give me back my vagina, didn't I?" She grinned. "Hey, Poopie; fuck this asshole!"

"Okay, Lynn!" The gleaming from the temple shone all over the creature, bathing it in a multitude of spotlights. The golden illumination made it look more horrible. Leaving shit-splotch footprints, it strode confidently towards Tom.

"Run, Tom!" Rose moaned. "It's so big!"

Poopie the shit monster came closer. Tom fought to unstick his feet. "I'm trying, Rose . . . I ca—"

That was the last thing he said. As Poopie reached Tom, he suddenly found himself unable to speak through his mouth. His tongue was missing. And his teeth.

A familiar musky smell reached his nostrils.

"Flee, Tom!" Rose screamed, only now, its voice was coming from Tom's face. He looked down at his left hand, saw that his mouth resided there now.

Poopie stood smirking at him, its brown mushy lips split in amusement.

"Surprised?" it asked.

Tom turned to Lynn with pleading eyes. "Please," he begged, speaking out of his hand. "You can have it back."

She ran fingers through her blonde hair. "Not yet. You both need to be taught a lesson." Her eyes gleamed. "Now deep-throat the shit-cock with your mouth-pussy."

"Hell, no!" Tom and Rose yelped simultaneously.

Poopie grinned broadly. "Hell yeah." It grabbed Tom. Tom fought against Poopie, but the creature's stink weakened him like nerve gas. Gripping his shoulders, Poopie pushed him down to his knees. Then it gripped his head and forced its massive shit penis into the vagina in Tom's face.

"NO!" Tom yelled from his hand as he felt the excrement phallus entering his head, curving down so it was going down his throat.

"Wow, honey," Lynn said. "Your gag reflex is fucked."

Tom hammered the monster with his fists, splattering shit left and right. To no avail. Mouth-in-palm shut tight, he gripped its grapefruit-sized testes and squeezed. His hands sunk into the testicles' fecal substance. Shit squirted between his fingers, then firmed again over both his hands, liquid shackles locking them in place in Poopie's body.

Tom's mouth-vagina was now filled with the shit-cock. He became a single massive urge to throw up everywhere.

Poopie's penis was six inches into Rose, the vagina now looking like an unwiped post-crap anus.

"His throat's real tight," Poopie said.

The blonde grinned. "You know how all these virgins are. Just persevere: you'll bypass his reservations."

Poopie yanked extra-hard on Tom's head. The shit-penis slid in deeper: first an additional six inches, then a full foot, then finally everything went in—two feet of excrement.

Poopie's crotch pressed against Tom's face. Poop squirted into Tom's nostrils, flooded up them. He shut his eyes tight against the solid wall of brown feces facing him.

He kept the mouth in his hand similarly clamped shut.

In his mind he heard Rose screaming in pain against the violation. There was however nothing he could do. The shit-cock was all the way down his throat now, past his sphincter, into his stomach.

He was dying. He couldn't breathe with the cock in his face, in his head. In addition he could smell that there wasn't any air to breathe—all was vomit-inducing stench, like he'd been shoved up an anus.

I'm being face-raped to death by a woman's shit. Traumatized, he fainted, overcome by the stink and degradation.

It however wasn't over. Outside of himself, he watched the shit monster now fuck his face fast and furious, until his head was so covered with excrement that it looked like a turd itself. His hands were both still buried—locked—in Poopie's testicles.

He stood disembodied, watching it slide its humongous cock in and out of Rose, the vagina a brown hole in his head.

"I'm gonna cum, Lynn!" Poopie yelped. "Damn this feels super good. I gotta do this more often."

"Go for it, honey. Might be awhile before you get a face to fuck again."

Poopie pumped and pumped and came. Tom watched his belly swell up as the shit monster ejaculated. Poopie visibly shrank as it came, while Tom's belly bulged like he was pregnant. Finally, Poopie disappeared completely into Tom's mouth. All the shit wiped off his head after it. Rose looked like a flower between his lips.

Freed of its anchorage in the monster, Tom's body now toppled over sideways. He now looked like a blimp with arms and legs.

"Wow!" Lynn said, rising from the floor and stretching like she'd just cum herself. "I really outdid myself this time."

She snickered at the prone body. "Dude, that'll *teach* your ass not to mess with mine."

She searched around till she found her golden axe, then walked back over to Tom's body. "Now to get my cunt back."

"No!" Tom shrieked, as with one slash, she chopped off his head.

He didn't bleed. All that pumped out of his neck was a river of shit. Even discorporate, Tom could smell its horrible stink. The stench filled the golden temple like a perfume of decay.

The blonde laughed. Carrying Tom's severed head, she walked off towards her throne, wading through the excrement.

Tom walked over to his decapitated body. He stared down aghast at it. Its belly steadily deflated as the shit pumped out of him. *Oh, fuck!* He looked over at the woman who held his head.

She looked dreamily toward him, unable to see him. She raised Tom's dead face to hers and began kissing it; pressing her lips to its labia, tonguing his vagina mouth, licking its clitoris.

"No! No!" Rose shrieked. "I don't swing that way! I love Tom. Tom, Tom. She's raping me! Save me, Tom!"

"Shut up, you retard. You're *my* vagina! Your stupid boyfriend's dead—murdered by my shit." She began licking Rose again.

After a while, Rose moaned back, "Oooo fuck, Lynn, I love you so much more than that Tom prick. You really know how to do me."

"That's because I am you, you dumb slit—I know what I like."

Amber light gleamed down fiercely on them, like the gold temple approved of their strange communion.

Tom watched Lynn lick her vagina in his head. His heart was broken. He loved Rose and she'd deserted him.

He broke down and began crying.

***

221

Tom jerked awake. Sweat poured off him like he'd been doused with water. He instantly grabbed his head, ensuring it was still attached to him.

What the . . . ? Not again. Lynn siccing a shit monster on me? Damn! It's getting worse.

A revolting stink of excrement plugged his nostrils and mouth. He snorted and gulped in clean air, then wiped his mouth with his hand, worried it would smear brown.

His hand came away clean. Relieved, Tom sat up. Morning sun steamed in through the window.

The door burst open and Harding entered.

"Get your ass out of bed," the burly cop growled at him. "We had company last night. The eaters got Anne and Tony."

Chapter 60

Detective Tony Jones woke up. His head hurt like . . .

Tony suddenly realized he was both naked and tied up. He shook his head to clear it, then examined himself. He was tied between two poles, arms outstretched overhead and lashed to the poles with cords around his wrists, his ankles secured likewise.

Goddam it—I nodded off again? I got knocked out in my sleep?

He was in a large chamber with earthen walls and a large number of eaters present busy with different things.

Directly in front of Tony, a group eaters were gathered around a table, a waist-high stone slab. Tony couldn't see what they were doing. He however saw the blood streaming around their yellow feet.

The others. What happened to the others? That's definitely one of the guys being . . .

***

Tony's attention was suddenly diverted. A little eater girl and her mother were walking toward him.

"Mummy, I want some ice cream," the little girl squealed suddenly.

Her mother rolled her eyes, creepy without eyelashes. She looked at Tony as if to say: 'kids.' Then: "Okay, honey, help yourself. You know how. But not too much now."

Tony rolled his eyes too. *And where the hell are you going to find a fridge, you little yellow horror?*

Tony then looked around for the first time. He shuddered. On his left, the copse of a fat bearded man lay on a table. Naked, and with his throat slit. His head opened, his brain excavated. Legs apart and with his torso stitched like he'd just been autopsied.

The little eater girl skipped over to the dead man and without ado, stuck her hand up between the fat saggy buttocks.

Tony's eyes widened in shock. *Ice cream? No . . . she meant ass . . . ass cream? Oh, God, no . . . !*

"It's *tight*, mommy."

"All assholes are, dear. You need to push harder to open a back door." She regarded her daughter. "You want me to show you how it's done?"

"No, I'm a big girl now."

"If you say so, darling."

"The last one wasn't this tight. My hand went in easy."

"I think she used to be a porn actress, darling." She smiled patronizingly. "Just push harder. Yes, baby, like that."

The eater child had taken firm grip of the dead man's testicles to brace herself, then forced her hand up deep inside his anus.

She grinned. "I'm in, mommy, whoopee!"

Her mother clapped. "Wow, you're so smart. Okay now, don't take too much. Remember, it'll soon be time for breakfast."

"Awwww, but, mum, he's *full* of ass cream."

"No, honey. One handful is all you can have. Don't be greedy; the other kids will want some too."

The little girl nodded. Tony could practically see the wheels of her mind turning as she worked out how to grab as much feces as she could.

Oh no, I really don't need to see this.

The girl's mother saw the sick look on Tony's face and laughed aloud. "It's not what you think."

"She's fishing for shit in a dead man's rectum."

The yellow woman shook her head. "Not shit. Ass cream is a new invention. Kid party fun. You stuff an emptied corpse with pulped human brains mixed with heavy cream, sugar, whisked egg-white, and cornstarch thickening, then the kids get it out by jumping on the corpse's belly so it squirts from the ass, hence the name."

Shortly, the little girl's fist exited the fat corpse's buttocks again. Her yellow hand was now coated with chunky white stuff.

"See what I mean?" her mother asked Tony.

He nodded mutely.

The little girl raised the handful to her mouth and took a lick.

Her mother asked, "Good, darling?"

She beamed back, see-thru teeth gleaming. "Oh, yes, mommy! Vanilla flavor! Delicious."

She skipped away happily. Her mother winked at Tony, then followed.

***

Tony's attention now returned to his own predicament.

A female eater stepped away from those working at the slab. Tony saw the female head behind her on the slab, the carrot-colored hair, staring amber eyes. Gashed throat with meat and windpipe exposed.

He winced. *Anne.*

"Hey," the eater woman said, tapping a man on the shoulder. "Breakfast is awake."

Fear flooded Tony at her words. The eater woman blew him a kiss. She was skinny, and heavily pregnant, her bared yellow belly taut like it would burst at the prick of a pin. She was quite a looker. An odd beauty, considering how she lacked hair and eyebrows, and her eyes looked like holes covered over with scotch tape.

The man turned to look disinterestedly at Tony. "He's dinner, Mary, not breakfast."

"But he looks delicious."

"You should have said that before we killed the girl."

Mary's yellow face twisted into a scowl. "But I want to eat him now."

"Fucking suck his dick then. Just don't bite it off—I don't want him bleeding to death on us; fresh food is always best."

"Okay."

She walked over to Tony and grabbed his penis.

"Leave me alone," Tony yowled, cringing at her touch. Her fingers felt dry and unpleasant, like reptile skin.

She giggled up a mouthful of teeth, her transparent eyes conveying lust despite their invisible pupils. "Now don't be like that baby; you should be grateful; it isn't every woman that wants to suck a condemned man's schlong."

All Tony's courage drained from him. *Her teeth are like transparent flick-knife blades. If she bites me down there . . .*

"Don't be scared," she said. "I give great head. My husband always used to say so before we ate him."

Tony didn't reply. He couldn't. She began to suck him lustily. Tony hated himself, when, despite his horror, he got an erection.

Mary lifted her mouth from his penis. "Now, *you're* the sort of man I like—a hard one."

Tony didn't hear her. The eaters around the stone slab had now moved away, and Tony saw what they'd been up to.

Anne's headless body lay spread-eagled; totally opened up like she'd exploded. Her belly, her arms, her legs all were split wide. Her limbs lay limp as cooked noodles, their muscles held in place by her skin. Her ribless chest looked like an unzipped handbag.

Her bones have all been removed, Tony realized. They were piled besides her corpse. *But why?*

An eater wheeled a metal butcher cart piled with vegetables across to Anne's body. Carrots, cabbage, giant red and green peppers, broccoli, onions, radishes, string beans. Simultaneously, Tony noticed the previously-hid cauldron on the other side of the slab. Fire burnt fiercely beneath it; steam rose from bubbling water.

Mary was sucking Tony fiercely now. His penis was incredibly hard, but didn't feel part of him. He never even noticed that she'd been right that she gave great head. His horror prevented appreciation of her fellatrix expertise.

Mary, however, was getting off big time. While sucking Tony off, she squeezed his balls with one hand; the other rubbed under her distended belly.

The eater with the metal cart scooped all Anne's bones into a bucket and stuck it under the cart. Picking out a knife from an arrayed selection, he proceeded to cut her muscles out of her hands and legs, then dropped them amidst the veggies on the cart.

"Hey, Joyce! Tammi! Give Dave a hand, willya! The water's been boiling now for ten minutes."

Two female eaters joined the man by Anne's corpse. Picking up cleavers, they diced up her flesh along with the vegetables. Their faces as they worked were serious, not maniacal like a human psycho's would be. As uninvolved as Tony would be whilst making a sandwich.

Tony watched in horror. He was unable to speak, no words existed inadequate enough to express his disbelief. He'd fought against eaters, himself killed many, heard stories of what they did . . . but never had it been like this.

I'm getting a blowjob while these monsters are turning Anne into soup.

Below him, Mary was groaning out an orgasm, two fingers stuck deep up her vagina. Several female eaters gathered round them, their gaze shifting from Mary and Tony to Anne's corpse and back again.

Dave cut Anne's heart and lungs out of her and deposited them on the cart. Joyce and Tammi quickly reduced the organs to a pile of chunks. Anne's liver and kidneys followed, then her spleen. Her intestines went into the bucket alongside her bones.

Dave turned to the women. "You ladies done?"

Tammi nodded. Dave dug his hands into the mass of chopped meat and veggies and mixed them up thoroughly. Then he started stuffing Anne's corpse with them. The women helped him.

Tony was forced to ask: "What the hell are you doing?"

Dave replied, "Relax with the questions, man; you'll find out soon enough."

He said no more. Neither did Tony.

Between Tony's legs, Mary had sated herself and was sitting on the floor breathing heavily. "I feel so much better now, Kay," she told one of the other eater girls between gasps.

"He hasn't cum yet," Kay replied. She was plump, with a thin nose. She pulled down her panties. "I'll have a turn too. I want to be pregnant like you."

Tony's blood chilled. *NO.*

Kay grinned at Tony. "Okay, stud, lets go."

She backed up to him, and, standing on tip-toes, slid onto his erection. "Fuck, this feels good," she groaned as she slipped all the way down on him. "Dammit, Dave, do we really have to eat him today?" She began pumping her ass back and forth on Tony.

Dave had in the meantime stuffed Anne full of the meat-veggie mix. While he sprinkled salt and spices into her and stirred everything up some more, Joyce and Tammi began suturing up the corpse's splayed trunk. Dave removed his hands and they stitched Anne all the way up from crotch to neck.

Then, while Tony both moaned in horror and groaned to the pleasure of Kay's vagina, the cannibal cooks lifted Anne's stuffed body off the slab by its emptied limbs and dropped it into the boiling cauldron.

Dave covered it with a metal lid. "Our girl dumpling should be done in say thirty minutes."

Mary, now standing to one side and watching Kay fuck Tony, licked her lips. "I can't wait."

It was the innocence she said it with that horrified Tony, the understanding that she saw nothing wrong with eating him.

Kay groaned through an orgasm. "He's not cumming," she panted accusingly when she was done. "I want to feel his spunk in me."

Pregnant Mary thought a moment. "He's just distracted. Keep screwing him. I know what to do."

Kay began slamming her ass on Tony again. Mary got on her knees behind Tony. She spread his buttocks and began licking his anus.

"Stop that," Tony moaned as her tongue flicked up and down over his ring.

Mary stopped. "Come for Kay, boy. She wants to have your baby." She laughed. "You're going to die; might as well leave some genes behind in the world."

She returned her mouth to tonguing his anus, working it inside him.

The feeling was too much for Tony. Horrified as he was, he began ejaculating.

"Fucking-A," Kay yelped. "I don't think he's cum in ages. Feel's like he's pumping an entire gallon of semen in me. I'll get a baby from this for sure."

Mary removed her face from Tony's ass and stood up. She wiped her mouth clean, then folded her hands over her distended belly. "If it's a girl, name it Mary; this is as much my doing as his."

Kay laughed. "Whatever you say, darling."

Tony finished cumming. Kay separated from him, and collapsed to the floor by his side. She lay there, looking up at him with a happy smile. "What's your name, darling? Just in case it's a boy."

Tony couldn't answer.

"Give the kid a nice tough name," Mary advised. "Something his cop dada will be proud of. Something like Tony."

Kay wrinkled her face. "Tony?"

"You know, Tony Montana in *Scarface*. Guys looooovve that dumb movie."

Kay waved from the floor. "Ladies and gents; hooray for little Tony. Damn, I feel flooded."

Tony, hung there as tied, utterly speechless.

A while later, Dave looked up from the cauldron he was boiling Anne in. "She's ready now. Someone bring plates." He grinned at the spent Tony. "Hey, lover man! Better sow all the oats you can; you'll be in this pot in nine hours."

Tony refused to accept that. His mind raced violently, seeking an escape.

"Forget your friends," Mary said, coming over to him carrying a plate heaped high with the mix of cooked Anne and vegetables. "They've forgotten *you*." The pregnant eater chewed a bit. "We're gonna eat you. Hope you're as delicious as she is."

Oh, hell no! Tony thought desperately, *they'll fuck Pussypalm's hand and find me before then.*

Mary forked some carrots into her mouth. "Too bad only three of us were out last night. More of us, and we'd have caught the rest of you. Then you'd have company now."

Kay got up from the floor. She squeezed Tony's ass hard, then waltzed over to get a plate of Anne. Watching her go, Tony couldn't help admiring her figure. She had nice buttocks and shapely legs.

He now noticed Dave in conversation with a dirty teenaged boy. Dave was scowling, angry, jerking his thumb at Tony, while the teen kept nodding emphatically.

The teen left. Scowling, Dave handed serving duties over to Tammi and walked across to Tony.

Tony almost crapped himself when he saw the bloody serrated knife the eater held.

Dave reached him and frowned.

"If there's shit I hate," Dave told Tony. "It's having my menu dictated by others."

"What are you . . . ?"

Dave's expression was extremely pained. "Sorry, dude. Normally I'd let you enjoy the girls till evening, but Big Sister Kelly just sent in a request for sautéed kidney . . ." He pointed apologetically to the slab where Anne had been butchered, and I already used up all of your redhead friend. So—"

"Please," Tony pleaded, suddenly caught in the grip of a horror that transcended the fear of death. "Refuse to do it, tell her no . . . just till evening. *They'll definitely screw Pussypalm's hand,* he thought, clinging to his single glimmer of hope. *I gotta buy time, gotta buy me some time.*

Dave looked really upset. "Sorry, dude. I'd like to help, I mean there's some utterly fantastic pussy around here—I mean you just got to see Melina and Cassie-Jo . . . But Big Sister's word is law."

"Aw man, give me a br—"

Tony went silent with shock as Dave, still looking extremely upset, stabbed him in the bellybutton. He felt incredible pain, which just increased. Looking down, he watched as Tony slit his belly across left and right, cutting through the abdominal muscle with a practiced hand. Blood streamed out of Tony's belly and poured over his genitals. Tony screamed with the pain, thrashed futilely against his bonds.

Meanwhile, Dave reached into the rive, fishing between Tony's guts till he found his left kidney. He cut it out, then searched for Tony's right kidney, and extracted that also.

He straightened up, holding both bloody organs like they were prizes. "Man," he told Tony, "you got big fatass kidneys. Big Sister Kelly will be overjoyed. Make a great sauté . . . I can already smell 'em sizzling, diced and spiced . . . in butter, with some onions and chili, a twist of lemon . . ."

His expression changed. "But you know, man. It's like I was saying, I just hate it when I got gourmet plans and Big Sister just wants fast food. It's like asking Picasso to paint a horse, dammit. Like asking Hélène Darroze or Jamie Oliver to manage a McDonald's. Like my kitchen art is being—"

"Go screw yourself, asshole . . . ?" Tony interrupted dully, picking the words through the pain flooding his body. He was incredulous. *I'm dying here. I've just been gutted like a cow, by a cannibal who's more worried about cooking ethics than my life?*

Dave misinterpreted the look on Tony's face. "Sorry, man," he said. "I shouldn't let you suffer like this. It's inhumane."

He slit Tony's throat from ear to ear.

Chapter 61

Forget it," Tom said. "It's not happening."

Harding scowled at him. "Consulting your hand is the only way we'll know for sure."

"No," Tom reiterated.

"Now you look here, you prick, this is all your fault to start with."

Brooke spat in disgust. "Harding, they're both dead by now. You know that as well as I do."

"That's right," Megan concurred. "If they're not, we've no chance of saving them. There are too few of us. From what we've seen, there may be hundreds of eaters up here. Too many to take on."

"I don't like the thought of just leaving them."

"Neither do *we*, Lieutenant."

Harding looked away in disgust. After last night, he'd come to trust Megan's instincts. She was right, of course, but it was against all his principles to not even attempt a rescue . . .

He looked from Tom to the others. "I just don't believe the amount of crap we're going through because of this piece of murdering shit. We've lost four good officers, simply because of this thieving bastard, this slime from a garbage dump—"

Tom had had enough of Harding's insults. He leapt at the cop, fists swinging.

The attack caught Harding totally by surprise. A punch connected to his jaw, then Tom barreled into him and they both went down.

Harding was stronger and a more experienced fighter, but Tom was *motivated*. It wasn't just the other man's constant abuse. Everything had stacked up to this point—the vagina in his hand, his arrival here, the stolen gold, Queen Shirley and Joe Bradley's deaths . . . and worst of all, the constant flashes he kept having each time he handled a gun, irrefutable testament that he was very likely someone else, someone he'd forgotten being.

Confusion, frustration, pain, anger. All boiled over in Tom now. Harding was simply a convenient focus.

The pair rolled over and over, punching and pummeling each other, hatred in their eyes. They staggered to their feet. Bruised and bleeding, they fought on. Grimly, silent as the reaper, except for the thudding of blows.

Brooke moved to separate them.

Megan held her back.

"Testosterone at work," she said. "It's good occasionally for men to work the machismo out of their systems."

"Megan, they're trying to kill each other."

"Neither of them are that stupid."

Brooke looked at her pityingly. "Wanna bet?"

"I'm enjoying it. Violence is sexy." She saw the angry look on Brooke's face. "Oh alright, I'll break them up."

She walked over to the pair, who'd now crashed onto a fungus sofa, Tom on top.

Tom, busily throttling Harding, who, purple-faced, was throttling him in return, was suddenly aware of a sharp pain between his legs. A pain like he'd been castrated.

He looked down between he and Harding's bodies, saw the white hand holding his crotch, then turned to stare at Megan over his shoulder.

"You've got nice egg-like testicles," she said, giving them another squeeze. "Be a shame if I popped them."

Tom nodded. The pain was unbelievable. He instantly let go of Harding, who kept choking him.

Megan let go of Tom. She winked at Harding. "You too, unless you want the same."

Harding obediently let go of Tom's neck.

"Both of you sit," Brooke instructed, "and let's figure this out."

"Like good boys," Megan added. "No more macho posturing."

Both men, faces bloody, sat on the sofa, breathing heavily. Tom held his crotch. Harding smirked at him. The policeman had the beginning of a black eye. Tom had a cut on his cheek.

Megan and Brooke stood facing them. Megan regarded Brooke coolly. "You're in charge of this mission; what's your decision?"

She frowned. "Harding's right. We can't go on until we know for sure where Anne and Tony are. Danger or not, there might be a chance to rescue them. She nodded at Megan. "Go love Tom's hand in the toilet."

Megan extended a hand to Tom. "Come on, you know you want to."

"Get up, dickhead," Harding growled.

Megan pulled Tom to his feet and led him off.

"For fuck's sake, Lieutenant; control yourself!" Brooke said behind them.

"Hey, the son-of-a-bitch attacked *me*!"

Tom and Megan returned five minutes later.

"They're both dead," Megan said simply. "Our orgasms were worth the inquiry, however."

Tom glared at Harding and Brooke. "I hope you two are convinced now."

"Screw your personal pride," Brooke retorted. "My officers' lives are worth more than your useless cum."

"A prophetic pussy is a priceless possession," Megan continued. "Penetrated, it provides pure pleasure, like—"

"My metal detector just started working," Harding interrupted. "The gold's around here somewhere."

They all gathered around to see. The indicator of Harding's detector bracelet, a converted sub-nuclear compass, pointed an unerring northeast.

"Well at least one good thing's happened today," Brooke said, her voice grim. "Let's get over there."

Part 5: Mountain

Chapter 62

Kim Fields kicked the basement door off its hinges.

There was a single sentry, a yellow-skinned man sitting on a stool.

His slanted eyes suggested he'd been Chinese before the Bizarro virus transformed him.

"Freeze, asshole!"

The eater reached for his gun instead. Kim and two other cops pumped him full of holes. His perforated corpse collapsed off his stool, draining pink onto the floor.

"I wonder why perps keep doing that bravado shit, Sarge," Officer Bobby Robbins said. Bobby was stocky, with curly brown hair.

"Cos they're stupid." Kim looked around quickly as other officers entered the room. A half-eaten little-girl-corpse lay in a corner. The body was gutted, emptied of organs—typical eater M.O. The child's hairless cunt poked from her bloody skirt—a pissed-off prediction of puberty never to materialize.

Kim scowled. To the right of the corpse was a barred and padlocked metal door.

"Don't like this, Sarge. Eaters installing a barred door here means long-term plans to use the place."

Kim scowled. He was right. "Their plans just got scrapped by the Boston City Council." She nodded at the door. "Open it. Keys should be on that dead motherfucker."

Bobby got the key ring. He and another cop got the metal door open.

Bright light instantly flooded the basement.

That's odd, Kim thought. *Like daylight.* She walked over to where Bobby and the other cop were gaping wide-eyed out the doorway.

"We're mass hallucinating, right!?"

They were looking out on a wide beach starkly framed under a clear morning sky. Overhead, the sun burnt bright orange. Below it floated fluffy clouds.

Bobby found his voice. "Sarge, we're currently two floors below Chinatown, which is in turn under Bizarro, how come there's sun everywhere?"

To that, Kim had no immediate reply. Toughness held no defense whatever for the sudden inexplicable inversion of the laws of science.

I got a fucking job to do here. Steeling herself against the unknown, Kim stepped through the door.

"Sarge . . . you sure bout this?"

She glanced back at the tough, conflict-processed women and men crammed into the room. All looked uncertain. These officers were Boston's finest. None of them were scared of death, but this wasn't death, this was . . .

"Haul ass, the lot of you," Kim said. "Eaters get in through here, means what's outside ain't killing 'em."

Everyone still looked unconvinced. There was some motion, but not much.

"Move your asses, you slackers! You don't see any eater corpses around here, do you!? Those cannibal shitheads can survive here, so can we!"

That got everyone in motion. Whilst her unit pulled itself out through the door, Kim moved farther outside and looked around properly.

They were exiting a cave on a short cliff projection overlooking a beach. Steps cut into the rock surface descended from the cave almost to the edge of the white water.

White water? Yes it *was* white, like paint.

Kim descended toward the beach, studying the water. The curvature of the shore suggested a lake or lagoon.

She groaned. In the far distance, wreathed in clouds, a mountain-tall naked woman stood buttock-deep in the water. She was middle-aged, with pale eyes and straw-colored hair. Her body was as flawlessly white as if carved from limestone. Her belly was massive, distended and taut with pregnancy. Dangling between her proportionately huge breasts was a silver pendant—the word 'MAMA.'

Her breasts . . .

Kim blinked twice in disbelief. She wiped her eyes with her hands, then blinked again. *She's squirting the sea from her breasts? This liquid is milk, not water?*

The white liquid spurted in endless jets from the distant giantess's nipples. Liquid over solid white, it streamed down her front, cascading from her pregnant belly to crash into the lake, from whence it exploded back upward in a wall of mist that obscured her mons.

The giantess's face was unemotional. Her gaze was set above them, like she was watching for someone or something.

Kim grinned. Something about the woman's cold detachment reminded her of Anne. *Yeah, that's it—she looks exactly how Anne does*

238

when we fight and she wants me to apologize first. Catch her cold in the act, Anne would rather die than admit she was wrong.

With the memory of her girlfriend, a nice warmth built up in Kim's crotch. Oh, last night had been just delicious. A major mistress punishment scene.

***

Kim slapped Anne. Just hard enough to get her attention.

"Fucking stop that! I'm clipping my toenails!" She scowled up at Kim, who'd just come in and was all sweaty. "Why the hell did you slap me anyway?"

"You stupid bitch. I saw you making eyes at Brooke Hayes again."

"I wasn't."

"Oh yes, you were, you little authority slut!"

Anne dropped the nail clipper. "Ohhh, look who's jealous." Her face burnt where Kim had hit her. She however felt a familiar warmth start down in her vagina. It occurred to her that the evening might get sleazy. She grinned. "Wow, Kim. You look totally hot, like sex barbequed on a skewer."

Kim slapped her again. Harder now. Anne fell back naked on the bed. Kim quietly stripped and got out her green 'firefly' dildo. Seeing the look in her girlfriend's eyes as she strapped it on—part fear, part anticipation, part rebellion—filled her with her own mixture of anger and lust. She felt powerful. She reached beneath the harness and dug fingers into her cunt. Sticky, sticky. *Teaching this bitch-slut-lover a well-deserved lesson is just what I need to unwind tonight.* She smelt her sticky fingers. Sex and sweat.

Intoxicated on the smell of herself, Kim advanced on the bed. "You need to realize who's boss in this relationship."

Anne yawned. "Darling, I'm not your property. Did you remember to pick up the hair gel I asked you to help me get?"

Kim got on the bed and grabbed her by the shoulder. "Listen to me, you little slut. You don't even blink at the sun unless I give you permission to do so."

Anne smirked. "Or what? You'll screw your way up to become police chief too?" She stifled a yawn. "You career girls are all alike, all bark and no dyke." She dropped her hand to her vagina, spreading its pink folds so her girlfriend could see the white smear of her arousal amidst its lips. "Screw your endless jealousy trip. Gimme me some loving instead, darlin'."

"Oh, you think this is a joke?"

"I look horny, not amused." She swirled a finger around inside her cunt, then lifted it to Kim's nose. "I smell fuckable don't I?" With her other hand she lifted her left breast to her mouth and licked its nipple, her eyes never leaving Kim's.

Oh, I'm definitely fucking you, honey.

Kim pretended like she was going to lick Anne's fingers. Instead, she grabbed her wrist. In a smooth cop-restraining-criminal motion, she jerked Anne off the bed and spun her around so she lay belly down. Kim cranked Anne's hand up behind her, keeping her in place. "Do you *still* think I'm joking?"

Anne's voice was bored, but there was excitement mingled in with it. "Stop being such a drama queen. Let me up. I'm going up to Bizarro with Chief Hayes tomorrow. I can't shoot if you break my arm."

Kim smiled coldly. Her eyes caressed Anne's buttocks—those gluteal hemispheres were perpetual winners with her. "Chief Hayes, eh? I bet that wasn't what you called each other whilst sucking clits."

"Oh, come on. You know as well as I do that Brooke's straight."

"Not if I let you convert her from her erroneous ways. And tell me it isn't odd that I, a crack shot, aren't on this very important mission, and you, who can't shoot straight to save your life, *is* on it. Stinks like dirty pussy to me."

Anne rolled her eyes. "Girl, you're almost as bad as Pam Andersen."

Kim cranked her arm up hard.

"Yeow! What you do that for?"

"Don't compare me to Longneck. From what I heard she ate Joe's ashes."

Anne's eyes widened. "*Ate?* What the . . . ? Who told you?"

"Don't change the topic."

Anne rolled her eyes again. "Okay. Just let me up."

Kim sniggered. "Not until you realize who's boss."

Anne lay motionless, a trembling mass of anticipation. Kim spat in her palm, creamed her strap-on with the sputum—

"Yeah, c'mon, darlin'. Give mama some femme-cock in her nice tight hole."

—Teased the lips of Anne's vagina open with the tip—

"Oooh, girl. I just love the way you do that."

—swirled the dildo around just inside her labia—

Anne moaned. "Stop torturing me."

—then withdrew the phallus and pushed it into Anne's anus instead.

Anne's eyes widened with shock. "Ouch! No, please!" She began bucking her hips.

"Shut up." Kim forced the dildo all the way into Anne's resisting anus, then tapped the other woman's shoulder. "Tell you what. I'll let you up if you admit that I wear the trousers."

"Fuccck!" Anne groaned. The dildo in her rectum felt like someone had planted a tree in her ass. Then she calmed. "No."

Kim shrugged. "Have it your way then." She knocked away Anne's free hand, which she was sneaking under herself so she could masturbate, then smacked her on the ear for good measure. "No playing with yourself. I'll decide when you get off . . . maybe never."

"Please, Kimmie . . . ouch! Ouch! OUCH! What the hell is wrong with you?"

"*You* are what's wrong with me."

She fucked Anne hard, pumping her down into the mattress. Deep, HARD strokes of dildo, each a testament of her frustration with this stupid relationship with this beautiful asshole of a girlfriend who was doing her absolute best to fuck up what could be glorious because she was a self-seeking dimwit.

"Ouch! That hurts!"

"It's supposed to hurt." She smacked Anne again. "Listen, you cop groupie. I'm going to fuck your ass till you've learnt your lesson."

***

At first, Anne totally enjoyed the scene. Kim was pitifully transparent. After a recent series of romantic failures, it was satisfying to finally have a girlfriend she could wrap around her fingers.

She moaned, bit her tongue, her sensations a blend of pain and satisfaction. *Oh, Kimberley Fields, you're so naive. So what if I screw Brooke? It ain't like she's about to get pregnant.*

Kim wrenched Anne's arm painfully up. "You're mine, you little slut!"

"I'm my own woman!"

"You'll do what I tell you and like it."

"Oh yeah? Says who?

"Says your anus!"

"Ouch! Lighten up, you jealous bitch!"

"You don't even know what jealous is."

The sodomy began to really hurt. Anne was surprised by how insistent on her power trip Kim was tonight. *Damn, she's really trying to break me, break my ass in two, rather. That fucking dildo feels like a chainsaw.*

"Beg for mercy. Promise to be good."

"Screw you, Kim, I'm my own—"

Another slap. Anne's left ear rang like a bell.

"—Shit!"

Her ass was really sore now. "Use some lube, will you, bitch? One would think you'd taken rape classes." Inwardly, she laughed. *You're mine, darling. I know how desperate you are, and . . .*

"No lube until you agree to be less of a slut."

Shit, Anne thought. *If she keeps pounding my ass like this, I'll be unable to make the trip to Bizarro. And what kind of cocksucker excuse is: 'Sorry, Chief, my rectum is in ruins?'*

"Okay," she groaned. "I'm only joking, Kimmie, you know I can't live without you."

Kim pulled the dildo out. Anne's anus looked red; really sore. She let go of Anne's arm. "Nice doggie. Now turn around to face me."

Anne turned around. Kim unstrapped the dildo and waved it in her face. "With all the garlic you eat, be glad I'm not making you lick it clean."

She flung the strap-on off the bed, then scooted up to kneel over Anne's head. She plumped her pussy on Anne's mouth, spread it wide with fingers. "Start eating cat, dog."

She leaned back, raising her hands to caress her breasts as Anne got eagerly to work.

Soon Kim was a trembling orgasmic mass. Anne gave great head. The girl was flighty as hell, but her quim-eating technique was first class.

***

It's a problem, Kim thought. *Now that Brooke's ascended the cop ladder to head girl, how do I hang onto Anne?*

She pulled her mind away from last night's superlative sex. A cold wind was blowing across the milk lake toward them. The distant giantess's face suddenly looked menacing, disapproving.

Bobby Robbins stepped up. He and the others had also noticed the endlessly lactating pregnant giantess. He grinned. "How'd you like this, Sarge? A lake full of *milk*? And *breast* milk at that. City council are going

242

to *love* this shit. They're always going on about the calcium shortage for kids nowadays."

Kim turned. The men and women were arranged behind her, waiting for orders. "I think we're up on Bizarro. With the sun overhead, it's the only explanation that makes sense."

Bobby squinted. "But how?"

"Leave that for Oppenheimer to figure out. He needs a new puzzle to jerk off to every now and then." She addressed her unit. "We wait for the eaters to show. They don't, we hide upstairs till they do."

"No need," Bobby said, pointing over her shoulder. "The cannibals are coming."

Chapter 63

"We're dreaming, right?" Tom asked.

"Even knowing better, I'm inclined to agree with you," Megan replied.

Following Harding's metal detector, they'd come onto a road a mile from the mountain. They'd followed it right to a beach bordering an expanse of white water.

"We've found White Lake," Brooke said.

"And a pregnant giantess with a 'Mama' pendant squirting it from her breasts," Megan added, nodding out at the distant form. "Which I suppose makes it Milk Lake."

"We've found a lot more than that," Harding said. He pointed down at three large rectangular boxes at the shoreline. "Those are Pussypalm's missing bullion trucks."

***

They walked down the beach to the shore.

The 18-wheeler trucks were sunken deep in the sand, their tires totally buried. The lower half of each tractor unit was completely submerged in the lake, milk lapping against their now-rusted metal. The vehicles were dirty as shit, their white paint peeled off in flakes and strips. Grime as testament to the passage of time. Their interiors were maps of guano and animal skeletons.

'Wu Dock Trucking' read the legend on the tractors' sides.

'Wu . . . Wu . . .' Tom remembered in shock. *That's the Chinese guy whose wife's nipples I shot off in that vision.*

Harding winced at bad memories. He looked pointedly at Tom. "They're all empty. Where's the gold?"

Megan replied instead. "Pussypalm's amnesia no longer matters. Boston's gold is clearly up here. His majesty will be delighted to have it back. All we need to do now is return downstairs and ask for a large force to be sent up here to search for it."

"And I'll be delighted to see justice served to—"

"What I would like to know," Brooke interrupted Harding, whilst peering into the nearest truck, its dim evacuated recess a-chirp with the agitated sounds of creatures disturbed by the unfamiliar human presence, "is how Pussypalm got these three behemoths up here."

"Me too," Megan said. She turned to Tom. "How did you?"

Tom said nothing. He felt on the edge of a revelation as to where the money was. Illumination hung in the rear of his mind; a curtain he needed to yank away to know himself for who he really was.

"Well, say something," Harding growled. "How did—?"

"Hey!" Brooke interrupted again, pointing out across the milk lake. "What's that weird shimmering over there?"

Chapter 64

Paddled by eaters, six odd boats approached the beach over the milk lake from Mama's direction.

Kim yanked Bobby Robbins sleeve. "Come, I've got to see clearly. Those things can't be what I'm thinking."

They made their way between the other cops, then scrambled up the cliff-face steps. Halfway up, they turned and squinted out across the white liquid expanse.

"I don't believe this," Kim said. "Human canoes."

Bobby was gaping. "This *confirms* we're up on Bizarro."

Each approaching boat was a giant hollowed-out human body. As they neared the shore their details became clearer. All were *male* bodies—they had penises and scrotums—with skin pale as the milk they traveled over. They were each thirty feet long and floated on their backs, the milk splashing up into their bodies. Their legs were together, their arms locked out from their bodies in an arrowhead shape.

Arranged four-a-side, eight paddle-wielding eaters sat inside the hollowed trunk of each man-canoe, taking instructions from a pilot sitting in the vessel's similarly evacuated head. Each canoe's black hair spread around its head like jellyfish tentacles.

The yellow rowers sat on the de-fleshed upper portions of ribs. More ribs were clearly visible inside the man-canoes.

"They've seen us," Bobby said. "There goes the element of surprise."

"What element?" Kim retorted. "We're more surprised than they are." She yanked his sleeve again. "Come on, we need to get everyone into position."

They raced back down to the beach. Meanwhile, the man-canoes had halted their approach thirty meters from shore. The eaters were dropping anchor and picking up weapons.

"Down!" Kim yelled, darting along the shore as the first salvo of gunfire came from the eater fleet.

The police officers were already hitting the sand. Those down blazed their guns at the eater boats.

The gunfight continued in earnest. Metal death shrieked back and forth like invisible arrows. Far out over the lake, Mama squirted breast milk and gazed across the sky.

For five minutes neither side gained an advantage. The Boston cops took cover behind a smattering of shore rocks. Likewise, bullets hitting the man-canoes ripped meat out of their bodies like shooting a side of beef, but the wall of protecting muscle was so thick no damage met the cannibals behind it. The canoes' side-splayed arms formed an additional protective barrier against gunfire.

"This is getting us nowhere!" Kim yelled above the shooting, "Someone give me a rifle with a telescopic sight!"

One was found and passed to her.

She scowled. *Okay, let's see how protected you fuckers are.*

She raised the rifle to shoulder, pressed right eye to sight, and began shooting.

Kim wasn't known as the best shot in Boston for nothing. Like magic, the eaters' heads began exploding—Pop! Pop! Pop!—with yolk-colored brains blowing out the rear of their skulls.

In one minute, Kim had killed all the eaters in the nearest man-canoe with head shots. She swung her gun to the next canoe and pumped the trigger again. More heads exploded.

The eaters began yelling in confusion. All they needed do was put their head up to look around and Kim popped them.

"They're turning tail," the woman next to Kim said. "Cowards."

Kim popped the heads of two eaters desperately scrambling for paddles. "We can't let them escape," she said. She ejected the rifle magazine. The policewoman handed her another. Kim slotted the clip in, banged it into place. "If they warn the others, we'll never find them."

She shouldered the rifle again, then lowered it. "Screw this!"

"What?"

"The canoes' feet are blocking the targets."

Bobby Robbins rushed over to her side. He pointed to the departing eater canoes. "Something's odd about this. They're not heading back the way they came."

Kim saw what he meant. Two crewless man-canoes bobbed on the milk nearby, eater corpses draped over their sides like hung laundry. The other four cannibal boats now floated parallel to the shoreline, their rear ends four pairs of large feet. At their sides, paddles rose and fell with heartbeat regularity. *Bobby's right. If they're running away, they should be headed back towards the giantess Mama. They're off to land elsewhere.*

"Up and after them!" she yelled. "Catch those fuckers!"

The cops ran along the shore after the eater boats. The man-canoes had a head start, but the cops quickly closed the distance.

Running almost parallel to the eaters, the police began firing again. The cannibals ducked low in their human boats to avoid the gunfire.

Then . . .

The foremost man-canoe disappeared, vanishing progressively like it was entering a hole in the air.

"Stop shooting!" Kim yelled. She needed to think.

The second and third man-canoe also vanished into what Kim now made out as a shimmering air distortion. Squinting hard, she dimly made out the transited canoes floating inside the shimmering, their shapes faint wavy lines. Viewed normally, though, the lake looked empty.

"Damn," she said. "Oppenheimer's right—there *are* doors to other dimensions."

The fourth hollowed man was about to enter the shimmering air.

"They're getting away for good," Bobby said.

Kim sniggered. "They just think so. They're not tougher than we are. Anywhere they can go, we can follow." She pointed back at the two abandoned man-canoes bobbing on the milk. "Let them go, we'll follow them through in those. It'll help us discover all their bolt-holes once and for all."

They turned back toward the shimmering 'airway.' The fourth eater canoe still hadn't gone through it.

"What the hell are they waiting for?" Bobby asked.

Then two eaters flung something over the side of the man-canoe. Kim squinted. The object—a large oblong yellow pod—hung motionless in the air beside the boat.

Immediately after they launched the pod into the air, the eaters dropped back into their vessel and paddled quickly through the shimmering.

The moment they vanished through it, the pod exploded, filling the air with yellow dust that blew unwaveringly towards the shore.

This is downright fucking bad, Kim thought as the yellow dust sped towards them, the extent of its spread too much to outrun. *Mustard gas?* "Get your gas masks on!" she yelled, pulling hers from her belt and snapping it into place. "Don't breathe that shit in!"

All the cops got their masks on. The yellow mist blew over them, settled on them and was gone.

Kim waited for her uniform to start melting, her skin to start burning. Her eyes to pop from her face. Nothing happened. She relaxed, heaved a sigh of relief.

She looked around at the others. "False alarm. Weapon likely had a dud fuse." She pointed to two officers. "Nick, Luke; get your jackets off and get into the milk. Bring those boats over to where we can board . . . yeooooow! What . . . ?"

Kim looked down at her leg. She gawked in disbelief. Her sniper's rifle, slung over her shoulder, was transforming into a metal dog. The dog was half-formed—what should have been its hind-quarters was still the gun's barrel. It transformed as Kim watched.

Its metal teeth were sunk deep into Kim's right thigh. Blood soaked her uniform around the punctures.

She quickly got over her shock. She unslung the rifle's strap, and gripping the dog by its jaws, forced its mouth open, pulling its teeth out of her leg.

The significance of the fact that its body shimmered with yellow spots wasn't lost on her. Nor was the fact that its eyes were dull gold oblongs. *Like the fucking pod. The dust from the pod . . .*

"Someone give me a hand here!" she yelled as the dog's jaws once again snapped shut on her thigh. It twisted its metal head, savaging her muscles. The pain . . . On the ground below it, its metal rear legs formed, massive and powerful.

The metal beast grew larger.

"Fucking help me, someone!"

No one came running. No one could.

Kim looked around, regarded the scene about her with total incomprehension. All the police officers' guns and knives had transformed into monster animals: huge dogs and cats and creatures she found hard to describe. All were busy attacking their erstwhile owners.

On Kim's right, a huge metal dog with knives for teeth was ripping into Bobby Robbins. The creature's teeth bit through his bulletproof vest like Kevlar was Doritos. The dog ripped the vest away and sunk its teeth into Bobby's chest, emerging with his heart between its jaws, its snout a dripping red mess.

Kim screamed. The dog savaging her leg—fully formed now and HUGE—had now gotten its teeth completely across her thigh and was sawing through the muscles.

She beat at its head. She grabbed its metal ears and pulled with all her strength. The metal jaws again retracted from her flesh, then clamped down tighter.

The dog bit completely through Kim's thigh muscles. Blood pumped like water from her severed arteries. The meat hung off her leg in strips, draped down over her knee like the hood of an umbrella. The agony was unbelievable.

The beast let go of Kim's leg. It leapt atop her, tearing her jacket open with claws like honed bayonets.

Her flak jacket fell apart. She looked sideways, her eyes pleading for someone to help her. *Shit, I don't wanna die like this.*

All around her was total carnage. Metal monsters ripping screaming police officers to bits. Like a painting of a nightmare. Blood flew everywhere, much of it splattering the lake surface, creating strawberry-yoghurt-colored streams.

None of the cops had escaped. The policewoman who'd handled Kim the rifle had been sectioned in two. A lion-sized metal cat had its head stuck up inside her ribcage, while another was fishing around inside her groin with a paw.

The cat examining the woman's lower half pulled out something. Kim vomited when she saw what it was—the woman's womb.

The cat wolfed the womb down, ovaries and all.

A dog bit off a policeman's entire lower jaw. He gaggled in horror and pain, his tongue bitten out, the bottom of his face a yawning chasm. Blood gushed from sectioned arteries in his neck.

Kim looked out across the lake. Mama still spurted milk from her breasts over her bulging belly. Only now, she was looking at the dying cops. Her eyes held no pity. No mercy, but no judgment either. A gaze as neutral as the face of the moon.

Mid-morning sun glittered off the murderous metal monsters' mustard-mottled bodies.

The metal dog ripped through Kim's breasts, slitting the white curvaceous skin so their contents of yellow fat gaped raw in the holes. Then it ripped her chest skin and muscle off altogether. Finally, using its paws like surgical separators, it pulled her ribs fully apart so they snapped and her chest lay open.

Its golden eyes glimmered in satisfaction at her exposed heart. The organ beat weaker as her body drained of blood.

The dog bent and ate Kim's heart.

Kim Fields died, her eyes fixed on the shimmering disturbance hanging over Milk Lake, wondering where the fuck it led.

Her absolute last thoughts were of Anne. She regretted that she'd never see her girlfriend again, never again feel her hot lips and tongue. Never again hold the other woman in her arms and tell her how much she loved her.

Once the police officers were all dead, the blood-soaked weapons-transformed-into-animals made no further attempt to eat their bodies. All sat quietly, watching the rippling lake surface.

Flies buzzed over the corpses.

Chapter 65

Tom, Brooke, Megan, and Harding studied the portal over the lake. It was fifteen meters out into the milk, thirty along the shoreline. Six meters high, it was a 'wobbly/furry' patch of air, semicircular in shape like it was half-submerged in the milk. Vague shadows were visible on its other side if one peered carefully and at the right angle; otherwise the lake looked normal through it, like looking through thick glass.

"That has to lead somewhere," Harding said.

"Nowhere good," Megan said.

"That portal might lead halfway across the universe," Tom said.

Harding scowled. "And pigs fly too, right?"

Brooke made a face. "C'mon, you lot; we're wasting time. There's nothing more to do here." She pointed. "We'll climb the mountain, try to locate—"

At that moment, the first man-canoe popped through the shimmering distortion, emerging like a newborn from its mother's cunt to bob on the milk surface like it had always been there.

"What the . . . ?"

It took them a moment to understand what they were seeing.

"That's a hollowed-out giant human body being paddled by eaters," Tom said, as three more man-canoes followed behind the first.

Bodies lay limp over the side of two of the man-canoes. Ripped meat lay in shreds along their sides, revealing white bone beneath.

"They're shot up," Megan said, "they've been in a gunfight."

"Back, quick!" Brooke whispered, "Behind the trucks!"

"Too late," Harding said as they dashed for cover. "They've seen us."

The eaters *had* seen them. Crews yelling loudly and paddling hard, the four hollowed-human boats made for the beach.

Brooke held a brief council of war behind the furthest truck from the debarking cannibals.

"There's too many of the shitheads to take on in the open," she said. "We'll have a better chance up on the mountain."

The others nodded.

Keeping the trucks between themselves and the landing cannibals, they ran for the mountain.

Chapter 66

The eaters didn't immediately set out after the fugitives. They were too surprised at being ambushed at their Chinatown door. They erred on the side of caution, letting the fleeing four run without attempting to shoot them.

They dragged their vessels up onto the sand and unloaded their weapons, all the while making certain there weren't any other humans coming down to ambush them.

Even then, they'd not have followed after Tom and his companions. Their original intent had been a hunting raid into Central Boston.

Once the transformer pods had killed off the cops it should still be possible to enter the city that way. Or, if that was too unsafe, there were other ways.

But one eater female, Gina Fieri, walked over to Donny Q, head of the raiding party. Donny Q was tall and thin, a xanthous version of Yul Brynner.

"Harding's among them," Gina told him.

Donny Q looked at her sharply. "Ryan Harding? Police Lt. Harding?"

Gina nodded. "Unmistakable."

Donny Q considered this. "Gina, are you *sure*?"

She nodded emphatically. "I'd recognize him with my eyes closed. I was with Pussypalm during the bank raid. When Harding shot Lynn, I guarded him." Her water-eyes glittered with hunger and lust. "Something else you should know—the other man runs like Pussypalm himself."

Donny Q looked at her like he'd been shot.

She nodded. "Same height and build, same gait. Odd pacing, like a guy who's out of breath."

Donny Q squinted down the beach. Brooke and the others were climbing up through a group of colored rocks to the mountain's base. "Pussypalm's supposed to be . . ."

He shrugged. Wrong or not, it would have to investigated.

He turned back to the others. "Hey listen up, you lot, we've got an emergency."

"What's up, dude?"

Donny Q grinned glass teeth. "Gina says Ryan Harding's one of those fleeing. Maybe Pussypalm too."

The other eaters gaped at him. "Pussypalm?"

Donny Q nodded. "Forget hunting. Catching Pussypalm just became our number one priority."

Chapter 67

The brown mountain rose above them in a gentle but slippery slope. The profusion of colored rocks studding its base rose well above their heads.

The mountainside was coated with mud that flowed to mire its base, making walking a tedious process of constantly unsticking one's feet.

"This mud smells like chocolate," Brooke said.

She scooped some up and took a tentative lick. "Yeah, it's chocolate alright, some caramel in it too."

She made a face. "It figures—a milk lake, a chocolate mountain . . . hope we don't meet wafer people."

Tom rapped his knuckles against an orange rock. Loud guitars/drums and The Beatles singing *Get Back* exploded from a beehive of perforations in its side. "And these are *rock* candies."

Harding scowled. "Turn that damn thing off, you idiot. You're giving our location away."

"Sorry." He rapped the rock again. The Beatles ceased rocking.

Brooke looked out from their cover of rocks, down at the beach. "Too late; I think we already failed the audition. The eaters are on their way over."

She looked to their left. "Hey, Megan, find any caves yet!?"

Megan, examining the mountain surface a short distance farther off, shook her head. "Everything's solid chocolate."

Harding looked up the maroon slope rising to a distant white peak. "We can't climb the sides: we'll either get mired or slip. But then, neither can the eaters." He frowned, scratching his hairline. "Our best defense is to move farther along the rocks, hide, and ambush them once they're well on the chocolate surface." He pointed to the brown wall, down which sun-melted chocolate flowed to further slicken the already slippery floor. "They'll be as un-surefooted as we are."

Brooke nodded.

They moved stealthily towards Megan's position, steadying themselves with the rock candies as their route inclined uphill.

Harding's gun hit a blue-red-yellow spiraled candy too hard, and Motorhead's *Ace of Spades* blared forth.

Tom, bringing up the rear, kicked the candy to shut it up.

Brooke looked back, her face pained. "Will you two please stop that shit?"

"Hey!" Megan called from up ahead. "Caves!"

They slipped up the last few meters to join her. Here the brown mountain face was riddled with large holes.

"It's like a honeycomb," Megan said. The melted chocolate flowing down the mountainside dripped into the cave mouths, running off along their floors.

They paused by the first cave. A slight bend in the mountainside offered them some concealment from below.

"Perfect place to make a stand," Brooke said. "Okay. We split into two groups. Harding and me in this one—" she pointed a bit farther up, "— Tom and Megan in that one."

"I think I should have a gun now," Tom said.

Harding guffawed. "In your dreams."

Tom looked to Brooke. She shook her head. "Not on your life. You'll never have a better chance to shoot us in the back now we know the gold's up here."

Megan laid an impatient hand on Tom's arm. "Let's hide ourselves. The cannibals are arriving."

He peeped down, saw she was right. The first eaters had entered the space between the last line of candies and the mountain wall. Guns held ready, yellow faces were peering up towards their place of concealment. The eaters' bald heads looked like an array of Korean melons.

Tom heard the word 'footprints' uttered.

He and Megan quickly retreated into the upper cave. Once they were out of sight, Megan pulled a pistol from her belt and handed it to him. "Hide it. Remember, it's only for emergencies."

"Don't you need it?"

"I've still got mine. This one was Tony's. I picked it up back at the mushroom after the eaters kidnapped him."

"Thanks." Tom suddenly felt a 'memory' start loading itself into his mind and spectral fingers turning his hands into gloves.

He was in a ransacked room, violently fucking a dark-haired woman's bleeding anus, his penis smeared red . . .

256

He quickly dropped the gun into his pocket. The horrible recollection instantly faded, his hands returned to being just his.

He shuddered, still seeing the confused look on the raped woman's face.

Grinning at him, Megan patted her jacket. "I've no idea why I carry a gun myself anyway. I'm better without it—needles are more personal. Stabbing someone is like having sex." She kissed Tom on the cheek. "It's all about the penetration, darling."

Chapter 68

Brooke and Harding waited. The eaters climbed cautiously, their ascent punctuated by loud music from the rock candies.

"It's atrocious how clumsy they are," Brooke said when one triggered *More Than a Feeling* from a green candy.

"At least they've a sense of city identity," Harding said, nodding his head to Tom Scholz's guitar riffs. "Great they let this track play on."

***

"They must know they're giving their pursuit away with all this noise," Tom told Megan.

(They'd now discovered that each rock candy played a complete album. The climbing eaters hadn't triggered any more music, but the 'Boston candy' had, after playing *More Than a Feeling*, moved on to *Peace of Mind*, the second track on the band's eponymous debut album.)

"They clearly don't care. There are only four of us."

"We'd be smarter to just head into the caves."

"No. We don't know what's inside there. The eaters likely do. This way we have a fighting chance." She smiled at Tom's disagreement. "They most likely think we're fleeing inside the mountain now, sitting ducks they can pick off at will."

"Something is wrong about this scenario. There are less eaters coming after us than were aboard those creepy boats of theirs."

"Calm down, we'll be okay."

***

"Okay, let 'em have it," Brooke said, stepping out from the cave mouth. Harding joined her. Their guns blazed downhill.

Their joint gunfire blew four eaters back down the chocolate slope, end over end. The rest ducked behind the rock candies. The one playing Boston's first album was now on *Foreplay/Long Time,* the music blared loud like a war film soundtrack.

The eaters returned fire. Bullets flew up and down the incline. The slugs split chips off the candy rocks, ricocheted between them, thudded into the mountainside. Dollops of mountain plopped to the ground.

Brooke and Harding ducked back into the cave. They simultaneously ejected their magazines and loaded new clips.

(Triggered by bullets, the candies were now playing a cacophony of different records. AC/DC, Anthrax, Patti Smith, The Stones, Alanis Morissette, Marilyn Manson, Men At Work, Bob Dylan, Green Day, Dream Theatre . . . the sound grew louder, became the indistinguishable white noise of a metal mesh.)

Harding winced. "I'm running low on ammo!" he shouted, straining to be heard over the noise. "Just one spare clip left!"

"I've three!" Brooke yelled back. "Here!" She passed him one. "This isn't working! They're all hidden behind the candies now! Impossible for us to hit them there!"

"Works in our favor! I suggest we step out again, give them a burst to discourage them from following us, then head up past the caves!"

"Yeah, this fucking cacophony is giving me a fucking headache!"

"It's too loud to even hear yourself shoot!"

Brooke grinned at that. "Let's hit the fuckers again!"

Chapter 69

Tom and Megan watched Brooke and Harding fire a new burst downhill.

"They have the situation under control!" Megan shouted.

Tom grunted. Something was wrong. He could sense it. But what?

The music got louder. The candies flanking the cave entrance began blaring out music. And all was Death Metal/Deathgrind/Pornogrind, layers of drop-tuned guitars that sieved his brain like wheat, bass that made him want to shit, drums that felt like his head was simultaneously both kick and snare, and demon-distorted vocals that possibly only made sense to Satan without a lyric sheet. Cattle Decapitation, Cannibal Corpse, Torture Squad, Cock and Ball Torture, Dying Fetus. The noise poured into the cave in incoherent overlapping layers.

Now it was almost too loud to think.

Tom didn't immediately understand why the noise had increased. His mind was otherwise occupied.

One tune amongst the clamoring melee was pissing him off big time—Cannibal Corpse's *Entrails Ripped From a Virgin's Cunt*. The band sounded like a one-man *Texas Chainsaw Massacre*. Lead singer Chris Barnes's voice stood out amongst the general cacophony like a cancerous breast.

After Tom's just-now vision of him raping a woman, this was audioshit he didn't need.

Tom thought he knew which rock candy was playing the Cannibal Corpse track: a purple one that pulsed in rhythm with the song.

"Hold on!" he shouted to Megan. "I've got to turn that damn thing off!"

"Dangerous! You don't know which it is!"

"It's *that* one! Damn thing looks like a tumor!"

He slid out of the cave at it, feet set so he was skiing on the chocolate mud. The music in the crevice had now reached a deafening crescendo. Tom reached the offending purple rock. He kicked it. Chris Barnes stopped adding his voice to the noise. Tom gave Megan the thumbs up. He looked down the slide, past Harding and Brooke, who stood in the pass like wolves. He smirked; the eaters were all out of sight, in hiding. He looked up the way they'd been climbing. The route was clear.

Then an eater stepped out into the open, fired a burst downhill and ducked into cover again. The bullets blew green chips off the candies next to Brooke and Harding. The pair leapt back into cave cover.

The implications of the loudly blaring candies by their caves now hit Tom.

Shit! He slid back to Megan's side. He noticed then that her hair was the exact same color as their chocolate surroundings.

She looked piqued. "Happy now!?" she yelled.

"It's an ambush! The eaters have circled round. It's gunfire from uphill that's activating the candies outside!"

Megan frowned. "We have to join the others!"

"Okay, let's—!"

Like speakers pumping out heavy bass, the cave began throbbing around them. Its floor and walls rippled in waves. Simultaneously, a thunderous bass noise overlaid itself over the already deafening cacophony. Tom felt his ears would burst.

"What the hell is that rumbling!?"

Tom looked at her confused. "It's coming from outside!"

He staggered to the cave door and cocked an ear up. The sound was coming from overhead.

Then a massive dollop of chocolate splashed down on the rock candies outside the cave. Another followed, completely coating them. The candies fell silent, like someone had slit all the musicians' throats.

The viscid brown mass seeped toward the cave mouth. Solid chunks of chocolate fell to join it, building up in a pile at the entrance.

Tom leapt away from the opening. "It's an avalanche! The noise has set off a chocolate slide!"

A huge chocolate boulder rolled into the cave, bounding over the corrugating floor toward Megan. Tom yanked her out of harm's way.

The cave entrance was now half-packed with chocolate. More dropped and slurped onto that already preventing their escape. The chocolate dam bulged inward toward them.

Megan scowled. "Looks like constipated shit fighting to exit an anus."

Her simile irked Tom. His waking dream haunted him. Poopie . . . *If that thing gets loose . . .*

He looked up. The cave ceiling wobbled unsteadily overhead. Tom's single consolation was that it was silent now, no more ear-splitting Death Metal, only an ominous rumble like far-off thunder.

"We'd best go before the choc-slide shuts out the light," Megan pointed out. We need to find a passage that links up with Brooke and Harding."

Tom nodded. They set off into the mountain.

Chapter 70

Brooke and Harding tramped into the mountain.

Harding grimaced with each step. He'd caught a bullet in the calf, a ricochet just before the cave ceiling collapsed on itself. A flesh wound, but it stung. He was however grateful for the silence. *Damn, I never want to hear Bruce Springsteen again in my life.*

"Shit!" Brooke growled. "I should have known they were trying to ambush us. There were too few of them."

Harding shrugged. "Chief, they've done us a favor setting off the avalanche. We're in stalemate now."

"They can't get in, we can't get out? I never was a fan of chess."

"The avalanche must have buried the majority of them."

"Maybe."

They'd reached a bend in the tunnel. Harding shone his flashlight over their brown surroundings. The rumbling had subsided now. Except for the occasional tremor, the tunnel walls had stopped shaking. "I'm worried about Pussypalm escaping."

Brooke pushed hair out of her eyes. "Megan will never let that happen. True, she's kooky, but she'll fight to the death for justice." She laughed coldly. "Besides, he's not going anywhere. Just like we're not."

***

Tom and Megan followed the tunnel till it widened into a high-roofed chamber. Light dappled them from holes high above.

On their left, a wide white stream cut a deep channel. It bubbled, gurgled, rushed off into the distance.

"It's the continuation of the milk lake," Tom said.

Megan's lips curled into a smile. "It leads somewhere. Meaning there's a way out; we're not trapped in here."

They traced the milk flow. "What are those things? Chocodiles?"

Megan laughed at the brown lizard creatures swimming against the milk current. "At least they're not attacking us."

***

Brooke and Harding turned in through a door.

263

"At last, somewhere not brown and slippery," Brooke said, looking around. "I was starting to think I was inside someone's rectum."

The room was small. Its white walls seemed made of plastic. Large lustrous silver flowers grew from its walls, wavering on white stems.

Harding rolled up his trouser leg. The bullet had gone clean through the muscle. Blood seeped from the wounds. He fished some chocolate out of his boots and used it to plug both holes, wincing with pain as he forced the brown confection into his leg.

Brooke sat cross-legged on the floor, gun in her lap. Her gaze played over the flowers. *Is it just my imagination, or did they all tense when we walked in?*

She experimented, moving a hand in front of the wall, left, then right. The metal blooms swayed with the motion of her hand.

Oops, they're tracking me.

Her fingers brushed one of the flowers. It reared back like a cobra. A mouth of metal teeth opened amidst its petals.

Brooke jerked her hand back. The flower's maw snapped shut on air.

Okay, that's it. We need to get out of here like yesterday. Already's not fast enough.

She turned to Harding, her face white. "Watch out for the—" She froze as the words did. *Oh, no.*

Harding had let down his trouser leg again. He was leaning with a hand on a wall, sniffing an argent bloom that dwarfed his head. Behind him, other silver flowers swayed, poised like cats sniffing him in turn.

He turned to Brooke as she did to him. "Funny, Chief. Despite their unarguably being metal, they smell like meat." He reached out a hand and gripped the flower's white stalk.

"No! Get away from them!"

Harding looked at her in puzzlement as the massive flower reared back in his grasp. Seeing her speechless fear, he turned to look at the flower just as it struck at his face, totally smothering it in its jaws.

Brooke sat horrified; frozen in shock.

The flower instantly pulled back again, ripping off Harding's entire face, eyes inclusive. The other hovering flowers now attacked him en masse, tearing portions of his body off.

Blood spurted everywhere. It drenched the flowers, drenched the wall and floor. The other flowers in the room became restive, licking the air with split segmented metal tongues.

Sightless, Harding fought back on instinct, trying to pull the flowers off him. Tongue eaten, he couldn't scream.

264

A flower bit through his right upper arm. Elbow and forearm dropped to the floor, where another flower instantly snapped them up. A flower bit off his entire left arm at the shoulder. It swayed off with the limb, fighting over it with six other silver blossoms.

A flower swooped up between Harding's legs and ripped out his crotch. Blood pumped like cum as Harding's armless body twitched insanely.

Make it stop, God! Please make it stop! The prayer filled Brooke's head. It was sickening watching someone die like this.

She unfroze then. Leaping up to a crouch, she raised her gun and splattered Harding with bullets. The slugs plastered him against the wall, their force keeping him upright.

The gunfire hit several of the feeding blooms. The bullets pinged off their metal petals. A ricochet grazed Brooke's thigh. She didn't notice.

Her clip clicked empty. Harding's body slithered down the wall. It dropped in slow-motion, the feeding flowers never letting go.

Finally, the flower that had eaten Harding's face covered the top of his head like a hat. Digging its teeth deep into his skull, it bit off the top of his head.

Brooke stared into Harding's opened skull cap, at his bloody pale brain. Then a little flower dug into the exposed meat.

Brooke leapt up. Swinging her gun like a club against snapping flowers, she charged out of the white room.

Fours steps outside, she slipped on the chocolate and caromed out of control down a winding tunnel.

Chapter 71

"Again? After all that shit this morning?"

"If we don't," Megan pointed out, "we'll keep going around in circles forever. This is the third time we've been past this point."

Tom grimaced. She was right. The milk river looped back on itself. They'd explored both left and right division of the point where it split, only to find themselves back at the same place.

"Don't worry," Megan said. "I'll love you gently."

In silence, Tom pulled his glove off and stuffed it in his pocket.

Megan stroked the back of Tom's hand. "Lovely tattoo."

He didn't reply. The etched rose was to him the mark of Cain.

Megan turned his hand over. She licked her lips on seeing the exposed palm vagina. She rolled down her trousers and pulled her panties aside, popping her penis out of harness. Her cock was limp; she caressed it hard, then inserted it into Rose.

Slowly, gently like she'd promised, she began fucking the palm vagina, holding it to her crotch by forearm and fingers.

Tom watched his wrist expand with each of Megan's penetrations, felt the bones separating around her penis.

He fought to distance himself from the sensations. It was impossible. Soon he had a hard on. He freed it from his pants so he wouldn't mess them up. He made certain not to rub himself, however. That would be getting too intimate with Megan.

Shortly after, Rose began its telltale moaning.

"Yes, do me, honey pie! Harder! A vagina needs it!"

Megan sped up her thrusts. She came. A second later Tom ejaculated. In his palm, Rose throbbed in a crescendo of pleasure that matched his spurts.

Megan pulled out of Tom's hand. She raised Rose to her lips and drank the semen out of it.

She laughed at Tom's shock. "I enjoy the taste of myself."

He nodded, too drained by his own orgasm to reply.

"Oh, Meg honey," Rose moaned as Megan tongued its clitoris "You're the absolute best." The vagina gasped. "Oh, holy shit! I feel like I'm falling endlessly! Okay, Tommy darling. What do you want to know?"

"We're lost. How'd we get out of here?"

"That's an easy one. Head back to where Milk River splits into two. Take the left tunnel. Six paces in, push against the left wall twice. A door will open into a white room full of flowers. Walk directly ahead to the opposite wall and push again. It'll open up a stairway to the mountaintop."

"Thanks," Tom said.

"One more thing," Rose said, its voice fading. "The flowers in the white room are dangerous. Whatever you do, Tommy; don't touch 'em."

Chapter 72

Brooke's sliding descent ended when she crashed into a soft white candy. Thankfully it didn't start playing music.

She was upset at Harding's death. She was also very pissed off at losing her gun during her fall. Whilst desperately skidding around a bend, she'd slammed into the tunnel wall. The gun had flown out of her hands and stuck in the chocolate. Her only weapon now was the knife in her belt.

She got to her feet and looked around.

She was in a massive cavern.

The cavern was *immense*—a hundred yards across and similarly wide. And high. Brooke easily imagined it reaching to the top of Mount Choc (as she'd come to think of this place).

It was brightly lit. Light poured from several huge 'windows' situated well overhead.

The chamber walls were in different shapes and shades and hardnesses of confection, from white milk chocolate panels to the mocha brickwork lining a nearby portion on her right, to the éclair-like formations that dribbled cream from punctures in their convex surfaces.

And this was just the beginning, the antechamber as it were.

The chamber was also full of the soft marshmallow-like candies that had broken her fall. All were taller than she.

Brooke walked in deeper.

She was careful not to touch anything.

Memory of Harding's horrible death floated through her mind. She imagined motion behind the placid surfaces of the white candies. Metal jaws tensed to rip her limb from limb.

She walked toward a massive 'choc-fall' at the chamber's far end—a chocolate cascade splashing into an extensive lake.

Halfway to it, she became aware of motion to her left. She froze, listened. It sounded like feet.

Apprehension thrilled in her. Animals? Or eaters?

Knife at the ready, ducking stealthily from candy to candy, she made her way toward the sound.

She peeked around the last candy. And froze again.

I don't believe it. I f'n don't believe . . .

Giant ants were climbing the wall facing her, digging their feet into the maroon bricks and walking up the vertical surface. Some of the insects were as large as horses.

But that wasn't what had shocked Brooke. *The ants . . . they're . . . they're made of chocolate!*

The ants were forming from the pool at the base of the choc-fall.

At the pool's 'shore,' well out from the liquid cascade, large bubbles were forming. Brooke watched as the bubbles lengthened, then differentiated into head, thorax, and abdominal sections, then grew out pairs of legs and antennae.

Then each new chocolate insect joined a procession from the pool to the wall, its initial wobbly steps becoming surer as it neared its destination.

The ants formed and climbed endlessly. Brooke squinted up. The ant trail led to a sunlit opening high above her, through which the chocolate ants all exited.

Her vision trailed across the chamber roof. Exactly opposite the point of the ants' exit, chocolate spurted from a slit crevice in the choc-face, forming the choc-fall that in turn formed the pool the ants were forming from.

Then Brooke understood. *The mountain's recycling itself. The sun melts it, it falls as liquid, then solidifies into ants that climb up to repair/form it again.*

Along with her understanding came a plan to get herself out of the mountain. But would it work?

The first test was to check the ants' reaction to her. *If they're hostile, I'm stuck here.*

She stepped out of concealment. The ants paid her no notice. She walked closer to them, ready to cut and run immediately if one of the insects made a belligerent motion in her direction.

None did. Their facetless eyes gave off the knowledge that they were simply mindless parts, axles and gears in the overall machine—the mountain.

So far so good then. Sheathing her knife, Brooke walked to the edge of the chocolate pool. There, she looked for the largest morphing mass of chocolate she could find. She waited till the horse-sized insect had finished forming, then clambered atop it. She sat on its thorax, legs dangling between its first and second pairs of legs.

The ant gave no sign of recognizing either her presence atop it, nor the additional burden she presented. It trudged inexorably for the wall.

This had better frigging work, Brooke thought.

The wall came closer. The chocolate ant immediately ahead of hers reared up like a horse, dug its feet into the sheer choc wall, then hauled itself up effortlessly.

Brooke blanched as her mount reached the wall. *Am I frigging mad? No way is this working!*

She calmed her intense desire to leap down off the ant's back and find another way out.

The ant reared up. Praying she'd calculated right, Brooke wrapped her arms around its neck. She locked her legs tight around its sides, imagining they were Tom's buttocks.

The chocolate ant began climbing. Step after step after step it rose, tireless as the mindless confectionary machine it was.

Brooke looked down once at the receding chamber, at the endless line of brown ants streaming from the chocolate pool to follow her. She looked up the brown shower to its origin, an endless pulsing gush. She realized it would go on forever.

Wow! was all she could think. *Wow!*

She rested her head on the ant's shoulder and let it climb, carrying her out of the chocolate mountain.

She forced all thoughts of Harding's death to the back of her mind. *I'll grieve later. Right now, I got a job to do.*

Chapter 73

"Rose wasn't joking," Tom said, pointing to the bones across the white room, the bloodstained wall and blooms. "We don't go near the flowers."

"It pays to have a vagina," Megan said. "They're the primary organ of female intuition. Being fucked a lot makes them extra sensitive."

"None of my girlfriends ever predicted the future correctly. Still, it's . . ." His eyes fell on the bloody gun to their right. "Megan, these are *Harding's* remains."

"Huh?" Unsettled, she looked quickly around, eyes taking in the tatters of bloodstained uniform everywhere. A backpack's contents strewn wall-to-wall. "Could be Brooke's," she said hopefully.

Tom shook his head. He walked over to pick a chocolate-smeared boot from a corner. The nearest silver flowers swayed towards him, sniffing him. He carefully avoided any contact with them.

He brought the boot back to Megan. "The foot's still inside it. Bitten clean through at the ankle. It's Harding's. Brooke has small feet."

Megan considered the boot. The sheared ankle bone pearl-white amidst a triple red-black-brown corona.

She sighed; dropped the boot. "What *a waste* of a good man."

"I feel much safer with him dead," Tom said. "Can we leave now?"

Megan sighed again. Tears filled her dark eyes. "You'd say that, wouldn't you?"

"He wanted to kill me."

Another sigh; this one lifting her breasts like she'd swoon. "You'll never understand—Harding was twice the man you are."

Tom hid a grin at Megan's reference to Harding's two penises. Looking around the room, he wondered which of the flowers had eaten them.

Megan stroked Tom's cheek, her hand warm against his skin. She looked him in the eye. "Tell me: are you fucking Brooke?"

Tom rolled his eyes. He grabbed her wrist, pulled her after him. "Let's go!"

She followed him meekly, swaying like she was drunk.

Tom looked back. She was swaying too much to the left. "Megan, don't touch the flowers!"

He made certain she'd heeded the admonition, then pushed on the opposite wall.

Blooms and all, a six-feet-high rectangle swung left out of the wall, revealing a stairway.

The stairway was a chute—a tunnel without landings leading up to a distant square of light. Its stairs were oak, with ornately carved bannisters. The stairs were paved with red carpet. The close-fit walls were decorated with paisley-patterned red/gold wallpaper. 18th-century-style gold lamps sat at intervals on the walls, and there were chandeliers in the wood paneled ceiling. Fifty feet up the ascent, a series of wooden doors began in the staircase walls.

Looks like something out of Lewis Carroll's head, Tom thought. *All we're missing are the funny bunnies.*

He pulled Megan through the door. It swung silently shut behind them.

Tom pointed up the ascent. "What do you think?"

Megan giggled. "My opinion remains unaltered. Harding was twice the man—"

"I *know* that. I mean about the light coming from overhead."

"Oh." She looked up the stairway, to the far-off rectangle of light. "Led Zeppelin would have loved this."

Tom looked at Megan oddly.

"Stairway to Heaven, get it?"

He looked at her more oddly.

"It's okay," she said. "I'm over the shock now. Harding's dead, but you're still here, my dear."

He looked at her pointedly, wondering if she was cracking up. *Oh no, don't you dare airhead out on me, Meg. Not here, not now.*

She smiled coolly back. "I'm okay. Lead the way."

That was more reassuring. Tom turned and began climbing.

Chapter 74

Brooke's ant reached the top of the wall.

She'd not dared look down again. Vertigo didn't even begin to describe what she was feeling now.

The ant clambered out of the opening in the chocolate. Ten feet to its left the previous ant out of the mountain was walking into a white square cave.

Brooke's ant turned to follow it. She leapt down immediately. *No way am I entering in there again.*

Her ant entered the white cave. She got out of the way of the next one in line, then turned to look around. She'd just realized something was different.

No not something . . . everything.

Then she relaxed. *This is just the top of the mountain, from a distance it was white. I'm okay, I'm—*

With the sun directly overhead in the sky, there was no warning shadow. In the corner of her eye, Brooke had the barest impression of something flailing toward her.

Quick reflexes saved her. She whirled round, saw the vav, and instantly flung both hands up to protect her neck.

The vav's tentacle wrapped twice around Brooke's neck. Its meat hook stabbed inward, but embedded itself in the back of her left hand. Not deep—the bones prevented that—but painfully.

Screw that, I'm alive.

The vampire vagina reeled Brooke in like a fish. Brooke kicked as she was hauled first sideways, then aloft into the plant woman's crotch.

The tentacle was tight around her neck, slippery and slimy. She however wasn't choking, her hands prevented that. Blood dripped from her wounded hand. The vav's tentacle sucked it up with vacuum-like efficiency. The vav groaned with the pleasure of the feed.

Brooke swung there in the giantess's crotch. The woman's thighs were golden-brown palm trunks on either side of her, exuding an intoxicating coconut scent. Brooke fought to keep her head clear.

Wow, this is the classic 'frying pan to fire' scenario. How the fuck do I get out of this? I've got my knife in my belt, but no gun, not that it'd be any use against this oversized cunt; and even the knife is essentially useless since I can't free my hands—

The vav turned and began moving. Walking off across a landscape that Brooke now realized was anything but what she'd expected the mountaintop to be.

—I've got to get lost before she joins her thirsty sisters.

Everywhere was huge white cubes—like sugar—stacked atop each other, like seating in an endless arena. Dunes and dunes of cubes, hills and valleys of them. At one point a 'river' of the white cubes flowed through rises of static cubes.

Brooke's intellect hit freeze. This made no sense, so she tried not to understand it.

As they covered more distance, Brooke saw herds of chocolate ants climbing up and down over the cubes. And people riding them. Bald yellow people.

Eaters? What the hell are . . . no, why are there so many of them?

Her mind was ripped from this side-contemplation by worry; worry that the vav bearing her off would shortly wonder why Brooke wasn't draining quick enough and lift her out of her crotch to rectify the matter.

And there was worse in store. Brooke could now see where the vampire vagina was headed. In the distance was a stark smooth expanse amidst the cubist landscape. An oasis of form in this geometric desert. And on the expanse, she could clearly make out other vavs. A *lot* of them.

How do I get out of this crap? she fretted.

Then she heard two gunshots in quick succession, and she was falling. She hit the white cube ground with a loud thud.

Above her, her vav captor began shuddering in pain.

Chapter 75

"I told you I wouldn't miss," Tom said, lowering the gun.

"You didn't," Megan said admiringly.

Tom had put two shots through the vav's vaginal tentacle. Unable to bear Brooke's weight with the damage, the tentacle had snapped.

Tom quickly pocketed the weapon again. He didn't want to remember what he'd seen this time. A shotgun up a woman's . . . ? What the hell . . .?

"Come on," he said. "We've got to retrieve her before the vav signals others."

They raced from the stairway opening—a vacant face of one of the white cubes—across to Brooke, who was now staggering to her feet.

The vav—an Ava Gardner—lay on her side, writhing. The look in her green eyes as she surveyed them was one of utter incomprehension. She was too traumatized by the agony between her legs to attack them. In a reflex reaction, her leafy tentacle fingers kept clenching on empty air.

Tom unwrapped the tentacle from around Brooke's neck. He kissed her full on the lips.

Megan smiled. "So *you are* fucking her. No wonder she's been so even-tempered of recent."

"And *you*, were screwing *Harding*, with his twin towers."

Megan's eyes widened in surprise.

Tom kissed Brooke again. "You okay, baby?"

She nodded, gripping his shoulders. "I've lost a little blood, but I'm otherwise—"

"Time to leave," Megan interrupted. "Trust me, this mute veggie is silently screaming fit to bring the house down."

Tom looked at Brooke.

She nodded, pointed. "That there's an entire plain-full of vavs. There's also eaters riding giant ants around the corner."

"I see reinforcement vaginas on their way over," Megan said. "Asses-in-gear time, love puppies."

Tom nodded to Megan and Brooke. "You two head for the stairway."

Megan raised an eyebrow. "And you?"

Tom raised the vav's tentacle. "I don't like watching a lady suffer."

"Tom . . . the vavs are coming!"

"Go on, I'll be fine."

Brooke and Megan ran for the stairway entrance.

Chapter 76

Tom walked over to the vav. She mouthed silently at him, too agonized to attack or repulse him.

He studied the plant giantess for a moment; her dashingly gorgeous face— bewitching green eyes, perfect nose, incredible lips. *But then I always was a sucker for Ava.* Her body was a plant's: mottled like snakeskin, perfectly sculpted with those magnificent watermelon breasts, but no more than aesthetically human.

The look in her eyes chilled him. It hurt to see anyone in this much pain.

Okay, now time to find out just how far a vav's regenerative powers go.

After first draping the severed tentacle around his neck, he forced the vav's huge palm-tree thighs apart and stuck his left hand into her cunt. His hand sluiced up into her moist genital cavern.

Damn, there's a LOT of space in here; I can fit my head in with ease.

The vav trembled with the penetration, but made no attempt to remove his hand.

Tom stole a glance back at the cube face where Brooke and Megan watched with anxious eyes. Then he plunged his hand deeper into the vav's vagina. Like a glans penetrating an anus, his fist bumped over her cervix, into her womb.

(Rose tingled in Tom's hand as it slid through the vav's wet tunnel. Tom suddenly realized he'd not put his glove back on after Megan fucked it.)

He felt her tentacle, coiled like a snake, writhing around with her tremors.

Tom felt around for the tentacle's severed end. Grasping it firmly, he unreeled it out of her body. The wound was raw, oozing green sap.

The approaching vavs were now two hundred yards away, a band of about fifty giantesses.

Tom smiled at the floored vav. He held both severed ends of her tentacle together, expecting joining roots to grow like had happened with the vav whose arm he'd shot off.

No roots formed.

Instead . . .

A green jelly squirted from Rose. Like a jade snake, it swirled up over Tom's hands, coating the damaged portion of tentacle.

Startled, Tom let go the severed end in his right hand. It didn't drop away from its fellow, but remained in place like it had been superglued, absorbing the green jelly. The tattered wound edges faded, leaving the tentacle like new. More jelly squirted from Tom's palm-vagina to coat the healing organ.

The vav stopped writhing in pain. Eyes glimmering like polished emeralds, she raised a hand and stroked Tom's head gently.

Once certain her tentacle wouldn't break apart again, Tom left the vav's side and ran across to join Brooke and Megan. He was very confused as to what had just happened. *Rose just healed that tentacle with pussy juice?*

He turned his hand over. His flower tattoo seemed alive, like his hand was part of a meat plant. Then it turned normal again.

Brooke and Megan hadn't noticed a thing.

"That was very gallant of you," Megan said when he reached them. "Now she'll love you forever."

He looked at her askance. "What was that?"

Brooke scowled. "She's just pulling your leg. C'mon; we're outta here."

"Which way?"

Megan stretched languidly, arms overhead. "While you were playing gynecologist, Brooke suggested we try one of the doors leading off the stairway."

"Might lead somewhere normal," Brooke confirmed. "If there's anywhere normal anywhere up here. Damn, I'm not even sure if we're still on the mountain anymore."

"We're not," Tom said. He pointed. "That's the mountain over there."

"It's also just downstairs," Megan added sweetly.

Brooke looked at the distant brown chocolate mound with its white peak and scowled. "Screw this Bizarro mindfuck! Let's get the hell out of here."

The others followed her down the stairs again.

***

The other vavs had now arrived. They helped their wounded sister to her feet. They examined her healed tentacle and questioned her. Then they all stood looking for a long time at the hole Tom had vanished into.

Chapter 77

Transition daze.

The doors were set in a staggered arrangement on either side of the staircase. The first was on the left. The next one, twelve stairs down, was on the right. And so on down.

The first door opened into a fire-blackened avenue.

Charred, half-demolished hulks lined the road. Melted, overturned cars were arrayed like they were viewing an art exhibition of demolition sculpture. It was raining lightly; smoke rose from the damp pock-marked earth. The air was heavy with the stink of recent burning. Far ahead, out in the distant sky, kaleidoscopic colors swirled amidst departing storm clouds.

They stood in what was here the charred doorway to a roofless bungalow.

"Thank God for somewhere normal," Brooke said. She made to walk forward.

Tom held her back. He'd instantly recognized this place as the Boston he came from. "This *isn't* somewhere normal. I used to live here."

Megan looked up and down the road. "You don't sound glad to be back."

Tom pointed across from them, at a pile of bones in a puddle. "That depression next to it isn't a pot hole . . . neither is that one. See the spiked projections at the front of each?"

It took a while for both women to register his meaning. Then Brooke gasped. "They're footprints? They're each over six feet long."

Tom considered how much to tell them. First, he peered back up the paisley-patterned stairway. The upper entrance was still vacant of an inquisitive face. He returned his attention to his companions. "There's a safe part of town. I assure you, this isn't it." He indicated the flickering lightshow beneath the far-off black clouds. "Those aren't things you want to meet."

"It's somewhere to hide," Brooke insisted. "That's all we—"

The dragon came in low and fast, playing a long blast of fire ahead of it like an auxiliary tongue. It was the size of two school buses placed side by side. Each of its teeth was larger than Brooke.

Tom had suspected the beast was still around. He pulled Brooke and Megan back inside and slammed the door, just as the fireburst scoured the bungalow's side.

Next, the door disappeared completely, the wall covering seamlessly over with wallpaper.

"It likely just stamped the bungalow to bits searching for us," Tom said. He felt Brooke shuddering against him. Her vulnerability touched him. He stroked her black hair protectively.

"I've never seen a transparent dragon before," Megan said. Then: "Why are both of you gaping at me?"

Brooke pointed. "Your arm's on fire."

Megan looked down. Her right forearm was burning. Bright orange plumes charred the skin above her wrist, curling it off like frying bacon or burning paper.

Megan quickly patted the flames out, smothering them completely in her shirt. "Oh dear, silly me." She looked up again. "My reflexes aren't what they're supposed to be. Normally, I'd—"

"You don't act like it's hurting you," Brooke interrupted.

"I *decide* what hurts me."

Tom shook his head. "Uh, uh. That makes sense if you knew you were burning, Megan. You didn't."

"And you burn funny," Brooke added.

The transsexual brunette touched her forearm, roving her fingers over blackened and taut flesh. "I'll heal."

"See what I mean?"

Tom shrugged. "It's likely a reaction to being on Bizarro. You just saw a door disappear, didn't you?"

Brooke wasn't convinced. She let it go, however. There was nothing to be gained by pushing for answers.

Megan had already descended the stairs and was opening the next door.

"Is that one better?"

She grinned back up, "If you're a can of beer, it is."

***

Here was just an expanse of freezing water with massive icebergs in it. The door opened onto a nine-feet-square iceberg with water sloshing up over its sides. The water froze on contact, pointing up as white needles.

"Looks like where the Titanic went down," Megan said.

"It's fucking *freezing*."

Tom agreed with Brooke. It was sub-zero cold. Their breath misted in front of their faces and the wind felt like knives cutting into him.

Brooke's face was blue, her veins visible as dark trails under her skin. She shook her head emphatically. "No way I'm entering here."

"Nowhere to enter to," Megan said. "Everywhere is ice floating on icier water." Like she'd not reacted to the fire; here too she seemed impervious to the cold.

Brooke pointed. "What's that?"

Tom squinted. "It's a giant penis. Nah, that's ridiculous."

Megan laughed. It *was* a penis, a distant massive purple erection like a mutant mushroom. "Maybe it's the North Pole. Somewhere this cold can only be the Arctic after all."

They shut the door on it.

***

Megan opened the next door. A wash of flame—like a ginger-colored wig—blew out through it.

She leapt back. Not fast enough. The right side of her face was afire. Brooke rushed to put her out, smothering Megan's face in her own jacket.

Tom kicked the door shut. Face grim, he turned to both women. "People are getting tortured in there; and there's demons with tridents."

Megan, okay except for a discolored patch of cheek and singed hair, grunted. "That's Hell, I suppose."

Brooke shrugged. "I'm cool with that, so long as it doesn't burn through the walls." She looked pointedly at Megan. "Girl, you've the oddest reaction to fire I've ever seen in my life."

Megan frowned. "You two open the doors from now on."

"Third one unlucky now," Tom said worriedly, stepping down to the next door in line. "Let's see what's next."

He pulled it open. "I don't frigging believe this shit."

Brooke and Megan joined him. They stared with Tom at the interior of a fridge packed with food and drink.

"I'm not saying I'm ungrateful for the chow," Brooke said, picking a chilled can of Coke from a rack, "But we need to leave here before the eaters show up."

Megan helped herself to a cheese sandwich and Dr. Pepper.

"Way I see it," she said between bites. "We keep looking. One of them has to be an exit, if only to where we entered the mountain."

Tom didn't take anything from the fridge. He climbed down and opened the next door. "I think you mean—to where we *exited*," he said grimly.

The door opened onto a white cubic landscape like that at the top of the stairs.

Leaving Brooke and Megan staring out over the strange geometry, Tom proceeded down the stairs opening more doors. His voice trickled back up to them, in expressions of increasing exasperation: "Rain forest with giant crocodiles fighting anacondas; sea world with giant sharks flying everywhere; undersea—don't ask me how that's possible—I'm facing a wall of water; chainsaw-wielding maniacs fighting zombie women; another white cubist landscape exactly like the one you ladies are looking into."

Door slam, next door open. "Another view of Hell. Here I've got a panorama: there's a burning landscape and a distant huge black throne shaped like a skull. Black trees and buildings and headless truckers on a melting highway with a burning sign reading: 'Welcome to New York.'"

He shut the last door in disgust and stomped back up the stairs to join them.

"We're trapped in a loop," he said.

Together they looked through the doorway, out over the endless array of white cubes. Lower in the sky now, the sun made the landscape seem a terrace of mirrors.

Brooke pointed out, then rolled her eyes up. "I doubt *here's* up *there*."

"It is." Megan pointed across the distance. "That's *this* chocolate mountain we're currently in over there."

"Whichever way, we're stuck with Lego landscape."

Tom groaned. "Worse still, we've got company."

A group of eaters were approaching, riding chocolate ants at speed toward the cave entrance.

"Aw shucks!" Brooke hissed. "The shitheads are back!"

Tom slammed the door shut. "Down! We'll head back through the mountain like before!"

They fled down the stairs, gripping the bannisters and leaping to cover the maximum distance with each step.

Tom had the sudden clear understanding that they weren't going to make it to safety, and *why*. It was simple mathematics: Each fifth door apparently opened onto the exact same point on the cubist landscape. There were at least thirty doors to pass on their way down. At the speed the eaters were riding towards the cave—

Even before he'd finished the thought, the bottommost two doors burst open and eaters spilled into the stairway.

Chapter 78

The cannibals instantly began climbing.

Tom, Brooke, and Megan stopped their descent and turned around.

Above them, the same group of eaters—Tom had no idea how this was possible—were both descending toward them, and streaming in from the other cube-landscape access doors.

He looked back and forth, seeing exactly the same faces approaching from up and down.

Megan pulled out her gun.

Brooke brandished her knife. "This is making me dizzy as hell."

Megan handed Brooke her own gun and pulled out two steel needles instead. "Hand-to-hand's my preferred form of combat anyway. I get to feel the life angrily departing my opponent's punctured body."

The eaters ascended/descended towards them, weapons held ready. They advanced slowly, caution in their colorless eyes.

Fearing the accompanying vision, Tom pulled out his gun.

Reversed time instantly flowed through his head.

He was having doggy-style sex . . . with an eater woman.

Her face was hidden, bent low between her shoulders. Her bald yellow head glistened with sweat, as did her back. She was plump, with small breasts. He gripped her love handles firmly as he thrust.

He looked around. On a table to their left lay a plate of roast testicles—human meatballs—that the eater woman had him brought as a sex offering. Cannibal oysters. He'd refused to eat them.

Both of them were greatly enjoying the encounter. Her yelps of pleasure were dog-like. "Oh fuck, Tom!" she growled. "Fucking give it to me!"

Caressing her breasts, her yolk-toned skin felt dry and scaly against his—reptilian. Her bald pussy was dripping and gripping. His orgasm was close; he felt semen rushing up from his balls, relentless as a bullet train.

He licked his thumb to wet it, then stuck it deep in her anus . . . she moaned . . .

The vision cut out, leaving him on the stairway again.

Tom was relieved. At least he'd not mutilated or raped anyone this time. He pondered, bemused, what he'd seen, as the nerves within his nerves took over, granting him the ability to kill on demand. *Me and an eater woman? And that clearly wasn't the first or only time either.*

He, Megan, and Brooke waited, watching the ascending/descending eaters.

"Something's wrong," Brooke whispered. They're not shooting at us."

"They can't," Megan replied. "They're all the same bunch—they'll likely just kill themselves."

"And us? Why aren't we shooting at them then?"

"We don't have enough ammo to kill more than a few of them," Tom explained. "If they shoot back, we're screwed anyway. No matter how many of themselves they kill, we won't live to celebrate."

Brooke's voice was irritated. "Then what?"

"We'll wait till the last minute, try to break through them."

The eaters stopped their approach four steps above/below the trio.

One stepped forward. He waved his shotgun menacingly at them. "This shit's as confusing for us as for you," he said. "I've no idea why there are eight different versions of me in here now, but I'll shoot you anyway if you fuck up. Dig?"

Tom nodded. The eaters' voice had come from all around him, like all eight versions were speaking at the same time. It was disorienting beyond belief. "Let's go outside where it's less confusing," he said.

The eater nodded. "Lead the way." He pointed with his shotgun. "Hand your weapons over first."

Brooke nudged Tom. "Don't," she whispered.

"We've no choice," he whispered back. "Trust me on this—I don't think they want to kill us."

"No, there's no fire available. Use your brains."

"Just trust me."

"Don't waste our time," the eater said. "This fucked up situation is doing my head in. I'm close to shooting you just to convince myself I'm not going nuts."

Brooke scowled. "I'm not handing *this* gun over."

Megan prodded her in the buttock with a needle tip. "*You will*, honey, or this goes all the way through your ass into your pussy. We're not getting sieved with bullets just because you want to be a tough guy."

Brooke cursed and handed her gun over.

"Your knife too," an eater woman said all around her.

Brooke handed her knife over.

Tom gave the eaters his gun. Smiling, Megan let them have her needles.

The eater leader nodded. "Okay, now pick any doorway and leave by it. No tricks, we've got guys outside."

Tom nodded back. Like before, the same voice came from eight different mouths on eight different stair levels. The illogic of seeing so many eaters duplicated was disarming in itself. It was: *Didn't I just see that guy behind me? And why's she both on my left and right at the same time?*

The nearest stairway exit was six steps down. Tom, Brooke, and Megan descended to it and docilely stepped outside into a semicircular corral of eaters on antback.

The rest of the eaters exited behind them a moment later. A single group from what was, after all, a single opening.

"We're gonna regret this," Brooke whispered.

"Maybe," Megan whispered back. "But I'm not sure."

Chapter 79

The eater who'd addressed them inside walked around to face them. He was accompanied by the girl who'd been simultaneously on Tom's left and right.

"Damn," he said. "I never want to experience that again. My brain feels like putty."

He squinted hard at Tom. "Gee, you sure this is Pussypalm? Dude don't *look* like him in the least. Tom's taller, better looking."

The eater girl, Gina, nodded emphatically. To Tom's eyes, she looked about twenty-two. "Looks ain't everything, Donny Q." She prodded Tom with her shotgun. "Let's see your hand. Left palm."

Tom showed Rose to them.

Donny Q's eyes gaped wide. "Tom?"

Next thing, he hugged Tom tight. "Dude, how in hell did you find your way back?" Then he remembered something, and stepped back. "Where's Lt. Harding?"

"Dead," Megan replied. "The metal flowers in the room at the bottom of the stairs ate him."

Donny Q winced. "Big Sister ain't gonna like this. She wanted Harding alive and well."

"One out of two ain't bad," Gina said. "Not our fault."

Tom stared at the eaters in bewilderment. "What the hell is going on? You *know* me? And who the hell is Big Sister?"

All the eaters burst out laughing, like he'd just told a hilarious joke. Those seated on ants hooted and beat the chocolate insects' sides till they cracked, spilling cream filling. Their teeth reflected sunlight like mirrors.

"Big Sister is the eater queen," Megan whispered in Tom's ear. "She most likely requires impregnation."

Brooke overheard. She looked sharply at Megan, then scowled from Donny Q to Gina. "I don't understand. What's going on here? Aren't you going to eat us?"

Donny Q stroked her cheek. She flinched at his touch. "Normally we would, babe. You in particular, have a great ass—fantastic amount of gluteal meat there. Chef would flip over you." He pointed to Tom. "In this case, however . . . no. Big Sister . . ." He shrugged. "Tommy here, he clearly doesn't remember a thing, so we're going to see someone who'll remind him."

He gestured to a couple of eaters, "Bring them some ants."

A trio of chocolate insects were duly led forwards.

"Where are we headed?" Tom asked as they mounted at gunpoint.

An eater pointed over the white cube landscape, "Home, man . . . Pleasure Bay, South Boston, where frigging else?"

Part 6: South Boston

Chapter 80

While they rode, Brooke was filled with moody reflection.

Riding beside her, Tom sensed her mood. "Don't worry," he whispered. "It'll be okay."

She turned to face him, her eyes dark. "You don't get it, do you? The wings just fell off the plane."

It bothered him how certain she sounded. "They want *me* for something."

She smirked. "Trust me, darling; it isn't anything good. *Big Sister*?" she shrugged. "Maybe you cheated them out of their share of the gold."

Behind them Megan laughed. "I just told you: the yellow queen wants an heir. Only a famous killer like you can be considered a satisfactory sperm donor."

The eaters steered the chocolate ants using their antennae. Pulled left, the insect went left, and vice versa. The three humans copied the guidance method without difficulty. The ants' motion was jerky but hypnotic.

"Look," Megan said. "There's the vavs."

Tom and Brooke looked over the giant women. At this distance, in their smooth oasis amidst the rolling cube landscape, they looked like palm trees with white faces.

Brooke's hand hurt badly where the meat hook had stabbed into it. The wound, a jagged slash, seeped blood. "Screw those vampire cunts."

"It's odd," Megan said, "the way they're staring at us."

Gina rode close. "They're just pissed off that they can't have you to suck dry. Vavs don't dare mess with us eaters." Face smug, she rode off again.

"Female intuition assures me it's more than that," Megan said.

Brooke grimaced. "With our luck so far, it's likely that they're all in love with Tom here, and are planning how to abduct him."

Tom said nothing. He considered his left hand, now gloved again. He pondered what had happened when he'd repaired the vav's vaginal tentacle. Though completely unexpected, Rose's behavior had had an odd sense of déjà vu to it.

***

The cubist landscape smoothed out into the beach enclosing Milk Lake. They passed Mount Choc on their right. The chocolate deluge that had trapped them inside the mountain was now literally lifting—breaking up into large chocolate birds that flew up the mountainside immediately after forming. As the brown confection turned avian, the rock candies were once again revealed. A dissonance of *Total Eclipse of the Heart, Smells Like Teen Spirit, Born in the USA, I Love Rock and Roll,* and *Hotel California* floated across to them on the air.

Tom felt his ant mount attempt to turn right and head off toward the mountain. He steadied its direction with a tug on its left antennae.

"A very strange ecological system," he said.

"But deliciously effective," Megan added. The ant she rode was exactly the same color as her hair.

They reached the beach.

"I'm curious," Brooke said loudly as they passed the three half-submerged trucks. "Where'd all the gold go?"

Their yellow captors didn't reply. Now for some reason, they all looked pissed-off.

Oops, so Tom did rip them off. But no, they looked pleased to see him.

They dismounted opposite the man-canoes. Once freed of their riders, the chocolate ants immediately turned around and marched off in orderly procession, off to recycle themselves back into the mountain's substance.

Chapter 81

The beached human-canoes were pushed back down into the milk. The captives were loaded aboard one of them. Tom was seated opposite Brooke, Megan behind her. Gina handed them paddles.

The fact of sitting inside a hollowed-out human body was almost too much to take. "Who thinks up this sick shit?" Tom said to no one in particular.

Donny Q laughed. "You did, dude." He waded off to inspect the other boarding eaters.

"Try to maintain a consistent stroke with everyone else," Gina said, sitting behind Tom, "else we'll turn in circles."

Tom traced the muscle meat joining the massive rib he sat on to the next. "What did you lot do with the internal organs? Eat them?"

The eater girl shook her head unaffectedly. "Nah, they didn't have any."

He turned to look at her. "No innards?"

"They were just meat inside."

Tom now got a good look at Gina. She was really pretty, with a large mouth and a snub nose. Her bald head was a smooth, streamlined curve. Her sunflower-yellow body was shapely and firm, her eyes like drops of water.

A strange, alien kind of beauty.

Alien. *Yes*, Tom decided, *that's the right word to describe her.*

Gina's dress was a bloody mass of rags—all the eaters' clothes were. The dress was ripped open on the left, from shoulder to navel, her left breast fully exposed. The breast was large, with stretch marks like she'd just had a baby. Its nipple looked like a huge yellow sweet.

Gina noticed Tom sizing her up. She smiled shyly and looked away.

"This boat stinks," Megan said. "It's decaying."

Gina peeled off a strip of rancid meat from between her feet and popped it in her mouth. Then immediately spat it out again. "Damn! I'd forgotten how crappy they taste. Yucky like you wouldn't believe. Ugh. I really wish they tasted better."

"Fucking shut up!" Brooke snapped. She simmered with displeasure, balanced the paddle in her hands like a weapon, a club she'd use to batter Gina and the other cannibals' heads to pulp. Okay, so her anger was unwise, but she didn't care. She couldn't help how mad the eaters' blasé attitude to eating human flesh made her.

Gina smirked at Brooke. "Just stop with the drama already."

"Take that sass out of your voice. I'm chief of Boston police."

A jeering laugh: "They must have a shortage then; or does the force now consist of just you?"

"Give her a break," Tom said. "She's pissed off that you're going to eat her."

Gina grinned evilly. "Now there's a nice thought."

Brooke quickly turned away. She didn't want Gina to see that she was about to burst into tears.

***

They were in the third canoe. Beneath Mama's uninterested gaze they paddled. Their paddles slapped the milk in hypnotic rhythm.

"We're about to go through the OD," Tom said a moment later.

They braced themselves for the transition. Their passage through the shimmering air went through them in turn—it felt like heat rippling through their bodies.

"We're still in the same place," Brooke said.

"We're not," Gina retorted. She pointed to the huge pack of metal animals seated along the beach, their bodies bloody from the kill; then, further ahead at the two man-canoes abandoned during the morning's fighting.

Opposite those, on the shore, a white stone stairway rose along the cliff face to a solitary door that glinted metal in the sunlight.

She scowled meaningfully at Brooke. "Now don't make nuisances of yourselves; we've some meat to pick up."

Donny Q gave orders to the fleet. The four man-canoes split into two groups. Donny Q's and the one carrying Tom, Brooke, and Megan moved directly to the shore. The other two rowed off to fetch the crewless man-canoes.

Brooke indicated the scattered corpses lying between the metal beasts. "From their uniforms, those are clearly Boston police."

The others said nothing. Even the imperturbable Megan was struck speechless by the carnage, the complete demolition of living beings into construction-kit body parts decorating a shoreline.

The giant metal animals—cats, dogs, lizards and apes with the wrong number of limbs, their bodies patterned with yellow mold—made no move to harm the eaters.

Donny Q and his contingent walked along the beach, bagging human chunks. There were a lot of parts to be collected, and it took a long time. The collected human meat was loaded into the two empty human-vessels.

Tom, Brooke, and Megan sat through the gory process. Gina covered them with her shotgun. Her gossamer eyes pleaded with Brooke to screw with her.

Tom looked out at sea, at Mama. *And you, pregnant giantess endlessly spurting milk. Are you really alive? And if you are, why haven't you moved from that spot all morning? And what are you pregnant with?* Tom was convinced—oddly, illogically so—that Mama wasn't gravid with any 'human' offspring.

Gina watched his eyes rove over Mama. "She's pregnant with the future."

"All woman are pregnant with the future," Megan said. "Children are the future."

Gina snorted. "A nice pat answer from a woman who's clearly never conceived in her life."

Megan smiled nicely. "It's complicated."

Brooke turned to face them. Her dislike of Gina had perked her spirits up again. "Speaking of pregnancy: How does sex with human men feel now that you're transformed, eater girl? Is it sweeter, or just duty to be endured, like visiting the dentist to have a tooth pulled?"

Gina's face visibly darkened, the angry hue flushed beneath her yellow skin. Her grip tightened dangerously on her shotgun. "You slut. How dare you allude dirt to our beautiful process of reproduction?"

"Whose corpses are those?" Tom asked quickly. The pickup crew seemed close to done with their gory task.

Gina took the bait. Her face lost its belligerence. "Just some asshole SWAT team that tried ambushing us this morning." She pointed. "That cliff-side door at the top of the steps leads into Chinatown."

Brooke's face turned white with horror. *Chinatown? That's Kim's unit?*

Chapter 82

Steaming like a clam cooking in its shell, Brooke was pissed off as hell.

Her personal pride was taking a battering. Her professional reputation was at stake. *I'm chief of police, dammit!* she thought, watching the cannibal mutants bagging up the remains of men and women recently under her command. *This crap shouldn't be happening!*

Brooke felt like grabbing Gina's shotgun from her yellow hands and knocking out all her glass teeth with it. *See how your cannibal ass eats us then.*

The young woman's smug top-of-the-food-chain expression made Brooke utterly mad.

Watching sack-laden eaters wade through the milk and hump their burdens into the two unmanned vessels, she rallied her emotions. She wasn't about quitting. Her sense of duty wouldn't permit it. *The city of Boston is relying on me and I'm not letting them down.*

It wasn't all bad. She looked up at the glittering metal door in the cliff face. *So this is where the infiltration is coming from. Gotcha, suckers. All I need do is survive this shit . . .*

Her thoughts turned glum. *But how? I seem poised for the eaters' kitchen.* But even in this despair, she found hope. *They're so confident of our surrender, they're not hiding anything from us. But that's 'cos we're not exactly likely to escape.*

She killed the negative thought. *No! I, Brooke Jessamine Hayes, will escape. I'll make it back to Boston and bring back a properly armed unit to deal with these cannibals.*

And I'll retrieve THE GOLD, the primary aim of this mission. We were all wrong—the eaters had the loot all along—it wasn't up on Bizarro. But Rose said . . . Screw Rose, the stupid cunt was protecting him! The gold . . . Pussypalm—Tom—had moved it elsewhere. But where? South Boston?

But if the eaters have the gold, why the hell did they seem angry when I asked . . .

And what does the eater queen want with Tom?

Then understanding hit her: *Oh Shit! How could I be so blind? Tom was screwing Big Sister—plumbing her yellow cunt—so the eaters would help him rob the bank!!*

Brooke's eyes strayed across to Tom. He grinned reassuringly at her. A bolt of heat rushed up from her crotch, flooding her belly.

She faked a return grin. *Oh, I hunger for your body, Tom, but I don't . . . No . . . can't . . . I can't trust you anymore. I can't afford to.*

Her thoughts set cold as ice. Her rising pussy heat was shifted to back burner.

She coldly considered her two paddling companions, both unreliable for different reasons. *Megan is too flaky with her sex-freak religious bullshit . . . Soon she'll be praising breast milk as the food of the gods and advising us to suck—"*

"The giantess has lovely nipples," Megan said. "Wonderfully pert for their size."

The eaters were finally done loading the bags of dead cop.

Meat ferrying meat, Brooke thought. *Can anything be more morbid?*

She looked at the metal animals with their odd patches of yellow mold, like crusts of peeling paint.

The huge robot beasts sat sentinel, motionless, their eyes staring at the man-canoes.

Brooke shuddered with sudden realization. *They're looking at me and Tom and Megan, awaiting the signal to swim through the water and rip us to shreds.*

She smiled grimly. *Oh no, I'm not making Kim's mistake. When I come back through here, it'll be with guns blazing. I'll see how you metal mutts and meow machines hold up under a barrage of mortar fire.*

Donny Q gave a signal. The boats resumed motion, turning towards Mama, the meat-laden pair in tow.

Chapter 83

Mama

Mama was titanic in size, colossal in conception, a humongous feminine extrusion from the lake surface.

The nearer to her they got, the more impressive she was. They'd grossly underestimated her size: each of her arms was wider than a house, and her massive gravid bulge . . . The shadow falling off Mama enclosed their approach to her in dimness like dusk.

Their paddles dug into the white surface with rhythmic slaps. Tom saw strange fish swimming in the surface, fish like carrots fused together.

"Where are we going?" he asked as their convoy entered Mama's shadow. "Why aren't we changing course?"

"Keep paddling," Gina said behind him.

Brooke looked up at the giantess's bulk. "He's simply pointing out the fact that we're on collision course with her milk waterfall. We'll be drowned."

"Don't worry 'bout it."

Finally, when they were right inside the shadow, their bodies wetted by the outskirts of the breast milk mist, Donny Q diverted the lead boat so it curved left around Mama. On their right, milk dropped off her massive pregnancy, crashing onto itself, ricocheting skyward in crotch-obscuring blurry white mist, sea-level clouds.

They travelled like this for a minute, then Donny Q diverted their passage again. This time right, underneath . . .

"How didn't I guess this?" Brooke said. "We were headed *under* her pregnancy?"

Then milk spattered them and they were through.

***

Underneath Mama's pregnancy was night-dark and cold. Light shone in from the other side of the tunnel formed by the milk-fall on their right and her crotch. A half-circle like a sinking moon.

Mama's belly was a taut sky overhead, one that bobbed occasionally. Milk escaped the falling torrent and streamed back down its slope, falling in tendrils to drench the travelers.

Mama's pubic hair was a dense forest.

Gina stopped rowing for a moment. She pointed to the chamber-sized slit on their left that was Mama's vagina. Inside it, strange white creatures glowed—semisolid mouthless man-things with four arms and three eyes.

"Those are the Barths," she explained. "They're created from Mama's genital secretion. They live a few days max, then dissolve into the milk, and another lot are formed."

"Do they fuck?" Megan asked.

Gina nodded. "To death. They're like incubi—they drink the spirits out of those they have sex with. When they dissolve away, those stolen souls become the spirits of eater children."

Brooke grimaced. *And where the heck do these pussy-ghosts find people to screw, you doofus?*

"An interesting—" Tom stopped speaking. The first two canoes had exited the end of the underbelly tunnel. Through the opening the sea looked totally different.

It looked normal.

"Welcome back down to Boston," Gina said.

Chapter 84

Pleasure Bay

The inlet on Mama's 'other side' *was* normal. A landlocked ring of clear blue water revealing bright coral—green, yellow, and red fish frolicking amongst pink rock formations. The water in the shallows seemed like transparent bricks or shingles laid in overlapping plates—like liquid crystal. Light fluttered down through the water, clearly illuminating the cove floor. See-through as eater eyes.

"Pleasure Bay," Gina said.

"It's beautiful," Megan said as they floated over a huge solitary octopus, "utterly lovely."

"My parents used to bring me here as a kid," Brooke said. "Then you eaters came along and abolished picnics."

Gina scowled, then grinned. "You just *wish* you were me, don't you?"

The two leading man-canoes were now on their right, heading for a palm-enclosed beach beyond which apartment buildings rose. They turned and followed.

Tom looked back. Mama was now transparent, like a sculpted block of ice. Here, her breasts gushed water. Her massive pendant still glittered silver.

Bizarro was back overhead. The floating mass hulked like existence's biggest pizza. Or a consolidation of rotten clouds.

Brooke followed Tom's upward gaze. "I've always felt it looked like a cloud of shit. Now I'll adjust that to chocolate."

***

Up ahead in the clear blue, arranged in precise orchard spacing, were giant people. Thirty-feet-tall pale-skinned men and women stood shin-deep in the water. Bodies arranged so they faced different directions, all were totally motionless, arms locked by their sides, eyes closed, faces set in expressions of serenity.

"Behold the source of the boats," Brooke said as they paddled nearer the motionless giants.

"Those are the mensch," Gina said. "They're odd. Each time we uproot one of them, another instantly sprouts to take its place."

Brooke pondered that. Her expression turned confused. "I don't get it: that suggests they're inexhaustible."

The eater girl nodded at Tom. "Pussypalm thought so too."

Brooke finished her train of thought: "Then why do you keep eating humans?"

"The mensch taste like shit—they're better used for transport."

Tom was bemused. "Are they alive?"

"No idea." She pointed up at a giantess they were passing, whose black hair descended to her buttocks. Her pubic hair looked like a black bear stuck in her crotch. "You were worried for a long time that they'd wake up and attack the camp in revenge."

Tom nodded. He was apprehensive as they neared their destination.

***

Human canoes skimming the pellucid surface like they were flying, they passed the rows of giant people, to the shore.

The eaters tethered the vessels to the legs of the foremost of the silent motionless giants. Everyone disembarked and waded ashore.

Brooke and Tom stared back at the giant sentinels. And beyond them, to Mama's transparent outline. "She looks made from the same stuff as the eaters' teeth," Tom remarked.

"I wish they tasted better," Megan said, joining them.

"Huh?"

"The meat giants, the mensch. Then we'd be spared all this nonsense."

Gina poked Brooke in the back with her shotgun. "Come on, you three; transport's here."

They turned. Donny Q was waving them up the beach.

"Time to go see Big Sister," Tom said, with misgiving.

They followed Gina up the beach, to a blue Hummer SUV parked on the Head Island Causeway.

Behind them, eaters lugged bags of human meat from the man-canoes to a truck.

Chapter 85

The blue Hummer rumbled past the roundabout at the William J. Day Blvd/East Broadway intersection, onto East Broadway Street, through Marine Park and across Farragut Road, then turned off immediately into a square complex bounded by a quartet of three-story apartment buildings.

The enclosure was roughly square and about seventy yards across.

Trees, sunbathing dogs, and a group of soccer-playing eater children on the clipped grass, made the scene normal.

Almost normal:

"Figures you'd use a human head for a ball," Brooke remarked as they alighted.

"Only after eating the brains," Gina retorted. The macabre ball rolled over to her feet. She picked it up so the captives could see it. Metal staples had been used to clip the separated skull cap back in place. Same with the lower jaw, which was filed smooth. "Brains taste just—"

"Now, Sofia, here's your mommy!"

The speaker was a thin teen girl carrying a baby. Tom noted the facial resemblance between the teen and Gina.

Gina's eyes brightened on seeing the baby. "Thanks, Nitty."

The teenager grinned glassy teeth. Tom had the feeling she was wondering what they'd taste like.

"My kid sister Anita," Gina explained to the captives.

She flung the skull-ball back to the soccer players and took her daughter from Anita. The child was duplicate of her mother—same pretty face, same clear-water eyes with blended-out pupils . . . Same rotted clothes—Sofia's yellow body was swaddled in rags. She stank too. Gina rocked and coddled the child.

Brooke was almost touched by the normalcy of the mother-child interaction.

Gina pointed to Tom. "Look who's here, Sofia darling. It's your daddy!"

Tom froze at the words.

Brooke looked coldly at Tom. "Stud service?"

"Daddy?" Tom managed to ask. He looked at the little cannibal girl in horror. The baby chortled happily at Tom. "My daughter?"

Gina nodded. "Yes, she's your daughter." She smiled smugly at Brooke, as if she'd determined the relationship between the pair, then handed the baby back to Anita. "I'll come breastfeed her after we take these prisoners to Big Sister."

Anita left with Sofia. Tom stared after her. "My daughter?" he repeated in disbelief.

Megan smiled and licked her lips. "Well, you've a reputation for being quite the cocksman, Tom."

The children had resumed their game. A sudden suspicion dawning on him, Tom looked first at them, then at Gina. She smiled smugly back at him.

"How many?"

"Huh?"

"How many children?"

She grinned teeth, paused for dramatic effect before replying. "Do you mean, how many kids do *we* have? Or how many *you* have?"

"Both."

"Me and you? Just Sofia. With the other girls? Let's see." She counted on her fingers. "There's Tommy Lee Jr., Geraldine, Mercy, Jude—that's that baby boy sitting over there watching the game; then Alexis, Alice Cooper, Nadine, Gary . . ." She stopped counting. "Too many to remember. About a third of the kids here are yours. Practically all the toddlers."

"I don't get it."

"Eaters can't fertilize their own women," Brooke said curtly, her eyes hard. "They use human men as babydaddies."

Megan giggled. "You've clearly spread a lot of love around, Tom."

Donny Q walked over from supervising the meat offloading. "Okay, guys, let's go see Big Sister." He grinned at Tom. "One of the girls has already informed her that you're back. She's impatient as hell to see you."

Chapter 86

Big Sister's office was an open-air space on the roof of the three-story building bordering Farragut Road and Marine Park. It had an unobstructed view of Pleasure Bay and Mama.

(Viewed from this height, the mensch's shadows fell at odd angles to each other, dappling water and sand alike with shades of not-quite-black. Some shadows fell thrice, in different directions, their ends overlapping others like shingles.)

Rising from her desk, Big Sister crossed the rooftop to them.

Brooke gasped on seeing the approaching woman's face. "*Gail? Gail Harding?* You're . . . alive? Ha . . . ha . . how?"

Gail Harding smiled coolly. She waved to Megan. "Hi. How's his little majesty doing?"

"So, so. The royal lollipop still calms his tantrums."

Gail turned to Tom. "Lisa already told me you look and sound different now, but wow!" She regarded Tom for a long moment, her eyes confused. "It is you, darling, isn't it?" Her voice was soft as silk.

He removed his glove. "Everyone I've so far met seems to think so."

Gail's eyes widened on seeing Rose. She gripped Tom's face in her hands, stroked his cheeks. "Darling, I've missed you *so* much. Once Lynn woke up again, I knew . . ." Her expression turned concerned. "*How much* do you remember?"

"Nothing," he replied truthfully. There was no doubt—she was clearly the woman with him in those 'gun flashes.'

(Now he was meeting her in person, now his vision wasn't being filtered through 'himself'—a hard concept to wrap his head around—Tom saw Gail's definite resemblance to Ryan Harding.

Both shared the same looks: fleshy face and dark hair, same piercing blue eyes, the same stubborn jaw. *Trouble there for sure*, he thought. *This is a lady who doesn't divert from a plan of action once she's decided on it. They hopefully don't share the same temper.*

Gail Harding was tall and large-boned; not fat—definitely not fat. Her clothes—army-green shirt and slacks—hung well on her, flattering her figure: small breasts, wide hips, slightly bowed legs. Her feet were small, cushioned in brown sandals.

Her small mouth was lipsticked purple.)

"We'll fix that," Gail promised. She kissed him gently on the cheek, then on the mouth.

He kissed her back. He couldn't refuse her lips and tongue—they had a telltale familiarity to them.

They broke apart. Her lips separated from his with reluctance. She linked her arm through his, turned to face the others.

Brooke got over her shock. "Gail, how are you still alive?"

Gail looked her over. "I think I remember you—Sgt. Hayes, isn't it?"

"*Captain* Hayes," Megan corrected. "Brooke just got promoted to Chief."

"Promoted? What happened to Joe?"

"Joe's dead."

"*Dead?*"

"Tom shot him."

A raised eyebrow. "Why? Jealousy?"

"Accident."

Gail shrugged. "Shit happens."

Brooke grimaced. "*Shit happens?* You were about to get *married* to him."

Gail laughed. "Just a ruse to see the robbery through. The sex *was* fun though. He was a wiz with his tongue." She grinned at Tom. "Me screwing Joe was part payback for you impregnating all the women in camp."

Donny Q and Gina, both silent since bringing the captives to the roof, chortled.

Gail lifted Tom's left hand to her lips, dipped her tongue deep into Rose. She slurped the vagina noisily, then wiped her mouth dry with the back of her hand. She smiled. "Tom here was always my first love."

Brooke nodded. "So you didn't love Joe. That still doesn't explain how the hell you're still alive when we autopsied and buried your body. That was no fake, Gail—it *was* you we stuck in the ground."

(Her mind shrilled an additional question: *And why the hell haven't these fucking cannibals eaten you!?*)

Gail looked out across the rooftop, then back at the other woman. "I had a little help from Dr. Oppenheimer."

"Oppenheimer's a traitor?" Megan asked softly. "I'd never have thought that."

Gail laughed. "Oh, he didn't want to, but darling Tom here convinced him otherwise."

She made an expansive gesture, "Okay, it's story time."

Chapter 87

Gail looked pointedly at Donny Q.

He nodded back. "Rich is bringing the mindspider." He walked over to the stairway entrance. "Hey, Rich, move your old ass, willya?"

"I'm coming!"

Rich stepped onto the roof. He was an odd sight—tall and scrawny with a wrinkled head and weak chin. His overalls were shredded memories of themselves.

Rich was carrying a football-sized black arachnid that looked like a mutated tarantula.

Megan wrinkled her nose. "It stinks like a rat. Like unwashed crotch."

"It likes dark places too," Rich said.

Gail stroked the spider's twitching hairy legs; it purred like a cat. She turned to Tom. "It's time to remember, darling."

He shook his head, stepped away from her. "I really don't think so."

"What does it do?" Brooke asked. "Eat brains?"

Donny Q shook his head. "It eats memories." He pushed Tom toward Rich. "Beastie here is how you forgot everything, dude."

Tom regarded the mindspider. Its multitude of black eyes regarded him back, like he and it were enemies . . . or friends. He considered more resistance . . .

"Okay," he said, stepping forward. "I'll do it."

Brooke grabbed his arm, held him back. "Are you sure?"

Gail's eyes narrowed to slits at the contact.

Tom smiled at Brooke. He nodded. "I have to. This odd journey . . . this trip of perpetual questions and half-revelations has brought me here. And it gets more confusing each moment. I need to know who I am."

"Okay then, if that's what you want." Ignoring Gail's displeasure, she kissed him full on the lips. She pulled back, her facial expression one of intense worry. "Just try to remember me afterwards."

He laughed. "Like I could ever forget."

He turned to Gail. Her face was a mask of smoldering rage. *Oh yeah, she definitely is Harding's sister.* He nodded. "Hit me with it."

Gail nodded to Rich. "Put it on him."

Gina had brought over a chair. Tom sat in it. Rich turned the mindspider over. Its belly was an open black crevice. No intestines or viscera. Presented like this, it looked like a living cap.

Rich pulled the edges of the mindspider's belly wide open, then popped it over Tom's head. He pulled the arachnid down till it totally covered Tom's face and its legs were treading his shoulders.

"Just relax," he said.

Gail looked from Tom to Brooke and Megan: "Okay, you two, I'll fill you in on what he's remembering. That way we'll all be on the same page afterwards."

***

Inside the mindspider was a wall-less gray cavern. For a moment, Tom was subsumed in the creature's musk, then, like fetid gas escaping a corpse, anamnesis came.

Memory unlocked her doors to him; Tom dissolved totally into his past.

Part 7: Bank Corridors Pt. 2

Chapter 88

When you plan on robbing your own bank, you need to be supremely resourceful.

Gail Harding planned the heist for two years.

She took her idea to Tom Pussypalm, whom she figured was the only person insane enough to dare pull it off. She'd never once bought into all his 'new leaf' behavior, his working for King Eric as a security consultant. Besides, from observing the pair during fiscal policy meetings in the palace, she'd realized Tom was screwing Queen Shirley.

Then, once King and employee had had their spat over pay . . .

***

To find Tom's hideout, Gail took to shadowing Queen Shirley. Her surveillance quickly paid off. Claiming she liked its rooftop view of the harbor, the Bostonian queen went twice a week without fail to an old waterside apartment on Old Atlantic Avenue between the Long and Central Wharfs.

Gail went to the waterside apartment herself on a cold Saturday morning when the clouds looked like fat frozen fingers. She rang the buzzer, Tom opened the door. He said nothing on seeing her, just indicated that she enter.

Shirley wasn't lying, Gail mused, looking out a window as she accompanied Tom into the living room, *the view's fantastic.*

They sat opposite each other. She explained why she'd come.

He frowned. "Can't be done, the Fed's practically a fortress."

Gail laughed. "Nothing is impossible if you don't mind what it'll cost you. And anyway, it's *my* fortress."

Her words visibly impressed Tom. He smiled, his lips a cruel crease in his face.

"Hey Lynn," he yelled. "Come out here a moment. Ms. Harding's got a business proposal for us."

A green-eyed blonde Gail didn't know appeared in a doorway. "Ms. Harding?" She raised an eyebrow in recognition, then quickly crossed to sit in the chair beside Tom's. She regarded Gail impassively. "I'm listening."

Gail repeated what she'd told Tom.

Lynn considered. "Making money isn't to be sniffed at, but . . ." she gazed pointedly at Gail, ". . . your elder brother's a cop—how do we know we can trust you? This might just be King Eric the Brat trying to screw Tommy again."

"My thoughts exactly," Tom said. His cold blue eyes bored into Gail's. She felt like they were drilling through her skull to her mind. Stripping her soul naked in their quest for truth.

She'd come prepared for the question. She pointed to Rose. "Why don't you ask your hand?"

Lynn scowled. "Watch your fucking tongue or lose it."

Tom laughed at Gail's suggestion. "You're smart. Rose never betrays me." He grinned at Lynn. "Let's have a consultation."

Lynn scowled. "With *her* here?"

He held out his hand. "Do it." He tapped the gun on the stool beside him, looked across again at Gail, his eyes like a snake's. "The benefit of Ms. Harding's being here is that she can't get away if she's lying."

Lynn snickered at that. Gail shuddered.

Lynn moved onto the arm of Tom's chair and began tonguing Rose.

Fascinated, Gail watched the blonde lick the hand-vagina, finger-fuck it, tongue the clitoris . . . Ryan had mentioned it to her once, but . . .

Tom groaned. He reached down and unzipped his fly. His penis sprung from his pants, already fully erect.

He jerked on it twice, then stopped. He nodded to Gail, tapped his erection: "Hey, make your mouth useful."

Gail had come prepared for that too. This took whatever it took. She crossed over to Tom and sucked his swollen member into her mouth.

They continued in their strange congress, with Tom alternately running fingers through Gail and Lynn's hair, till Rose began moaning in ecstasy.

Next moment, like a dam bursting, Tom flooded Gail's mouth with semen.

She swallowed quickly. There was a lot of it, like he'd not had sex in a while.

Though scared, Gail played it cool. After licking Tom's penis clean, she returned to her seat, got out her compact and touched up her lipstick. She was aware of his appraising eyes on her. She sensed that he approved of her pragmatic attitude.

That, however, was secondary at the moment.

"I love you, Lynn," Rose was saying. "What do want to know?"

Lynn laughed. "You always say that. Okay, Rose, can we trust Ms. Harding?"

"Oh yes. She's greedier than both you and Tom combined. And ruthless too. She'll do *anything* to get that money."

Tom raised a sated, surprised eyebrow at Gail. She affected not to notice.

"Oh, Lynn, I feel incredible. So tired too, like I could sleep for a billion years—"

Rose's voice was fading.

"—so quickly, hon: anything else you'd like to know?"

"This robbery plan of hers, will it work?"

"It's a good plan—it *might*. But there's details to work out . . ."

Rose fell silent.

Lynn grinned at Tom; they both grinned at Gail. "We're in," Tom said.

***

They discussed how:

"Gold weighs too much," Tom said, "cash would be better. There's money in the vaults too, right?"

She smirked. "A hundred million. Chick feed. Not damn near enough."

He looked surprised. "How much *gold* is in the Boston Fed?"

"Six point two billion dollars worth at last count. We're a repository—no one ever removes anything—everything's internal transfers between buyers and sellers."

"Gold it is then. How much do you intend taking?"

She shrugged back. "Why leave *any of it* behind? We're not a charitable organization, are we?"

He laughed. "King Eric'll have a fit."

"So? Let him. We'll leave a note saying we'll donate a small percentage of the proceeds to UNICEF."

They both laughed at her wit.

A silent moment followed. She met Tom's questioning gaze evenly, her eyes assuring him she was totally serious.

He nodded, scratched his forehead. "Now, how to move it. Six billion dollars in gold is a lot of weight—"

"A hundred and fifty-one metric tons," Gail said. "Over twelve thousand bars."

Lynn whistled. "We'd need a fucking aircraft carrier to get it out of the harbor."

Tom shook his head. "Moving the gold by sea isn't practical anyway. Harbor Patrol will be on us in a flash. There's nowhere to hide out on open water. We'll use trucks instead." He did some math in his head while gazing at the ceiling. "Three 18-wheelers will do it. They're bulky, but maneuverable enough. Now, how to load up fast 'cos of the cops . . ."

Gail grinned. "We'll work that out."

Lynn poured three whiskeys, handed the glasses around. "Here's to being rich and infamous."

Chapter 89

Gail had found herself powerfully attracted to Tom. She'd begun a relationship with him, and then, to further the robbery plan, with Joe Bradley.

She'd never loved Joe. Her engagement to Boston's head cop was simply to keep she and Tom up to speed on what the police were up to.

Sex with Joe was great though. Gail was a concupiscent woman—she liked to fuck. In some ways, sex with Joe was even better than with Tom, whom Gail had now fallen deeply in love with.

Whatever the case, both men—the one she loved and the one she didn't—were essential to her robbery's success.

***

"They'll know it's me for sure," she said one night, lying on her belly whilst Tom rimmed her ass. Gail like having her anus tongued. After a hot, sweaty Boston day, it was a nice cleansing feeling. "Then we'll have an endless manhunt."

Tom looked up from her saliva-slick anal pucker. "They'll think you're dead."

"You're forgetting Ryan. My brother's bullheaded as shit. He'll never let it die if there's no corpse." She giggled. "And my fiancé's Chief of Police. If he thinks you've abducted me . . ."

"I'll think of something," Tom grunted. He lowered his tongue to her buttocks again, resumed laving the moist crack, slipping a finger under to rub her clitoris.

"I got it," he said a short while later.

"A new name for my anus?"

He slapped her buttocks. "Be serious. I mean how to fool the investigation afterwards."

"You're not thinking of cutting off one of my hands again, are you?"

"Nah, we'll go see Oppenheimer."

Gail turned to look at him over her shoulder. She frowned. "Waste of time. He's loyal to King Eric."

Tom's eyes were broody. "Loyalty has its limits. Oppenheimer dearly loves his aged mother. Be a shame if anything were to happen to the old girl."

315

Gail grinned, "But what *can* he do for us, darling?"

"You'll see." Tom bent to lick her anus again.

Gail pouted with suspense. Then Tom dug his tongue especially deep into her rectum and she forgot all about the future.

Chapter 90

"The choice is yours," Tom said, sliding the shotgun deeper up the old woman's vagina, "I either pull the trigger now, or later." His voice turned savage. "But I damn sure will."

Gail, leaning on his shoulder, grinned. "Which will it be, Doctor? It's a simple question, nothing like your usual quantum physics."

White hair even more disarrayed than usual, Dr. Karl Oppenheimer looked aghast at his wheelchair-bound mother.

Gail had cut the old woman's plaid skirt open up to the crotch, and her panties off, exposing her skinny thighs. Ma's legs were forced apart. Blood seeped slowly from her vagina, trickling down the shotgun barrel sticking from her pussy like a metal cock.

Ma's eyes were round with disbelief. Her glasses hung off her large nose, her bony hands hung off the side of her wheelchair, twitching. Her toothless gums worked furiously. "This is an outrage, Maximillian! Take your rotten manhood out of me this instant, you bastard. Head on back to your whores and bar floozies."

Dr. Oppenheimer sighed. This was the only good part of this nightmare. Ma was eighty-seven and senile. She thought his dead father was trying to take advantage of her after a Friday night's carousing. It had been a regular scene in his childhood.

It wasn't bravery that had Dr. Oppenheimer speechless, it was horror that anyone could be so callous as to treat his mother like this.

"Look," Tom said, "I haven't got all night here." For emphasis, he jerked the shotgun in and out of Ma's pussy.

More blood spurted. Ma shrieked. "I'll have the cops on you for this, Maximillian! You're going to rot in the slammer. Karl now works for the King!"

Gail stuffed the old woman's mouth with a napkin. She looked pointedly at the doctor. "We might be doing you a favor by killing her."

Dr. Oppenheimer nodded. "I'll do it." Of course he would. Once they'd started on Ma, there'd never been any real question in his mind about it.

Tom looked at him cold-eyed. "No tricks, Doc."

He nodded. "No tricks."

Tom slid the shotgun out of Ma's ravaged cunt. The opening yawned bloody like the mouth of a kid who'd been fighting.

Ma jerked upright, then slumped. Her scrawny chest heaved rapidly like she'd just cum.

Gail covered Ma's thighs and pushed the wheelchair away.

"How long?" Tom asked.

Oppenheimer looked over at his mother, slumped in her wheelchair like she was dead. He was shaking. "Two . . . Two months at most." He'd not believed the legends, but . . . but . . . this man Pussypalm was nothing but a monster.

Gail came back from parking Ma in a corner. "You're sure about this? Remember: you screw us up and mama won't like it. She'll get pregnant with a metal baby."

The doctor sighed heavily; he polished his glasses. "It'll be ready."

Chapter 91

Two months later.

Dr. Oppenheimer's lab looked like a morgue. Cool and brightly lit. Machines hummed everywhere.

The doctor walked them over to a naked body on a bed. "Behold your doppelganger."

Gail gasped on seeing the sleeping woman's face.

Tom grinned. "Yeah, it's her all right." He slapped Oppenheimer on the back. The man flinched. "Well done, Doc. I guess mama won't be getting fertilized with metal sperm after all."

The clone woman was connected to a profusion of tubes. A catheter connected her urethra to a half-full bottle of urine. A larger tube ran from her anus into another machine.

Tom tangled fingers in the clone's dark pubic hair. She opened her eyes and gurgled like a baby. He raised a hand and squeezed her right nipple. It stiffened under his touch. "Feels like you too."

Gail shuddered. "Ugh. Why's she looking at us like a retard? All the drool and stuff?"

Oppenheimer dabbed the spit from the clone's chin. He removed his glasses to polish them. "She's only adult in appearance. Mentally, Grace is two months old. She also has an infant's lack of muscle control."

"Grace?"

He shrugged.

Gail examined her duplicate closely, running her fingers up and down the soft white expanse of her skin. *Grace. The mirror me made flesh.* Grace gurgled and grinned as Gail probed her, making pedaling motions with her feet. Her hands playfully tapped her thighs.

"What about her fingerprints?" Tom asked.

"A perfect match. Grace is like Gail in every detail."

Gail turned from probing her clone's crotch. "Not exactly—I lost my virginity ages ago."

Oppenheimer said nothing. These people were so hard to please. He just wanted this mess to be over. Whatever would little King Eric think if he found out?

"Don't worry about that," Tom told Gail. "I'll handle her deflowering. You can watch."

Her face contracted into a scowl.

319

Tom ran a hand up the clone's thigh into her crotch. He parted her pussy lips, felt her maidenhead. He smiled at Gail. "You're not jealous of *yourself*, are you?"

Chapter 92

Tom told Gail a story:

"A year ago, down in Techxas to buy guns from Pablo, I came on this dying vav in a forest. I'd stopped my car to pee and there she was, lying by the roadside with an infected tentacle. The organ was swollen purple; thicker than my leg and covered with scabs. In several places it was cracked and seeping pus. Impossible to pull up inside her again. You could see from her face that she was in horrible pain. She was withered down like an old person too."

"And instead of fleeing like any sensible person would," Lynn said, "my intrepid cousin walks over and plays doctor."

"Doctor?"

"Rose healed the tentacle," Lynn replied. "One vagina cured another."

Gail looked at Tom in disbelief.

He nodded. "True. I was clearly in no danger. The vav was wheezing like she'd die any moment, so I walked over. You should have smelt that tentacle . . . Anyhow, when I was about three feet away from the vav, Rose spurted green goop all over the tentacle and it healed immediately."

"That's too odd to be true."

"It's what happened. Everything—scabs, stink and all—vanished like it had never been. The swelling went down like it had been deflated. A lovely slick tentacle was all that remained."

"And afterwards?"

"I was confused as hell. Then I saw the lady in question was smiling at me like I was her boyfriend, and it occurred to me she might be considering draining me of blood to get her energy levels up again. So I hightailed it out of there, got in my car and drove off."

Lynn sighed. "That wasn't the end of it however. A week later, he had the same experience again. This time in Clarksburg, West Virginia."

Tom took over the narrative again: "This time the vav's tentacle was snapped. She was lying on her back, staring up at the sky in agony." He shrugged. "Anyhow, I knew that vavs heal automatically, so I located the broken-off portion and carried it over to her. She was real pretty—Ava Gardner's face—"

"And Rose spurts goop all over the ends and fixes the tentacle again," Lynn finished.

"This time I wasn't as surprised; and apparently, neither was the vav. I was prepared to run back to my ride the moment she showed any signs of ingratitude—I had two rocket launchers I'd just won from Pablo in a shootout wager—but she just got up, stared at me for a loooooong moment, then walked off into the forest."

"That's a fucking odd tale," Gail said.

"Odder still is the clear impression I got that she knew who I was. I knew that the first one I'd helped would have told her sisters; I just had no idea of the range of their telepathic transmission. We're talking here of a distance of over a thousand miles."

Gail wrinkled her nose. "You're saying all the vavs in the US now know about what you did?"

He shrugged. "No way to tell for sure."

"The point," Lynn said, "is that Tom has something that the vavs want. You know how they auto-heal every kind of injury except to their pussies. So we offer them Tom's services in exchange for their help robbing your bank."

Gail mused on this awhile. "I dislike the idea of my boyfriend playing with other women's vaginas," she said finally, "but . . . in this case we've no real choice." She scowled. "Okay, we do it. But how do we talk to them?"

"Don't worry about that," Tom said. "Lynn has these telepathic bugs she found somewhere."

Gail looked questioning at Lynn.

The blonde nodded back. "Ugly stinky things. I call them mindspiders."

***

Armed with three mindspiders, Lynn, Tom and Gail took a speedboat out to Castle Island to converse with the vavs.

"We'll look like aliens from 40s sci-fi," Gail said, referring to the flamethrower tanks on their backs. They also wore metal collars for neck protection.

Lynn laughed. "We'll be safe though." She swung the boat toward the quay, then cut the engine and let it glide in. She docked the boat, climbed up and secured it to a post. "Okay, darlings, from here on we walk. Here, let me have my creepy-crawlies."

Tom handed Lynn her bag of mindspiders. He and Gail climbed out.

Together, they stared up at Fort Independence. The star-shaped fortress's granite walls extended left and right, ending in its trademark arrowhead-shaped corners. Inside it resided the vavs.

"Odd they chose this place," Gail noted.

Lynn shrugged. "Not really. This is 'Castle' Island, and they're ruled by a queen. Guess the location makes sense to them."

"Yeah, right. Like they took political science classes."

Lynn reached in her bag and brandished a mindspider. "Okay, guys, time to really look alien." The black insect kicked feebly, its bristly legs seeking purchase on thin air.

"Ugh." Gail pushed Tom forward. "You first."

Tom presented his head. Lynn slipped one over his head, then did Gail and herself.

Inside the mindspider, the outside world was a limitless grey space. People and objects were depicted as black outlines of varying solidity. The Fort wall was a 'blackening' that was as much there as not.

Gail lifted a hand to her face. She 'saw' her fingers, but then they wobbled and dissolved like melting ice. Then they were back again, an artist's depiction of a vibration. Then another dissolution.

"I look like a badly-drawn cartoon character," she thought at Tom.

He laughed inside her head. "You don't say?"

"Let's go," Lynn thought to them both. "The vavs have sensed us. We're expected. Just remember if we need to use the flamethrowers: the vavs are the *tall* ones. Don't either of you dare fry me."

Enveloped in the stink of arachnid musk, they walked into the vav camp.

***

The vavs very readily agreed to join Tom's robbery plans.

"Don't fear us," the vav Queen said. "We will not hurt you. We know and like Pussypalm." The muddle of black lines converged into Marilyn Monroe's face, then dissolved again. "Of course we will help you. But afterwards . . ."

Tom and Gail both rolled their eyes at the vav's request.

"Okay," he agreed.

***

Outside again:

"How greedy can you get?" Gail said immediately Lynn slipped the mindspider off her head. "That's so typical. Offer another woman an inch of your man and she wants the whole shebang!"

"They have a point," Lynn said. "Except Tom lives with them permanently, there's no way they can guarantee his safety. As far as they're concerned he's an invaluable resource that must be protected."

Gail still fuming, they got back into their motorboat.

Lynn pointed back at the walls of the vav fortress. "We're lucky they didn't insist he stay now."

Gail tapped her flamethrower. "Not difficult to explain that." She scowled. "I disliked this from the get-go. Now what do we do? No way am I agreeing to him staying there!"

"Calm down," Tom said soothingly, reaching an arm around her.

"You'd like that, wouldn't you? Being the only man surrounded by—"

Tom shut her up with a kiss. She resisted awhile, then melted into his embrace.

"If you two dare start taking your clothes off, I'll upend you into the water," Lynn warned.

Neither paid her any notice. Arms folded, Lynn sat in the boat's prow and watched them kiss.

Love really is mysterious, she thought. *I've still absolutely no idea what Tom sees in Gail. I mean, she isn't even pretty, just passable-looking at best. And it isn't the promise of making money attracting him to her either. I'm certain of it. And the corresponding hunger in Gail's eyes whenever Tom's near? No, that isn't faked either.*

After a while of being comforted, Gail looked up at Tom. "What are we going to do? We need their help."

He grinned back. "You're worrying over nothing. We agree now, disagree afterwards."

Lynn grimaced. She doubted it would be that easy.

Tom looked at her. "Why aren't we moving?"

"It isn't noon yet," she said, "We can still go see the eaters today." She looked pointedly at Gail. "Shouldn't take more than an hour or two. We'll still deliver you home in time for your lunch with Joe."

Gail considered it awhile, then shook her head. "We'll be slicing it too fine. At the moment Joe's still convinced I'm working overtime on Saturday mornings. If he suspects I'm not and puts a tail on me, we'll be sunk before we're even afloat."

Lynn looked unconvinced.

"She's right," Tom said. "If the eaters turn out as dumb as the vavs, we might have to fight our way out of their camp."

Lynn grimaced. "Your darling's 'Saturday only' availability is slowing us down."

"Better we're patient than penniless," Gail said. "I'm still thinking up a good excuse to leave Joe on Sundays too."

Lynn shrugged. She started the motorboat, then swung it around in a smooth curve towards Boston. She relaxed into the vessel's power, the throb of its engine as it sliced apart the sea surface.

She looked back once. Tom had Gail bent over the rear seat and was fucking her hard. Lynn watched his penis glide in and out of Gail's wet vagina for a moment, then shrugged and altered the boat's direction, swinging it north towards Logan Airport. Best she allow them to bump and grind the lust out of their systems.

Chapter 93

On the Saturday morning slated for the trip to the eater camp (Gail's first 'all-free' weekend), Lynn woke up with really bad period pains. Gail and Tom waited to see if she'd get better. By noon she was still hurting, so they went alone.

Tom showed the eater guards at Pleasure Bay beach his left palm. That got them instant access to Big Sister.

Following their escort, Tom understood why the cannibal guards hadn't bothered disarming him. He estimated there were well over a hundred eaters in the camp, far too many to fight if things went pear-shaped.

***

The eater society was Matriarchal, ruled over by a 'Big Sister.'

Big Sister Cassiopeia Evans was in her sixties. She was doted on and pampered and her word was law of life and death—much like King Eric the Young of Boston.

Gail and Tom met Cassie in her rooftop office—the top of the three-story apartment block overlooking Pleasure Bay.

There were three others present: Donny Q, Cassie's Head of Security; a pretty young woman named Gina Fieri; and Trudi, Cassie's pregnant daughter, who sat in a beach chair silently watching proceedings.

Cassie was obese, like a mustard-coated walrus. A face like dough, with features like excavations. Eyes scary in their pellucid vacancy. Massive floppy breasts like throw pillows. Flab rippled her sides like meat ribs. Each of her arms was the size of Gail's thighs.

Cassie's hairless sex, visible through her ripped dress, was veneered with slime. Her humongous thighs were crusty with dried secretion.

She heard Tom and Gail out, then smiled. "Yeah, we're interested. We need money to buy better guns to kill you humans with." Her voice was sandpapery. Stink rolled off her.

Hiding his disgust, Tom smiled back. "Work with us then: There's more gold in that bank than any of us can spend. You'll be able to buy enough weapons to take on the fucking US army."

"The vav have already agreed," Gail added. "If you eaters come in too, the plan can't fail."

Cassie's flabby features compressed in thought.

(Tom looked past her, out over Pleasure Bay. The mensch filled the foreground, pale sentinels dripping mid-afternoon shadows across the rippling water. Tom had no idea how shadows formed under Bizarro without direct sunlight.

Mama's transparent form dominated the bay. To the left of the water cascading off her humongous belly he made out Castle Island, the vavs' camp.

Closer to home, a pack of dogs were mating down in Marine park. Their coupling howls and barks carried like ghosts on the wind.)

Finally, Big Sister belched, filling the air with yet more stink. "You make a convincing case," she said. "We just *might* join you."

"What's the *might?*" Gail asked cautiously. She didn't like Cassie. It wasn't the woman's unkempt ugliness—she just didn't trust her. *And for heaven's sake cover yourself. Get a new dress or wear some panties; even a blind lesbian would be turned off by that mess you call a vagina.*

Cassie laughed, her expression shrewd. "Nothing complicated. No tricks either. Just a simple question you must answer—are you worthy of us?"

Tom and Gail looked at themselves, then back at her.

"You gotta pass an initiation," Donny Q explained. "A contest to show how tough you are."

"I'm not here to fight," Tom said.

"Eaters don't work with weaklings," Gina said. "Fight or fuck off." She put special emphasis on the 'fuck.' Tom had the idea that was for his benefit.

He sized her up, then laughed. "Okay, tough girl, I'll fight."

"What sort of fight?" Gail asked worriedly. This was a complication she'd not foreseen.

Donny Q shrugged. "His choice. Only thing is—it's a three on one combat. You fight all three opponents at once. Kill them if you can, don't if you can't. They'll be trying to do the same to you. Once we're sure—"

"Three on one's unfair," Gail objected.

"So is life," Gina said. "So is eaters eating humans. So is humans eating cows." She squeezed Tom's bicep. "Girl, if your boy here ain't up to the challenge, take his ass on home. I for one want to see if he's as tough as his reputation makes out."

Tom and Gail looked at Cassie.

She nodded. "You're free to leave if you choose. You'll have safe passage this time, but watch out next time we see you."

"You'll be dinner," Gina said nastily.

Cassie's daughter Trudi adjusted herself in her beach chair. She waved to Tom, grinning a transparent smile. "I in particular look forward to eating *you*."

Gail shuddered; Trudi's pregnancy looked like a massive yellow tumor. In true eater fashion, her dress was a rotted web dangling over her belly like curtain strips. Gail couldn't understand why eaters never changed their clothes.

Tom shrugged. "Let's do it."

"You sure about this?"

He grinned, looked at the eaters. "Three on one? To the death?"

Big Sister nodded. "Or till we think you aren't a pussy, Pussypalm."

"You're on."

Gina smirked. "I like a hero. What kind of fight?"

"Old fashioned gunfight. Pistols." He smiled coolly at Gina. "If women are included, ensure you're aren't one of them—I kind of like you."

She smirked again, then looked away shyly.

Chapter 94

The gunfight was held in an empty square. Eaters of both sexes watched from the second-floor windows of the enclosing buildings. Gail, Big Sister Cassie, and pregnant Trudi watched from a sofa in the 'royal box,' a room furnished in purple.

The ground floor was left vacant in case the gunfight spilled over into the houses.

Tom's opponents were three mean-looking men who struck the fear of God into Gail.

("Don't worry," he whispered to her before she was led off to the royal box. "They're assholes now? They'll be *dead* assholes soon.")

He and they all had pistols—old western six-shooters Donny Q had found somewhere—holstered at their waists.

Only thing Tom didn't understand was the weird figure drawn on his forehead in blood. A mouthful of teeth with a bone in it.

"Remember the rules," Donny Q said. "You each back off ten paces first. No climbing the stairs and no shooting overhead." He looked pointedly at one of the three men. "Josh, if you accidentally KILL somebody again like last time . . ."

Josh nodded hastily.

Donny Q turned back to Tom. "You ready?"

He nodded.

"Good then. Once I'm inside with Big Sister and Trudi, I'll blow a whistle and the fight starts. It continues till I blow the whistle again."

Tom nodded again. Donny Q left them.

"You're dead meat, punk," Josh told Tom as Donny Q walked off. "I'm having your pecs for dinner."

Tom said nothing; he stared Josh down. The eater wilted under his cold gaze, looked away in discomfort.

The other two eaters smirked at Tom. "Oh, so you think you're a tough guy, eh?" one said.

"A delicious tough guy," the other added.

Tom said nothing; just gave them the same cold eyes.

Donny Q's whistle sounded.

Hands held out from their sides, they began backing off. The crowd counted paces for them in an expectant roar: "One . . . Two . . . Three . . ."

The atmosphere felt to Tom like Ancient Rome and the gladiators.

". . . Eight . . . Nine . . . Ten!"

A hush fell over the square. The air was tight with tension.

Tom and the eaters stared at each other, watching to see who'd draw first.

The apprehension became solid, something to shatter with a hammer. Overhead, Bizarro seemed to descend like a ceiling, canning the tension on contestants and spectators.

"Better go for your guns, assholes," Tom said loudly, his voice returning in punctured echoes.

Three eater hands simultaneously flew to their pistol butts.

Tom was faster. Cocking and firing in a lightning-fast blur, he shot all three eaters in the head before any could draw. The spectators gaped in shock as the men collapsed. There was graveyard silence for a moment, like the eaters thought the dead were playacting—that they'd get up and resume the fight—then Donny Q blew the whistle again.

He descended from the royal box and walked over to Tom. His eyes popped wide on noticing the perfect alignment of the bullet hole in each dead man's head—two inches above the bridge of the nose to form an equilateral triangle with their eyes.

"You'll do, dude," he said quietly, then turned and raised Tom's hand, yelling to the crowd. "And the winner is . . . Pussypalm!"

Gail ran downstairs from the royal box and across the grass to Tom.

Tom kissed Gail's hair as she held him tight. He wasn't sure, but he thought he'd seen several eater women faint when Donny Q announced him as victor.

That should have warned him there was trouble in store.

Chapter 95

"What?" Gail said, aghast.

Big Sister Cassie nodded. She looked at Tom pointedly. "You're an eater now, aren't you?"

He stared back, confused. "Me? I thought the fight was just to test my courage."

"I recall Donny Q calling it an initiation," Trudi said, sucking marrow from a human finger bone, "That should have warned you."

They were up on the roof again, evening setting in. Trudi was eating a boiled human hand, the smell of which made Gail nauseous. She'd already puked once, vomiting over the edge of the building, regardless of who she splattered.

Big Sister pointed to Tom's forehead. Tom remembered the bone-in-mouth symbol drawn there. "That's the initiation symbol."

Donny Q slapped Tom boisterously on the back. "You're an eater now, dude. We couldn't eat you even if we wanted to."

"But . . . but . . . ." What the eater matriarch was demanding was simply . . . Then he remembered something else. He pointed to Gail, "What about her?"

Big Sister scowled. "Technically, she isn't one of us, but—"

"She's my woman—"

"Don't interrupt me. I was about to say that since she's your woman, she's a honorary eater too. No one will mess with her."

"Particularly once you start doing what's right for the tribe," Trudi added.

"And that," Big Sister finished, "is knocking the girls up."

Gail shook her head. "Hell, no. There are so many women here, I'll never get to see him."

Trudi sniggered. "It's not an every-night or romance thing. Most of the women have boyfriends. We're not seasonal breeders like you humans with your menstrual cycle. We get pregnant real easy. Most times, once is all it takes."

"Eater women are fertile all year round," Big Sister said with pride. She looked coldly at Tom. "You do your duty by us, we'll do ours by you. Anyone who wants a baby can come see you in the morning. Gail has you to herself at night."

Tom looked at Donny Q. The eater nodded. "*Please agree*. Saves me having to keep giving family planning classes to guys we catch for food."

Tom looked at Gail. Her face was conflicted but she nodded. "Do it for me," she said.

He looked at Big Sister. "Okay. But no romance, right?"

Big Sister nodded back. "Of course. You're still Gail's property. The girls will be made to understand that she's sharing your semen with them, but no more."

Trudi laughed softly. "And don't think too highly of yourself. You humans look like shit to us—like slugs . . ." she tapped her bulge, ". . . except when there's babies involved."

Wobbling like a bowl of yellow Jell-O, Big Sister got to her feet. "But, first, the new eater sleeps with *me*." She grinned lewdly at Tom and Gail's astonished stares, then crooked a finger at Tom. "Come on, Pussypalm, I want to see if your lower pistol fires as good as your upper one."

"But you're too old to have a child," Gail objected.

Big Sister smirked. "Never said I wanted one." She pointed to Trudi. "I already had more than my fair share of rugrats. Now I'm just carrying out quality control. Much more fun."

Tom looked helplessly at Trudi.

She shrugged a 'don't look at me/it's not my fault' shrug. "Go get your groove on, stud. You can't say no. Being queen means mum gets first pick of all the men, whenever she wants."

Tom followed Big Sister downstairs to her apartment.

Chapter 96

To Tom's surprise, the sex wasn't bad. True, Big Sister was dirty and stank rankly, but once laid out in bed naked, the maize-colored expanse of her flesh with its marbling of pink veins was eerily erotic.

"Relax," she said, "I'm not going to eat you—queens don't suck cock, except they're gay, of course. *You* eat *me* instead."

Tom couldn't help but grin at that.

Big Sister's fingers manipulated him deftly, stroking up and down his shaft while he sucked her breasts, till he warned, "If you don't stop I'll cum in your hand."

She stopped stroking, parted her massive thighs. "Get to work down there then."

He bent to lick her cunt, dreading the experience. To his surprise, it smelt and tasted *clean*. Nothing like its distressing unwashed appearance. It was the one part of her that didn't stink. He licked and tongued the yellow slit, while she moaned and purred, fingers working in his hair.

Either side of his head, her elephantine thighs rose like sulfur cliffs, monuments of cellulite.

Big Sister came, squirting into Tom's mouth.

He tried pulling his head away. Her body shuddering with her orgasm, she held Tom firm in place, wedged between her thighs. Her colorless, odorless flow filled her crotch and rose up into his nostrils.

"Drink it," she ordered, "Mama's sex water is good for you. Makes weak men grow big and strong."

Unable to free his head, in danger of drowning if he didn't, Tom swallowed. Like her cunt, her orgasmic secretion tasted pristine clean. She squirted it out in warm jets, splattering his face, sending some up his nose, into his eyes. Tom drank it down, swallowing endlessly, till finally the gush subsided to the trickle of a turned-off tap.

Tom pushed himself up on his elbows.

Big Sister's fat face creased into a smile. "Now that's what I call head."

Tom smiled weakly back. His cock felt about to burst. He slid up and inserted himself into her wet pussy.

Big Sister was slack and orgasm-slick, with little vaginal friction. Tom fucked her hard for a while and came, spurting deep like he wanted to make a baby with her. The orgasm was a deep release of all the tension he'd felt since arriving in Pleasure Bay.

He felt shattered afterward, and lay corpse-still on her elephantine bulk. Her immense breasts spread under him like pillows.

Big Sister giggled throatily. Her stink wrapped Tom like a blanket.

"You're good," she said softly, thick yellow lips stretched in an almost ear-to-ear grin, squeezing his ass with both hands, "the girls are going to be delighted."

Chapter 97

Back upstairs on the roof again, there was tension between Big Sister and Gail. Gina and Trudi, being female, recognized the latent hostility for what it was—claims of territorial integrity.

Tom and Donny Q had no idea of the violent undercurrents of passion swirling around them.

Big Sister regarded Gail coldly, angrily noting how she gripped Tom's arm with taut fingers, hiding her distaste over what she'd agreed to behind a smile. *This human bitch will have to go. I'm a reasonable woman, but . . . I foresee only trouble from her.*

No longer human, the eater matriarch couldn't comprehend Gail's unwillingness to share Tom. *It's not like we want the man himself, just the content of his balls, you dimwit.*

Big Sister's incomprehension was simple biology:

Since male eaters didn't fertilize their womenfolk, eater family units were much looser than human ones. Family was a loose aggregation of children, mother, and whichever 'father' caught her fancy. Eaters paired up and broke up as they pleased. Neither sex took offense when their current partner went off with someone else.

And so, to Big Sister, Gale's territorial jealousy was petty and pathetic. *I'll have to get rid of her*, she concluded. *But not yet. Not till Tom's properly integrated into the tribe—which will have to be after the robbery. Too long, but I've no choice but to wait. Heaven knows we need the money—*

She grinned dishonestly at Gail. "I've tested the goods, darling. I'm satisfied that my girls will be satisfied."

—And we need Tom's little prude to get it.

Gail grinned back just as insincerely. The battle lines were drawn. She was well aware of Big Sister's dislike for her. *I'll have to do something about this slug masquerading as a woman*, she thought, the gears of her mind whirling to manufacture a plan. *This camp isn't big enough for both of us.*

Chapter 98

"What's your deal with Lynn?" Gail asked Tom one night after an intense lovemaking session.

Tom leaned up on an elbow and stroked her nipples. He'd been expecting the question for a while. "She's a witch."

"I *know* that. She's got so many books of magic, she's practically a one-woman coven."

"Don't tell me you're jealous."

"I'm just watching my investment. I'm a banker, remember?" She peered intently into Tom's eyes. "We're about to become *very* rich. I'm not having you dumping me for the older version."

"Lynn's *younger* than you."

"I mean older version as in 'old girlfriend's club.'"

He laughed, then sat up. He pulled Gail up to snuggle against him, then splayed his left palm in his lap. "This is Lynn's vagina."

Gail's eyes widened to the size of chicken eggs. "What? Ha . . . ha . . how?"

Tom frowned with memory. "First thing: Lynn's my cousin, that's why I never sleep with her."

"She licks Rose regularly."

He laughed. "It's *her* vagina; don't tell me you don't wish you could lick yours."

"Ugh. Go on with the story. What's *her* cunt doing on *your* hand?"

"Two years ago, Lynn had an accident during a sex-magic ritual. It was . . ." His brow wrinkled. ". . . I honestly don't remember what it was about any more. But what she happened, was, she duplicated herself."

"Like, make a clone?"

He shook his head. "No. This one was in another dimension. The problem is, there was a cock-up during the magic ritual—Lynn performed it with some magic dildo inside herself—and both women were left with only one vagina."

"Huh?"

He grinned. "Yup. That's the problem: while Lynn has the pussy here; the other Lynn—let's call her Twin Lynn—has none."

Gail laughed. "You can't honestly believe all that talk of other realms. And a shared vagina's even more absurd." She shook her head.

He laughed, but more somberly. "I didn't originally. But there's *more* to it. Whichever Lynn has the vagina . . . is the living one."

Gail gaped at him.

Tom nodded. "The other one's dead until she gets their shared pussy. It transfers between them. Remember, they're both the same person—at least that's what Lynn assures me. The other one's just in another version of Boston."

Gail mused on that. It had the ring of implausible truth—urban legend—to it. "So why is it on your hand?"

"Safekeeping. Lynn is scared of her duplicate scheming to kill her across the dimensions if she holds on to it." He shrugged. "It's a silly fear if you ask me."

Gail nodded. "But a rational one—no one wants to die."

He shrugged. "Anyway, I'm looking after it for her till she works out how to duplicate it so the other Lynn can have one of her own."

Gail's face turned suddenly serious—she hugged Tom tightly. "Don't ever leave me, darling."

He looked at her in surprise. "What's with you all of a sudden?" then: "You're not pissed off about me and the eater women, are you? I've told you, I don't feel a thing for any of them. Besides, you agreed to it."

Gail couldn't fully express her fears. The sudden image of a lonely woman, stranded in another dimension tugged at her heartstrings. It seemed the ultimate abandonment. "I don't give a shit about you and the eater women. Just don't leave *me*."

She looked up at him, eyes teary. "I love you, I don't ever want to wake up to find you're not beside me." Her breasts heaved with the emotion of her words. "I may not be the most beautiful woman in the world, but I love you. I'm not perfect—hell, I'm far from perfect—but I fucking love you." Her eyes burned like lamps. "Do you understand that?"

Her words sobered Tom. "We're murderers—violent criminals," he said. "You carved my initials into Kiki's cheek yesterday after I shot her nose off. Do we also love like the innocent?"

"Everyone loves, Tom. And no one's really innocent. Evil makes us human."

She stated it so matter-of-factly that Tom had no reply. He kissed her.

Gail pulled away from him. Her stare was icy. "I don't want to be patronized and placated. I want your assurance that you'll never leave me."

"You're taking this very seriously."

Her icy stare didn't alter. "I'll never betray you, Tom. You can trust me with your life. I'll never leave your side, or be less than the partner you expect. I'll have your kids, as many as you want. I will love you until the stars fade in the sky." Her cold resolve faltered, her voice broke. "I just want your assurance that this isn't a one-sided deal. I *need to know* that you care about me exactly the same way."

Tom looked at her for a while. Then nodded. "I love you too. I mean it, Gail—I'll *never* leave you. Your heart's safe with me."

He kissed her again. This time she didn't pull away. She sunk into the warmth of his body.

When they broke apart, she was calm and happy again. "Very odd about Lynn; you mean she really has no pussy down there? How in Hell's blaze does she have sex?"

"She doesn't. She claims celibacy helps focus her magic. Same claim for her veganism—meat weakens her aura."

Gail thought on that. "I guess she knows what she's talking about." She stroked Rose, probing its urethra. "Does it pee?"

"Nah, the opening's just for appearances: Lynn kept her pee hole to herself."

Gail laughed. "Can't say I blame her; else she'd be pissing out of her anus. Why does Lynn call her vagina 'Rose' anyway?"

"It looks like a fuck-flower."

Her brow creased in thought again. "Is Lynn's magic really any good, or does she just keep engineering trans-dimensional pussy screw-ups?"

Tom recognized her tone of voice. "What are you *thinking*?"

"Just that, maybe Lynn can help resolve our problem with Big Sister Cassie."

Chapter 99

Big Sister Cassie fell ill the next week.

"Never seen anything like it," Donny Q said, leading Tom and Gail through the matriarch's apartment. "She's . . ."

He pushed the bedroom door open, so they could see.

They stood and stared, speechless. "This all happened just yesterday," Donny Q said.

Big Sister had mutated. What lay in her bed now looked like a monstrous white insect, but with a shell soft like boiled egg-white. Her arms and legs too were plated with the same soft armor. Like a garden slug, she was slimy all over, more clear goo pulsing from her pores as they watched.

She was secured to the bed by metal handcuffs at wrists and ankles. Her hands and feet were white reptilian claws.

Big Sister's corpulent face was still recognizable as hers, but her eyes were now orange. Bright orange like they'd been plucked from a tree. Her teeth were gone, replaced by strips of flesh dangling from her gums like curtains. She had no tongue, could no longer talk.

Her eyes held no recognition of them. She growled, fighting to break her metal restraints and attack them.

Tipping Big Sister's breasts now were two flexible metal spikes.

Donny Q pointed to the spikes. "Stay away from those." He walked over to a side table and returned carrying a yellow football. He flipped the ball over, so they could see the single blinking eye on its other side. "This used to be Davey."

Tom and Gail both gaped. "Her son, the doctor? What the hell happened to him?"

Donny Q sighed. He pointed the ball at Big Sister's breasts. Both metal spikes now dribbled a black liquid. "Davey was trying to give her an injection to calm her, when . . . she pulled him down on her—she wasn't bound up then—and jabbed him with those. She pumped him so full of that black shit, it was squirting from his ears." He threw the yellow oblong up and caught it again; rolled his eyes in despair. "He became like *this* in *one* hour—his hands and legs shrunk, his head . . ."

Gail involuntarily stepped back toward the door.

Donny Q looked at Tom. "Dude, it's a good thing you two both got here now. Davey was our only doctor. Do you know anyone who can come look at her?"

Tom pretended to think. When Lynn had told him Big Sister Cassie wouldn't be a problem anymore, he'd been skeptical, but now, looking at the monstrosity on the bed . . .

"My cousin's a witchdoctor," he told Donny Q. "She might be able to help."

"She used to a nurse too," Gail added.

Donny Q grimaced. "Oh, what the hell, whatever. We'll take any help we can get."

***

After injecting Big Sister with a magic potion to ensure her hex wouldn't ever wear off, Lynn called the others outside the bedroom for a conference.

She shut the door quietly on the transformed matriarch.

"It's incurable."

Trudi gasped. "Incurable?"

Lynn nodded. "I've seen similar cases in the past, back when I worked with Boston EMS. It's a constantly morphing viral infection—lacks any stable form that could be researched on." She pushed a stray blonde hair out of her eyes. "The virus isn't done with Big Sister yet. It'll continue to transform her till it reaches a final form."

"What's that?" Donny Q asked quietly. Behind him Tom and Gail nodded solemnly.

Lynn shook her head. "I honestly don't know. One patient became a cat covered with eyes; another ended up as a green winged cow, yet another—"

"Mum looks like she's becoming a bug," Trudi said, "a cow-sized bug!"

She burst into tears. Donny Q stared helplessly at Lynn. "What can we do?"

"Kill her. Put her out of her misery."

Trudi immediately wiped her eyes dry. She glared knives at Lynn. "You dare murder my mother, human, and I'll eat you for lunch."

Lynn raised her hands to pacify Trudi. "Just a suggestion." She looked at Donny Q. "The only other thing you can do is quarantine her—lock her away somewhere. She's a danger to everyone as she is."

Donny Q winced, remembering how Davey had transformed into a football. *A football?* "Don't I know it."

He looked at Trudi. "You saw what she did to your brother. The doctor's right: quarantine is our only safe option."

Trudi glared at Lynn like she was personally responsible. "Okay, we'll lock her away."

Tom and Gail nodded. "Does this building have a basement?" Tom asked.

Donny Q pointed down. "Yeah, for sure. I'll have some guys come move her."

Chapter 100

Donny Q looked at Trudi. "We'll have to prepare for the succession contest," he said quietly.

She looked back at him, gasped. "But . . ."

"There's no shame if you opt out. You're pregnant."

Trudi stared back coldly. "No."

"The baby . . ."

She patted her massive belly. "If I lose it, I can always have another ankle-biter. After this, I might never have another chance to be Big Sister."

Donny Q's eyes showed his displeasure. He liked . . . loved . . . Trudi, but this was *her* choice to make. "Are you sure?"

"Like I've never been in my life."

He nodded. "Okay, then, I'll set the fight up."

***

"I want to compete for the succession," Gail said.

"No," Tom said. "You'll have your ass handed to you on a plate."

"Trudi's fighting, isn't she? And she's pregnant. Besides, I'm tougher than you think. Ryan taught me some self-defense moves to protect me against rape."

He rolled his eyes. "You're fighting *women*, duh? No testicles to knee."

"Screw you, darling. Tell Donny Q to include me."

His face tightened. "No. This once, you do what I tell you."

She held his gaze with her own. "Do this *for me*. Just trust me, okay?"

He sighed. "Okay."

She chortled. "Don't look so worried honey. Okay, how about I cheer you up with a blowjob?"

***

Tom and Lynn consulted Rose about Gail's interest in the succession contest.

"What will be, will be," the vagina replied.

Lynn grinned at Tom. "It's your love life, cousin. Me, I'm off to the basement to dope Cassie up again."

"Fuck, no," Donny Q said. "Not happening ever."

"C'mon, man; do this for me. I'll be forever grateful."

The eater stared coldly at Tom. "Don't play the friendship card—she's not an eater."

"She's an honorary. That's been enough so far, hasn't it?"

Donny Q's cold façade collapsed. "Dude, you don't get it: What if I put her in and she accidentally *wins*?"

Tom burst out laughing. "*Gail?* Are you *nuts*? Who's she going to beat? Herself?"

Donny Q pondered that. "You sure of this?"

"Of course. The only reason I'm agreeing is 'cos you said the first three rounds aren't to the death; once the opponent's subdued, it's over. Dude, I love Gail more than life itself—no way I'd even *suggest* this if I thought she'd get hurt." He grinned. "She, however, needs a large dose of humble pie."

"Yeah, I know lots of chicks like that." He laughed. "Share a secret? I'm expecting Trudi to get her ass kicked too."

Tom nodded sagely. "Pregnant chicks shouldn't brawl. Man, I wondered why you let her in the contest in the first place."

"She used to fight a bit back before we all got transformed. Minor MMA stuff, never up to championship level. Besides, her mother was the last Big Sister, so she's an automatic entry. Trudi's the only one who can opt out, and she won't. I see her point though—whoever becomes Big Sister now might be matriarch for the next twenty or even thirty years, forty even, before dying, by which time Trudi will be much too old to compete again."

Tom winced. "Pregnant chick? One well-placed punch and her lights are out."

"That," Donny Q said, "is what I'm counting on: that she gets knocked out before anything happens to the baby."

***

It's odd, Tom thought afterwards, *how alike humans and eaters actually are. Sure they eat us and see nothing wrong about it, and for some reason they never change their clothes, but . . .*

We both love our women.

Chapter 101

The succession contest was held in the same square where Tom had been initiated. This time—with no shooting anticipated—the tribe watched whilst leaning against building walls.

Lynn begged off attending: "Don't want to watch your girlfriend get her ass kicked, Tommy."

Sixteen women—Gina included—aged from eighteen to forty-two were assigned numbers at random and split into eight groups.

Nothing went as planned.

First Round.

Trudi flattened her first opponent with a single punch. She sidestepped the girl's lunge, connecting as she went past with a hard right to the jaw. The girl crashed to the grass unconscious.

Gail broke her opponent's arm. She tripped the woman up and stomped on her elbow. The loud 'krak' ricocheted across the combat square like a bullet. End of fight. The screaming woman was carried away.

Donny Q and Tom eyed each other darkly. Ooops.

Second Round.

Trudi's opponent punched at her belly. Rather than ducking, Trudi leapt impossibly high, clamping the woman's punching hand between her thighs when she was in midair. She landed, her weight pulling the woman down. She wrestled her to the ground, then put her to sleep with a legs-around-the-neck chokehold.

Gail simply smashed her opponent's head against a stone till she was pulled off her. The woman was dragged away dazed and cross-eyed, pink blood gushing from her dented skull.

***

Tom and Donny Q met.

"Semi's are next. Neither of them can keep this up, right?"

"Right."

"Why don't we sound convinced?"

344

The excitement levels had risen as contestants were eliminated. Now the air was taut with anticipation.

Trudi's opponent Cheryl was an experienced fighter—an ex-army colonel. She was limping, her right ankle bandaged from her last fight.

She didn't rush in on Trudi, but circled her cautiously, sizing her up for an opening.

Trudi was equally cautious. Her swollen belly made her sluggish, but also created separation from her opponents and made her hard to grapple with.

She was however tiring. All she could think of was winning this contest and relaxing for the rest of her life. That end definitely justified this means.

Bring it on, bitch, she thought.

Cheryl closed with her. Trudi instantly swung them both right, forcing Cheryl to put weight on her bad ankle. She held on tight, forced them both in an endless circle till Cheryl's ankle twisted underneath her again.

"Shit!" Cheryl gasped, letting go of Trudi and falling over as the pain hit.

Trudi quickly grabbed Cheryl's bad foot. Holding it tight to her breasts in an ankle lock, she twisted it HARD.

Cheryl slapped the floor. "I quit! I quit!"

***

Gina was Gail's semifinal opponent. The pair squared off.

Gina smirked. "Look what the rats brought in!"

Gail smirked back. "Look who's talking." Through the rounds, she'd slowly grown in confidence. She'd have however preferred to face Trudi's opponent Cheryl, rather than Gina, who would insist on being an asshole and try to make a species superiority issue out of their fight. She didn't dislike the eater girl, just found her too full of herself. Gina always had something sharp and bitchy to say.

Gina sneered at Gail. "Just lie down and give up, eater wannabe. When I'm queen, we'll threesome—you can lick my pussy clean after Tom cums in me."

The amusement left Gail's eyes. That statement had cut deep. "You talk too much, no-eyes. If you're so tough, what are you doing over there?"

345

No-eyes was the ultimate eater insult. Gina rushed at her.

Gail kicked her in the belly. Gina pulled up sharp, like she'd been shot.

Gail kicked her again, this time in the vagina.

The eater girl's eyes widened in disbelief. Clutching her crotch, she doubled over in pain. Gail rabbit-punched her. Gina collapsed to the ground.

Gail kicked Gina twice more in the belly. Hard. Gina grabbed her middle and wheezed, sucking for air.

Gail scowled down at her, "You had enough, bitch?"

Gina slowly picked herself up. "Screw you, human cunt. Your boyfriend prefers me anyway."

That did it. Gail saw red. She waited till Gina was halfway to her feet, then kicked her in the head like she was punting a football. Gina's head snapped sideways, she crashed to the grass unconscious.

A disbelieving hush fell over the spectators.

***

Tom and Donny Q snuck away for an emergency conference. Both were horrified.

"I should never have listened to you," Donny Q said angrily. "You assured me she couldn't fight."

"So did you. Pregnant chicks can't fight, remember? We're both at fault for not being able to control our women."

"Control? I never met a man who could control a woman who had her mind set on doing something."

They stared at each other in silence for a while.

"We've got to stop them," Donny Q said finally, speaking in a rush. "The final's a no-holds-barred knife fight. It doesn't stop till one of them is dead."

"Can't you simply disqualify Gail? You said yourself that she's not an eater."

Donny Q cupped a hand to his ear. "Listen."

Tom listened. He heard it: a low rumble of voices chanting 'Gail . . . Gail . . . Gail . . .' "No, I guess not." He looked at Donny Q. "They'll accept her as Big Sister?"

"Without a doubt. But *they're not fighting*." The eater's voice was almost histrionic. He paced rapidly back and forth, then turned to Tom. "Only one thing to do."

"Yeah?"

"Tell Gail to forfeit. Just have her quit. Crowd won't like it, but it's happened before. She can claim injury."

Tom nodded. "I'm on it."

***

"Hell no!" Gail said. "You want me to give up the chance of a lifetime to that pregnant piece of cannibal shit?"

"It's *to the death*, darling. She'll murder you."

Gail looked at him pityingly. "Why is it you never have any faith in me?"

"It's not like that. I just don't want to see you get killed."

She smirked. "Don't worry your dick over it, I'll still be around for you to fuck tomorrow."

Defeated, Tom turned to leave.

"Wait, darling."

He turned back to look at her.

"If you dare get me disqualified, we're quits—finished. I need you to believe in me now."

***

"She said no. She's ready to fight to the death."

Donny Q looked pained. "I'll go get Trudi to quit. We'll explain it away as threatened miscarriage."

***

"No!" Trudi said. "How dare you even *suggest* that an *eater* throw in the towel in favor of a *human*? She's inferior to me."

"This is bigger than your personal pride. She's dangerous enough to kill you."

Trudi stared coldly at Donny Q. She prodded him in the chest. "I'll fight and kill that human bitch—"

"If you die, it's for nothing."

"—not for personal, but *tribal* pride. No human woman will be Big Sister."

Donny Q pointed to her belly. "You're not . . ."

347

"That's what you said before. I reached the final, didn't I." Her hard gaze softened. She leaned up and kissed Donny Q tenderly on the lips. "I know you *love* me, man. Have some faith in me."

The Final.

The air was thick with heat and anticipation. Once again, Bizarro's overhead bulk seemed like the lifted top of a pressure cooker. The crowd spoke in hushed whispers, awed by this totally unprecedented turn of events.

Tom and Donny Q stood side by side looking glum. They stared pointedly at Gail and Trudi, now being painted with ritual signs on their foreheads. Both women just as pointedly affected not to see their men's pleading glances.

"Never let a woman fight," Tom said. "It always turns out badly."

"One of our girlfriends is about to die," Donny Q said.

"I'm trying not to think that far ahead."

The eater turned and stalked off, muttering. He was angry at Tom, angry at himself, angry at the world.

Emotionally incapacitated, Tom sat on a window-ledge and watched.

Donny Q stomped back to his side and sat also.

They watched together.

***

Gail received her knife from Oprah, the old eater woman overseeing the final.

Oprah handed the other knife to Trudi. Both weapons were exactly alike: slim sharp blades with bone handles.

"These are the knives of queenship," Oprah intoned. "Two go in, one comes out." She peered at both their faces. "One dies, one survives . . . Only *one* survives . . . do you understand that?"

They nodded.

"There are no rules, there will be no interference. One of you will be Queen, one a corpse."

Two more nods.

Oprah moved out of the way and yelled, "THEN FIGHT!"

Gail and Trudi immediately backed off from each other. Knives held in front of them, they circled each other.

"Glad you joined the party," Trudi said. "I'll be the first Big Sister to actually *eat* her opponent."

Gail didn't reply. She was focused as hell. Shit, she was focused. Tom had warned her about Trudi's MMA background.

"I'm having you for dinner. Hope you taste good."

She shut Trudi's voice out. *Don't listen! If I let her freak me out, I'm dead! This is the real deal, literally no second chances!*

They circled one another like vultures inspecting a corpse.

"Once you're dead, I'll chain your ugly boyfriend in the basement with my mother and have him fuck her insect ass morning, afternoon, and night. Maybe she'll turn him into a football like my brother."

Ignore her—she's just trash-talking! But Gail couldn't resist a side-glance at Tom. *Damn, he looks more scared than I feel, and Donny Q looks worse than he does.*

Trudi noticed her distraction. Smiling coldly, she leapt at Gail, knife slashing. The blade cut a shallow line down Gail's arm.

Gail backpedalled quickly. Trudi came on after her in a rush, forcing her advantage. She slashed again. Gail blocked the swipe with her own knife. She closed with Trudi, grabbing her wrist. Trudi similarly grabbed Gail's wrist.

They strained against each other in stalemate, muscles taut, Trudi's swollen belly separating them.

The crowd were yelling, but Gail couldn't hear them. The world had contracted to just herself and Trudi.

Trudi tried biting Gail, snapping at her neck like a gator. Gail leaned as far back as she could. Trudi kept biting at her. Gail momentarily wondered why she wasn't kneeing Trudi in the pregnancy. But one didn't do dirty shit like that, did one . . . ?

Trudi freed her knife-hand then and stabbed Gail in the chest. The knife punctured Gail's left lung, just missing her heart. Gail gasped, coughed up blood.

Trudi twisted the knife in the wound. Flesh ripped, more blood spurted. Gail screamed.

Unheard by either woman in the pinpoint universe of violence they now inhabited, the spectators moaned their excitement.

Trudi laughed, her yellow face glowing with the joy of the kill. "I told you you'd die," she said.

Gail clamped down on her pain. "Someday, no-eyes, but not yet. I don't want Tom writing 'I told you so' on my tombstone."

Incensed by the 'no-eyes' insult, Trudi tried to pull out the knife for another stab. Gail held her wrist and the knife in place. While her opponent fought to free her weapon, Gail spat blood in her face, blinding her.

She let go Trudi's wrist. The blade slid free. Trudi staggered back, wiping her eyes.

Gail ducked down and stabbed Trudi in the vagina.

Trudi stiffened as the knife penetrated her sex. Gail forced it in up to the hilt.

The pain hit Trudi. She stopped wiping her eyes and stabbed Gail in the back.

Gail, however was relentless. Ignoring the pain in her chest and back, spitting blood, she sliced up through Trudi's vagina, cutting open her crotch, splitting her pubic symphysis.

The knife was super-sharp. Trudi's yellow skin and flesh parted with ease. Pink blood spurted from her ripped-open cunt.

Trudi stabbed Gail one last time in the side, then froze, paralyzed by pain. She slowly sunk to her knees, her descent accelerating Gail's opening up her belly.

Gail, her hands totally colored pink, yanked the knife out. She kicked Trudi over. Now she was aware of a hush from the crowd. Gail remembered the rules.

This is to the death, right?

She walked around Trudi. Her opponent was leaning up, looking into her ripped-up abdomen in disbelief. Then she looked at Gail. "You . . . you . . ."

"You'll be missing dinner tonight." Gail slit Trudi's throat, slashing through it savagely.

Trudi fell back dead.

Gail sighed. *Guess this means I'm Big Sister now.*

The hush from the crowd continued.

Now what the hell is wrong with all of you?

The silence continued. She saw Oprah was staring at her in disbelief. She looked at Tom. He was looking at her like she was a ghost. Donny Q too.

The silence pissed Gail off. Totally pissed her off.

You goons want to stare, eh? I'll give you something to stare at. It had occurred to Gail that she needed to make a statement of some kind, something that would remain indelible in the mind of the tribe forever.

She knew just what.

She quickly moved to Trudi's corpse. The woman's belly yawned open. She pushed the sides of the wound apart, pulling out the expanded womb. The eater's womb was transparent.

Except for its daffodil-yellow color, the eater fetus looked human enough—small body, large head, spindly arms and legs. About three-quarter term.

Considering the size of Trudi's bulge, Gail was surprised at how small the infant was. Most of Trudi's belly was her womb's spongy transparence, a thick layer like solid water, marbled with pink and green blood vessels. *No wonder she could fight.*

The fetus wasn't dead—the water-womb had protected it while Gail butchered Trudi. Its legs kicked weakly like it was trying to awaken its mother.

Gail raised the knife so all present could see it. Then she slit open Trudi's womb and yanked the baby out.

She quickly severed its umbilical cord, then held the fetus high above her head. She looked around. Everyone was still waiting to see what she'd do.

Without killing the fetus, she brought its head to her mouth and bit into it. She bit hard and deep, quickly before anyone could stop her. The soft cranium crunched and then her mouth was full of the eater child's brains. She ate these, then scooped the rest out of the baby's head with her fingers and ate them too.

She laughed out loud. "I'm Big Sister, you bastards! You will all respect me!"

The crowd broke into noise. "Gail! Gail! Gail!" The noise ascended toward heaven, bounced off Bizarro and cascaded back down on its creators.

Gail saw Tom running towards her. She set off in a fast jog away from him, in a circle around the spectators, cutting the baby up with her knife and wolfing down its soft flesh.

And all the while, the eaters cheered her on, punching fists skyward and singing songs of affirmation, of praise to the new Big Sister. She ran and ran and ran, finding somewhere strength to outpace Tom, who she could hear behind her, screaming, "Gail, stop! Wait! What are you doing!!?"

And all the while she ran, Gail kept eating the baby. She ate its lungs, its still-beating heart, its guts . . .

At some point Gail's strength wore out, her wounds and blood loss overtook her will, and she collapsed smiling. *Oh, yeah, I fucking did it.*

She was aware of soft hands lifting her up. Of everyone still cheering insanely. Of Tom peering down at her, his expression mingled love, relief, disgust, and admiration. Of Donny Q staring at her in the sort of awe normally reserved for divinity.

Smiling, she handed Donny Q what remained of Trudi's unborn child—its two legs. "I'm not sure if it was a boy or girl."

He grimaced at the grisly remains.

Donny Q's voice: "Quick, get Dr. Lynn here!"

Tom's voice: "Better we carry her over."

More soft hands bearing her off. And while she was being carried off, a strange thought: *How is it that we humans don't eat eaters? They taste like fish.*

Chapter 102

It took a major magic spell for Lynn to heal Gail. Even then, she wasn't totally alright.

She just looked okay enough to fool Joe Bradley. "An eater girl jumped me down in Chinatown."

Joe, face pale with worry, rolled his eyes. "Shit, Gail, what the hell were you doing down in Chinatown?"

She smiled weakly. "I was thinking of Boston's money, honey, and took a wrong turn. I stopped to make a U-turn back, and next thing I know this lemon-skinned chick is leaning into the car, stabbing me."

Joe nodded soberly. The interior of Gail's Honda Prelude had been a mess of blood. Of course, no one bothered checking that the blood was actually hers.

That passed.

The stars aligned right. Tom, who still kept his twice-weekly liaison with Queen Shirley at the waterside apartment on Old Atlantic Avenue, convinced the Queen of a potential eater threat up in Charlestown. Shirley, as unwilling as anyone else to move house on one of King Eric's whims, asked her little husband to have Joe investigate the claim. King Eric, in typical bombastic royal flourish, insisted that his police chief not return to Central Boston till he could categorically either report that the eater rumors were false, or had 'killed all the terrorist cannibals.'

This meant two whole weeks when Joe didn't see Gail, in which she was—by taking sick leave off work—both able to heal properly, and to consolidate her hold on power in the eaters' camp.

There was little change at the helm of eater affairs: Donny Q remained as head of security and Gina (though still full of sass, and a guaranteed pain in the ass) became Gail's personal assistant.

Gail now discovered that her status was semi-divine amongst her adopted tribe, that she was set for a lifetime of worship.

She might even have called off the robbery, but she hated having to eat human meat, the one inescapable condition of being Big Sister that the eaters, not seeing anything wrong with it, had neglected to inform her of. Ironically, if they had, Gail would have immediately unenrolled from the queenship contest. If either Tom or Donny Q had thought of mentioning it to her before the final, Trudi would be alive and eater queen now, by Gail's instant disgusted forfeit.

353

And Gail's eating Trudi's baby? She wasn't proud of it later, but she'd never admit that fact to anyone, least of all Tom, who'd been pampering her like an egg since that fucked-up incident.

Chapter 103

Oppenheimer's lab: Ten days later.

Dr. Oppenheimer had tactfully left his lab.

Tom stood between Grace's legs, her feet up on his shoulders. His pants were down around his ankles. Like a battering ram, his turgid cock was poised at the clone-woman's labia.

He looked at Gail, who sat looking bored and playing with her cunt. "Ethical question: Deflowering a retard clone? Isn't this rape? I mean lack of content."

"She's *me*. I consent for her."

Tom grinned. He pushed firmly. Grace's hymen broke.

The clone moaned, her expression one of pained confusion. Her hands clenched into weak fists, her toes curled beside Tom's ears.

Gail watched impassively while Tom thrust into Grace's pussy, his cock now coated with a thick red sheen.

"There's a lot of blood."

"She's me alright. Was the same thing when I lost my virginity—I bled like a hog."

She got up and walked over to them.

"Ga ga ga ga," Grace mumbled.

Gail tapped Tom on the shoulder. "You're not supposed to enjoy it—you're just breaking her in now so she's clearly not a virgin when we grab the gold." She ran patronizing fingers through Grace's brown locks. "New version here's simply a means to an end."

Tom pulled out of Grace. He rearranged the clone properly on her bed again, then grabbed Gail's hair, forcing her down to her knees so his bloody erection pointed in her face. "Clean me up, then let's fuck properly."

Gail took his penis in her mouth and licked and sucked it. When she'd gotten all the blood off, Tom yanked her to her feet again, then bent her down over Grace's thigh.

"Let's show the clone how it's done. he forced Gail's mouth into Grace's crotch. "Lick her pussy clean while I fuck your ass."

Gail tried to pull her head back. Tom forced it deeper into Grace's crotch. "Lick that blood off her cunt."

She opened her mouth to protest, then gasped instead as he penetrated her anus from behind. His entrance . . .

Gail was caught up in a sudden swirl of blue mist inside her head. Compassion for Grace rose in her, like it was her own innocence Tom had just cruelly snatched away.

She began licking the virginal blood from Grace's cunt, swiping it up on her tongue, sucking it down into her belly.

I'm a vampire, she realized, dropping a hand to rub her clitoris as Tom slid in and out of her rectum, *Grace is my victim, born to die that I might be rich.*

She licked the bleeding vagina faster and faster, feeling her orgasm sneak up on her, an erotic marauder.

Tom shifted his grip from her buttocks to her clothed breasts. He pumped harder.

Grace moaned suddenly, her thighs tensing. "GA GA GA!!!!"

The clone arched her back, then went limp. A drooly smile settled over her face.

Gail moaned in sympathy with Grace's orgasm. *Always best that a girl enjoy her first-ever fuck. Gives her a healthy perspective on sex for life.*

She rubbed her clitoris harder, slid her middle fingers into her wet sex.

Gail's orgasm hit her. It rose from her crotch like a phoenix, smothered her like a blanket. Hand moving at speed between her thighs, she moved her head from Grace's crotch to suck and bite on the clone's engorged nipples.

"Ga ga ga! Koo koo!"

Tom tensed behind Gail. She relaxed, felt him spurt cum into her.

"Oh, fuuucck!" he gasped.

Deep, deep. She imagined his semen as a liquid snake slithering up her gut.

They descended together from bliss.

They wiped clean. Tom hitched his trousers back up, Gail dropped her skirt.

She smiled at Tom. "That was fun."

He grinned. "You're *always* fantastic." He looked over at Gail's clone, now giggling at the ceiling and rolling her blue eyes in delight. "She's creepy."

Gail shrugged. "Like I said: she's a means to an end. The money justifies her existence."

"I'll get Oppenheimer in here. I almost forgot; he has to duplicate your new scars on Grace's body."

Gail slipped a finger inside her top, traced the scar on her left breast. "Is this really necessary? He's already matched my teeth to hers."

"Joe's seen them, hasn't he? If they're missing after you're dead, it's a clear giveaway."

Gail moved to stroke Grace's head. "She won't like it."

"Don't get soppy. She won't feel it—there's anesthesia."

Gail nodded. She smiled down at her clone. "Sorry, hon, the drama of your short life just got turned up a notch. You're about to get your first tattoos."

Chapter 104

A week later.

"Gaa . . . ga!"

Tom was fucking Grace in Gail's office in the bank. For realism, they'd ransacked the room, smashing her computer and scattering her papers.

The floor rumbled from explosions on the lower two floors. The noise of gunfire came in through the window.

The clone was dressed in Gail's clothes and splayed out over her desk. "Ga ga ga," she cooed as Tom slid in and out of her, her arms and legs moving in a baby's uncoordinated motions.

"Don't be selfish," Gail said. "Make certain I cum too."

Tom rolled his eyes. "You're serious?"

"Best she goes out with a bang." Gail walked to the clone's side and ripped her top open, then pulled her bra down. She fondled Grace's breasts with one hand, moved the other to her clitoris. The clone's 'ga ga ga' immediately deepened in pitch.

The clone's 'ga ga ga' immediately deepened in pitch. She gleefully patted Gail's skirt.

It's my clit, Gail thought. *I definitely know how to get myself off.*

Grace came. Her body went stiff as a board, then she went limp. The floor rumbled like the building was cumming in sympathy with her.

"Okay, I'll do her ass now."

Tom slipped his penis out of Grace's vagina and forced it into her anus. Grace's eyes instantly opened wide in shock and pain. "GAAA!"

"Sorry, girl, playtime's over," Gail said. "This has to look realistic."

Tom fucked Grace's ass brutally, leaving her bleeding. She twitched spastically at the anal abuse.

He pulled out. A stream of blood accompanied his cock's exit. "Wow. It's like she had a hymen in there too."

"Put it back in her pussy. Hurry up and cum."

He slid his penis back into Grace's vagina and ejaculated inside her. Then he wiped himself clean on her blouse and zipped his penis away. Grace stared at him blankly. Her crotch was a mess of blood with cum in it.

Gail giggled. "Ryan's going to be mad at you. And Joe . . ."

"It's strange. She's not you—she's different inside."

"Just not been fucked enough. Takes a while for a cunt to reach its full potential. Vaginas are like wine—they get better with age." She giggled at his surprised expression. "Megan said that."

Tom checked his watch. "Ryan should be on his way over. The guys watching you must have alerted headquarters by now."

She looked out of her office window. "We'll know once the South Terminal Precinct guys arrive. Damn this lack of telecoms." She calmed, turned back to him. "The vavs are restless."

He shrugged. "A hungry pussy is an angry pussy."

More rumbles, more gunfire.

Gail walked over to open her office door.

"Okay," she told the two eaters waiting there.

The two yellow men entered. Both stared at Grace's prone, splayed form with hunger in their eyes. She stared back, something akin to horror blossoming in her baby brain. *"Ga?"*

Tom nodded at the eaters. "Kyle, Dan; now remember, this has to look right, Okay?"

"Okay, sir."

"You eat at least half of her face. Then rip out her guts and feast all you like. But leave her left breast intact; Joe will remember her scars."

"Don't kill her first," Gail added. "Let her die of her wounds. We need blood spurting everywhere like I resisted. Also, don't move her off the table or shift her too far—the semen between her legs has to be noticed."

Both eaters nodded obediently. "Yes, Big Sister."

Tom checked his watch again. He looked pointedly at the eaters. "Don't get carried away. Hurry up, and once you're done, join us at the vaults." He turned to Gail. "Let's go."

"We'd better take the back route around the balcony, so I can reassure the vavs that lunch from the precinct will shortly be delivered."

Gail and Tom left. Behind them, Grace began screaming in agony as the eaters ate her.

Chapter 105

Downstairs, the noise of battle was loud and clear. It got louder as they descended the stairs to the basement.

Lynn, naked beneath her black robe, was seated on the tailgate of the truck nearest the massive steel vault doors, eating a radish. Seeing Tom and Gail, she leapt down from her perch and hurried to meet them.

"Done?"

"Done," Tom said. "Now we just need to be patient."

They strode back together to the vault doors, by which a large number of eaters waited. Gail nodded to the yellow men and women. "So far everything's going according to plan."

Gina jogged across from the door to the bank foyer.

She bowed respectfully to Tom and Gail. "Your brother just arrived with about thirty SWAT guys."

Tom grinned coldly. "We're on schedule then. He peered between the massive trucks, each with its conveyor belt primed for descent into the vault. "Now where the hell are those—?"

On cue, rapid-fire gunshots thundered from the back lot. Tom waited till he saw the vavs whirling their vaginal tentacles and flinging them at the approaching police officers, then turned back to the others.

"The girls are happy now, lunch just arrived."

Behind him, the first policepersons were snared up into waiting vampire crotches.

Gail smiled tensely. She crossed her fingers. "Time to see if our gamble paid off. Donny Q should be hitting the precinct about now."

All the basement lights cut out. Tom flicked on a flashlight. The beam reflected off Gina's teeth. "Okay, get ready."

A hiss of decompression. The vault doors swung open.

"Get those wedges in place," Tom yelled at the eaters around the doors. "Move, move!"

He turned back to Gail and hugged her. "We're rich, honey."

***

Once the gold was loading, Gail went to sit in the front of the first truck. No way must Ryan or any of the cops see her.

360

(Joe Bradley was up in Charlestown. Tom had had Shirley once again convince the King of an imaginary eater threat up there.)

Tom and Lynn supervised.

"I never imagined there was this much money in the world," Lynn said, tapping a gold bar as it streamed up into the endless recess that was the truck's interior. She turned round to grin at Tom, "Just imagine what we'll—"

Lynn's brain exploded out of her forehead.

Tom grabbed her as she slid floor-ward.

"I'm dead," she said, with a bloody grin. "But don't worry. I've enough memory of myself left to finish pulling this off."

He winced at the mess the bullet had made of her head. His eyes scanned the upper basement walls, settling on the stairwell landing. "Bastards were shooting at me, not you."

"I'll see who it is." She faded to nothingness.

Tom waited.

Lynn materialized again some moments later with an unconscious Ryan Harding in tow. "Look what the rats brought in."

Tom nodded at Gina. "Wake him up."

***

Tom coldly surveyed Harding, as the other glared back at him. It would be simplest to kill the cop, but Gail would never stand for him murdering her brother. Damon, a third, younger brother of theirs had gone missing and Gail still insisted he wasn't dead, but off adventuring somewhere. *Yeah, right.*

He smiled coldly at the cop. "Welcome to the gold rush, Lieutenant."

361

Chapter 106

Six Minutes Later

The last of the gold clicked over the conveyors into the trucks. The conveyors retracted back into storage. The rear doors were shut and locked.

Gina regretfully tore her eyes away from Harding's slumbering form. If she looked at him anymore, she'd rip open his jacket and sink her teeth deep into his muscular chest, rip the flesh up like she used to do with turkey. Gina liked muscular human men—more to eat. Biceps were her favorite part of a man, delicious meat on that upper arm bone that she could hold in both hands and bite into with the blood (or broth) running down over her chin and splattering her breasts.

(She knew girls who liked eating penis best, but not Gina: there wasn't enough meat in them, and the misandric sexual symbolism sucked. Gina *liked* men.)

Harding here? His biceps were HUGE. Oh yes, he'd certainly taste delicious.

But the cop was Big Sister's brother and as such off limits.

Gina sighed. *What a waste of food*. Leaving the unconscious policeman, she walked round to the front of the truck and climbed up into the driver's seat.

Chapter 107

Gail pressed the pistol muzzle hard into Tom's side. "Fuck your pussy-saving gallantry, we're getting the hell out of here."

Tom stared at her in disbelief. "What?"

Gail's voice was ice cold. "Forget Shirley."

"King Eric already suspects our affair. He'll have her killed."

"Let him."

"Gail, be reasonable."

She smiled coldly. "I am being reasonable. I'm not in this for the competition."

"I was dating Shirley before—"

"You met me? I know. But you *did* meet me. Your Greyhound bus just reached its last station, buster."

She waved the gun. "We leave together. Let's go."

His face was adamant.

She scowled. "You *still* don't get it? I already told you, I don't mind about you and the eater girls. They're not human, and all they're after is your cum anyway. But a human woman? No, no, no. I'm enough woman for you." Her voice softened, "Honey, we're rich now, we've got each other, no third wings wanted. Believe me—Shirley's safer over there in the palace—I'll kill any woman who comes between us."

"Damn, Gail. You sound like Longneck Pam."

"*All* women are that possessive. Pam's problem is she's bad at hiding it."

Tom nodded. "Okay, let's get Lynn into the truck."

Chapter 108

Lynn rode in the first truck, held upright by Gail. Tom was driving. She sensed Gail's nervousness. "It's okay, I got this."

She checked the rearview mirror on their side. The last truck—the one Gina was driving—was just pulling out of the bank lot. Vavs—several dangling police officers from their pussies—strode beside it. Beyond the vavs, two military transports full of eaters waited to join the convoy.

Lynn's vision faded in and out. Like her eyes were leaking out her skull along with her brains. First the world was celluloid bright, then old black-and-white, then hazy soft-core mist, then fiercely pixelated like Japanese *Pinku* erections. It sharpened again, bloomed like a rose.

Dying sucks. She felt the bullet hole through her head—evacuated space in her brain—like a psychic vacancy.

Already she could feel her trans-dimensional twin's delight. The woman's joy was palpable.

Lynn's head wound had one positive—it had shut off her twin's harrying voice. Lynn had *hated* it: hearing her own voice speaking in her head like she was schizoid. Urging her to kill herself. Sometimes cooing softly, sometimes yelling.

Sometimes the pressure had been so much, she'd have gladly slit her throat to end it.

She saw *her* now, form without substance, smile dancing on wisp-of-gas lips. A face like holes in rising smoke, but still her own.

Okay, our pussy's yours now. Don't wear it out. I fucking mean that, Lynn. DO NOT dare get a job as a hooker or porno actress.

Her twin shrieked in silent glee. Lynn felt her mind collapsing. *Not so fast, girl. I've business to handle.*

The convoy rumbled down Summer Street.

Tom turned to Lynn. "Need to do this soon. The cops . . ."

She nodded. "Get ready."

She began chanting:

"Nenors Torps Starri,
Jananyn Lissor Elinox Haroz . . ."

A slit developed in midair fifty yards ahead. It ripped open, its edges 'peeling' off the air behind it then folding over, leaving a shimmering semicircle, an arch spanning the road, its ends buried in buildings on either side.

Through the shimmering, Lynn saw a white beach and Mama spurting breast milk over Milk Lake.

She grinned. "There you go. Hit the gas, Tommy."

Tom floored the pedal. Purring like a sated lioness, the 18-wheeler surged into the shimmering.

***

"Nono Nenors Starri Torps Zeno,
Itx mena mana itx moix,
Lenord Nana Nono!"

On Lynn's last word, the shimmering arch wrenched itself away from the top of the beach. It slid down through the sand, past the three parked trucks and disembarking eaters, into the lake.

"That's major impressive," Gail said, watching as the arch's view of Central Boston slid past them like a photograph.

"No one's out there yet," Tom said, "but if we can see them, they can see us too."

Lynn—held up between them—coughed. "Not for long." She raised a finger, chanted again:

"Taras, nix nien Toblor."

The view through the arch altered to normal lake surface.

"Where's it lead now?" Gail asked.

"Just closer to Mama."

Mission accomplished, Lynn thought. *We're all richer than fucking Croesus now. One more thing to take care of, then I rest in death's arms.*

***

Lynn's gaze became piercing, like laser light fixing an eye. "You know what happens now, right, Tommy?"

"The pussy transfer?"

"Stop making it sound like a bank transaction."

"Sorry, it's the current environment."

365

"Tommy, understand this: I'm *dead*. Right now, you're talking to a ghost, get it? I'm dead *dead* until I get my vagina back." Her eyes probed his pleadingly. "I don't want to stay dead. Don't let that happen, okay?"

He nodded. "Don't worry, I won't. I'll go look for it." He pointed at the shimmering over the water. "How do we open the space-time portal?"

"The spell's written on a card pinned behind my bedroom door. There's two of them. The top spell takes you to that other Boston, the lower one brings you back. Drawl the words like you're Techxan."

He looked sharply at her. "You've been planning this awhile?"

She looked over at the three trucks, their noses parked right at the white lake's edge. A few eaters were passing around bars of gold for inspection. "Cousin, you don't pull off the biggest bank robbery in the history of the USA without expecting to become a casualty." She peered into his eyes. "We're lucky any of us came back. You did take that risk into account, didn't you?"

He raised the hand with her vagina in it. "Rose said we'd get away with it—I believed her."

Lynn winced. "*Oh*. Well, remember you promised . . . just leave my corpse in my bed; it won't rot."

Tom nodded.

"Okay, goodbye you two." Her eyes brightened momentarily. "One last thing—Tell Rich that Cassie's drugs are in my kitchenette, the drawer over the sink, and to remember to feed the mindspiders." She grinned at Gail. "Bye, Big Sister, see you in a bit."

Her eyes closed in death.

Tom and Gail lowered her to the ground.

"Yeow!" Tom yelped.

Gail turned to him in alarm. "What?"

He held up his left hand. Lynn's vagina had vanished.

Gail considered his hand. "Is that supposed to happen?"

"Huh?"

"Well, I assumed that if she was keeping it on your hand so her twin wouldn't kill her, it wouldn't vanish when she died."

Tom sighed. "Maybe the other Gail worked out how to get it off her."

Gail frowned down at the dead blonde. A fly was now walking about on Lynn's brain. "Or maybe she just wanted an excuse to leave her vagina with you so she wouldn't be tempted to have sex." Her expression turned thoughtful. "Darling, how much of what Lynn told you was actually true?"

"Honey, please . . ."

Gail grinned. "Doesn't really matter I guess." She felt Tom between the legs. "The important one's still here."

Tom pointed down the beach to where ten man-canoes waited. "Let's get everyone home; we'll shift the money later."

Gail walked over to organize her cannibal tribe. The eaters were jubilant, their yellow faces wreathed with smiles. They'd brought several blood-drained police corpses back and were sharing their meat around.

The vavs had already left the beach, their distant forms headed for the White Cube Plains beyond Mount Choc.

Tom slung Lynn's body over his shoulder and walked towards the man-canoes.

Chapter 109

"No," Gail said. "Not yet. We've only been back a week."

"I promised Lynn."

"I know. I was there." She climbed out of bed, and walked over to the window, her body sleek and svelte in the penetrating darkness. She turned to face Tom, the sheen of their recent lovemaking a mirror on her inner thighs. "I'm not saying, *don't* go. Only I want you to myself for awhile. You can't leave now—we've no idea how long you'll be gone for."

Tom propped himself up on pillows. "The longer I wait, the longer the other Lynn has to get in trouble."

"Might be to our benefit." All she has to do is get killed and you don't have to make the trip at all."

"I'm thinking more along the lines of her getting pregnant."

Gail smirked. "Do you really give a damn about that?"

"The paradox will only make killing her more fun. She'll only be able to have the baby when *our* Lynn dies again."

Gail laughed. "Think of the religious implications—a woman without a vagina becoming pregnant."

Tom laughed too. "Okay, I'll wait a month before going. By then—"

"Three months."

His eyed widened. "But why?"

"Because . . ." Lithe as a cat, Gail strode back to their bed, lust twinkling like starlight in her eyes. She climbed in, squatted over him, and guided his erection into her dripping sex. ". . . Because, darling, by then my vagina will be screaming for rest from the six-times-a-day cock-assault I intend subjecting it to."

Chapter 110

One month later

The mindspider was hot and gooey on Gail's head. She felt Rich adjusting it over her face. Her nose filled with its musky smell, like she'd stumbled into a rat's nest.

In the spider's interior, the vav Queen was black paint on grey canvas, luscious overlapping brush strokes by a master artist.

"Where is Pussypalm?" she asked, her voice soft and pleasant in Gail's head. "Our agreement was for today, a month after the robbery."

"He's missing," Gail replied in thought. "He fell through a portal similar to the one by which we left the bank."

The Queen's disappointment was silence made audible.

"This is very annoying," she said. "Where is this portal? We might be able to—"

"It vanished. Like he was being kidnapped."

"Kidnapped? That is even more annoying."

***

Annoying? You think that's 'annoying?' You've no fucking idea of the word's meaning.

Gail was livid. They'd all been so jubilant over the success of the heist that they'd forgotten their deal with the vavs—Tom's agreement to be their permanent gynecologist:

"Of course we will help you," the Queen had said. "But afterwards— one month after—you must live here and take care of us forever."

Oh shit. *One month later.* Donny Q had reminded them two days ago.

"There's no way you'll *ever* get Tom back if the vavs take him," the eater said. "Best he disappear till they're prepared to talk a compromise."

"But he doesn't even have Lynn's vagina anymore."

"That makes it worse. If he can't heal them, they might interpret it like he *doesn't want to* heal them, then . . ." Donny Q theatrically dug two fingers into the side of his neck and gagged.

Gail wasn't in the least bit amused. "Okay, so we hide him away."

"Hey, what about my baby?" Gina said. "Tom promised me one."

"No time for that now," Gail retorted testily. "You should have pulled rank on the other women rather than playing prissy princess prude."

369

Gina settled back, muttering angrily, "Not my fault girls from other camps began flooding here."

"Calm down, Gee," Tom said. "We'll do it before I leave."

She looked dubious. "For real?"

He nodded. Gina looked at Big Sister for approval.

Gail scowled. "Okay, okay; he'll impregnate you before going. Now let's work this out."

They thought and discussed awhile.

"That takes care of everything," Tom said finally. "Through the portal it is then. I have to go look for Lynn's vagina anyway."

"We need to wipe Tom's memory," Gina said.

They turned to look at her. "Huh?"

She nodded, pleased to be the center of attention. "The vavs are telepathic. They'll recognize him by mental patterns. And you know they're persistent. They might begin sending vavs through the portal up on Bizarro till they somehow trigger it—"

"Or through another," Gail agreed softly. "Lynn mentioned that there are others dotted all around, like the one that leads through Mama to here . . . or there."

"My point is: if they somehow enter that other place after Tom and find him there . . ."

Gail winced. "I guess the question now, is . . . how?"

"Use the mindspider. Rich says it can do that too."

11.15 p.m.

Gina gaped in disbelief. "Fuckin' what?"

Framed in the bedroom door, Gail shook the glass of semen at her. "I said: Here's your baby."

"Bu . . . but . . . !"

"Keep your voice down! But *what?* Tom?"

The eater girl nodded. "He . . . he . . . *promised,* Big Sister,."

Gail nodded over her shoulder. "He's too *tired* to screw you." She grinned wickedly. "I've been draining him all afternoon." She indicated the quarter-full glass. "Do you know how much sex it takes to get this much cum out of a guy? You should be *grateful* to me."

Gina looked over Gail's shoulder. Tom was naked in bed, snoring. "But Big Sister . . ."

Gail raised the glass of semen to her lips, swirling the translucent liquid like wine. "Normally I swallow instead of spit. Now, do you want this baby or not?"

"Stop, don't drink it!" Gina croaked hoarsely.

She stared meekly at Gail, her female hostility defeated by ingrained respect for the tribal matriarch. She realized Gail was doing this simply to demonstrate her dominance as the superior woman. Gina doubted it would work,—she'd heard sperm cells died almost immediately they left a man's body—but she was desperate to have a baby.

Children were very important to Gina. She just loved the little darlings, their innocence, how guilelessly funny they were. Since her teenaged years she'd imagined how her own kids would look; how it would feel to hold them close and tell them she loved them; how she'd love their daddy . . . This last had altered somewhat with her being transformed into an eater, but hell, getting one less than everything you want wasn't bad.

"You promise you won't tell anyone? I'll never live this down if the other girls find out."

Gail stroked Gina's cheek. "Of course not, Gee. I'll even promote you, so long as you continue to not make a nuisance of yourself."

Gina nodded meekly. "You can count on me." She pointed to the glass. "*How* do we do this?"

"Like normal sex—you lie down and spread your legs, I spurt it up you."

Gail looked back lovingly at Tom, then stepped into the living room, shutting the door behind her.

She pointed across at a sofa. "Make yourself comfortable. Legs up. Masturbate to open your cervix up. That way, I'll be able to squirt Tom's seed directly into your garden."

"Big Sister, where are you going?"

Gail tapped the glass of semen. "To the kitchen, to get the turkey baster we'll use. "

Cheeks turning bright pink with embarrassment, Gina made her way to the sofa and rucked up her tattered skirt. *Oh, yes. I'm having this kid*, she thought, spreading her hairless yellow labia and slipping a spit-moistened finger between them into her vagina. *I'm most definitely having Tom's kid.*

Next morning.

A soft wind rippled Milk Lake. Gail, Gina, and Donny Q sat in a man-canoe bobbing before the shimmering arch of air.

Tom sat beside them, solitary passenger in a small rowboat.

He read the spell to open the space-time portal. The shimmering broke open like a shattered mirror.

Donny Q nodded with satisfaction at the revealed vista. "That's Fort Point Channel." He pointed. "And Summer Street Bridge. Strike out for shore, dude, start walking and you'll reach Chinatown."

"It looks really different," Gina said. "I ain't never seen rushes that huge before."

Tom nodded dully. He no longer remembered who any of these people were. Or who *he* was. *Eaters are dangerous cannibals, so what am I doing with them? And why does this eater girl, Gina, keep smiling shyly at me? And the other woman—the brunette. Is she really my girlfriend? But why would she lie about that? Damn, she's hot, I hope she's not lying.*

His memory had huge holes in it; he scavenged what he could.

They say I'm an assassin; off to kill one woman, to save another woman. Then this paper I'm holding brings me back home? But why the hell? Where is home? None of this makes sense. And why aren't we all going? Why just me?

Tom packed the paper with the spell into the black gym bag containing his clothes and supplies, placing it inside the envelope of instructions, which also contained a photo of his proposed victim. He'd so far resisted all urgings to look at the picture. *I really don't want to see her face just yet. And when I do, can I even kill her?*

He'd read the papers later, when he felt less confused.

He checked his watch. The portal would shut by itself in eight minutes. *Five minutes left.*

Gail leaned over the side of the man-canoe and kissed Tom passionately. He kissed her back equally fervently, feeling the beginning of an erection. Her lips were something he remembered. *But how, and where?*

She began weeping; profuse tears streaming down her cheeks. "I'll really miss you, darling. Ensure you come back. All the gold in the world means nothing without you."

He nodded. "I will." His heart felt like it was jumping into his mouth. He suddenly didn't want to leave this woman he couldn't remember.

They disengaged. She sat back down, now crying heavily.

Her soft lips had reassured Tom. He gripped the oars and rowed towards the opening to the otherworld.

"Bye, Tom," Gina called.

"Remember to read the instructions in the envelope," Donny Q called.

Then there was just the wind and Gail's loud weeping, an emotional rain.

Tom entered the arch to the dark waters.

All at once, he realized he wasn't alone in the water. He peered down into the blue. A fat blob of silver was streaking toward him, glittering like a submerged mirror. Behind it, a large brown armor-plated hump with a sail-sized fin cut the water in pursuit.

Tom's memory fog was instantly replaced with panic.

He looked back. The portal was shutting. Its edges were falling to its middle, rising up from the water, crackling like lightning. Beyond it— unable to see what he could—his companions waved goodbye.

I'd better row hard for shore.

The silver flash leapt out of the water. A swordfish that dwarfed his boat. Its sword looked like a lightning rod. It flailed over him, ten meters above.

The brown hump reared up also, flailing out of the water after the swordfish.

Tom gawked in disbelief. The monster was an ichthyosaur—the dinosaur version of a porpoise—streamlined body and paddle-shaped fins. Twenty times larger than the sword fish it was pursuing. For the brief period it was airborne over Tom, the sky didn't exist.

As the ichthyosaur soared overhead, its tail smashed into Tom's boat. The rowboat shattered into bits.

It happened fast. One moment, Tom was gaping at the massive dinosaur passing over him. The next he was flailing in the water amidst wood fragments.

Both hunter and prey crashed back into the water, throwing up spray like rain.

Aw shucks, Tom thought, treading water, watching the pursuit continue into the distance. *Couldn't you two just go around me?*

The boat's shattered prow bobbed up. He grabbed it to steady himself, then looked around for his gym bag. The black bag was nowhere in sight.

It's sunk. The weight of the spare gun clips . . .

This wasn't good. Tom looked through the portal, catching Gail's reflected distress as it closed.

On Tom's side, the oversea air was normal, undisturbed, like nothing had ever been there.

Cursing as he bobbed in the cold water, his memory once again a patchwork of shit he couldn't remember, Tom struck out for the Boston shoreline.

Just do it, he thought. *Like fucking Nike.*

***

Mouth open in horror, Gail watched the ichthyosaur rise out of the water and smash through the boat.

"Honey, no!" she yelled as the boat disintegrated.

She watched Tom grab hold of a bit of driftwood, then . . .

The portal slammed shut.

"He's safe," Donny Q said after a pregnant pause. "That's a relief."

"He lost his bag," Gail said. Her eyes remained focused on the once-again 'plain' arch.

Gina considered speaking, but thought better of it. She'd seen Tom's gym bag containing the enveloped instructions and spells fly through the air as the boat fell apart.

"He's lost his bag," Gail repeated.

Gina and Donny Q now realized what she was getting at. The pair looked at her in shock.

"Hell!" Donny Q said. "Now Tom doesn't know who he is, where he is, or even who he's going there to kill."

"Worst of all," Gail added miserably, "he's got no way of getting back home again."

***

You think you're pissed off!? Gail thought angrily now. *You've no idea; I should never have agreed to this bullshit!*

She wasn't worried about the vampire vagina 'hearing' her. The mindspider only transmitted thoughts designated as conversation.

The only good thing is, I'm not lying now when I say I don't know where the hell Tom is.

"We will search for him," the vav said. "Maybe we'll find him."

Well at least we were right about that. Good thing we wiped his memory.

374

"But, we're not fools. You might be trying to trick us out of our doctor."

"Huh?"

She felt the vav Queen's soft, sardonic laughter. She looked up at the plant woman, trying to see her through the body of the creature covering her face. The smudge of lines condensed a little sharper, then filtered to pencil strokes again.

"We will take a ransom against Pussypalm's return."

That threw Gail for a loop. *"Wha . . . what do you mean?"*

The Queen laughed louder in Gail's head. "The gold. The gold we took from the storage place. We will take it home with us. It will be ours until we either find Pussypalm, or accept that he's dead. We will protect it for you. If we leave it here, the kidnappers might steal it away too."

Gail was outraged. "But you can't do that! We need the money—"

"You can't stop us, Big Sister. Warn your children not to attempt to. It will hurt us to hurt them."

Defeated, Gail nodded. She spat in anger. *There goes all our weapons! The medical supplies Rich needs! The . . . ! Shit! Shit! Shit!*

***

The gold—twelve thousand, two hundred and forty-six bars—was all stacked in the opposite square to the eater camp. It was tarped over to prevent unexpected air surveillance. A clump of oaks prevented view of the pile from the road.

Gail felt in her mind the vav's satisfaction.

Gail was incensed. She felt around blindly till her hands found Rich's tattered overalls, then began tapping the mindspider, indicating that he remove it.

The slimy arachnid slipped up off her head.

"What are you trying to do, Rich? Drown me in stink?"

He didn't reply. He was staring past the vav Queen, out across the road.

All the eaters around Gail were staring in the same direction, like their eyes were glued to what they were watching.

Gail followed their gaze, peering through the giantess' legs.

A procession of vavs were walking into the opposite quad where the gold was stored. Other vavs were exiting the quad and walking toward the bay.

What now? You girls intend living opposite us?

The vav Queen gave Gail a Marilyn Monroe wink, then walked off to join her sisters.

Donny Q ran out of the opposite quadrangle. He looked around till he saw Gail, then began signaling furiously at her to come over.

She set off running, still unsure what the problem was. The vavs didn't seem to be taking anything with them.

Outside, in the road, she stopped and stared. The procession of oncoming vavs seemed endless. The line of giant women reached down to the bay and beyond. *There's hundreds of them*, she thought incredulously.

She crossed to Donny Q's side. Two vavs walked out of the square and past them. She looked up at the two giantesses. One had Lauren Bacall's face, the other, Joan Collins's. Both pointedly ignored her. More followed them out.

"What is going on in there?"

Donny Q said nothing, just indicated that she follow him inside.

***

Gail stared speechless at what was going on. *How come Tom and I never thought of that? We'd never have needed trucks!*

The vavs were stuffing themselves with gold bars. Once each plant giantess reached the gold stack, she slit her belly open with her meat hook, loaded ten or twenty glittering bricks into herself, then waited for the wound to heal. Then she walked off again.

"What do we do, Big Sister?" Donny Q asked.

"Nothing," Gail replied heatedly. "The bitches came prepared to fight; that's why there's so many of them." She sighed. "Even without the crap of their not dying easy, they outnumber us at least three-to-one."

Donny Q winced. "No shit. It looks like half the vegan vagina population of Massachusetts coming this way."

A gold brick fell from a vav's hand. Donny Q took an instinctive step toward it.

The vav—an Elizabeth Taylor—instantly blocked his path, snarling and slashing her meat hook at him.

He stood back, hands up in a gesture of peace. "Okay, lady. The cash is yours. I'm also a great fan of your movies—love your Cleopatra."

Closely watching Donny Q, the vav retrieved the gold brick and inserted it into the tear in her belly. She turned to get more from the rapidly-reducing pile.

Gail tapped Donny Q on the shoulder. "C'mon. Let's leave them to it. At least we'll know where it is. We've still got the forty million Tom packed to pay Pablo. That'll buy us some rocket launchers and bombs. Your helicopters will have to wait."

"Damn! I was looking forward to those."

She glanced up at Bizarro. "Don't know why you want them anyway. Thirty million each for aircraft you can't fly because of that lump overhead?"

Donny Q was angrily silent.

Part 8: Finale

Chapter 111

"So," Gail said, grinning at Brook and Megan. "That about brings you two up to speed." She looked at Rich, pointed to Tom, who sat twitching while the mindspider wobbled like black jelly on his head. "He's not ready yet?"

"Should be, best to leave it on a few more minutes for safety's sake."

"I always wondered why Pussypalm left Harding alive," Megan said. "It made no sense."

"I vetoed killing him."

"He's dead anyway," Brooke said dully.

Gail's expression instantly altered to one of alarm and shock. *"What? How?"*

Brooke explained.

Face pale, Gail looked sharply at Donny Q and Gina.

Donny Q nodded. "We've been wondering how to tell you."

Gail walked over to sit on the edge of her desk. Wrapping her arms about herself, she stared miserably out over Pleasure Bay. The shock was so sudden—she had no words. *Ryan, dead?*

She'd dreamed of one day—when she and Tom had relocated to Techxas—contacting her brother again. But to have him die so needlessly, so stupidly . . . *And in a roundabout way it's me and Tom's fault. If we'd not stolen the gold . . . if Tom hadn't left me . . . if he'd not turned up again in Boston . . . If, if, always fucking if!*

It hurt badly, like a knife in her heart. For a long time she stared out over the shimmering water, past the giant people planted in it, at Mama's transparence. She felt as empty as Mama looked. *All is illusion,* she thought. *And Tom and I? Are we also imaginary? Are our plans and dreams nothing but mirage, just air we clasp?*

She wiped away tears, then turned back to the others.

"Please accept our condolences," Megan said.

Brooke smoothed her wind-ruffled hair and nodded. "We'll all miss him."

Gail nodded. She calmed herself, nodded to Rich. "Get that damn thing off Tom. I can't stand to be alone now."

Rich bent over Tom and removed the mindspider.

Chapter 112

Tom's memories floated in his head like versions of himself. Like a movie he had no choice but to view; one he'd also scripted, directed, and starred in.

The mindspider slipped up over his head. The silver-screen panorama coalesced into his brain as his actuality.

As it came clear, dripping final impressions on him like rain, Tom had a sudden conviction, clear understanding that a grave mistake had been made, that even originally, he'd been wrongly infused with another man's memories.

I am the man I was, not the one I'm becoming. The feeling was so strong, panic filled him as the logical impossibility of everything he'd viewed hit home like a derailed bullet train.

Help! I don't want to be stuck in another man's life! I'm not Tom Pussypalm! That murdering son-of-a-bitch is dead, eaten by a dragon— serves him right—or walking around somewhere, trying to remember who he is! I, Thomas William Palmer, clearly remember my life, childhood, adolescence, adulthood, girlfriends, breakups, different jobs, every fucking thing up to the moment I met Lynn in that bar! I can't be Pussypalm, I'm not Pussypalm! I REFUSE to be Pussypalm! I'm me!! I'M ME, ME, ME!!!

The horror, the panic, the feeling passed. The time for doubt was over. The download of himself had passed the point of no return.

No undo. Right or wrong, he was who he now was.

The mindspider disconnected from Tom's brain.

Tom opened his eyes.

His perspective had altered. Everything was different. Alliances had shifted. Enemies had become friends; friends, enemies. His ethics, beliefs, worldview—all were new by the reinsertion of the old.

He looked at the four women on the rooftop, all four now looking at him with concern in their eyes: Gail, Gina, Megan, Brooke.

He loved Gail. She was the most wonderful woman in the world. The only woman for him.

The eater girl, Gina was cute and fun-loving. They already had one kid, she said she wanted four. That of course depended on what Gail thought.

Megan was a fun fuck, nothing more—sort of like a permanent one-night-stand. Thrills, thrills, and more thrills, the more pervy the better.

And Brooke. She looked most worried about his mental state. He dimly remembered sleeping with her, and her trusting him, and their joint plans. Water under a long-demolished emotional bridge. Brooke, Boston's head cop, was automatically the enemy.

He smiled sadly. Brooke was beautiful, intelligent, STRONG . . . Everything a man wanted in a partner. If he'd met her before Gail . . . Now there was no one but Gail, never would be anyone for him but Gail.

"Dude, you okay?" Donny Q asked.

Tom grinned. "Yeah, feels great to be me again." He looked across at Gail, who still looked worried. "Don't worry, hon, it's really me."

He walked over to her and took her in his arms. He kissed her hard. She kissed him back for a while, then pushed him away.

He looked at her in surprise. Her face was flushed with desire, her pupils dilated with lust. Her nipples had felt like pebbles against his chest. "What? I thought you missed me."

"Your dick's getting hard," she whispered. "We've business to attend to."

"Oh." He turned round to look at the two captives, Brooke and Megan. "Ah, yes. Now what do we have here? Boston's finest and King Eric's lapdog."

"Yes, this sounds like the real you," Megan said. "A wonderful asshole."

Tom smiled. "Coming from you, Meg, that's a compliment."

He saw Brooke regarding him warily.

"No more Mr. Nice Guy, right?" she said.

"You have me confused with someone else, lady. I never was Mr. Nice Guy in my life."

Yeah, Tom thought again, *you're damn pretty, Brooke. You're also one dangerous chick, cop girl. We need to get rid of you.*

Chapter 113

Brooke was horrified by the change in Tom. It was like a sheep transforming into a wolf. The difference in him was as clear as night suddenly become daylight. By an imperceptible adjustment of muscle tensions, his facial expression was harder . . . ruthless. By a similar subtle shift, Tom's body posture now conveyed a sense of physical confidence . . . and menace.

Even his voice was now deeper.

This isn't the man I fell for, Brooke knew instinctively. *That Tom is gone for good, banished to heaven knows where. This one . . . Hell, no!* The look in Tom's sea-blue eyes now chilled her. *They look like marbles.*

But who then was that man she'd desired and melted into ecstasy with? Certainly not just a figment of the mindspider's imagination, a mental avatar built to fill Pussypalm's emptied cranium. It was a horrifying thought.

She looked at Gail. The woman was frowning at her, her blue eyes colder than Tom's. Brooke recognized the look. *Alpha female sees competition—bad things about to happen to competition. Okay, girl, now you've discovered the eater's hideout and the big secret, it's time to fucking leave.*

But how? She glanced surreptitiously around. Rich had departed, taking the mindspider with him, which Brooke was thankful for. The arachnid's musky stink had been addling her thinking.

Gina and Donny Q were behind her, both relaxed now Tom was himself again. Gina was on her left, Donny Q on her right. Most important of all, Tom was unarmed. Pussypalm with a gun was trouble she didn't need.

She smirked. The most obvious plan was to take Gail 'Big Sister' Harding hostage. The eaters would clearly do anything to keep her safe.

She began edging behind Megan. Megan was certain to back her up once the fight started.

"I've been gone a whole year?" Tom asked, looking out over Pleasure Bay.

"And I'm delighted to have you back again, darling." Gail said.

Chapter 114

Brooke calculated the angles and swung into action.

Shielded from view by Megan's body, she kicked Gina, while at the same time elbowing Donny Q in the gut.

Gina fell sideways, her shotgun discharging as she fell. She crashed hard against the roof parapet.

Donny Q doubled over, grunting. Brooke darted behind him, grabbing his semiautomatic. Donny Q recovered and fought with her for possession of the weapon.

Gina sat looking stunned.

"Megan! Get Gina's gun!"

Megan didn't respond. Still entangled with Donny Q, Brooke managed to see why.

Not again, goddamit! The blast from Gina's shotgun had set Megan on fire again. Orange tongues of flame licked her left hand as Megan beat out the fire on her pants.

Donny Q gave up trying to wrest the gun away from Brooke. He snapped at her with his teeth.

"I ain't lunch, you son-of-a-bitch!" She swung the barrel up under his chin and pulled the trigger.

The top of Donny Q's head blew off in a pink eruption. He slumped against Brooke. She flung his corpse off her, swung the gun to face Gail.

Shit. Tom had found a gun somewhere and was pointing it at her.

Brooke kept her finger tight on the trigger.

Gail smirked. Her eyes were however unsure as she pointed at Donny Q's corpse. "That little stunt isn't going to endear you to anyone."

"The hell with that. You're coming with me, Gail! The City of Boston wants a word with you!" To her left, Brooke was aware that Megan had put herself out and was closing on Gina, who was now staggering to her feet. She thought Megan had pulled some fresh needles from her jacket, but wasn't sure.

Tom laughed. "Gail's not going anywhere. Neither are you, Brooke."

She saw the look in his eyes. *Fuck! The bastard's going to kill me anyway, no matter what I do. So Gail dies too.*

She pulled the trigger. She was surprised when Tom instantly leapt to shield Gail. The bullets hit him in the side.

Simultaneously Gina's shotgun went off.

Brooke watched Tom go down, his shirt turning red. Then she looked around. Gina's shotgun blast had blown Megan halfway across the rooftop, which Brooke found absurd. Yet more absurd was the fact that Megan was picking herself off the floor and dusting herself off like nothing had happened to her.

She was also patting out tongues of fire spurting from her chest.

What the . . .?

"Hey, bitch!" Tom called.

In her surprise, Brooke had forgotten Tom. *Oh, you fucking want more?* She spun around.

He fired at her from the floor. Two pistol 'kraks!'

Both bullets hit Brooke in mid-turn in her upper right arm, shattering the bone. With a yell, she dropped the gun.

Tom regarded her with snake-cold eyes. "You're not good enough to take me down, Brooke—no one is." Spitting, he looked at Megan. "Kick the gun over here. One smartass move and I shoot Brooke in the brain."

Megan toe-poked the weapon over.

Alerted by the gunfire, armed eaters had begun arriving on the rooftop. They formed a silent semi-circle around everyone, covering Brooke and Megan with their weapons.

Kneeling, Gail bent over Tom, her face pale with worry. "How badly are you hurt?"

His gun lay beside him in the blood from his wounds. " I don't think anything vital got punctured. Help me stand."

Gail helped him to his feet. Holding his side, Tom sat on her desk.

Gail scowled at Brooke, her face livid with rage. "You're going to pay for this, you bitch. I just got him back after a year, and you're trying to take him away from me again?"

Brooke scowled back, blood streaming down her broken arm. "Collateral damage. He got in the way. I was shooting at *you*."

Gail motioned to the cordon of eaters. "Take them both away."

The cannibals strode forward and grabbed both women. Brooke winced when they held her broken arm.

"Wait," Megan said.

Gail smiled coldly. *"What?"*

The aging brunette's beautiful face was impassive. "What happens now?"

"To *you*? Nothing—we'll talk later." Her gaze shifted to Brooke. "Now, to the head honcho asshole here . . ." She smiled evilly, crooked a finger at Gina.

The eater woman rushed over. Gail whispered to her.

Gina nodded. She turned back to the others. "Okay, let's get them downstairs."

The eaters resumed ushering Brooke and Megan towards the stairway. Two of them picked up Donny Q's corpse.

"Tommy! I came as soon as I heard!" shrieked a female voice from beyond them.

The group of eaters and prisoners parted to let her through.

The speaker, a tall blonde naked under her black robe, walked hurriedly through their midst.

Tom grinned on sighting her vagina-less crotch. "Hi, Lynn," he said weakly.

"Just who we need," Gail said.

Lynn's green eyes widened on seeing Tom was bleeding. She rushed over to him, ripping his shirt open to examine him. "Who the hell did this?"

"The cop bitch you just passed."

Lynn stared angrily after the departing throng.

"Forget her," Gail said, "she's already history."

Lynn returned her attention to Tom's wounds, a pair of punctures down his left side. She studied them a while longer, feeling and prodding, then sighed in relief. "You're EXTREMELY lucky. Both shots went right through you. Too low to puncture your stomach, too high to rip your guts up."

Tom nodded. "Other than Kim Fields, Boston cops were always lousy shots."

Gail frowned. "Lynn, he's still bleeding."

"A few nicked blood vessels. Likely subcostal or intercostal arteries. Nothing life-threatening."

"Stop sounding like fucking Oppenheimer. Can you fix him up?"

She tossed her blonde hair. "Yeah, sure. Let's get him downstairs to your apartment. He'll be okay by morning."

Chapter 115

Brooke was separated from Megan a floor down. The eaters opened a door and pushed Megan inside.

"See you later," Megan told Brooke.

Gina laughed. "Yeah, a lot later."

The door shut on Megan. Brooke was led down to the ground floor then back along the corridor. The ends of her shattered arm-bone ground together as she walked, ripping her arm with pain. Fighting the agony, she sized up her captors. She could see no immediate escape.

Woman, you've really gotten into the shit this time.

Gina opened a door. The eaters hustled Brooke through it.

It took a moment for Brooke to take in the horror she was witnessing.

The room was large and tiled like a bathroom. A wall of wide windows watched the quad yard.

Brooke gasped. What immediately magnetized her eyes wasn't the huge steaming pots, or the meat being chopped up on side work surfaces. Or the gutters by the wall ferrying away a runoff of blood.

No, it was the naked human bodies suspended upside-down on meat hooks hung from the ceiling.

The nearest male corpse had a slit throat. An eater was removing a bucket of drained blood from under it.

"Hey, Peter! Where's the spices for the blood sausage?"

Peter hurried over.

Another eater arrived with a knife and began eviscerating the corpse, collecting its innards into a pail.

A tall fat eater wearing a rotted apron walked over to Brooke and her captors. "Who's this?"

"Tomorrow's lunch, Chef," Gina replied. "Big Sister says to garnish her well."

Brooke looked at Gina in horror. "No!"

"Yeah," the eater girl said with a smirk of satisfaction. "You really shouldn't have killed Donny Q. Welcome to the kitchen."

Chef gaped at Brooke. "Lady, you killed Donny Q?"

Brooke didn't reply. Gina leaned up and whispered in Chef's ear.

Chef nodded coolly, then looked Brooke over.

Brooke suddenly realized that she was dreaming. The impassive look on Chef's fat face as he scrutinized her body like a housewife would meat in a butchers' shop, feeling her muscles like she was already dead . . . *No, this is impossible, this is just a nightmare.*

Chef finished his appraisal. "Great meat on her ass. Prime cuts. Thighs'll make good steak too." He nodded to Brooke's guards. "String her up."

"No!" she shrieked as she was borne towards a vacant hook. "Fucking let me go, you bastards!"

"Shut her up," Chef growled.

Next moment, Brooke's mouth was covered with duct tape. Her arms were wrenched behind her back and her wrists bound. Her ankles were also secured.

She fought them in panic, forgetting the pain in her broken arm. "Mmmmph, mmmmph!"

The eaters got Brooke to the hook. They hung her up by the duct tape securing her ankles. Hoisted her off the floor till her head swung at knee level.

An eater placed a bucket under her head. He looked over at Chef. "Ready?"

Chef looked back over disinterestedly. "Yeah, sure. Tie up her hair, willya? Or she'll end up looking like a paintbrush."

The eater fished a rubber band out of his pocket, twirled Brooke's black hair into a bun, and secured it behind her head.

"Hey, Jenny!" he yelled. "We're ready."

Brooke's eyes widened as a short eater woman holding a hunting knife walked over. "Mmmmph!"

"Bye, girl." Gina waved at Brooke.

Brooke began thrashing wildly, regardless of the pain in her arm, flinging herself back and forth on the hook. "Nnnyyyaaaaaaaaahhh!!!!"

She knocked the bucket below her over. It rolled noisily across the kitchen floor.

"I said shut her up!" Chef yelled.

The eater woman, Jenny, kicked Brooke in the head.

The kick stunned Brooke. She stopped fighting, hung dully.

She looked pleading up into Jenny's eyes. There was no mercy there. Infinitely more horrifying, there were no qualms of conscience over the rightness or wrongness of what she was about to do.

Brooke looked desperately at Gina. Gina was licking her lips. There was no malice in her eyes now, just hunger.

The rollaway bucket was retrieved and replaced under Brooke.

"Okay, let's get this over with," Jenny said. "I got more meat to cut up." She squatted beside Brooke and unceremoniously slit her throat from ear to ear.

"Lower her a little," she said as Brooke's neck began spurting blood.

Brooke was winched lower till her head hung out-of-sight inside the bucket.

Brooke gaped at the bucket's interior as life fled her in red spurts. *No. . . this isn't happening to me. I'm fucking Chief of Boston Police, for God's sake. This isn't happening to me; it's not happening . . . It's not!!!!!*

Chapter 116

Megan sat on the bed in her cell and thought, her middle-aged face tranquil. Her thoughts weren't complicated—Megan's thoughts never were: *Survival is imperative. Pragmatism is essential in the present circumstance. Heroineism is only a virtue if it achieves its aim.*

Megan's jacket, with its racks of needles, had been taken from her. She felt naked.

She unbuttoned her shirt, then fished the shotgun pellets out of her chest, dropping them on the bed. The pellets were embedded deep in her breasts, their holes charred pits.

She didn't bleed.

She felt flustered, not as calm as she'd like. That had to be dealt with.

She unzipped her pants and freed her penis and scrotum. She spat in her palm and began masturbating, running her fist up and down the white shaft, over the knob of her glans and back again, in slow practiced strokes.

She ejaculated two minutes later, catching the semen in her cupped palm. She raised the pool of cum to her nose and sniffed it, then drank it all down.

She sighed with satisfaction, then licked her hand clean. She zipped up again, then lay on the bed looking at the ceiling.

What does Gail want from me? she wondered. Now, like she'd intended, her mind was much calmer.

While she thought, the wounds in her breasts healed, her burnt skin turning smooth and creamy again. Her burnt face and hands also mended.

Chapter 117

"Come closer, I want to whisper something to you."

Smiling, Lynn bent over Tom. "What, Tommy?"

Tom slapped Lynn hard.

She reeled back in confusion, then gaped at him.

"Why the hell did you hit me?"

"Thanks for all those stupid dreams you sent me."

Lynn's green eyes flared with anger. She punched his wounded side, slamming her fist so hard into the dressing she'd placed over the bullet wounds that blood seeped through the plaster.

Tom's eyes widened as the pain went through him. It felt worse than being shot the first time. He went rigid. "Shit!"

"They were meant as nighttime *entertainment*," Lynn said acidly. "You didn't know who I was anyway." She scowled, drew back her fist to punch his wound again. "So what was the big deal?"

"I was fucking *you* in one of them," he gasped. "I don't do incest, cousin."

Lynn lowered her hand. "Oh, that?" She grinned. "I just wanted to see what it felt like."

"And?"

"The butt-sex was fantastic—I came loads. Also, it was hilarious, seeing your face when I was a young man giving you head." She laughed. "Incest is a fun taboo."

"You had a *shit-monster* fuck me in the mouth."

"Not in the *mouth*—in the *vagina*." She rubbed her crotch. "*My* vagina."

"Which was on *my* face. That's gross."

She waved it off. "It was just a dream, Tommy."

"A nightmare."

"Okay, a black dream." Her expression brightened. "The good news is I've worked out how to duplicate Rose, so Twin-Lynn can have one of her own."

Tom gaped at her. "For real?"

"Believe it."

He grinned, then his expression turned thoughtful.

"Lynn?"

"Yes, Tommy?"

392

"How'd you know when and where to put the portal to bring me back?"

She grinned. "A lucky guess."

"Huh?"

"After I woke up, I found the house where Lynn had died, but didn't know if you were still there. So I set up a transit gate out in her street. I did it six different times, each two hours apart, hoping you'd find you way through it."

"Odd then that Gail wasn't expecting me."

Lynn nodded. "I didn't tell her about the portals. Be cruel after all this while to get her hopes up, then dash them again. Besides, I doubted myself that you'd attempt to enter the portals."

"I wouldn't have, except for the smoke."

"What smoke?"

"Thick green. It was fucking everywhere. Couldn't see a damn thing."

"That wasn't me. Maybe a side-effect of the portal's appearance."

Tom nodded. "Doesn't matter. What's important is that I'm back with Gail again."

The bedroom door opened then. Gail entered, followed by two eaters bearing covered trays, and another with two bottles of white wine.

"Dinner is served," she said gaily. She nodded at Lynn. "How's the patient?"

The blonde smiled back. "Good. He'll be fine for the party."

Gail grinned. She indicated the eaters place their food trays on a cleared table.

"What party?" Tom asked.

"Tomorrow's welcome-home party."

He winced. "Is that really necessary?"

Gail dismissed the servers and sat on the bed. She stroked his chest. "It's not just that. We're burying Donny Q and the others who died today tomorrow morning. I've told Gina to spread the news of your return, and tell everyone that after the funeral we'll have a beach party; sort of a camp holiday."

Tom pointed to the food trays. "What's for dinner?"

"Eater special. Grilled steak and ribs."

Lynn gagged. "I really don't know how you two can eat this shit. It's cannibalism."

"We can't all be vegan like you, Lynn, subsisting on fruit and nuts like make-believe squirrels. I for one *like* meat."

"Gail, in this case meat really is murder."

(Tom watched. It was a old argument. As matriarch, Gail had no choice but to eat human flesh. Lynn, however, had already made it plain to the eaters that she'd quit doctoring them if they insisted on making a cannibal out of her, so they left her to her veggie ways.

For his part, Tom couldn't stand the taste of human meat—too salty, he'd never liked pork either—but he'd eaten it whenever he was in camp.)

Gail scowled back. "Trust me, girl, the food is the one aspect of being Big Sister I hate. The sooner we can get our gold back from the vavs the better. We scram, get our asses over to Techxas."

"You've been saying that for . . . Shit!"

"What now? You're not going to start puking again, are you?"

"No, no," she retorted quickly. "Seeing Tommy wounded made me forget something: The vavs know he's back."

"What!?" Gail and Tom stared at each other, then at her. "How can they?"

Lynn pulled up a chair and sat. "A 'Grace Kelly' told me while I was cleaning some fungi out of her cunt, that one of her sisters up on Bizarro had her tentacle repaired by a man with a vagina in his hand."

Gail looked sharply at Tom. "You've been playing gynecologist?"

He winced. "Result of losing my memory. I helped out this vav with a severed vaginal tentacle and green goop spurted out from Rose and healed it. I was totally confused."

Gail sighed, a worried exhalation. She looked at Lynn. "Do they know he's here in the camp?"

"They suspect it. They saw him with Brooke and Megan. Then later, several of them saw Donny Q and the others riding the chocolate ants heading for Milk Lake. But . . . the one healed said Tom both looked different and his mind was wrong."

"That's a relief," Gail said. "Maybe they think it's someone else."

"Uh uh," Lynn said. "They're not stupid. They'll expect side effects from him falling through the space-time portal like we told them." Her expression turned questioning. "We call off the party?"

Gail shook her head. "Too late. The news has to be all around camp by now." She got off the bed, walked to the window and flung it open. "We'll hold the party as planned. On the beach."

"I don't think that's wise." She looked at Tom. "It's you the vavs are after; what do you think?"

He nodded. "Gail's right. They've got our gold. They know we desperately want it back. So they'll expect us to come negotiate for it."

"Tom, those women are persistent bitches. What if they insist on you coming to live with them full-time?"

"That is so not happening," Gail said forcefully, returning to Tom's side and gripping him so tight he winced.

"Ignore Gail's vagina's objection," Lynn said, her green eyes boring into her cousin's. "What if the vavs *insist* on you coming over? What then?"

Tom thought a moment. "Gail will suggest to them that we fuse both camps into one."

Gail looked up at him in surprise. "Eaters and vavs living together? It'll never work."

"Why not?"

"Don't be obtuse, cousin. You know they *hate* each other."

"So do lots of humans. We'll also propose to them that both tribes hunt together. They feed on different part of humans anyway."

"Some of the eaters—Peter for instance—like using drained human blood to make blood sausage."

"Screw Peter. He's German. They invented blood sausages."

"Peter seems to think it was during the Holocaust."

Tom winced. He looked at Lynn, "What do you think?"

She shrugged. "Best plan we've got at the moment. Give the vavs something to think about anyway." A worried expression flickered over her face. "That's the problem, though: In all the time I've dealt with them, the vavs have never struck me as a species that thinks particularly deep about anything."

She yawned. "I'm totally bushed, gotta get to bed. I've been sticking my hands up vav pussies all day. Those ladies get some really crazy diseases. Tree fungi, blight, rot; whatever plant infection you've heard of, they get."

Gail winced at the imagery.

Tom raised his left hand. "When do you want Rose back?"

"I *don't*. Hang on to it." She scowled at his raised eyebrow. "I told you—sex screws up my magic. I'm only copying it so my twin stops shrilling at me to kill myself." She gazed searchingly at Gail. "Or would you like two kittens, darling?"

"One panty pet's trouble enough to look after," Gail quickly replied. "Besides, I don't want you licking me whenever you need to know the future." She thought a moment. "And I'd murder you the first time I had my period out of two holes."

Lynn shrugged. "Sorry, Tommy, but the Queen says no." She yawned deeply. "Guys, I really gotta go. I'll leave you two to get properly reacquainted."

"Okay," Tom said. "We'll do the vagina duplication ritual tomorrow?"

"Yeah. While everyone's partying."

Chapter 118

Once Lynn was gone, Tom pointed at the covered tray. "Let's eat."

Gail shook her head. "Let's make love first. I need to work up an appetite."

She stripped off before he could object. "You've no idea what it's been like for me this past year without you around."

He adored her body, plush but not fat, generously padded in all the right places. "Lynn says not to move."

She grinned wickedly. "You *don't* move. I'll do the work."

She moved down his body, pulled off his pants, then took his erection in her mouth. She sucked him a while, then lifted her mouth off it. "You've no idea how I've missed this piece of white meat."

***

"Keep your eyes closed. You'll love this surprise. Hands behind your head. No touching either."

Tom kept his eyes shut. As always, Gail's lips on his cock were incredible. As she sucked him, he felt his worries recede, all his recent stresses become recent memories. She sucked him till he got so hard . . .

Her lips slipped off him.

"Now for my surprise," she said. "Keep your eyes shut—no peeking."

Tom squeezed his eyes tight. Her lips were replaced with something else—a tight, tight sheath. This new enclosure around his cock felt like her pussy, but was somehow different.

He laughed. "You had yourself tightened while I was gone."

She laughed. "You're not even close, baby."

Her womanhood rose and fell on his manhood.

"Damn, Gail, you're so incredible." Unable to resist the temptation, Tom removed his hand from behind his head, felt for her breasts. She knocked them away. "No cheating."

Tom let his hands fall back limply. He relaxed into the sensation, it was incredible, exquisite, the rise and fall of her body on his, of her ass . . .

That was the problem: Despite the incredibly tight grip on his cock, Tom couldn't feel Gail's buttocks on him, like they should be if he was in

397

her vagina or anus. And she definitely wasn't fellating him. She wasn't even on the bed. And it wasn't her hand.

So what?

The pleasure peaked. Tom ejaculated. His semen spurted in a hot stream that felt almost solid. The release forced his eyes open.

What the . . . ?

Gail was stroking his penis with a wet ridged object like a small pale football.

That's a—

At that moment, she turned and looked at Tom's face. Saw that his eyes were open. "You cheated," she said, ramming the wet, lobed object down HARD on Tom's erection.

—A brain! . . . a human brain! I'm fucking a human brain.

Tom froze in shock as she forced the brain down on him. He felt wet meat tear, like a teenager's hymen, as his cock ripped through it. Heedless of his concerns, he pumped cum into the horrible object.

Gail grabbed his testicles so he couldn't get away.

Tom collapsed back, let the last of his cum dribble from him into the brain. He remembered Gail whispering to Gina on the rooftop.

Brooke? Oh God, no!

Gail carefully slid the brain off Tom's penis. "I'm not sure Brooke would approve of what we're doing with her remains."

"How could you?"

"I just wanted you to have her one last time."

Tom scowled. "You're sick."

"Pot calling kettle black." She tapped his arm. "Move over."

Tom shifted. Gail lay beside him. She lifted her hips so they were well off the bed. Then she aligned Brooke's brain in her crotch—

Careful, careful now.

—and poured the semen into her vagina.

"What are you doing?"

She looked at him coolly. "Not letting this cum go to waste. Eater bitches aren't the only ones who want your kids."

Tom's face assumed a pained expression.

Brooke scooped a remaining thread of cum out of the brain into her pussy. "Put a pillow under my ass, will you, honey" she said, forcing the semen inside herself with a finger.

Tom did as she asked. Then he knelt beside her. Gail relaxed back, buttocks in the air.

"What the hell is this about?"

"I'm sorry, honey, I've cheated on you. I'm having another woman's baby."

Tom was filled with a sudden impulse to hit her, to make her stop this madness. A bloody mouth would cure her.

He thought better of it. *She just feels insecure over my relationship with Brooke. But how the hell can one be jealous of a corpse?*

Gail fondled the brain, manically running her fingers along its slick grooves. "I'm having Brooke's brat; darling. Now don't be jealous—if it's a girl, we'll call her Policía."

She began tearing the brain to bits, smashing her fist into it, pulling chunks of pale meat out of it with her fingers. She grinned at Tom, her eyes one step short of insane. "Oh, I'm so sorry; now look what I've done."

Tom sat beside her again. "Okay," he said quietly. "I get the point. There's no other woman for me anywhere in the world, except you."

Gail grinned up at him. Her eyes however, were teary, pleading with him for reassurance. "You mean that? You *really* mean that?"

He nodded. "You know I do, honey." He pointed to Brooke's shredded brain. "You totally rip up the competition."

***

They didn't have sex again after that. Gail flung the brain off the bed, then held Tom tight.

"I'm scared," she admitted. "We're right back where we started. Once the vavs discover—"

He ran soothing fingers through her hair. "Stop worrying. We've got a plan."

"If it doesn't work? Lynn just reminded us how the vavs aren't hot on thinking."

Tom frowned. He lifted his hand, rubbed the vagina against her lips. "Tell you what. Let's consult Rose."

She shook her head. "Uh uh." She snuggled closer. "I'm not in any mood for lovemaking tonight—too many morbid thoughts in my head."

"Tomorrow then."

"Promise me, Tom, that everything will be alright."

He forced a smile. "Nothing bad can happen now we're back together."

Tom found Gail's worry infectious. To be so bothered was totally unlike her. She normally focused on the positive attributes of negative situations, not the negatives in positive ones.

"Hold me tight," she whispered.
He held her tight.

Chapter 119

Tom regarded Megan, who lay placidly in bed.

"Have you decided yet about me?" she asked.

"Depend on where your loyalties lie."

"Currently, I'm loyal to the royals."

"Fair enough. Now, you've two choices: Either join with us or we'll douse you with gasoline and burn you—you seem impervious to bullets."

"I'll join you."

"Okay, but no tricks. We'll have an initiation ceremony during the beach party."

Megan nodded. "What sort?"

"A fight to the death. Three on one, until the tribe deems you tough enough."

Megan smiled. "My pleasure, but . . . are you *sure* you want to waste three people's lives?"

Chapter 120

The eaters used the Gate of Heaven Catholic Church on East 4th Street as a mausoleum. After a brief exhortation from the pulpit by Rich, and sincere words of comfort from Big Sister Gail, Donny Q's and the other eater corpses were stacked like bricks in a first-floor room, on top of several previous layers of dried corpses.

"Totally fitting that the dead are laid to rest in the house of God," Gina said, wiping tears from her eyes.

Rich locked the door on the corpses. "Party time," he soberly told Gail and Tom.

Chapter 121

The Overhead's underside writhed with soil tentacles that intermittently dripped dust in a fake rain. Transparent octopi snared equally see-thru fish over the coral in the crystal clear water.

Tom and Gail sat in brightly colored deck chairs, facing Mama, who dominated the lake, her ghostly face serene. Either side of them, tables and chairs were laid out along the bay's sandy curve, occupied by eaters laughing and having fun.

Few of the eaters wore beachwear, most preferring their normal rotted clothes. In keeping with this general trend, Gail had steered away from wearing a swimsuit, dressing instead in a white cotton sundress. Tom matched her choice of clothes, wearing a blue shirt and brown flannel pants.

As Lynn had promised, Tom's gunshot wounds were practically healed now. He felt only slight pain when he exerted himself.

***

"They give me the creeps," Tom said, pointing to the motionless giants and giantesses arranged out into the water in their orchard rows. The female menschs' waist-length black hair whipped about in the breeze like drying laundry. Bright Bizarro-filtered noonlight etched the giant people sharp as paintings against the landscape.

"Still, darling?" Gail replied, "I thought you'd be over it by now."

"I would have been if I'd hung around. Now I'm experiencing them anew, I can't shake the feeling that they're alive."

"Come off it, cousin," Lynn said, joining them. She plumped herself down in the chair on Tom's left, then pointed to the water-rooted giants. "We already determined that they're not. They're just meat plants— mutant coral that somehow evolved in the bay."

She pointed up at Bizarro. "With *that* overhead we should expect such mutations. I've been thinking: the mensch are likely broken-off chunks of Bizarro that took root and grew. Explains why they've no nervous system. The matter tried to adapt itself to the dominant species of the planet, but only copied the exterior."

"They have ribs and bones," Gail pointed out, crossing her legs.

Lynn shrugged. "Most creatures that stand upright do—even human-constructed skyscrapers have steel skeletons. It's just bracing—a natural requirement for stability." She laughed. "Their skulls are solid masses, bone all through. Okay, granted, they have eyes, but they're not connected to anything."

Gail laughed too. The day felt good. She grinned at Tom. "I remember, darling, the sick look on your face the first time Lynn cut one of the mensch open, and how relieved you were to discover they were nothing but meat and bones inside. You know, Tom, for a sociopath, you're occasionally a real pussy."

Tom remembered too. He forced a smile. "It's hard to be perfect."

A short distance along the beach on their right, Gina, dressed in a blue bikini that strained to contain her lactating breasts, was well out of her depth with trying to organize a group of rowdy toddlers who appeared intent on drowning themselves.

Gail kissed Tom, then left to help Gina.

Tom watched both women quiet the children, handing them several balls to play with. He winced—the balls were dried-up human fists. One ball was a baby's head. The children yelped happily, running around, kicking and throwing.

Tom's unease poked fingers into the pleasance, turning his smile into a grimace.

"What's bothering you?" Lynn asked him.

"Huh . . . what?" He withdrew his mind from the scene of the playing children, raised his left hand. "We intended asking Rose what to do, but overslept—Gina had to wake us for the funeral."

Lynn smiled. "Not your fault. You had a long trip. Gail also had a lot of pussy angst to work off. That generally exhausts you." She grabbed his left hand and licked the vagina.

"Stop that!"

She giggled. "You're such a prude, Tommy. No one's watching. Besides, why can't I lick myself in public? Oh, stop looking so damn serious. Today's intended to be fun." She tapped her vagina. "Tell you what: we'll do the consultation later, after duplicating it."

He thought a moment, then nodded.

At that moment, a loud cheer went up from the eaters. They both looked towards the access road. Megan was being led down to the beach.

"Initiation time," Tom said.

The thought of bloodshed made him feel a lot better.

Chapter 122

Megan squared off against her three opponents. Two women, one man. Gina had angrily vetoed her request that all three adversaries be men.

"An eater is an eater," she'd retorted. "Don't be sexist."

All four combatants carried hunting knives. Guns had been deemed unfair, as Megan seemed impervious to bullets.

The blood-written initiation symbol shimmered on Megan's forehead. She felt like the blood was singing into her brain, urging her on to violence.

She looked at all three eaters and saw corpses in their places, death in their faces. The grave vault, their final resting space.

The combatants were surrounded by a wide circle of eaters—an inner ring of chairs, an outer ring of standing people. Banished kids peeped through the legs of the adults.

The atmosphere was electric, knife-edged with tension. Megan was vaguely aware of Tom and Gail's concerned stares.

"Fight," Gina said. "To the death, or until I blow my whistle."

Gina got out of the way. The eaters charged at Megan.

She ducked inside the first woman's swipe, digging her knife into the woman's belly and yanking it up hard into her chest.

The woman screamed. Her intestines poured out of her. Dropping her knife, she fell to the ground cradling her spilled innards.

The male eater stabbed Megan in the side. She ignored the pain and slashed him across the throat, ripping his neck open from ear to ear. Pink blood pulsed, then jetted. The man gaped and gurgled. He stood panicking, vainly trying to stop himself from bleeding to death.

The second eater woman closed with Megan. The pair twirled around like dancers. Megan maneuvered the woman so she stepped on the intestines of the woman with the ripped-open belly.

The wounded woman, far from dead, screamed with pain.

Megan's opponent looked down at the noise. Megan wrenched her knife from her grasp, reversed her grip on it, and stabbed her simultaneously in both breasts. The woman froze, gaped at her in shock. Megan punched both bone hilts with her palms, forcing the knives through the woman's chest, so they exploded out of her back.

She crumpled dead to the beach sand.

Megan looked around the crowd of shocked spectators. She looked pointedly at Gina, then pointed to the gutted woman. "Are you going to blow your whistle? Or should I kill her too?"

Gina quickly shook her head and blew the whistle. She raised Megan's hand. The applause was subdued—the speed of the fight and Megan's ruthless brutality had rendered everyone near-speechless. Whispering loudly, the crowd dispersed.

Two eaters carried the gutted woman away. Wincing, Lynn got up to go treat her. Megan walked over to sit beside Tom and Gail.

"Sad to lose those two," Gail said, "but believe me, your eater credentials are now incontestably in order."

Megan accepted a cold lemonade from a server.

Then a loud cheer went up from the crowd. They looked up the beach to the road junction, where food trays were being offloaded from the rear of a white bus.

"Lunch is served," Tom said.

Chapter 123

Lunch was roast Brooke Hayes. Boston's erstwhile Chief of Police had been slit open, stuffed with Irish potatoes and parsley, then oven-cooked at medium heat for four hours. Her intestines had been cleaned, rolled in dough and fried up as meat sticks and pretzels. Her emptied skull, shaven of hair, was stuffed with potato mash.

Tom stared with revulsion at the swollen gravy-dripping body on the serving tray. It was pig-bloated, letting off wraiths of savory steam. It bore no relation to the woman he'd passionately fucked—had it only been two days ago?

Chef—in blood-splattered rotted apron—presided over the roast, sharpening a pair of carving knives by rubbing them against each other.

Tom grimaced as Chef began cutting Brooke up for an impatient line of eaters. "That's utterly disgusting."

"Can't help it," Gail said, her face expressionless, "it comes with the territory."

"They look delighted," Megan said, stepping out of her pants.

"They love roast pig," Tom said. He regarded her pale legs for a moment.

She laughed. "Might as well work on my tan. It's nice and sunny." She folded her trousers up, then took off her top as well.

"You sure healed up fast," Gail said, pointing to Megan's breasts. "One would think Gina never shot you."

"Masturbation plugs holes in your skin as well as your sex life."

Gail rolled her eyes. She'd forgotten what Megan was like.

The dispersal of Brooke was proceeding in earnest. A young eater woman brought them a heaped tray of meat and potatoes. "For you, Tom, and Megan, Big Sister."

"There won't be enough of her," Gail said. "I hope Chef made back-up."

The eater woman nodded, smiling. "The policemen's corpses collected yesterday were also roasted." She licked her lips. "Chef also made brain cheese soufflé and liver salad. He also made—" her yellow face crinkled in confusion.

"What?"

The eater woman was gaping at Megan's crotch, at her bulging 'womanhood.'

Megan giggled. She tapped her silk-covered penis. "You've never seen one before? At your age?" She grinned. "Why not come over tonight and I'll show you how it works?"

The woman gulped and left.

"The news'll be all around camp in ten minutes," Gail said. "I hope you like stud service." She grinned. "Nice of you to show up; means I can have Tom to myself more."

"I'm unfortunately infertile," Megan said.

Gail frowned, rolled her eyes. "You don't say." Her eyes narrowed. "Megan, what the hell are you? You burn like wood, you didn't even bleed when shot, you healed over—"

"Let's eat," Megan interrupted her. "I've been hungry forever." She took a potato from the tray and bit into it. "I liked Brooke, eating her would be improper."

"Be glad you're not me," Gail said. She searched out a bit of kidney and bit into it. "Ah yeah, say what you want, Chef can cook."

Tom winced. "You're not actually enjoying this food now, are you?"

Gail grimaced, her eyes suddenly a miserable sheen he'd never associated with her. "Believe me, darling, I hate it more and more each day."

"Doesn't look like it."

"Oh, don't be silly. I don't have . . . *neither of us* have any choice in the matter." She pointed across the water at Castle Island. "Not till . . ."

Megan swallowed some potato. "Like a pit you've fallen into, and can only escape by tunneling yourself deeper into."

Tom regarded the meat coldly. "What annoys me is how this simply never seems to end. Each day we become more like them."

"We don't believe *it's right* to eat human flesh."

"But for how long? We remain here long enough, and it's just a matter of time. We're already cannibals in practice, becoming so in principle is mere steps away."

Gail shrugged. She took a sip of beer, swallowed. "I view it as keeping up my strength for the getaway."

Megan sipped her lemonade. "I share your pragmatism. Tom, you're not eating."

"My belly aches," he lied. *No way am I eating Brooke*, he thought. *Ejaculating in her brain last night was bad enough.*

Gail looked at him with concern. "Not even some potatoes?"

"I'll go check on Lynn, get something for the pain. I don't think it's the gunshots. Just . . ." He looked up momentarily, then froze. "Fuck!"

Seeing the sudden horror that had leapt into Tom's eyes, Gail looked out over the water also.

It took her a moment to see what had spooked him. "Those two of the mensch with their eyes open? Is that it?"

Tom nodded.

Megan regarded the two open-eyed mensch. "They seem to be watching us three."

Tom considered her words. It was true. The staring giants' eyes did appear fixed on them. "I've a bad feeling about this."

Gail sniggered. "Oh yeah. Now what? They've suddenly become smart?" She took a bite of meat, chewed, swallowed. "Lynn said they're meat plants."

"And now their eyes are open. That's *never* happened before."

"Maybe they're *ripening* or something. Tom, it's just *two of them*. For God's sake, stop worrying. You're making *me* worried."

Tom forced a grin. "Okay, honeycakes, you're right."

He got to his feet. Gail gaped at him. "Where are you going? Don't tell me they're scaring you off."

He shook his head. "I'm going to see Lynn about my stomachache." He'd just remembered they'd planned to consult Rose during the beach party. He now also intended asking the palm vagina about the 'awakened' mensch. True, only two of the giants were looking their way, but . . .

"Okay, honey. Kiss me."

Tom bent and kissed Gail. As their lips locked, he was filled with a sudden sadness, a horrible premonition. He held her tight, kissed her extra-hard.

Giggling fiercely, she broke away from him. "I need some air, Casanova."

Then she laughed. "What was that for?"

"I love you," he said. "I love you more than anything else on this fucking planet."

Gail was about to retort saucily, when she saw how serious he was. She nodded. "I love you too. More than you'll ever know."

"How nicely romantic," Megan said. She reached a hand down into her panties and scratched her scrotum, which had suddenly started itching.

Tom left both women.

Gail watched him climb the beach for a moment, then turned her attention back to the staring mensch. *Oh yes, Tom's right: there is something menacing about them now.*

409

Then she smirked. *Screw you all. I'll be scared when you start moving your arms and legs.* Smiling, she compared her breasts to a giantess' for shapeliness.

Beside Gail, Megan fished a fat insect out of her panties. Grimacing in disgust, she popped it like a pimple. She wiped the bug-goo off on her bra.

Both women continued eating. A short distance from them, a DJ played records in a sheltered palm grove. Eaters danced. Some found secluded spots and fucked. Watched by Gina, the toddlers frolicked in the shallows.

The party went on.

Chapter 124

The mensch were young; the mensch were eternal; the mensch were unsure what they were.

Unknown to Tom and the eaters, or even to the vav, the white giants rooted in Pleasure Bay were alive.

The mensch were an ancient race, from ages away, unwilling ambassadors transported an unfathomable distance. In this new place, however, they were prisoners. Their bodies, for all their imposing immensity and physical perfection of their forms, lacked nervous systems. Their muscles were useless—as dead as if nonexistent. They didn't even possess brains in their skulls.

The mensch could sense the world around them, however, and communicate between themselves. Like the vav, they were telepaths.

And they were angry. VERY angry. With Tom, with Gail, and with the eaters, for turning them—gods in their realm—into mere boats.

The mensch had waited for ages to settle the score, and now they saw their opportunity.

***

The conversation—a flow of thought between interlinked brains that seemed to come from all of them at once proceeded as follows:

"Fortune and fate are now perfectly aligned in our favor. We strike now?"

"It seems good; they suspect nothing."

"This is a good time to take our revenge."

"More than revenge."

"They are truthful, intending no harm. They wish peaceful coexistence."

"The vav plant women don't know that. We will project to them an alternate version of what the humans and eaters are thinking and saying about them."

"There are ethical considerations—good and evil. We are good—"

"Spare your pacifism! We have lost our glory; the oppressed have nothing to do with honor!"

"What I mean is—"

411

"We all know what you mean. It has no meaning anymore. Its meaning died, was stillborn upon our arrival on this accursed plane. What remains now is survival."

"And truth."

"Yes. Truth, but not your version of it."

"Truth is objective reality. Black is black and white is—"

"Truth is an aroused subjective female dog who accepts penetration from all shades of interpretation."

"Stop bickering, both of you. We do now what is pragmatic; I do not intend to become a boat for an inferior species to paddle across Bizarro."

"It is agreed then, moderator? We mind-fuse?"

"Unless anyone has any other objection. Does anyone . . . ? No . . . ? Then it is agreed. We fuse minds and project."

"To where?"

"The golden palace. Enough questions. You two who were arguing . . ."

"Yes, moderator?"

"Stream up to us accurate real-time pictures and dialogue of what Tom Pussypalm, Gail Harding, and Megan Fox are discussing."

"At once, moderator."

"The rest of us will alter it and project it to the vampire vaginas."

The two mensch opened their eyes and recorded Tom and Gail and Megan.

Chapter 125

The vavs' palace had been built from the stolen gold.

It was the vavs only ever architectural accomplishment and one they could have been rightfully proud of, if it had been in their nature to be proud.

The palace was not visible as such from the outside. In their part-belief of Gail's story about Tom being kidnapped, the vavs had masked the building, first smearing it with secretion from their vaginas, then plastering cuttings of their hair over it, till now, from the outside, the palace seemed a massive heap of palm fronds.

***

Inside the cavernous gold palace, the vav Queen sat on her gold throne. Her Marilyn Monroe face was pensive, her cornflower-blue eyes oceans of displeasure.

The tip of her meat hook protruded from her vagina, dripping blood onto the temple floor. The human body it had just drained lay wasted to the side of her.

The Queen never hunted. Food was brought to her in the palace by her sisters.

The vav elderess council stood around the Queen. The topic of telepathy was the sudden reappearance of Pussypalm.

"It has to be he," said a 'Bette Davis' councilor.

"We can't prove this," a Dietrich vav retorted. "It may be another."

"We have a deal with the human Big Sister," the vav Queen said. "If she breaks it, I will personally drink her blood. I will."

"Humans lie."

"So they'll die."

"But if they don't?"

"Then they won't."

The air between councilors and Queen shimmered. A life-sized holographic image appeared. Two people sitting in beach chairs.

"Pussypalm and Big Sister," the vavs thought at each other.

"Quiet!" the Queen said. "Listen."

***

(It made no difference to the mensch that Tom had left the beach and that what was transmitted to them were really images of Megan and Gail, and that both women were actually discussing the abysmal state of their pedicures, and afterwards, how Gina was really good with children.

The vavs saw and heard what the mensch wanted them to.

Essential to the deceit's success was the limit of the vavs' plant intelligence, else they'd have questioned why they were now able to both hear and understand what the humans were saying, something previously impossible without using a mindspider.)

Tom kissed Gail. "So what about the vavs demand that you hand me over to them?"

"Fuck the veggie bitches. Stupid cunts. They should be more careful, stop continually picking up venereal diseases."

Tom raised his hand and licked Rose. "They'll come calling."

She laughed aloud. "We'll just tell them you're a twin—your brother's still missing. They're so stupid they'll never guess the difference!"

Tom nodded. "I wonder why they're not satisfied with Lynn treating their pussies."

Gail giggled. "They don't like how she has to stick her hand inside them. With you it's more holistic, more . . . *holy*." She shrugged. "That's what they say."

Tom scowled. "They can all go burn in Hell. Why does God keep sending humans to Hell anyway? Plant girls make better fuel."

She hugged him tight. "You're mine, honey, mine only." She frowned. "And heaven help any vegetable snatch who attempts snatching you from me. Stupid thatch-heads."

Tom pushed her off him. "That's easy to say. I've a better idea."

Gail looked seriously at him. "What, darling?"

"I've been thinking: maybe we're being too greedy."

"How'd you mean?"

He scratched his chin. "*Six billion dollars?* Whatever were we thinking? We'll never spend that much in six lifetimes. Right?"

Gail nodded enthusiastically. "Go on, darling. I'm all ears."

"I suggest we make a deal with Boston. We tell King Eric where the gold is, in exchange for just half of it."

"And the vavs?"

"Boston has enough explosives to kill off the dumb cunts for good."

Gail looked at him in surprise. Then she leapt off her chair and began dancing. "Oh, honey, you're so smart, you are. Yes! Let's do it! Let's kill off all the vavs."

Gail now knelt between Tom's legs. She freed his penis from his pants and began fellating it.

Tom ran fingers through her hair. "Yeah, honey, once the skanky plant women are extinct we'll do this everyday. Ahhhhhhhh! I'm cumming!"

He pulled out of Gail's mouth and ejaculated a flood of semen over her face, her hair and dress.

"Yeah, bomb me, darling!" Gail shrieked as he drenched her, squeezing his testicles so he came and came. "Just like Boston is gonna bomb those vav cunt bitches to smithereens. I can already see Agent Orange falling on their palm-tree heads." She stopped a moment. "You know what I'd like to do personally, Tommy darling?"

"What, hon?"

"I'd like to stuff a flaming torch up into each of their vaginas. Burn them down cunt-first like the overgrown clumps of grass they are."

***

The holographic projection winked out. Vav Queen and councilors stared thoughtless at the space it had occupied for a full five minutes. The Queen ran worried fingers through her palm-frond hair.

Then the Queen looked from face to face. "They intend to burn us down like grass?" Her fright was evident in her thoughts.

"Horrible, horrible, horrible!"

"Yes, horrible. Terrible!"

"Can't be allowed. Must be stopped!"

"Immediately!"

The Queen's eyes turned cunning. Her massive beautiful lips curved in a smile. She didn't question how the holograph had appeared—it just had. For her, things either happened or didn't: the rain fell, the sun shone . . . eatable humans lived in Boston . . .

"Pussypalm is back. And he is ours," she said.

Her councilors grinned back. "Yes, ours by right."

"We agreed, we agreed."

The Queen stood up. With a shake of her hips, she squirted her meat hook fully out of her vagina. It dropped past her knees before she halted its fall with a yank on its wet tentacle. Womb-slime squirted out between her fingers as she gripped it. She slung the meat hook in a gentle arc, golden palace light reflecting off the black mirror of its slime-slick surface.

Her councilors extruded their meat hooks also. The Queen walked between her courtiers toward the palace door.

"We will visit the eaters and ask for Pussypalm back. And if they refuse . . ." She whirled her tentacle fast and furious over her head.

The other vavs smiled at her. "They dare not refuse to hand him over."

"It would be suicidal of them."

"Stupid humans."

"Stupid and suicidal."

"Stupid Big Sister Gail, dares to think of burning us!"

"Horrible! Terrible!"

At the palace entrance the Queen and her council were met by more of their mentally-summoned sisters. All gripped their vaginal tentacles in their hands, dangled their scythe-like meat hooks.

The vavs left Castle Island. In purposeful procession, they strode around Pleasure Bay beach towards the celebrating eaters, leaving deep footprints in the sand.

Chapter 126

Tom pointed to the green tentacles—some up to two feet long—growing along the base of Lynn's living room wall. "What the hell are those?"

She sighed. "Occupational hazard. Remember Big Sister Cassie?"

Tom nodded. The transformed Cassie-bug had been stowed in the basement. *The basement.* His eyes widened with understanding. He pointed down.

Lynn nodded. "Yup. Directly underneath me."

Tom indicated the tentacles—slowly waving like part of an underwater organism—again. "And . . . ?"

Shortly after you left, the entire basement transformed into some kind of tentacle jungle. Of Cassie, there was no sign. We've not seen her since."

"She *vanished?*"

"Or *became* the jungle. Likely she disintegrated into mush and it grew out of her remains—"

Tom winced.

"—Which is less farfetched than it sounds. There are loads of little white beetles down there. Remember I turned her fat ass into a beetle. Maybe they're her offspring."

Tom nodded.

Lynn shrugged. "You need to see what the basement looks like now. It's odd like you won't believe. These tentacles grow through the floor, like grass. They don't bother me. They smell nice too."

Tom nodded. The air had a slightly minty scent to it.

He forgot the tentacles. "We need to consult Rose—two of the mensch just opened their eyes."

She looked at him sharply. "You think it's connected to . . . what?"

"No fucking idea."

"Don't be paranoid. What's this? Big Meat Brother is watching you?"

"I just don't like coincidences."

She considered a moment, then nodded. "Let's clone Rose first."

"How long will it take?"

"Ten minutes at most."

Tom sat on the sofa and waited while Lynn set up to perform the duplication spell. His attention was drawn back to the wavering tentacles at the base of her wall. *Maybe I am being paranoid,* he thought. *They seem aware of me too.*

Chapter 127

Seeing the approaching vavs, Gail called Gina over. "Leave the kids for a moment. Get a mindspider over here double-quick."

Gina nodded and turned to leave.

"Hey wait!"

"Yes, Big Sister."

"If you see Tom, tell him to keep well out of sight."

Gina yelled to her sister: "Nitty, keep them all in one place and out of the water! Michael, put that goddamn octopus down!"

"Awww, Miss Fieri! I like it!"

"I said drop it! Emily, don't you dare . . . !"

Breasts bobbing like buoys in her bright blue bikini, Gina sprinted off. Gail stood and waited.

"I don't like way they're carrying their meat hooks," Megan said.

"Dumb bitches are spoiling for a fight." Gail prepared to bluff them.

The eaters got out of the way of the plant women. Mothers grabbed their children and retreated up the sand to safe vantage points. The male eaters warily watched the oncoming procession of giantesses. Several rushed off to get weapons.

Gail counted. *There's almost two hundred of them.*

The vav Queen reached Gail just as Rich dashed to her side with a mindspider.

Gina ran past them both. She hurried through the ranks of vavs back to the kids she'd been watching, began hustling them up the beach to the road.

"Tom?" Gail asked before Rich slid the arachnid over her head.

"Over in Lynn's apartment."

Gail nodded. Lynn's apartment was on the opposite side of the square, without a view of the bay.

Then she was enclosed in the slime of the mindspider's interior.

Chapter 128

"Tom's not here," Gail explained patiently in response to the vav Queen's enquiry.

She sensed in her mind the giantess' amusement at her reply. "You are lying."

She was shocked, but feigned anger: "How dare you insult me with such allegations?"

"Because it's true." The Queen laughed. "Listen, Big Sister: I will ask you one more time, and then . . ." she let the threat hang. "Now, tell the truth. Where is Pussypalm?"

Enveloped in gray, Gail sensed disaster looming. Her mind—the voice of reason—screamed at her to hand Tom over to the vavs. Her heart, however, rejected logic's pragmatism.

"He's not here," she answered.

"I see you are stubborn."

"He's *not* here."

She sensed more than actually heard the vav Queen's next thoughts. The giantess was yelling to her sisters: "Attack! Kill! Destroy! Find Pussypalm!"

Oh shit, Gail thought. *What have I just done?*

"Okay!" she shouted, "He's—"

Then she felt someone knock her off her feet. Blind inside the mindspider, she rolled until she managed to stop herself.

There was a fumbling around her head and the mindspider was removed and she found herself looking up at Megan.

"I'm assuming you refused to hand Tom over," Megan said.

Gail didn't reply. She pulled herself up to a sitting position and looked around the beach.

All was pandemonium. The vavs had split in two groups. One group was advancing up to the main road, the other was fighting the eaters on the beach. There were already several dead eaters on the beach.

A short distance away Rich's corpse lay in the sand, his torso shredded like a bomb had exploded in it.

Gail smacked her head in dismay.

"They actually slashed at *you*," Megan said, "but I was faster."

"Thanks."

Staring at the fast-growing number of yellow corpses, of old and young alike, Gail was suddenly incensed. Rage built up inside her, stacking on itself in layers. *How dare you vavs attack my people?* Her previous intent to negotiate with the giantesses, even concede Tom to them, went out the window. *You bitches want a fight, right? I'll give you one you'll never forget.*

She sighted Gina. "Hey, Gina!"

Gina didn't hear her. A yellow streak, the eater woman was running towards two screaming children cut off from the others behind the attacking vavs. She ran like the wind, ducking meat hooks left and right, once flinging herself to the ground and rolling as two tentacles flailed at her. Finally, she reached the kids. Picking both up, she ran the gauntlet again back to safety.

Gail couldn't help but admire Gina. "That woman has kids on the brain."

Megan pulled Gail to her feet. "What do you intend to do now?"

"Donny Q stashed some rocket launchers as a birthday surprise for King Eric. Several flamethrowers also. We'll have to get those out."

"Hope you've got enough." She pointed; Gail followed her finger. In a battle tactic Gail hadn't seen before, four vavs were simultaneously slashing at an eater—looked like Chef—with their whirling meat hooks. The meat hooks ripped through Chef, separating him into bits. He exploded into chunks of yellow meat in midair.

Gail winced. Then she realized that Megan was staring pointedly at her.

"It's not too late to put the mindspider back on and agree to a truce with them," Megan said.

Gail hated Megan intensely at that moment for her suggestion. "I was about to do . . . Would *you* give up the man you loved to those palm trees?"

"If he was exceptionally bad in bed. Emotion only goes so far. I need friction to get off."

Gail considered the brunette's unruffled smile. "Fuck you."

"Maybe later . . . if we're still alive. For now, fighting is more in character for a leader. Where are the flamethrowers stashed?"

Gail bit down on her retort. "In the basement of the opposite quad, the one where the gold was originally kept."

Megan nodded. "We need to pick our way through the vav attackers. Our best tactic—"

"Just let's go," Gail interrupted. "I can't wait to give those cunts a taste of their own douche."

Chapter 129

Lynn rubbed a minty oil over Rose, then stepped back.

She and Tom stood inside a chalked pentagram in a space on her living room floor. The windows were shut, leaving the room in midday twilight.

Lynn retrieved a time-yellowed scrap of paper from the floor and began reading:

Nenonys, Natrix, Narna.
Nar Rose, Ders Ders . . .

Tom's left palm grew hot. "It's burning!"
She nodded at him and chanted some more:

Teer Nar Rose, Teer Na, Teeeeer!

A small 'shimmering' appeared in midair between them. A 'hole' the size of a dinner plate. Inside it, Tom saw Lynn's twin painted in faded watercolors. A gas ghost less substantial than her self-awareness.

The spirit glared at him, enraged by her impotence; an impotence heightened by sexual frustration.

Lynn stopped chanting. She let the scrap of paper fall to the floor. "Okay, we're good to go."

Tom looked up from staring at Lynn's duplicate. "Hurry up. My hand feels like—She-iit!!!"

Dipping her index finger into Rose for purchase, Lynn had grabbed both of the vagina's large labia and ripped it out of Tom's hand.

"Done," she said, holding the pink meat tube up for his inspection.

Tom gaped down at his palm, expecting a bleeding wound. But no, Rose was still there. The pain was already fading.

He looked back up at the duplicate organ. The cunt was like a pink slimy flashlight, a plump four-inch-long meat-flower giving no impression of the immense pleasure it would afford any penis shoved into it.

Ugh. To think I've still got one of them in my arm.

Lynn pushed the vagina through the shimmering portal. With a shriek of glee on seeing what she was being offered, the ethereal Lynn grabbed the cunt with wisp-fingers.

The portal slammed shut.

Lynn grinned at Tom. "Well that's one happy camper." Her expression turned lewd. "What was I like in bed?"

"Huh?" Then he understood what she meant. His expression turned cold. "Lynn, for heaven's sake."

She gave an exaggerated sniff. "Yeah, yeah, right. Big bad cousin is scared of incest." She giggled at his irritated face. "Lighten up, willya?"

"Look, I'm sorry for overreacting, but I'm on edge. I've got a huge case of jitters."

She frowned. "This is *so* unlike you. You're normally so calm."

He forced a smile. "Not today, I'm not." He pointed to Rose. "Can we do the consultation? That way I'll be able to relax."

She nodded. "Give me a minute to clear my magic gear away. We might as—"

Tom silenced her with a raised hand.

"What's that noise outside?"

She frowned. "Tom, there's a party going on. It's going to be rowdy." She saw how serious he was. "You really have to—"

"Shh! Listen."

Lynn listened. "Sounds like the party's gotten well out of control."

"Sounds like explosions."

"Explo . . ." Lynn ran and flung open the closest set of windows.

She stared with incomprehension at the Shirley Temple vav standing outside her living room. Lynn noticed the vav was whirling her tentacle.

"What . . . ?"

"What is it?" Tom asked, stepping toward the window.

Lynn turned to run. The meat hook streaked in the window after her. It looped twice round her neck then embedded itself deep in her throat.

Lynn gaped at Tom in horror as the vaginal tentacle yanked her off balance.

Tom grabbed the tentacle as it pulled Lynn to the window, but his fingers slipped down its slickness. *Shit! My gun's upstairs!*

He looked around for a knife. There was none in the living room.

Lynn's face was now purple. Her tongue protruded between her teeth as she gasped for breath that wouldn't come. Bracing himself against the window ledge, Tom turned her clockwise, seeking to unwrap the tentacle. It was futile—the organ coiled like a python, and there was always the danger of the meat hook ripping her throat to shreds.

Lynn couldn't even mouth a spell to help herself.

Meanwhile, with a pumping motion, a rhythmic swelling and deflating of her tentacle, the vav was draining Lynn. Blood streamed down under the strangling coils, coating Lynn's naked breasts.

Tom glanced out the window. The Shirley Temple vav's brown eyes were thinned to pleasured slits; she was oblivious to the suffering she caused. He had an impression of other plant giantesses behind her, battling with eaters.

"Kni . . .!" Lynn gasped. "Knife!"

Tom raced into Lynn's kitchenette. He looked around, grabbed a vegetable cleaver, and raced back to the living room. Lynn, arms limp by her sides, was just being dragged out of the window.

"Fuck!"

Tom dashed to the window. Lynn was halfway through it now. Her eyes were wide shut—open but seeing nothing. Tom had no idea if she was alive or dead. He dropped the knife on the windowsill, grabbed Lynn's legs and pulled her back inside.

Lynn pissed herself, an amber gush from her purple urethral puncture. The warm liquid squirted profusely in Tom's face.

The noise of yelling and explosions was coming hard and fast now.

Fear for Gail gripped Tom. He calmed himself.

He adjusted his face, so Lynn's urine arched over his shoulder. Holding her ankles fast, he retrieved the cleaver.

The vav gave an almighty tug on her tentacle. Death-piss streaming down her legs, Lynn surged out of the window again. Tom dragged her back inside. He stretched to chop through the vav's tentacle above her head.

Then the front door swung open, catching him hard on the shin. He let go of Lynn. Trailing a stream of amber drops, she flew out of the window.

Tom leapt back to the window. It was too late. Lynn's corpse dangled, swollen tongue in blue-lipped mouth, in the vav's crotch.

He whirled angrily toward the apartment door. *Who . . . ?*

Megan stood there. Her chest was opened up by a deep crosswise slash between her now bared breasts. He dully noted that the slash wasn't bleeding. The flesh in the wound was white and flaky like that of a sun-dried fish.

"The vavs have Gail," Megan said.

Tom's eyes widened with horror. *No!* "Which way!?"

She pointed out the window. "Down toward the beach."

Tom rushed past her out of the room. Megan followed hot on his heels.

Chapter 130

"I need my gun," Tom said, turning to climb the stairs.

Megan pulled him off the stairs. "There's a dead eater with a pistol at the end of the corridor."

They resumed running.

"How the hell did it happen?"

"Gail was getting out the flamethrowers in the quad opposite when a tentacle jerked her out through the window. I think they'd been stalking us."

Tom's face turned white. *Just like Lynn?*

They stopped for Tom to pick up the dead man's gun, then burst from the building.

Across the road, four eaters with flamethrowers had the vavs pinned back. Several of the plant giantesses were ablaze, massive mobile torches.

All the vavs had vacant crotches: eater blood held no nourishment for vavs.

"That way," Megan said, pointing toward the beach. "I can see her dangling."

They turned and ran for the beach alongside the streams of fire keeping the vavs at bay.

***

An airborne car came flying down the road. Tom and Megan watched it streak past. The automobile crashed down on an eater handling a flamethrower. A moment later, man and machine both exploded as the flamethrower's fuel tanks blew up.

The vavs immediately began flinging more rusted automobiles at the fire-wielders.

Tom hardly noticed the flying cars, some of which spun through the air like wheels. He was only vaguely conscious of a loud explosion behind him and the walls beside him brightening in a red glare as another flamethrower was neutralized. His mind was trained beyond the vavs flinging the vehicles (and trees, and chunks of building and beach road) to where he could now make out Gail dangling like a penis between a retreating vav's trunk thighs.

Watching her swing there, Tom felt like he'd been shot. He felt his blood was draining along with hers.

The vav's walking away from them prevented any clear shot at her tentacle. Tom ran with his gun held out, desperate to overtake them.

"Oh, God, please let her not die; please." He had no idea he was praying aloud.

Chapter 131

"Hey, Tom!" Gina yelled as Tom ran past the room where she and twenty eater children were hiding, "in here!"

Then a flung car crashed down on its side outside the window, completely blocking off view of the outside.

Gina, showered with dirt and detached rust, staggered back. Since leaving the beach, she'd hastily pulled on a red dress over her bikini. It made little difference to her general appearance—in true eater fashion, the dress was mostly holes, strips of dirty rotted cotton that swished about her like drapes.

Gina silently looked around at her charges. The twenty children she'd managed to bring inside looked back at her expectantly, yellow faces taut with fear, water-clear eyes frightened.

Across the room, she and Tom's three-month-old daughter Sofia was being minded by her teen sister Anita, who sat on a metal chair rocking the sleeping child.

Gina raised a warning finger to her lips. "No noise, you lot." With kids' lives at stake, she wasn't risking any gung-ho heroics.

She was relieved that even the youngest of the kids seemed to understand that this wasn't the time to be a pain in the ass.

Chapter 132

Tom and Megan reached the Farragut Road intersection. The row of vavs flinging things were mere feet ahead of them. Engrossed in repulsing the flamethrowers, consumed by fear of their primary enemy—fire—the plant women hadn't noticed Tom and Megan approach.

Megan pulled Tom down behind a palm. "Remember they're looking for *you*."

Tom regarded Megan. Though totally unselfconscious that her breasts were exposed, her expression was very strained, worried about the fire around.

He nodded. He *had* forgotten. If the vavs saw him, his rescue attempt was over.

He peered ahead through the giantesses' legs, to the beach. The vav dangling Gail stood by the bay, its crystal water a rippling mirror behind her. She'd now turned so she faced them. Tom recognized her as the vav Queen. She stood hands on her hips, swaying left to right, her face blissful. In her crotch, Gail kicked spastically, hands weakly beating against the Queen's tentacle.

Tom heaved a sigh of relief that she was still alive.

"She's draining her slowly," Megan said. "One queen killing another to show her power."

Unknowing, by facing them, the Queen had left herself open to a clear shot.

Tom sighted at her crotch.

Bang! Bang! Bang! Bang! Tom emptied the gun. With the noise everywhere, the shots sounded like snapping twigs.

The vav Queen's blissful expression instantly became one of incredible pain. Tom's four shots had severed her tentacle right at the opening of her vagina.

He stuck the gun in his belt.

Gail fell out of the Queen's crotch. She crashed to the ground, then—

Oh, hell no! Tom thought.

—rolled down a sand slope to wind up face down in the water.

Tom stared at Megan in horror.

"I don't think she's strong enough to turn over," Megan said. "We need—"

Tom didn't hear what Megan said next, he was already up and running for the beach.

Ahead of them, the vav Queen slowly knelt to the ground.

Chapter 133

The vavs were so perplexed by their queen's sudden shrieks of pain that they made no attempt to stop Tom and Megan as both rushed past them.

The pair sprinted past the writhing vav monarch, her beautiful face an agonized rictus.

Down, down to the water.

Tom splashed into the shallows. He grabbed Gail's shoulders, lifted her head out of the water, turned her face-up. Megan picked up Gail's legs. Together, they carried her up onto the sand.

Tom gaped into Gail's sightlessly staring eyes. He shook her. "Baby, baby, please, say something." The world faded from around him—his consciousness zoomed on her.

He unraveled the vaginal tentacle from around Gail's neck. The meat hook was sunk deep into her throat—a black sickle curving under her skin like a rib.

Tom stared at it helplessly.

"She's dead," Megan said softly, voicing his fear. "Empty. Her wound no longer bleeds."

Tom looked at Megan. He felt like he was dying inside—his heart felt like a stone in his chest. "Dead?" He fought down the hot tears bubbling up to his eyes. *Dead?* He looked down at Gail again. Her beautiful staring eyes, her small soft mouth . . . *dead?*

Tom looked out at the water-bound mensch, his gaze pleading, as if the giants were gods able to revive his beloved. The array of impassive white faces gave no hint they knew he watched them.

"We've got trouble," Megan said softly.

Tom looked down again. He turned, saw what she meant.

Several vavs had now gathered around their wounded queen. All were glaring angrily at Tom and Megan. Moody blues on beautiful white faces.

"We have to leave," Megan said. "They'll soon work out who you are."

Tom made to pick up Gail. Megan shook his arm. "Leave her."

"No."

"She's not going anywhere. We'll come back for her."

Tom let Gail fall back gently to the sand. He stared belligerently at the vavs. "Why aren't they attacking?"

"They're scared you'll shoot their vaginas too." She nudged him along the beach. "Our advantage to get away. Run! Before they get their courage back."

Chapter 134

They ran up the beach, past corpse after corpse. Their path diverted around the flaming remains of vavs who'd been racing for the water.

Megan was right: Scant moments later, the thunder of pursuing vav feet reached them.

They raced across the Head Island Causeway and William J. Day Blvd, through Marine Park—

Now there were additional pursuers; the vavs had summoned their sisters. More plant giantesses were advancing on them from the road.

—Burst through the trees onto Farragut Road—

"We're surrounded," Megan said.

"Not yet." Tom pointed. "There's a side door hidden behind that oak. The gap's too tight for the vavs to squeeze through."

—And charged across the road toward the eater camp quad.

Flames raged at the intersection on their right, thick smoke billowed from the streets beyond. The road was piled with the corpses of shredded eaters and burning vavs, along with incinerated dogs.

As they crossed, another wave of vavs emerged around the side of the building.

"They recognized you!" Megan yelled at Tom.

"Can't be helped." Seeing the mass of vavs after him, Tom's previous anger dissolved to grief. It was ludicrous that Gail was dead. *Because of me?*

His anguish boiled in his head as they reached the house and trees.

Running ahead of Megan, Tom leapt into the gap between oak and wall and opened the door. He turned back.

"Quick, in he—!"

He froze. Four vav meat hooks simultaneously hit Megan just as she reached the space. One dug itself deep in her right shoulder, two into her back. The fourth meat hook slung over her head, puncturing her left eye and anchoring itself in the eye socket.

Megan's mouth gaped in shock.

The vavs yanked on their tentacles.

Tom leapt and grabbed Megan's arms as she was pulled back. His mind replayed Lynn's recent death. He jerked the meat hook from Megan's left eye and flung it away.

The removal ripped the eye to shreds. White stuff like Styrofoam bubbled from the wound.

Megan twitched. "I am truth, about to be revealed," she groaned.

"Megan, help me free you!"

Megan made no attempt to get free. "You shall know me as I am!" she gasped. "In true impurity!"

Tom ignored her. The meat hook in the eye had clearly fucked up her brain. The white plastic foam was still spurting from her eye.

The vavs cautiously approached. Tom fought to unplug the black scythe embedded in Megan's shoulder.

He worked it free, but then another two meat hooks slammed into Megan. One in the waist. The second slammed into the top of her head, it's entire length disappearing into her brain.

"Sex is truth!" Megan yelped, then slumped as dead weight against Tom. "I am reborn as porn!"

Tom tensed, sensing what would happen next.

All four meat hooks were yanked out of Megan at once.

She literally blew apart. But not into meat—not even odd white-like-squid meat. No. Megan disintegrated into a mass of white fluff and sheets . . .

Sheets of paper.

Tom stared at her remains, as confused as the plant women by this odd turn of events. *Paper? She's made of paper?* Odder still, Megan's paper filling was covered with writing.

Fluttering fragments of the transsexual brunette were now blowing everywhere. The bemused vavs swatted the sheets of paper away like they were swatting flies. Megan's shattered head rolled away between the vav, trailing toilet paper brains.

Tom's confusion ebbed. He remembered the vavs were after *him*.

Megan's left forearm lay by Tom's feet. Paper stuck out of its severed end. He grabbed the arm and darted through the door, into the building.

Chapter 135

The side door led through a storeroom into a corridor. The corridor was empty. Soundless, as if all the eaters were dead.

Turning left, Tom padded quickly along it. Sad thoughts trailed him like vengeful ghosts. *But, why? I only wanted to remain here because of Gail, and now Gail's dead. And, and . . .* The memory of how his lover's corpse had looked threatened to derange Tom.

Why?

He lifted Megan's forearm, plucked a piece of paper from it. *Shit, even her bones?* He didn't read the writing; he dropped the sheet so it fluttered to the floor.

Half a color photograph now stuck out of the forearm. Tom ignored it. *And, what? Yes what?*

Megan's oddity sheened Tom's grief with just enough surreal gloss to enable him to still function. Maybe it was all just a dream.

Tom suddenly realized he was walking through a mass of tentacles. He stopped and looked around. The walls were covered with writhing thick green prehensile outgrowths that also punctured up through the floor and up through the ceiling. The tentacles throbbed like heartbeats.

He understood where he was. *I'm standing over the basement. But . . . Lynn's apartment is on the other side of the square—I thought she meant just her block's basement. She gave no inkling the transformation extended this far.*

The door opposite the basement door was open. He looked into the room. Its floor was an expanse of tentacles. Its outer windows were open. A vav's barky ass faced Tom.

He turned quickly back toward the basement door. *Oh, no. Not going down there.*

Then he became conscious of a commotion at the other end of the corridor. He turned and saw a screaming mob of eater children jostling out into the corridor.

Chapter 136

Gina watched in horror as two leafy hands lifted the crashed car away from the window. *Oh, heavens no!*

She looked around her at the roomful of children, dreading the worst.

Two vavs—a Brigitte Bardot and an Audrey Hepburn—peered in. Their expressions were cold, merciless. The smaller children began screaming. The Brigitte Bardot vav stretched in a hand to grab one of the older boys. Gina leapt at her, sinking her teeth into the giant brown creeper fingers. The vav gave a mute shriek of pain, then flung her off. Gina crashed to the floor then leapt up again. She wiped blood from her nose.

"Outside, outside!" she yelled at the children.

They rushed out. The Brigitte Bardot vav had now caught the boy she wanted, and was pulling him to the window. The kid was screaming blue murder.

Anita had vacated her steel chair. Carrying the slumbering Sofia in her arms, she was busy hurrying others out the door.

Gina grabbed the steel chair and leapt at the clutching vav hand. She smashed down the chair. Scowling, the giantess let the boy go.

"Go out," Gina told the boy. "Tell the others to wait for me."

Chair in hand, she stood poised between the scowling vavs and children while the room emptied. Then she exited herself, to find Tom running toward her.

Forgetting herself, and that he was Big Sister's property, she ran into his arms. She gripped him hard, drawing fresh strength from the feeling of his arms around her.

He pushed her gently away, kissed her cheek. At that moment, Gina realized that in his own way, Tom loved her, though she wasn't Gail.

Chapter 137

"What's that you're holding?"

Tom raised Megan's arm so Gina could see it clearly. "Don't even ask; it's a loooonng story."

He looked around at the children. The older ones carried the babies. The sea of young yellow faces was strained, their transparent eyes bulged with fear. The toddlers clustered around his legs, little fingers clasping his trousers tight.

He noticed Anita was again carrying he and Gina's daughter. What was her name again? Susanna, Serena? Ah yes, Sofia.

He was struck by sudden amusement.

Gina regarded him narrowly. "What the hell is funny?"

"According to you, about half of these children are mine."

Gina rolled her eyes. "Oh, brother. *Now* you're having paternity issues?" She looked earnestly into his eyes. "Tom, the vavs have killed everyone else. What do we do?"

"Yes, *everyone*," Tom agreed dully. "Gail's dead too. You're Big Sister now."

Gina suppressed the sudden thrill of 'Yes!' that went through her. This was neither the time nor place to gloat.

Tom, reminded of Gail's death, stared glumly at the children.

Gina slapped him. "Snap out of it! There's vavs trying to get in and kill these kids!" She pointed down the corridor at the barred side entrance.

He tucked his grief away, nodded at her earnest yellow face. He pushed open the door she'd exited from and peeped. Brigitte Bardot and Audrey Hepburn were still peering in. Behind them Sophia Loren, Ginger Rogers, and Lucille Ball stared angrily on.

He shut the door again.

"The safest place is down the basement," he said.

"The children can't enter there," Gina replied flatly. "I've been down there once. It's darker than night and dangerous as shit."

He thought a moment. "Here's what we'll do then. I'll lead the vavs away from you. There's two SUVs out in the quad, right?"

She nodded. "Yeah, Donny Q's Hummer and the ammo truck. Both were too heavy for the vav to throw around." She scowled. "I don't see—"

"Both are fueled and have the keys in them?"

"Yeah, we hit the dump yesterday."

"I'm going to call attention to myself now. Once you see the vavs pulling away from the house after me, cross the yard and load up the kids into Donny Q's Hummer. Then get lost. Head for the church where we held the funeral."

She nodded. "And you?"

"I'll meet you there once I can get out."

"Out?"

"I'll hide in the basement. You know the vav, once they're certain I'm underground, they'll forget everyone else and start digging."

She looked at him worriedly. "Are you sure this will work?"

"You got a better plan?"

"Not unless we can find a mindspider and negotiate with the murdering bitches."

"Gail already tried that. They murdered her."

Gina nodded. She leaned up and kissed Tom hard, her teeth clicking against his. "Take care of yourself, baby." There it was; she'd dared say it.

He smiled. "Remember the plan: wait till the vav move. Don't worry about me; the basements all interconnect, there have to be several other exits."

Gina nodded. "One comes up under Lynn's apartment." She turned to organize the children, then turned back to him. "Take care down there; it's fucked up like you wouldn't believe—like Bizarro come down to Earth."

He didn't hear her, he was already racing toward the last room, the one opposite the basement door.

Chapter 138

Tom opened the basement door.

Then he rushed through the opposite room's carpet of tentacles and peered out the window.

The vavs stood facing away from him, huddled in some sort of conversation.

Shit! There's hundreds of them.

He suspected every vav who'd come to the eater's camp was now on this side of the building.

"Yaaay!"

They spun around en-masse. Tom waved his hands out the window, swinging Megan's arm like a flag. "Hey, darlings, I'm over here! Your love doctor's here! The gynecologist is accepting patients." The words sounded inane, intensely daft to Tom's ears. He shrugged. *Hey, whatever works. As long as Gina gets the kids out safe.*

He found his actions odd. He'd never been family-oriented. Even now, Tom was unsure if he was saving the children because he felt they were innocents, or if it was because they were *his* children, or if because they represented the only legacy Gail had left him.

Memories of my love are children I didn't even have with her? Kids who aren't even human?

As one, the vavs walked toward Tom. He waited, checking to ensure none were additionally coming around the front of the apartment block, from the road Gina would have to take to escape.

Okay, here goes. Slowly, so the approaching vav wouldn't suspect anything, he backed out into the corridor and waved Gina away.

She nodded back. He watched to ensure she'd gotten the front door open and was hustling the eater kids through it, then turned back to the window.

A Greta Garbo was peering in at him. Behind her a multitude of gorgeous giant faces were ranged: Hedy Lamarr, Jayne Mansfield, Elizabeth Taylor, Ingrid Bergman, Mary Pickford, Jean Harlow, Ava Gardner, Loretta Young, Joan Collins, Lillian Gish, Kim Novak, Diana Dors, Shirley McLaine, Joan Fontaine, Louise Brooks, Clara Bow, Carole Landis, Olivia de Havilland, Claudette Colbert, Barbara Lawrence, Ella Raines, Sally Blane, Vivian Leigh . . . the faces went on in an endless duplication.

Tom was almost struck speechless by their beauty. *It's like a movie premiere out there. Okay, a murderess's movie premiere.*

He smiled. "Okay, ladies. Looks like it's just us now."

None made any attempt to attack him. They just stared, smiling. He found their looks interesting. *It's like they're love-struck. But with me?* He glanced at Rose. *Or with this?*

The Garbo stuck her hand into the window, seeking to touch him. Tom drew away from her thick brown creeper fingers. Like tentacles they swished in front of his face.

He heard the front door slam shut. *Okay, almost done here.* He retreated back to the door, then across the corridor to the basement door.

He pointed down. "I'll just be downstairs if you ladies need me." He kissed Rose and blew the kiss at them.

The foremost Garbo's grin altered to a scowl. She gripped the side of the window and ripped the concrete out of the wall.

Tom gaped at the hole. The steel in the concrete support had ripped like liquorice. His faux blasé attitude departed him like a startled mouse. *Shit! I never realized you chicks were this strong. Who the hell am I fooling? Didn't I just watch you throwing cars through the air like Frisbees?*

Tom faked calm. He lounged in the door. Opposite him, a Natalie Wood and two Grace Kelly vavs joined the Garbo in ripping the window to shreds. Concrete crumbled like plaster of Paris.

Tom imagined he heard a distant car start up.

Job done. Gripping Megan's arm tight, he hightailed it down the stairs.

Chapter 139

Outside in the deserted quadrangle, Gina skidded the child-full blue Hummer out of the quad. The vehicle crunched up over five burnt corpses onto East Broadway Street.

The kids screamed as the car slewed across the road. They were packed like sardines; on top of each other in every conceivable arrangement.

Gina ignored them all, including Sofia, who'd now woken and was bawling the loudest. She hit the brake, then sat quietly for a moment amidst the child pandemonium, staring down the clear line of asphalt facing her.

"Hold on, ya'll!" she growled.

Then she floored the pedal to the max.

The Hummer surged forward like ocean waves.

Part 9: Basement Jack

Contrary to Gina's assertion, the basement was well-lit. Tom had no idea how; there simply *was* light down here.

He stood on the bottom step and looked around.

Damn!

The basement was a tentacle forest. Green wavering prehensile appendages grew everywhere, exploding in an insane profusion up from the floor.

Sea anemones minus the sea, Tom thought. He was conscious that he mustn't dally; he needed to make his way across to the basement's far side. The sound of the vavs' demolition of the outside wall reached him loud and clear. He also realized that it would take them a while to reach him. *They have to destroy two more walls then rip up the floor too.*

The smell of the basement was of decay and mold, of rotted cardboard.

A twittering reached his ears. He spun left, saw a fist-sized white beetle scurrying into cover.

I can see why Gina's little charges wouldn't like it down here.

Additional tentacles dangled from the ceiling, knotting and unknotting like hangmen's nooses. Yet more tentacles grew out of the basement's support pillars.

The wall beside Tom (and what he could see of the one opposite) was a surface of constantly moving vegetable serpents.

The tentacles were wet and slick, dripping liquid on the floor. Interspersed with the clumps of writhing green were massive white fungi that blocked off his view.

Tom leapt over a puddle onto the floor, then set off to his right, between the tentacles. To his relief, those in his path recoiled on his approach. The basement fauna grew in no fixed arrangement, meaning there was no clear route through the space. Tom turned left and right as each fresh obstruction dictated.

He brandished Megan's forearm like a club. With his gun empty, it was his only potential weapon.

Something fell from the ceiling, splashed into the water. He leapt back, looked down. It was another white beetle, this one larger than the first. The beetle was on its back. It kicked futilely, trying to turn over. The bug reminded Tom of Big Sister Cassie, Gail's predecessor. It looked exactly like she had after Lynn hexed her.

He remembered then how the transformed Cassie-bug had turned her son into a meat-football.

Shuddering he stepped over the kicking bug.

Another clump of tentacles faced him. He stepped around them and wound up facing a wall.

He winced, realizing that he'd lost his way. He looked around, searching for the stairs. He couldn't locate them—the tentacles rose too high, fell too low.

Worse still, the basement seemed to extend farther than he remembered. Like it now continued beyond the boundaries of the quadrangle.

He could also no longer hear the vavs breaking down the wall to reach him.

That's a relief; but where the hell am I?

Tom set out again. This time he walked beside the wall. After ten yards, a thick clump of tentacles halted his progress. He turned left and walked to their end, walked around them, then headed back for the wall. A huge mushroom now blocked his path. He detoured around it. Back at the wall again, Tom now found no sign of the clump of tentacles he'd been avoiding in the first place.

He traced the wall again, with the same result. Five yards into his trek, a huge fungus forced a detour that left him as lost as before. Still there was no sign of the stairway, or sound of smashing concrete. Walking away from the wall had the same result. Like he was in a maze that looped on itself.

Understanding hit Tom. *It's magic. I'm stuck inside a side effect of Lynn's hex. Didn't she say the basement began altering after Cassie-bug was banished down here? Shit. Okay, now how do I get out of here?*

A short distance ahead of Tom was a brown fungal mound. He walked over and sat on it.

Chapter 141

Tom stared around the surrounding walls of pulsing tentacles, then down at Megan's forearm, now resting in his lap. Now that there was no chance of his immediate capture (as far as he could tell), Tom permitted his sense of the surreal to override his sense of danger. Grief—images of Gail dead—sneaked into his thoughts; he forcibly evicted them, concentrating on the puzzle the arm presented.

Megan was made of paper? That's why she didn't bleed, and why she burnt. How can anyone be made of paper? She looked normal. He stared at Rose, remembering the vagina in his hand for the first time since the breakdown of everything. *She fucked normal too, and she ejaculated. How the hell is that even possible? Rock-hard paper transsexual cock came in me?*

The hand he held, externally seemed flesh and blood. Like her penis had in Rose. Like Megan had . . . Megan had never seemed less than a total woman.

He turned the white arm over. Its pale perfect hand, with its pampered fingers, feather-soft palm, green fingernails. He sniffed it. The dead transsexual invaded his nostrils as a goddess of scent. Semen and roses, shit and spittle, sweat and hairspray. Mingled male and female musk. A combination of human smells more animal than spirit.

Tom sat bemused for awhile. Then he reached into Megan's arm and pulled out the photograph half-stuck in it. Once he had it out, he found it was actually two pictures.

He gaped at the top photo. An image of a spiky-haired punk chick sitting on a chair with her skirt rucked up and stuffing a cucumber into her vagina. Her expression was manic. A red magic-marker caption read: 'Josie Kutchner feeding her vegan vagina.'

Tom stared at the odd image a long moment. Then he looked at the bottom photograph. The same woman—no, a twin, the hair was different, the facial expression less drug-infused—in a business suit was feeding a sausage into her vagina. 'Ali Kutchner feeding her carnivorous vagina' was the caption.

He nodded sagely, and placed the pictures in his lap. *Twins with a similar affliction.*

Tom now carefully unpacked the rest of the paper in Megan's arm. The arm deflated, looking like a glove for a woman with a severed hand.

The extracted papers were covered with large writing. He smoothed them out. Megan's two forearm bones were rolled sheaves of photographs. He smoothed these out too. Placing the pictures under the papers, he began reading:

'Love is the payment for sex. Sex is the payment for love.'

'Love is never free. It's an emotional commodity, on auction to the highest bidder. But it's like poker too, you can bluff yourself to the pot; something many people are expert at.

You can buy love; all you need do is offer the payment the seller wants.

Money, sex, class—the smell of exclusivity, or simply bragging rights—all are perfectly valid currency in the emotional marketplace.'

'Between her thighs is a great magic, a mind-control device no man can resist. Except they're homosexual of course.'

'There is no racism in vagina, all women are pink and wet where it matters. If you're a woman, no matter your sexuality or ideology, at some point in your life, your feet will be spread wide apart up in the air in a bed somewhere.'

'Butthole; why is it called that? It is the 'but' hole, the unholy one. First, it voids our waste: what exits it stinks, we want nothing to do with it; and also, we want everything to do with it—we want to go where no man naturally should.

Then it's dark, like a cave; we wonder what wicked secrets it hides.'

'Drinking cum is like taking medicine—the more you swallow the healthier you'll be. Three times a day is what Dr. Fuck recommends.'

'Pleasure and pressure are the same. Coercion is a function of the brain. Rape is a state of mind; it will be defeated by a mind that doesn't recognize it.'

There was more; a whole lot more:

'And If I'd asked you to shit in my mouth instead of using the toilet? Why not? In a loving relationship there are no limits, no taboos—only

bodies enshrined, cocooned in mutual trust. Except you told, who'd ever know I ate your excrement? A little toothpaste and we're back to normal.'

'Sex is war. To lust is to plan a murder. To fuck someone is to kill them. To make them come is to destroy them, to make them crave your body—to obliterate their individuality.'

'The vagina is the primary organ of female intuition. Being fucked a lot makes them extra sensitive.'

'Love makes you another's slave. But it is a delicious slavery, full of passion, pleasure, and pain—everything that makes life worthwhile.'

'You must be careful around her. Otherwise, her pussy power will overcome you. Or maybe, you'll be dominant, and penis power— penetrative procreative persuasion—will triumph in your battle of the sexes.'

As Tom read on and on, a clear picture of Megan formed in him:

The trembling painful pleasure/orgasm of the bleeding deflowered virgin, the jaded satiation of the double-fisted geriatric whore, Megan was both extremes and all in-between. S and M, sex without end, and so much more than mortal mind could comprehend. Thoughts to make the Marquis de Sade run insane. This was Megan.

'A vagina is an empire of piss, an anus a kingdom of shit—Neither is pure, both are the abyss, bottomless pits.'

'There is sex, then there is the conception of sex, which is merely a mental construct, where (for want of a better word) a fetish—either an object, a sensation, or a person—is required to sheen the sexual process, to provide additional 'dirtiness,' or 'kinkiness,' over the orgasm. The fact that orgasms are not kept in memory is invalid here; what is important is the memory of having done what one did during the sextreme encounter.'

'My anus is mine and mine alone, but I'll lend it to you if you're hard as a bone.'

'I have an addiction to penetrative friction.'

447

'The pleasure of an orgasm must never be measured against public opinion as to its propriety.'

'Vaginas are vampires leeching manseed into childfields.'

'Oh, to bathe, to swim, and finally, to drown in my lover's cum.'

Then Tom *understood*. Megan was a mass of thoughts and concepts. Not a person but . . . The word made flesh? Maybe. But whose word? Definitely not God's. There was no religion in here, no truth other than a deviant/perverted/defiant understanding of flesh as a source of pleasure; the schematic of a sexual realm where there was no difference between absolute selfishness and giving oneself utterly to the other.

***

He examined the photographs. All depicted sex—people fucking hard.

There were several glossy prints of Megan screwing Tom's hand. Two of her being fucked by Harding. One of her sucking both the cop's cocks simultaneously. One of Megan fucking Harding doggy-style, his eyes glazed with ecstasy.

Most pictures, however, didn't involve Megan. They showed women and men having sex of the kinkiest, most perverted sort. A man with two fists up the ass of a bound pissing woman. A woman screwing a horse, cum flooding from her vagina. A man being sodomized by a horse whilst he blew a goat. A man and woman covered with bleeding wounds and holding knives performing sixty-nine on each other. A woman using a severed hand as a sex toy. A fat boy fellating a pig . . .

Each photograph was more extreme than the previous. A disgustingly obese woman fisting a screaming little girl whilst scooping out her eyes with a spoon. Another man fucking a dead toddler while a Doberman ate its head. A withered old woman sucking the cock of a man with severed arms and legs, and whose head had been popped in a vise, so his brains had spilled over his face. A lesbian foursome—three women wearing strap-ons fucking another who was bleeding copiously from all three holes.

Tom doggedly thumbed through, just managing to keep from puking.

The pictures became 'normal' again. Two men performing sixty-nine. Two mating pigs. Megan screwing Rose inside Mount Choc. A dreamlike image of King Eric the Young in his throne room surrounded by nude blondes with humongous breasts from one of which he was filling a glass with milk. Pam 'Longneck' Andersen giving herself head. A woman with an entire foot in her vagina . . .

The implication of these pictures forming Megan's bones wasn't lost on Tom: At her core, the late Megan Fox had been nothing but sex. Raw sex, without any conception of 'right' or 'wrong.' Sex in word and image, in thought and deed.

Tom put the pictures and papers down. He now had a painful erection. He was disgusted at himself for being turned on by the images he'd just viewed; but then, he'd found Megan attractive in person.

He looked around. The surrounding, obstructing, direction-obliterating tentacles seemed to have increased in profusion.

I need to leave this place, but how?

His eyes fell on the top photograph of the pile—Megan fucking Rose. Tom was surprised he'd not considered that. He unzipped his fly. *I need to deflate this bed zeppelin anyway.*

He spat on his cock, then slid it into his left palm. The vagina spread like a flower, greedily accepting the penetration. Tom felt the oddity of his penis sliding up into his forearm. Then pleasure flooded him like water.

He leaned back on the fungus and fucked himself silly.

Chapter 142

Tom ejaculated into Rose. It felt like his semen was streaming up into his heart and being pumped around his body.

"Oh, Tommy honey," the vagina gushed when he withdrew from it, "You're the absolute best." It groaned delicately. "What do you want to know, darling?"

"Rose, I'm lost. Tentacles everywhere I turn. How do I get out of here?"

Rose laughed. "You know Tom, I do love you."

"Yes, yes, and I love you too. You know that. But how—"

"I'd like us to become one."

Tom stared at the vagina in his hand. "It's better we discuss this later."

"No." Rose's labia pouted tight with displeasure.

Tom sighed. He already regretted having sex with it. *I should have kept searching. An exit has to be around here somewhere.*

"Okay," he said. "I'm listening. But make it fast, the vavs are after me."

"Okay, darling. Keep stroking my clitoris so I don't fall asleep on you."

Tom felt foolish tickling the base of his left index finger, while Rose giggled beneath it. The vagina yawned wide, its walls smeared with his semen. Some flowed out into his palm.

"What I mean is—Lynn's dead and I feel lonely. I need you to be a permanent part of me."

"But *I am* part of you." He didn't enquire how it knew Lynn was dead.

"Not like that. *I'm* currently *part of you*. It should be the other way around, you as part of *me*."

Tom was bemused. "'Vagina with man attached' is an odd concept."

"Sexist reasoning. Gender discrimination. Wives are 'penis with woman attached'."

"Rose, you're not a woman, you're a fuck appendage."

"I'm a woman's essence—what separates her oppressed sex from you patriarchal male chauvi—"

"Screw your reverse logic. For your info, it swings both ways; husbands are really 'vagina with man attached.'"

Rose didn't reply. It pouted again under Tom's rubbing finger. He rolled his eyes at it.

450

(A football-sized white beetle nudged Tom's shoe. He kicked it away in irritation. It slammed into a grove of tentacles, which caught it and proceeded to rip it apart.)

"Okay, okay, so you feel marginalized being on my hand. Where is all this leading? We've never had this problem before."

The vagina's lips curved into an almost human smile. "The vavs love me, you know. 'Almighty Vagina,' is how they refer to me. They think I'm God. They pray to me."

Tom gaped at it. "I never knew that."

"Lynn did. They kept asking her to hand me over so they could worship me, and she refused. She was scared of being killed, she said."

He frowned. "Hold on a minute. Was this *before* I left for the other Boston?"

"Yes, certainly. They never wanted you, just me."

Tom regarded Rose, wondering if it was lying. "You're telling me I could have been rid of you for good if Lynn wasn't so paranoid? That Gail would still be alive?"

"I don't like your tone of voice. You make me sound like a parasite."

"What the . . . ? Rose, Gail fucking died over you! Lynn died. Everyone's dead except Gina and a carload of kids, and I'm not sure *they* made it out alive!"

"Oh, I didn't know that. I'm sorry."

"And now you're saying *none* of the deaths was necessary!?"

"Truth, Tommy, I didn't know. I'm sorry."

It sounded honestly contrite. Tom nodded. "Okay, it's not your fault. You've been good to me, Rose, and I appreciate it. I'm sorry too."

The vagina 'smiled' again. "Make-up sex?"

"Maybe later."

"Okay."

"Now, what do you really want?"

"I already feel better now I've gotten that off my G-spot. You know how it is, when you've got all this emotion bottled up inside you like menstrual blood? When you feel like you're just being used and discarded like a tampon?"

"Yeah, occasionally."

Rose laughed. "I'm delighted you understand, Tommy darling. I feel so hostile sometimes, I wish I was an anus so I could shit on everyone." It giggled. "I don't mind being part of you, you know. But it's really time for a change now."

What is this stupid sex organ yapping on about? He calmed himself. "Sorry, I'm under great strain now, and—"

"Another quick fuck might help. You rubbing my clit has me all buzzy. If you penetrate me, we'll cum real quick."

"No, no. Not that sort of strain. I'm getting worried. I can't remain down here forever. The vavs will find me. Gina will also be waiting for me at the Gate of Heaven church. Where's the exit?"

"Oh, sorry. I'd forgotten." A brief pause. "Go left. Walk straight, then turn right. You'll meet someone who knows the way out."

"There's someone else down here?"

"You're not the first person to get lost down here."

"Who is it?"

"Just some kid."

Tom thought he detected a note of cunning in Rose's voice, something he'd never heard before. He decided he'd just imagined it.

"Thanks," he said.

"You're welcome. And since you're not ready to fuck me again, you can stop rubbing my clitoris now."

"I need to take a crap."

"Remember to wipe with your *right* hand."

He shat beside the mound, afterwards using Megan's papers to wipe clean. *Okay, this is sick,* he thought, *I'm actually wiping my ass with Megan?*

Chapter 143

Tom found the child Rose had mentioned.

A little blonde girl stuck into a white fungus. She was embedded deep into the white surface, her feet well off the floor. She seemed glued into it—it had grown over her clothes.

She gazed plaintively at Tom. "Help me, mister. Please, help me."

Tom nodded. "How did you get down here?"

"The eaters caught me and my family. I escaped while they were eating my mother."

She began crying. He moved closer and stroked her cheek. "There, there, it's okay now."

She smiled at him. "You really mean that, mister?"

He nodded. "Someone said you know the way out of here. Is that true?"

She nodded slyly. "But if I tell you, you'll leave me behind here."

"No I won't. We'll go together. Promise."

She grinned. "Okay then." Then her expression turned curious. "Say, mister; why'd you have a peepee on your hand?"

Tom realized she was talking about Rose. He grinned with embarrassment. "A woman lent it to—"

"Fuck, fuck!" the little girl screamed suddenly.

Tom gaped at her. "What?"

"Fuck! Gonna fuck you!" The voice was now an adult's.

She was already changing, her pink skin bleaching to a pale white. She was also getting larger and fatter, her face filling out to a florid mass of fat, with huge faceted orange eyes.

The fungus she was embedded into slowly reshaped itself into a shell. Her legs grew longer so her feet touched the ground. Four more jointed appendages popped out of her sides.

Tom gaped. "Big Sister Cassie?" With a sinking feeling, he understood that Rose had deceived him. Betrayed him.

Fuck! Now that Lynn's dead, it's no longer loyal to me!

As confirmation, twin metal tentacles erupted from the bug-woman's nipples. Dripping with black fluid, they flew at Tom.

"Fuuukkkkk Youuuuu!"

In a surge of panic, Tom turned and ran, sprinting left. He ran so fast it felt like he was flying. He looked back once, saw that the monstrous bug-woman was hot on his heels, her orange eyes aglow with insane lust. Her purple tongue looked infected.

"Sex you! Sex, sex, sex man! Right now, now! Noooooowwww!"

She was gaining on Tom. He felt one of her appendages touch his neck. Hot and wet. With a final burst of speed he turned around a clump of tentacles and ran straight into a wall, only just managing to stop before he knocked himself senseless.

Like white on rice, Big Sister Cassie was on him in an instant. She grabbed both his heels and pulled him off his feet.

Tom slammed down face-first onto the wet floor. His head cracked hard on the concrete, stunning him.

Cassie turned Tom over and began ripping off his clothes. In a rush, she stripped him completely naked, flinging his clothes out of sight over the tentacle bushes.

Then she lowered her massive insect bulk down on him. "Aah . . . fuck you," she moaned softly. "Yesss, lovely fuck!"

***

Tom felt a horrendous pain in his belly. Then another. The pain instantly wiped the daze from his mind. He gaped down at his naked body.

"Hell no!"

Cassie's metal nipple-tentacles were stuck into his belly. Blood spurted from the punctures in Tom's skin as she slid them in and out of him. Her expression was of the deepest lust.

"Cumming!"

Tom writhed in agony. He struggled to get up, but wasn't allowed the opportunity. With a sudden grunt, Cassie began spurting into him.

Tom felt her emission fill him up. His belly swelled.

"Stop it!"

His belly was now expanding monstrously, like it was being inflated with air. Like he was about delivering sextuplets. Black goo like an oil spill began spurting out of the punctures along with the blood.

Just when Tom felt he'd burst from what she was pumping into his belly, Big Sister Cassie gave a sigh of pleasure and yanked out her nipple tentacles.

Her horrible fat face grinned at Tom. "Lovely . . . ss . . . sex. Was it goo . . . goo . . . good for you tt . . . too, baby?"

Then she fell over on her back, dead.

Tom tried to get up, but couldn't, his belly felt packed with rocks. It rooted him to the floor like cement. He pushed on it to expel the cum/liquid inside him, but the wound had sealed over.

He lay in a wet puddle while the tentacles stroked his body.

His mind was becoming dull. He felt an odd buzzing in his left palm, and raised it to his face to see. He watched with surprise as Rose now slithered through his flesh, moving from his hand up into his arm.

Horrified and confused, Tom watched the vagina's progress. Sailing like a boat through his flesh, it travelled up his arm to his shoulder, and then down across his chest into his bulging belly. It situated itself on his navel and grew bigger, becoming a monster slit that extended up through Tom's chest and down into his crotch.

Fuck, Tom thought weakly. Thinking had become a chore, replaced by an odd desire to be penetrated.

He looked across at the dead Cassie-bug, now dissolving into a white sludge.

Tom suddenly became aware of a new note to his own transformation. He looked back at himself in dull alarm. His legs were shortening at speed into his crotch, as were his arms into his shoulders. His head and face shrunk into his neck and disappeared.

His head, limbs and penis vanished totally into the slit white oblong he'd become. His internal organs all popped out, then transformed into humongous female labia.

I have become . . . no . . . I am Vagina, Tom suddenly understood, *Vagina Almighty.* Then his thoughts extinguished for good.

Chapter 144

Vagina formed. Vagina became self-aware.

As Big Sister Cassie's remains dissolved into goo, so the hex on the basement dissolved also. The tentacles shrunk back into the concrete, the white fungus all evaporated, the white beetles broke down to powder.

The basement once again became an ordinary space. Four walls and support pillars. Both the entrance Tom had taken in, and his proposed exit were clearly visible.

The vavs suddenly found themselves able to pull up the concrete floor that had previously kept repairing itself.

Chapter 145

The vavs found the massive vagina. Vagina was already packed with green goo. It was a white man-sized meat-football with a musky-scented four-feet-long slit down one side.

The vav considered Vagina's perfect lips, the massive perfect clitoris, the curly brown pubic hair (that had recently been Tom's hair), the deep orifice that clearly went deeper than the oblong it occupied.

Vagina commanded respect.

The vavs sighed with communal pleasure, joy that lit up their beautiful faces.

Vagina spoke in the vavs' minds—a radio blast like arousal. "Kneel and worship me, vavs."

Almost orgasming from the divine communion, the vavs bowed, then knelt before Vagina. Vagina was beautiful beyond belief, truly a divine orifice. But a question was in all their minds: *Does She have the power?*

"Worship me," Vagina growled at the vavs. "Revere and adore me, for I am your God, the triumph of the female sexual principle over the male. Tom is no more!"

"Tom is no more!" the vavs screamed in mental unison. "Vagina is all!"

"I will prove my divinity to you," Vagina said into the vavs' minds. "Take me down to the beach to your wounded queen, and I will heal her tentacle."

Enraptured, the plant giantesses picked Vagina up and bore Her speedily off. Out of the basement, out of the building, down to the beach where the vav Queen writhed in agony.

The vavs began searching for the severed part of the Queen's vaginal tentacle.

A 'Jean Harlow' sighted it in the shallows. In her rush to reach it, she trampled Gail's head into the sand, shattering it open, mushing her brains.

The vav carried the tentacle and meat hook to the writhing queen and placed both severed ends together.

"Smear her with my jelly," Vagina commanded.

A Fay Wray vav quickly smeared the join with a scooping of Vagina's goop.

The royal tentacle was instantly, seamlessly, healed.

"See?" Vagina said, "I am your God, your true God."

The vavs burst into silent applause.

They carried Vagina aloft, and danced and jubilated all the way home to Castle Island, to install Her as God in the golden palace and worship Her forever more.

Their silent song rolled in the ether:

"Worship Vagina, that men cheer and jeer,
The complementary hole every penis fears.
From which no man escapes, ever-strong despite rape,
The secret burrow of the trouser snake.
Cunning and wise, you grip like a vise.
The ultimate pleasure, the ultimate pain,
Cum, babies, blood; glory and shame.
Sweet odor eternal, hymens so vernal,
Child-abused pussy, feminist hussy.
Sinner and saint, pink like fresh paint,
Worship Vagina, for She is King.

Almighty Cunt, the route out to life,
Perfect penis pathway, both slack and tight.
Slippery with semen, beloved of he-men,
Revered by she-men, proclaimed by Femen.
Addictive as crack, lick Her with tact,
Spread the soft ass, tongue deep in the gash, respect Her like cash.
Lips like pink wings, birdsong She sings,
Once She's licked right.

Almighty Cunt, the hidden truth,
Man's true religion, needing no proof.
Unstoppable object, immovable force,
Scorned you are venom more evil that war.
Paradise lust, Heaven unbound,
Asses to asses, pussy profound.
Pleasure like death, flesh mother earth,
You kill the erection, then grant it rebirth.

Almighty Vagina, Almighty Vagina,
None is beyond Her, none came before Her,
Nothing is like Her, all cum inside Her,
None will succeed Her, nor supersede Her,

Worship Her all, praise Her or fall."

Behind the dancing, jubilant vavs, Gail Harding's corpse lay unnoticed on the beach, her brains spread across the sand like butter on toast.

Beyond Gail, out in the bay, the mensch watched from the water, all their eyes open now. They were very pleased.

Endings

I

Monica Dawn, the Boston EMS coroner, was a tall fleshy woman with long curly auburn hair. Middle-aged and handsome, but with an overly serious face. A devoted wife and mother of two, with a loving husband.

Monica Dawn liked fucking corpses.

Her necrophilia had built up slowly through her years of working with dead bodies. Initially she'd felt repugnance, deep disgust at the endless stream of death she was forced to autopsy. In those early years, many times she'd leave the morgue, claiming she needed to pee, and puke her guts out in the ladies' room.

But slowly, death had moved from being an unliked acquaintance to a good friend, and then, when boredom with her work set in, it became her extra-marital affair.

Monica's husband Donald was loving but unimaginative. Their sex life was a pleasantly predictable procession of orgasms. They lay in bed, gave each other head, she came; two days later they did it again.

Her children, a boy and a girl, were both well behaved. No teen rebels to have her pulling out her hair. There was nothing in her world to bother her, but that also meant there was nothing to excite her.

Except the stiffs she worked with.

Her necro-eroticism had crept up on her unawares. One night, with the lab empty, finishing up the autopsy on a teen gang member who'd had his throat slashed, Monica had found herself wondering what it would feel like to suck his cock.

What a silly thought, had been her first response.

She'd finished sewing up the y-section and returned the body to its locker, in a hurry to meet Donald for dinner at The Oceanaire.

She'd been unable to leave, however. She sat in her Honda SUV in the parking lot, her head full of a vision of her lips wrapped around the dead boy's withered penis. As the images flooded her head, her vagina moistened.

What the hell is wrong with me? She wondered, horrified. *Stop this nonsense. I'm leaving here right now!*

But she hadn't left. Instead, filled with a lust that had her knees wobbling, Monica reentered the hospital. Informing the security guards that she'd forgotten her purse, she returned to the morgue.

And once there, Monica Dawn had sucked the dead teen's cock for thirty minutes, simultaneously masturbating herself to a series of orgasms, the glory of which flooded her vagina with juice.

Then she'd cleaned herself up and met her husband for dinner.

"You look especially well today," Donald had joked, "found a young lover?"

Monica had flushed with embarrassment. "Don't tease me darling; who'd want aging me?"

But it was true: she did feel wonderful. She'd found what had been missing in her life.

***

Tonight, Monica got out the woman she called her 'girlfriend special,' Lynn Harriet Jones, aged twenty-eight, cashier at the State Street Citizen's Bank. Brought in three months ago. Cause of death: Suicide – Single gunshot wound to the head.

Monica wondered at people's behavior. This woman for instance: crazy bitch had shot herself in the head while giving a blowjob. And she'd waited till the last moment, too: her throat had been splattered with the guy's cum.

Lynn's corpse had refused to decay. Monica had insisted on keeping it for study. Her other reason for holding onto it—other than to screw it— was its strange lack of a vagina.

"An incredible medical occurrence," she told people, "all she's got down there is a little hole to pee through. No clitoris even."

"She must fucking *love* anal," a female colleague joked.

"Amusingly, her womb's intact. There's just no access way leading to it."

The colleague wrinkled her nose. "How the hell did she menstruate with no hole?"

"She didn't, that's the whole point."

"Whew, that in itself is enough reason to off herself."

Now, Monica arranged Lynn as she liked her best—on her side with her white buttocks sticking out over the edge of the mortuary cart. This way she had unrestricted access to Lynn's anus. *North, South, slide it in her mouth, East, West, asshole's best,*

464

Seeing the dead woman arrayed like that, her anus slack from Monica's previous use, the bullet wound in her head like a floral explosion, had Monica so hot she almost came from the sight alone. *She-it, my clit feels like it's burning!*

Monica quickly removed her clothes. She draped them over a chair, then strapped on her pink femme cock. She greased the dildo with Vaseline and pushed it up Lynn's anus.

She fucked the corpse violently. *Woman's dead, no need for consideration.* While pumping her ass, she played with Lynn's breasts. She slid excited fingers over the corpse's bone-white skin, dipping them into the bullet hole and caressing the destroyed brain.

She felt her orgasm coming on fast. She removed her hand from caressing Lynn's toes, slid a finger under the strap-on harness. She flung her head back with the additional pleasure, her reddish-brown curls swirling round her head like sea waves.

She had her first orgasm. *Oh fuck!* The waves of sensation flooded Monica. She forgot fingering herself and grabbed Lynn's cold backside with both hands and pumped hard. Her first orgasm melted into a second one. Monica let go of Lynn's ass, and grabbed her own breasts, squeezing them hard. She slid the dildo in and out of Lynn's rectum with a steady rhythm.

She turned Lynn around so she lay crosswise on the cart, then raised her left leg up (draping it over her own shoulder) to penetrate her more deeply.

A boat of warning sailed over Monica's sea of pleasure. *I need to be careful. Donald will likely want sex tonight, I can't be too tired for him. Okay, I'll have one more cum, then I'm done.* She stroked Lynn's cold dead face, said aloud, "But, honey, you're so damn beautiful, I could fuck you all night long."

Then she noticed that the bullet wound in Lynn's head was closing up.

Monica froze in shock, her strap-on deep in Lynn's rectum. Paralyzed by fear and disbelief, she watched Lynn's head finish repairing itself, watched the corpse's y-section become uncut skin again. Felt her icy skin grow warmer.

Monica glanced down between Lynn's legs. She shuddered with fear: Lynn now had a vagina.

Lynn sneezed, then opened her eyes. She stared at Monica in confusion, then felt herself between her legs.

Monica was still unable to move. *What's going on!?* her mind screamed at her.

The recently dead woman glared at Monica, her green eyes enraged. "What the hell do you think you're doing?"

"Oh, holy shit!" Monica gasped.

Lynn nodded coldly. "Well, you're in my asshole, which qualifies you as a piece of shit. But you definitely aren't holy."

Monica fainted. She slumped to the morgue floor, her pink femme cock loudly popping out of Lynn's anus.

Lynn sat up. Her anus hurt like a knee scraped on concrete. She scowled down at Monica. *For exactly how long have you been raping me?*

Then she ignored the pain and grinned down at her vagina. "Welcome home, Rose. For good this time."

Lynn got down off the mortuary cart. Ass smarting, She walked over to the chair with Monica's clothes. She looked down at the unconscious woman. "I'm leaving you just your strap-on, you necrophile rapist bitch. Serves you right when you get fired."

Lynn pulled Monica's shoes off her feet. Then she dressed in the coroner's clothes and left the morgue.

Wow, I really need to think up a good reason for not being at work all this while, she thought, heels clicking along the hospital's dim nighttime corridors.

466

II

Boston 2: South End; Late Evening.

The kids were hungry.

Gina frowned. *Now the excitement of their flight from the vavs has worn off their little bellies remember food.*

They were in the woods on the corner of Melnea Cass Boulevard and Washington Streets, the blue Hummer concealed in a grove of trees. Above was open sky. To their north, far beyond Ramsay Park, Central Boston's skyscrapers penetrated Bizarro like concrete erections.

Every now and then, the sound of a passing car blew through the trees. *The kids need food,* Gina thought.

She opened Donny Q's glove compartment, took out the pistol there.

"I'm going hunting," she told Anita, "keep everyone out of trouble."

"Okay, sis."

Leaving the kids, Gina stalked through the trees, emerging on Washington Street. She knew this part of the city well. Before the eater virus transformed her, she'd worked at Orinoco, a popular Venezuelan eatery up around the corner on Shawmut Avenue.

Gina was relieved. She and the children were safe. All twenty of them. She now needed a place to hide everyone, but that wouldn't be too hard. She'd find somewhere. She suspected they might even return home to the Pleasure Bay camp someday.

Gina was sad that Tom hadn't joined them. She suspected he was dead. Sorrow pierced her breast like an arrow. She winced. *He died saving us.* Or if he wasn't dead . . . then the vavs had caught him. Her sunflower-colored face flushed pink; impotent anger surged in her breast. Either way she'd lost out. *Sheeeiiitt! Damn those plant bitches!*

She squatted in the bushes bordering the road and waited.

A short while later, she heard a motorbike approaching up along Washington Street. She smiled as the rider came into view. A Boston cop, riding slow, likely watching for eaters like herself. He was taking the breeze, his helmet off and in his lap.

She licked her yellow lips with her yellow tongue, then drew a bead on his head and fired.

The cop's head jerked back. His body went slack on the bike. He and it careered off the road, crashing into a tree ten meters ahead of Gina.

She was up in a flash. After checking that no one else was approaching, she rushed up the road.

The crashed bike was smoking like it might explode.

She checked the cop, whose eyes now stared sightlessly upward. He was young and dead, a small entrance hole above his right eye partnered a large brain-dripping one in the back of his head.

Gina licked her lips again. Her meat lust was tinged with regret. *Wow, he's really handsome. Too bad he'll never have a chance to get me pregnant.*

Then she looked towards central Boston and grinned. *There's lots of other tasty guys in there. Hot bodies galore.*

She dragged the cop's corpse through the trees, over to the parked Hummer.

"Okay," she called out to the kids. "Dinner is served. Help yourselves, but don't make a mess."

The eater children covered the dead policeman like yellow rats, like a swarm of ants. They ripped off his clothes and ate him, ravenously biting chunks out of his flesh with their diamond-like teeth.

Big Sister Gina supervised them with a proud, maternal eye.

III

Boston 2: Techxas

Far away in the Lone-Star State, on the outskirts of Abilene, a swirling mass of paper and photographs slowly began forming into a beautiful middle-aged brunette.

The End.

About the Author

Wol-vriey is Nigerian, and quite tall.

He currently resides in a state of uneasy stalemate with his threatening-to-thin-beyond-redemption hair, and believes there actually are things that go bump in the night.

Wol-vriey recycles the ridiculous into reasonable reality for the reader.

His WEIRRRD philosophy?

WEIRRRD = Warp/Write Everything into Realistic Ridiculous Readable Distorted Dream Dimension Descriptions.

Wol-vriey blogs at:

http://oddityfarm.wordpress.com

OTHER GREAT TITLES FROM

Burning Bulb

PUBLISHING

WWW.BURNINGBULBPUBLISHING.COM

ANTHOLOGIES
BIZARRO AND TRANSGRESSIVE FICTION

THE BIG BOOK OF BIZARRO

The Big Book of Bizarro brings together the peculiar prose of an international cast of the most grotesquely gonzo, genre-grinding modern writers who ever put pen to paper (or mouse to pad), including:

NIGHT OF THE LIVING DEAD horror writers John Russo & George Kosana; HUSTLER MAGAZINE erotica contributors Eva Hore, Andrée Lachapelle, & J. Troy Seate and established Bizarro genre authors D. Harlan Wilson, William Pauley III, Wol-vriey, Laird Long, Richard Godwin and so many more!

From Alien abductions to Zombie sex, The Big Book of Bizarro contains OVER FIFTY STORIES of the most outré-landish transgressive fiction that you'll ever lay your capricious and curious hands upon!

WARNING: This book may be one of the most controversial and dangerous books you'll ever read.

WESTWARD HOES

Nine outlaw writers rode into town from obscurity to pen nine tantalizing tales of horror and fantasy, and leaving once they branded their own personal marks on the weird western genre and became living legends of the American Frontier experience.

Like drunken Indian scouts, the writers fervidly tracked down and captured the Western genre, tore off its fashionable veneer and ravished its exposed essence.

So belly up to the bar with your favorite soiled dove and enjoy perusing these thrilling tales of Old West debauchery, danger and desire; compiled by the publisher of The Big Book of Bizarro and featuring the bizarro novella Big Trouble in Little Ass by Wol-vriey.

Burning Bulb
PUBLISHING

ANTHOLOGIES
BIZARRO AND TRANSGRESSIVE FICTION

THE BIG BOOK OF BIZARRO SPECIAL KINDLE EDITIONS

GARY LEE VINCENT'S
DARKENED
THE WEST VIRGINIA VAMPIRE SERIES

DARKENED HILLS

When evil descends on a small West Virginia town, who will survive?

Jonathan did not start out his life to become a rambler, it just worked out that way. William was a troubled youth with something to hide. Both were from Melas, a small town tucked away in the West Virginia hills... a town where disappearances are happening more and more frequently.

After the suicide of a wanted serial killer, the townsfolk thought the nightmare was over. But when a centuries-old vampire is discovered they find out the hard way it's just getting started. Dark secrets can only stay hidden for so long and when the devil comes to collect, there will be hell to pay. Can Jonathan and William find a way to stop the vampire before it's too late? Find out in *Darkened Hills!*

DARKENED HOLLOWS

In the heart-stopping sequel to the award-winning *Darkened Hills*, Jonathan and William must return to West Virginia to face possible criminal charges stemming from their last visit to the damned town of Melas, where both had narrowly escaped the clutches of a vampire seethe.

And as livestock start mysteriously getting murdered with all of their blood drained, worried farmers are searching for answers - leaving the local Sheriff and his deputy racing against time to learn the cause before a more violent crime is committed.

Burning Bulb

www.DarkenedHills.com

GARY LEE VINCENT'S
DARKENED
THE WEST VIRGINIA VAMPIRE SERIES

DARKENED WATERS

When the world goes to hell, the chosen must arise!

As Talman Cane orchestrates a flood of epic proportions in this third installment of the *Darkened* series the towns of Melas and Tarklin are caught completely off guard by the deluge. Hell-bent on finishing what they started, the evil brothers return to the lunatic asylum to take care of the witnesses and add to the ever-growing army of the undead.

Aided by Lucifer himself and the insane vampire demon Legion, the stage is set to channel all of the forces of hell to come forth. In an all-out race to survive, Jonathan, William, and Amanda soon discover they are up against impossible odds as Lucifer opens the Gateway to Hell, ushering in the zombie apocalypse and the End Times.

DARKENED SOULS

Melas and the Madison House are about to be rebuilt.
True evil is about to be reborne!

Young ex-priest and vampire-killer William is drawn back to the West Virginian town that almost killed him, where his vampire arch-enemy Victor Rothenstein still stalks the earth.

The town of Melas lies destroyed after the battle of the End of Days. But why is wealthy Jackie Nixon so eager to rebuild it using the bone dust of murdered souls?

Terrible evil has visited before, but the Gateway to Hell is about to be reopened in a horrific climax. And this time – it's personal.

www. DARKENEDHILLS.COM

Burning Bulb
PUBLISHING

WEST VIRGINIA-THEMED HUMORROROTICA

BY RICH BOTTLES JR.

HELLHOLE WEST VIRGINIA

From the heights of Mothman's perch high atop the Silver Bridge in Point Pleasant to the depths of Hellhole Cavern in Pendleton County, evil lurks within the shadows as the sun sets upon the haunted hills and hollows of West Virginia.

Bizarro author Rich Bottles Jr. blows the coffin lid off horror genre clichés with this tour de force cast of Eco-friendly vampires, beach-yearning zombies and sex-starved she-devils.

LUMBERJACKED

If you are easily offended or do not possess a truly depraved sense of humor, this story may not be the light summer reading fare you desire. As for the four feisty female freshmen stranded on top of West Virginia's third highest mountain, they have no choice but to experience the sick, twisted debauchery and perverted mayhem described deep inside the tight unbroken bindings of this horrific missive.

Lumberjacked takes the reader to a nightmarish world where character development and aesthetic integrity are prematurely cut short by the swinging axes of maniacal lumberjacks, who are hell bent on death and destruction in the remote forests of Appalachia. And at the climax, when paranoia crosses over to the paranormal, Lumberjacked makes Deliverance look like a family raft trip down the Lower Gauley.

THE MANACLED

What happens when twin brothers lease out the former West Virginia State Penitentiary with the false purpose of filming a documentary on supernatural phenomena, but their true intention is to make a pornographic movie?

Chaos ensues as the disturbed spirits of murdered convicts, along with the reanimated dead from the neighboring Indian Burial Mound, take their vengeance on the unwary and undressed trespassers.

Zombies, ghosts, mobsters and porn collide in this bizarro tale from horror author Rich Bottles Jr.

Burning Bulb
PUBLISHING

WOL-VRIEY

BIZARRO AND TRANSGRESSIVE FICTION

Burning Bulb
PUBLISHING

BOSTON POSH

In 2028 AD, the USA is a nation ravaged by hungry dragons and dinosaurs. In Boston, Massachusetts, private eye Bud Malone is hired to rescue a kidnapped heiress. But nothing is as it seems. Malone works to unravel a tangled web involving Boston China-town, a 200-year-old woman with a 9-year-old body, white robots, a human-liver-eating psychopath, a golem, a porcelain dragon, and a snake goddess with a crush on him. There's also a woman obsessed with chicken sex. Then Malone meets Posh Lane, a gorgeous call girl who's desperate to quit her pimp. Romantic sparks ignite be-tween Posh and Malone, but Posh's past suddenly catches up with her in a BIG way. To save Posh, Malone agrees to run a quest for Earth's new rulers, the Forks. But, Malone has no idea that agree-ing to the Fork's odd request will send him on the weirdest trip he's ever been on in his life.

VEGAN VAMPIRE VAGINAS

The biggest bank heist in US history. And Tom Palmer can't remember pulling it off. And no, this isn't your standard case of amnesia. After a one-night-stand gone horribly wrong, Boston salesman Tom Palmer wakes up with a vagina implanted in his left hand. Then his day gets worse:

Tom is transported across space-time to a nightmare version of Boston, one where the Bizarro virus has transformed half the population into cannibals. Worst of all, Tom discovers that in this new Boston, he's the infamous gangster Pussypalm, wanted for robbing the Federal Reserve Bank of Boston a year ago. He also learns that the vagina in his hand is prophetic, i.e. it talks . . . after sex. With 130 people left dead during his bank heist and six billion dollars missing, Tom knows he's living on borrowed time. It is in his best interests not to remember anything. Because once he does . . .

VEGAN ZOMBIE APOCALYPSE

In the post-apocalypse worlderness, zombies rule the earth. They're allergic to meat, and brains literally make them explode. Zombies now eat blood potatoes, parasitic tubers grown in the flesh of humancows corralled in maximum security farms. Two fugitives meet in the ancient ruins of Texas. The first is Soil 15-t, a womancow who's escaped her farm a week before she's due to be killed and her blood potato crop harvested. The second fugitive is Able Kane, former head necros food technician, now sentenced to death for heresy. But Soil is no ordinary humancow. Unknown to herself, she's the vegan zombie agricultural revolution, and the zombies desperately want her back. And the necros equally desper-ately want Able Kane dead. He's fled with a forbidden discovery which will reshape the world for the worse if used. And Able is just hardheaded/misguided enough to use it.

MINOR CONFESSIONS OF AN ANGEL FALLING UPWARD

by Planner Forthright, as edited by Joey Madia

Confession. Revelation. Rant. *Minor Confessions of an Angel Falling Upward* is all of these... and more. Set in modern times and spiraling back to the swirl of Pre-Creation, this postmodern blend of genre-bending pop-prose and socio-political commentary is a classic tale of the (anti-)hero's quest for Reason and Redemption in a Universe gone mad.

Who is Planner Forthright? A fallen angel made Man. A once-winged evil with un-Divine purpose on this Plane. A cannibal prince chosen to inherit a castled landscape of destruction and despair. An Alchemist of sorts—a mental magician; a mortar-and-pestle wizard converting carbon lies to golden Truth, whose language is his own. A Vampire by nature and condition whose been walking the waters and thorny highways of our planet for over 40 years. And he's seeking a way out...

PASSAGEWAY

by Gary Lee Vincent with illustrations by Andy Hopp

When an archeological dig goes horribly wrong, the team is trapped in an alternate world where evil awaits them at every turn. Find out who will survive the *Passageway*!

From Gary Lee Vincent, the author of supernatural vampire thriller *Darkened Hills*, comes an unforgettable tale that spans four continents and takes the reader to the very realm of Hell itself.

Skeleton warriors, zombies, other undead beings and werewolves are allvery real inside the *Passageway*! In this Bizarro-genre tribute to H.P. Lovecraft and Indiana Jones, this deadly tale will keep you guessing and leave you breathless to the end!

THE TWELVE STEPS

by Zachary Crabtree

"A Man who Cannot Keep Awake Cannot Keep it Together." There is always something that pulls an alcoholic deeper into his unquenchable thirst – something degenerative to the human spirit. Indeed, there have been incidents in my life that carry tragic significance to me, yet I know they pale in comparison to the tragedies experienced by others.

When the jagged pieces of a disfigured past become a troubled, broken-up, glass-bottled mosaic in one's present life, all the innocent souls affected along the way become entangled in one's conscience; while the depression, pills, manic behavior and soul-searching coalesce in a series of twelve steps.

Alcohol affects the lives of hooligans, stubborn old fools, lovers, and families torn apart by drunk drivers – drunk drivers like me.

Burning Bulb
PUBLISHING

Bright little children, at school and at play,
until their minds are stolen away...

A Novel of Terror by

JOHN A. RUSSO

THE ACADEMY

THE ACADEMY

The Academy. It's every parent's dream, turning their little darlings into geniuses, superachievers, perfect little children.

And if there's a problem, the Academy fixes that too. It's a simple operation. Just a little device. Then a teeny pink scar on a tender little skull . . .

One boy knows the secret. Now he wants his mind back. But it's much, much too late. Too late for anything but the ugly feelings. The bad feelings. The messy sexy feelings. The knife-cold hatred, the murderous rage, for total, screaming, blood-drenching revenge . . .

www.TheJohnRusso.com

Burning Bulb
PUBLISHING

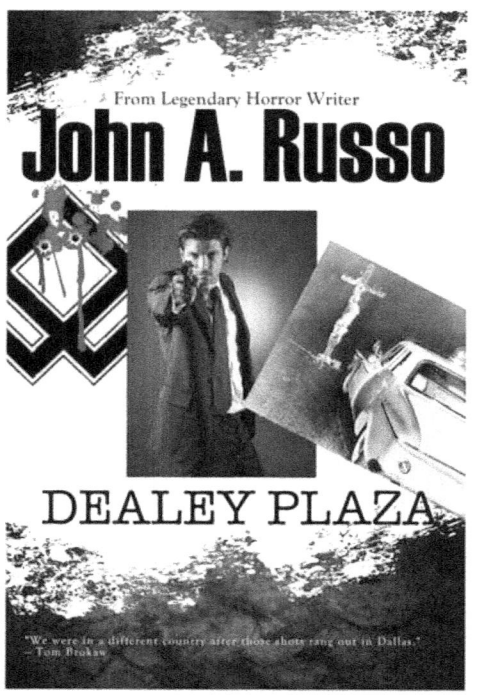

DEALEY PLAZA

From legendary horror and suspense writer JOHN RUSSO comes a harrowing tale where no one is safe!

Dealey Plaza is one of the most notorious places in America, and when youthful conspiracy buffs go there in 1964 to stage their own reenactment of the Kennedy Assassination, four of them are brutally murdered ~ the first victims of a hate-filled legacy that continues for four more decades.

The survivors of that long-ago Dallas trip, each of them now icons of the American way of life, are about to be honored ~ or killed.

Who will live and who will die? Will it be country-western star Lori McCoy? Her loving husband? Her scheming ex-husband? Or the case-hardened FBI agent and longtime friend who risks his life trying to protect them?

www.DealeyPlazaBook.com

Burning Bulb
PUBLISHING

THE FALL OF TOMORROW

Hopelessness... How do you protect your loved ones when Hell itself opens its insidious mouth?

Horror... Nightmarish Creatures invade your world and there is nowhere to hide.

Blood... How long can you hold out before they come for you?

Pain... Where do you run to avoid being eaten alive by monsters with a voracious appetite for your flesh?

Screams... While you selfishly run for your own life.

Questions... Who is to blame? Where did they come from? How many people survived...and how does the human race find the means to fight back?

THE FALL OF TOMORROW is man's last tale of desperation told by those that are striving to salvage some hope against a ravenous bastion of evil beasts bent on ruling our world.

"David Fairhead writes compelling stories that offer very human characters and very inhuman monsters. There is no subtlety in Fairhead's imagination - he is simply dying to scare the hell out of you."
    - Nelson W Pyles - author of DEMONS, DOLLS AND MILKSHAKES

Burning Bulb
PUBLISHING

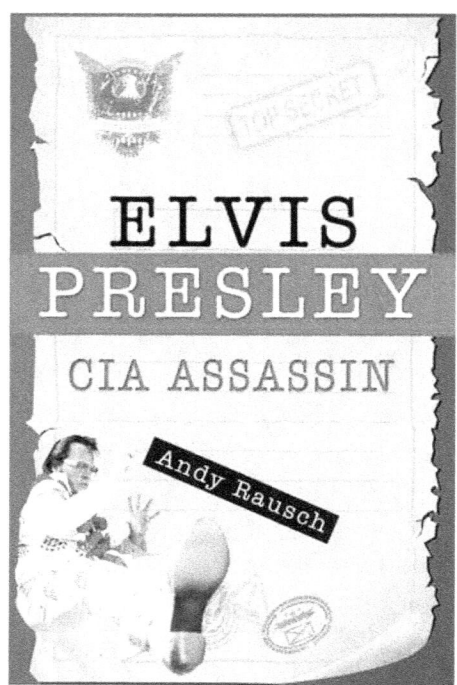

ELVIS PRESLEY, CIA ASSASSIN

"*I can guarantee you. Read this book and you'll never look at Elvis the same way again!*"
~ Douglas Brode, author of ELVIS CINEMA AND POPULAR CULTURE

SOON TO BE A MAJOR MOTION PICTURE

In 1970, singer Elvis Presley secretly met with President Richard Nixon. This new comedic novel imagines that Presley became a Central Intelligence Agency operative, eventually moving up through the ranks to become a skilled assassin.

Presented in an oral history fashion, the book tells us about Presley's secret transformation by the people who knew him best.

Did he fake his death in 1977? Was Presley involved with the Watergate scandal? The Iran hostage crisis? Communicating with aliens?

Read this book to find out the answers to these and many more questions.

Burning Bulb
PUBLISHING

www.ingramcontent.com/pod-product-compliance
Lightning Source LLC
Chambersburg PA
CBHW071339020726
47502CB00001B/163